THE MISSING ACTIVIST

A BRITISH POLITICAL THRILLER

LOUISE BURFITT-DONS

Louise Burfitt-Dons is an author and screenwriter of TV movies shown on television networks worldwide. She was born in Kuwait and has lived in the UK, Australia and France. Louise is married with two daughters and one granddaughter. Her home is now London with her husband Donald.

For Donald, my campaign manager

Praise for The Missing Activist

'This book sparkles because of its fine detail and nuances of London life today.' *Trip Fiction*

'Page Turner! A cracking political thriller. The insecure, paranoid world of the political candidate collides with the equally insecure and paranoid world of a Jihadist bride recruiter. It's twisty, clever and a real page turner.' Emma Curtis, *The Night You Left*

'The knowledge and perspective of the different characters/elements involved in this highly political "fictional" thriller was brilliant! Louise definitely knows her stuff.' Hazel Butterfield, Women's Radio Station

'The world of British Jihadi brides and internal bullying of political parties. Domestic violence, trafficking, sharia law... a terrific book for our times.' Harriet Khataba, *Her Story Matters*

'Ambitious, fun and chillingly real.' LBC

'Jihadi Terrorists and Tory Party politics combine in a thriller written by an insider.' Goodreads.

'The complexity of the terrorist threat undermining British society today ... Original, compelling.' RSA

A NEW CENTURY PAPERBACK

First published in Great Britain in 2018

A CIP catalogue record for this book
is available from the British Library

ISBN 0-9538522-9-6
ISBN-13: 978-0-9538-5229-1

newcenturydigibooks.com

Also by Louise Burfitt-Dons

CHAPTER 1

Zinah al-Rashid recruited more brides for Isis than anyone else. *Alhamdulillah.* Praise be to God.

Her fifth teenager crossed to Syria without any hitches. The accolades this brought meant she was now after her sixth. She dressed in her abaya and got ready for the interview with the schoolgirl who'd been messaging her nonstop to meet.

Already a jihadi website hailed Zinah a superstar and the write-up, short as it was, got rated with yellow smiley faces. The Brotherhood applauded the brave sister for her skill at teaching the ways of Allah. They commended her ability to work undercover so not a soul could pick her true western identity.

So this was fame. How great it felt! Zinah hoped her biological father learned it was his very own daughter being praised for heroic missions. It was payback for the twenty-five years since he'd adopted the Islamic religion, changed his name to Mohammed and headed east.

At that moment Zinah regretted her mother and stepfather weren't still alive to see how well she and Mohammed worked together for Isis. They'd have a fit.

It was nearly time to leave the room for her meeting. Tying the laces on a pair of green suede trainers she reflected on how the two people who had brought her up mocked Mohammed's open-toed sandals and bushy beard. *Infidels.*

Still high on the Islamic honours, Zinah resisted checking the net once more to see if she'd got more glowing comments from her fans. Instead, she left her hotel room early and headed for the coffee shop.

Because the girl she had a date with was late, Zinah had time to kill. To begin with, at the rear of Costa, she updated her note-taking app. Stay organised. It was vital to keep her jihadi profile hidden from those who worked with her in her other world. Her public relations on behalf of Isis depended on it. Was she the only one calling out Western media's lies? It sure seemed like it.

How the press spun things! Wasn't it in the UK where kids cut themselves with designer knives and got high on drugs? They were the ones in need of saving. Not Muslim women.

The teenager fitting the description she'd sent Zinah entered the coffee bar. She slouched in, head in an iPhone. Who was she speaking to when she should be focused on this important meeting? Maybe her mother? The silly woman was dead set on her becoming an electrical engineer, not studying the words of the Prophet? Didn't she think her daughter could do both? But the mum could be a danger to the operation, all the same. So Zinah knew the tack to take and used it. She welcomed the teen with smiling eyes.

'Hello, Amirah.' The adopted name. 'The name means princess or leader.'

Zinah had read it right. The girl flushed pink. She was more excited by her new persona than Islam.

Amirah was now in with the 'in crowd'.

'A person's name says something special about them and their character,' Zinah enthused. 'It's how people interact with you.'

'And when I call myself Amirah they see straight away I'm a Muslim.'

While Zinah could call up a show of empathy in an instant, it took time to develop real influence over these girls. *You can't hurry things.* So when Amirah fiddled endlessly with her hijab, Zinah stopped herself saying, 'Leave it alone.'

Don't nag.

Amirah was the same as the others she'd converted in this respect. Her first rush of passion for the Caliphate was more to do with the 'look at me' factor than anything else.

'It's a beautiful name, isn't it?' With the spark ignited, fifteen minutes later it burst into flame. Zinah had not lost her touch, had she? She had a way with these girls. Amirah now ached to become more devout. Another win.

'When can I wear the full-face veil like you do?' Amirah was longing to copy her, she could tell. Cover up completely. The parents were the blocking force because they'd not allowed Amirah to buy an abaya. But even though Zinah hated them for it, because they represented the major obstacle to her ambitions, she didn't show it.

'Your parents are right.'

She *understood* protective mothers and fathers. She'd dealt with dozens before. Find the point of agreement! To begin with, Zinah tackled the clothing issue which was usually the first to concern them. Yes, the hijab was indeed different to the niqab or the burka. To move from the scarf to the veil in two weeks would likely provoke people in the supermarket and on the street. The best way to wear what Amirah wanted, which was full Islamic dress, was to leave the UK. To up sticks from the place of her birth and travel

5

east to join her sisters in Syria.

When she did that, she'd be an instant celebrity, coming from the West. Just like the girls in the top show business magazines. But better. Much better. They didn't have immoral size zero requirements where Amirah was going. 'Out there women are beautiful in their natural form.'

Not only did Amirah love the flattery, but also the travel sounded fun. It was 'like' the most cool idea she'd ever had.

'You will live in a maqar at first.' *A shared house for women.*

Then, unlike her parents, Zinah addressed Amirah as an adult. 'You don't have to worry about meeting someone perfect for you because Isis do it all. You don't have to go clubbing and be disrespected.'

With this final detail one more recruit was well on their way to a new life with Isis. Straightaway the sixteen-year old wanted to leave boring school and become a married woman. Like *tomorrow.*

'Can you believe where my mum is right now?'

The girl had been bloody jabbing at WhatsApp, so no surprise she wanted to spill.

Mum Linda Clark was at an anti-sharia conference and been sending updates. It couldn't be worse.

They googled it and that's when Zinah learned it was not only being held in the town but at the very hotel she was staying in. How had she missed that? She seethed at her slip up. Then vowed it would never happen again. She'd travelled halfway across the damn country for this conversation.

But Amirah saw the twist of fate as an opportunity. 'Oh

cool. If you go back there she'll see you.'

These feminist rallies were happening right across the UK. The same ill-informed crowd ran them every time. Alesha Parkhurst was their leader. Alesha Parkhurst was responsible for denigrating the Prophet.

Another message arrived with a chime. Amirah read it out. 'Islam counts women as half of men.'

Messages were firing through. What Alesha Parkhurst was saying. How Islam treated Lindas and Amirahs as second-class citizens.

'But sharia is a perfect system which looks after all,' Zinah reassured the schoolgirl. 'The West makes it out as chopping off hands and stoning fornicators which it's not. That's only the Saudi way.'

Amirah seemed satisfied when she left.

'We'll be in touch,' said Zinah departing at the same time. It was as darkness descended and, by her mental maths, exactly when the conference should be closing up. She planned her entrance to the second, picturing the glorious scene ahead.

Zinah would enter the hotel foyer just as Amirah's mum was leaving. She would be SO gobsmacked to be faced with the epitome of all the evil she has been hearing about. Startled. She would want to ask Zinah something. Like 'What are you doing here?'

Zinah would then ask, 'Do you believe the rubbish you heard in there about women in the burka being subjugated?'

Zinah had learned her name from Amirah, but she wouldn't use it because their meeting was to remain a secret. But what she would say to Linda Clark was, 'What you've listened to for the last two hours from Alesha Parkhurst about Islam being an insult to women's rights is drivel.'

It was all planned. She gathered her cloak around her. It blended with the unlit buildings as icy wet air sprayed from the alleys. The night was harsh and her mood turned bitter as she rehearsed over and over the speech she would soon deliver. But when she reached the hotel lobby all was quiet.

The seminar must have gone over time, she thought. Zinah was too early. Damn.

The only person who noted the paradox in style between the feminists and the fully cloaked Islamic woman was a bulky man loitering in the shadow of the lifts.

So Zinah al-Rashid got no audience reaction. Naturally, she felt deflated. There was little point in hanging around, so she proceeded up to the fourth floor. Only after she'd tucked herself away upstairs in the last single room with its heavy purple drapes and overhead fan did she disrobe. A full head of golden blonde hair was revealed. She slid a pair of plain glass spectacles into their case and flicked out coloured contact lenses. Her eyes changed from chestnut brown to blue.

She examined herself. The foreboding figure was no longer. Instead, reflected in the glass was a woman early thirties wearing jeans and a pleasant expression who you'd cross on the street and take no notice of at all. She promised one day all this would change.

But for now Zinah al-Rashid had to find some other means to express her resentment at those who made her mission so hard. God willing. *Inshallah.*

CHAPTER 2

In the predawn dark, Filipino room girl Mary Mendoza arrived for work. She sang 'I want to find me a hero' into the scarf around her neck. A couple of guests, early checkouts, rumbled past dragging suitcases along the rough pavement. Otherwise, everywhere was peace and quiet. Life was *goooood.*

She entered the hotel by the staff door off the car park. Mary, the girl who'd seven months back escaped a bullying household, today felt free as a bird. She admired her first inking, a sun tattooed on the underside of her wrist. It was a reminder of home and made her look modern. Sunshine and laughter.

The usual work pattern applied. To begin with, she hung up her puffer jacket, put on an overall and went into the kitchen. A bit of joking with the chef who only clowned around before breakfast, never after. Fun. Height-wise she barely reached his elbow.

What had Mary done on her night off? And look at her. She'd washed and glossed her hair until it shone and caked her face with powder and applied mascara to her lashes. Why? Where was she thinking of going at six in the morning?

'Yeah, I go to London,' she said, which everyone, including the chef, knew about because this weekend off Mary had spoken about over a hundred times at least. He was teasing her, of course. Life was better in Wales, no? The Big Smoke was dirty, crowded, noisy and she shouldn't

9

return there in case she got caught.

No. Six months since her escape from the Saudi bosses meant it was safe to go back.

Anyway, nothing this morning would deter the twenty-five-year-old from returning for her weekend to the city where she'd one day become a star.

She bounced from foot to foot. 'Maybe I get a job as singer tomorrow night in a fancy club. If not, I am back working here on Monday. Beds. Cleaning.'

The sluggish lift took her leisurely up to the fourth level. Most guests still slept, the two she passed earlier were an exception. She wouldn't have to hang around late. Bless them.

As Mary pushed the heavy service cart along the passage towards 403 the ancient floorboards creaked in protest. She was super quick. The first room was done in no time but finishing the bathroom she checked her watch all the same. No way was she going to miss the train and the party which had been on her mind for weeks. Two Filipino girls who'd be at the hostel were also runaways from abusive families. And Mary knew the ropes. So they looked up to her as an old hand which made her feel great.

Madame beat me, or, the Master's sons rape me. The stories were always the same and after they heard the newcomers tell their tale they would all cry together. There'd be lots of cake eaten and they'd sing and clap hands. It was like being back home. That's why she had to be in Willesden by twelve, no later. The fun wouldn't wait. Mostly, the women's refuge was a joyful happy place. She didn't want to miss out.

She ticked off the first 'clean' in bright red ink. She

dropped the pen in the pot, put the clipboard on the trolley and headed on. Next up, room 425 right at the end of the corridor under the name of Parkhurst. Nearly done.

Because of her excitement, the noise of a hairdryer only briefly interrupted her dreaming. Mostly planning what she needed for the trip to London. Was she dressed ok? What should she take? Maybe she'd stop by Sainsbury's and pick up a six pack of San Miguel? They were for when one of the girls FaceTimed a mother or a sister in Manila. When the others would wave their bottles of beer into the camera to show how hard they were partying. It gave their families at home great comfort to see them chatting, looking radiant, doing well. 'We are fine, mothers. Look how happy we are, now we free from our bad bosses. Did you get the presents we sent? Miss youuuuuuu. Luv you.'

As Mary pushed her way down the passage, she hummed in her head. She noticed the door ajar at 410. This was not on the project sheet, but perhaps they'd left early, anyway.

'Hello. Housekeeping.'

She tapped, but there was no response. She stepped inside. No sign of life, no suitcase, no towels dropped on the bathroom tiles, nothing. Mary knew the procedure was to check with Reception before the clean-up. So she took the lift to the ground floor to get the go ahead. Was it ok for her to service 410 now?

The girl behind the desk said she'd call up the computer system. At first she thought Mary had got the rooms mixed up.

'425? It's on your sheet.'

'It is not 425. It's 410.'

'410.'

The receptionist saw no problem as there was zero balance on the account. She could service it if she wanted to.

Room 410 took no time to clean. The bed was unused. Mary changed the sheets, all the same. But there was something strange with the bathroom. Whoever had been in there had taken the face cloths and towels. While this was not abnormal, none of the free packs had gone with them which was usually the case when guests stole hotel linen. Mary hated the strong smell of bleach and this area stunk of it so bad. As if the occupant, the thief, had emptied an entire bottle into the sink. Clanging the pedal bin shut, she hurried away. She longed to be out of there.

One room more and she'd be through. To be sure it was unoccupied she gave four light knocks as a precaution. 'Housekeeping!'

Using her override key she opened up.

The closed heavy blackout curtains pulled to meant it was pitch black inside. Often the case when you did early rooms. But something wasn't right. The sour air hit her first. The skin on her upper arms prickled like it'd done so many times back in Jeddah, a sign to be careful.

She groped for the light switch. Flicked it, but it seemed nothing happened. Why not? She'd started the ceiling fan instead. As her eyes adjusted, she saw a shape moving. Whatever it was, it appeared to be dead centre in the room. It was now hard to breathe. Where was the light when you needed it to see? She fumbled and found it.

Hanging from the overhead fan a body swung in ever faster circles as the unit picked up speed. She gulped. Mary would carry the image to her grave. A face as purple as the yams she'd eaten as a child. The strap noosed around the woman's neck, eyes bulging from their sockets and the corpse carving a smooth circle in the room like a huge life-size puppet.

She heard herself scream as though it was from someone else. Then she tore down the stairs back to Reception.

CHAPTER 3

The morning of August 31st was one Karen Andersen would never forget. It was the end of summer in calendar terms, but you'd have thought it was the beginning. The sun shone when they'd forecast rain and everyone wanted to be outside. But for her that was nigh impossible. She had far too much to do. Her head was spinning with so many indoor jobs the last thing she needed was the further distraction of good weather. To add to it, she had a strong sense something mega was about to happen and if so, whatever it was, she couldn't cope. Her place was a shit heap.

Only two weeks prior she'd moved into the flat. But, no excuses. The small front room which served as the main living and working space was cluttered with black bin liners full to brimming. In addition, the corkboard and office equipment, such as it was, needed setting up and plugging in. Wires spread over the carpet still required sorting. But she couldn't focus on any one task. It was her first property transaction. She was too *excited.*

On top of this, rather than concentrate on essentials, she was mucking around with a second-hand foil she'd bought off the internet so she could practice her fencing. This was also complete wood from the trees.

Karen Andersen was a private investigator with a healthy dose of imagination. So when her phone went off while carrying out a pretend parry riposte, in her mind she was Diana Rigg from the Avengers. It could have been anyone on the other end, even John Steed. In fact, it was the BBC asking was she free to come into the studio to comment on a cyberbullying piece they were running?

The story was related to suicide caused by online bullying. It was a look at the death of Alesha Parkhurst, a high-profile feminist who'd killed herself six months prior. A 'did she jump or was she pushed?' type of debate. A detective from the Met had raised concerns. He reckoned the UK ignored too many mysterious deaths like the Parkhurst case.

Now her mind was racing because she couldn't see at first any direct link with her actual work, which was mostly checking CV claims, finding missing people or dealing with internet fraud. Why did they want her? What could a little-known private investigator add to a debate on suicide?

'Who put you on to me?' Karen asked, searching for clues.

After a barrage of questions, Karen sensed the researcher giving up. Losing the will to live. Wishing she hadn't bothered with her in the first place.

A deep sigh. 'An anti-bullying charity I called suggested you might help.'

Aha, so there was the connection! Karen had helped out a small victim support group pro bono because of the work they did with children. She'd given a couple of talks and answered questions on cyberbullying. But nothing as glamorous as appearing on TV for them. Then again, why Alesha Parkhurst? Alesha was a grown woman. But it sort of fitted. She'd been bullied to the point of wanting to take her own life which was pretty serious, wasn't it?

The BBC wanted two poles-apart views. Karen's one

that being cyberbullied was a big, big deal and they should continue to bang the drum as often as possible. Was everyone doing enough to stop this cruel behaviour?

'And the other?'

'The other side is putting the view that last year only fifty percent of unexplained deaths in the UK were reported to the coroner. So some suicides may not be suicides.'

In other words, if someone had a known history of being stalked or bullied, their so-called self-imposed death could provide a killer with the perfect cover for committing a crime.

It was very scandi noir and seemed too far-fetched for real life. But according to Ms BBC, the detective taking that approach, Donald Partridge, had a lifetime of murder experience. So he should know. Karen didn't pick up on the name at this stage because she'd always known him up until then by his nickname of Quacker. It came from Donald Duck. He was famous on the security circuit for being rather long-winded. But, as the most regarded expert on stalking in the Force, he could also make mincemeat of anyone who crossed him.

What Karen Andersen thought of next was exposure and to be on TV! It didn't occur what could come from it. Any negatives. Any backlash. Or even any good. Decisions like these are often major turning points. If Karen hadn't agreed to the interview, who knows whether one of the most audacious terror attempts on the then Prime Minister would ever have been thwarted. Because life is a series of unintended consequences. As it was, she saw the offer to be on TV as a golden opportunity for self-promotion. She said 'I'll do it.'

'So when would you be able to get into our Westminster studio?'

Karen's motorbike flashed into her mind, which she'd ditched after a nasty skid in the London traffic. The claim to repair it had caused her insurance quote to treble. So it'd been hastily dumped. However, at that instant, she regretted this decision. She told the researcher she'd leg it.

It shouldn't take too long, she assured her. She enjoyed walking. It's was hardly a hassle on her to stroll along the Thames on such a great day.

'Ah. Well, we need you here soon. So we might send a car.'

No other consideration on her part was required. She was to be on the world news. They would go to air as soon as she arrived. Could she make it quick? She imagined being swept into the studio in a limousine. Something out of a Bond movie.

The moment Karen finished the call reality set in and nerves with it. What to say?

There was plenty, of course. Waiting for the car, she called up old headlines to refresh. *Alesha Parkhurst found dead in Welsh hotel. Cyber abuse drives feminist to suicide.* But she didn't really need this. Karen Andersen had known Alesha Parkhurst if only briefly or to nod hello in passing on the street. Alesha had even told Karen about her cyberbullying when they talked at a woman's event. At that moment, faced with a live interview, KA was wondering whether to keep this to herself or not. How Alesha had made light of it all and joked she was more trolled than Emma Watson! Small wonder, thought Karen at the time. Because Alesha was dead against stay-at-home married mums who she believed undermined the feminist cause. This put her well at loggerheads with quite a few.

Karen also had suspected something else at the time they spoke. While Alesha Parkhurst pretended it didn't bother her that much, it was all a bit of an act. Inside, she'd been struggling to remain sane. Obviously. The vicious name-calling and nonstop attacks must have finally driven her round the twist. To top it all, Alesha suffered from a manic-depressive condition which she spoke about publicly because she was also a mental health campaigner. If she had asked Karen for advice, which she didn't, she may well have told her, 'You don't help yourself. You are too public.'

As a cause, the whole women's rights issue didn't for the most part interest Karen. She could take or leave the age-old male bashing bit. The anti-patriarchy movement. But when it came to a safety issue, she was very much on board the feminist cause. Women escaping abusive relationships or being stoned or killed for not wearing what they're told to was a *totally* different matter. And Alesha Parkhurst stood up for these women a lot at her own peril, which Karen admired.

But she needed an example of this. So she called up a YouTube video where Alesha was condemning strict sharia law being brought into Britain. She'd slammed the Imams big time. This had generated the foulest hate mail. Some of it from the part of the Islamic community who strongly disagreed with her stance. The rest from God knows where. The sum total of the rape and death threats had finally taken her toll.

Karen knew Twitter could be brutal. Alesha Parkhurst had built a following in the hundreds of thousands which added to the pressure. Even the reaction to her suicide had been pretty heartless.

As an example, 'Celebrities love good publicity so why can't they take the bad?' Or, 'She got what she deserved for speaking out against the Prophet.' They used the hashtag #manhaters too which made Karen hopping mad because more cyber abuse increased as a result.

In response, she'd posted back to one woman in particular who'd been harassing her, 'Fuck you.' It was a longer message, same sentiment. She'd received her first Twitter warning for abusive language.

That morning Karen's ride to the studios was in a gunmetal grey people mover. It was no polished limo. The car sped past the great city sights and magic buildings and as it did, she wondered at it all. She was at her wits end to find the right things to say about why someone like Alesha would suddenly crack and want to finish it all.

But radical feminist or not, Alesha Parkhurst loved British freedoms as much as Karen Andersen. Moreover she'd fought publicly to preserve them. Now Alesha was gone it was up to Karen to defend her corner.

CHAPTER 4

Robin Miller liked his red hair, but not the pale skin tone which went with it. He suffered badly from the sun, turned pink and peeled. Exposure to the elements was all part of political activism, which is why he always wore a hat when out campaigning and longed for autumn to get established.

He arrived at the luxury central London hotel feeling hot, and at his Election Day trot of four 'knock-ups' a minute in party language. The mental state of the twenty-one-year-old was between caution and excitement. Today he'd vindicate himself. He'd clear his name. Otherwise, it didn't bear thinking about.

Fearing not being in exactly the right place, he perched on a chair beneath a large television screen in good view of the ultra-modern lobby. He'd see Simon King arrive that way. He watched the news to take his mind off things. The BBC had a story running on the circumstances surrounding the death of feminist Alesha Parkhurst six months before. There was a suggestion from an investigating officer in the Met the suicide may have in fact been a murder.

Miller had to focus on his meeting. Despite this, he inclined his head to pay attention to the Parkhurst story and not miss a word. His eyes fixed firmly on the monitor taking it all in.

Suicide was something he'd certainly not wished on the well-known feminist. Of course not. But, in a way, it would help him. It put cyberbullying of campaigners and activists on the map. Showed how awful it was. Isn't that exactly what Robin had been coping with himself over the last twelve months?

Most people assumed Parkhurst killed herself because of hate mail from the 'opposition'. Anti-feminists. That was pretty bloody bad. Robin knew just how lousy it felt to be singled out by rival groups like Labour, UKIP or the Lib Dems. Even the Greenies could be brutal. But in a way his situation was far worse. Because it was mostly coming from members of the same party. He'd never expected that. His colleagues were supposed to be on the same side.

But then no one gave a hoot, really. No one saw bullying as an issue until an eight-year-old boy hanged himself from his wardrobe. Or some desperate teenager stabbed three of his classmates.

Occasionally Miller checked his messages. He didn't feel at all ready for the meeting, let alone here at a place like this. It was a jacket and tie job for sure. And for once he'd not worn a collared shirt to work expecting to go out campaigning for the local association straight after his shift in the phone shop where he worked.

He looked again at the text message from Simon King MBE. 'Suggest informal meet to discuss report submitted by you to Party. Are you free 5 PM?'

For a heart to heart chat, a pub would have been a better place. Maybe somewhere near party headquarters where the director could go over in more detail the next steps for Robin to take.

This five-star hotel is too heavy, he worried. Why here?

The fact he was now early too was super annoying. A follow-up text came through from King. 'Be half hour late. Apologies. Simon.' Had he known ahead of time, Robin would have had ample opportunity to change clothes, look more appropriate. How long had he got? At least forty-five minutes to kill. He'd not passed many clothing outlets on the way in. Was there enough time to find a charity shop which might have something? The next hour might be the most important meeting of his entire career.

Miller had been active in the Party since school days. As a late developer who'd only made five foot seven after turning eighteen, he'd never fitted in with the confident cool crowd in the common room. They were more into dating girls and drinking than studying. But politics had attracted him. The Conservatives welcomed him and government became his passion. What they provided too was a social life, a set of friends. Where else to hang out with like minds? Where else to meet others who idolised Maggie and Churchill, knew the only chance for the UK was an end to the bloody EU, to have a successful economy, to support the NHS? The most amazing healthcare system in the entire world!

After moving to London, having graduating in history from Nottingham Trent, Miller had hit the ground running on his long-term plan. He'd joined the Westminster West Conservatives and even got himself on the council list in an area where they were short. Somewhere they were desperate for people to stand. Difficult opposition areas such as Churchill Ward. Step one ticked.

He loved campaigning. For the super keen like Miller, plenty of streets awaited every day after work. Church Road, a marginal ward, was holding a by-election so they needed foot soldiers more than ever. Plus, the chair of the association was nearing retirement. Not standing again.

Miller had started dreaming of being elected Deputy Chair. So it was doubly important to show his commitment. If he got the job, it would build rapid credentials.

He wouldn't let the likes of Oli Harrington destroy that. Bullies such as him only did the Party a disservice. They created a toxic atmosphere with their House of Cards behaviour. It was counterproductive. Robin hated this side of it all.

What about his bag? Should he leave the canvassing carrier around his neck for the meeting? It was almost a permanent fixture. That might impress King.

He totted up the number of leaflets still to deliver from the night before. A hundred, tops! Maybe he should head straight on out after he'd seen King. He could finish delivering them before heading back to his bedsit.

If he pictured the face of his mother, it usually calmed him down. So looking at her photo in the small circular frame on his WhatsApp list he smiled. He sent a message 'Don't call now. In meeting'. He didn't want her contacting him, embarrassing him at the wrong time.

Then another. 'Talking with party director about bullying complaint. Tell you and Dad all later.' He switched the phone to silent.

The danger was clear. Robin had to save his political career. Otherwise, any application to go on the Approved Candidates List for a national seat, known more commonly as 'the list' would fail. And with it his ultimate dream of becoming an MP.

So he had to fight off this challenge. Oli Harrington was very aggressive, had actually said he'd crush him like an ant, would block him from any job in Westminster if he caused trouble. Robin would 'be finished in politics' if he complained.

This alone was enough to nail him for blackmail, surely?

Miller didn't consider himself a wimp. He'd stood up to Harrington well at first. But the nastiness didn't stop. It'd gone on and on. So Robin had reluctantly dobbed him in for bullying. But after the official bit, writing in, there'd been a big fat silence from Party HQ. Why? Hadn't he done the right thing? Surely they'd want to discipline an activist who also constantly hit on female supporters, harassed them endlessly, and phoned them at three in the morning? *Of course they would.*

Oli Harrington was a bully; there was no doubt about it.

The TV was doing the suicide piece again. God. He'd been waiting half an hour already.

The newscaster spoke into the camera, 'Initially, it was thought Alesha Parkhurst had been the victim of a cyberbullying campaign by Justice For Rape Lies, a group acting for men wrongly accused of sexual assault. But now a detective in the Met has raised the possibility the campaigner may have been murdered.'

The BBC had brought in a cyber abuse expert Karen Andersen who challenged this. Robin was only half listening.

The surprise meeting coming out of the blue threw him. It's how the system worked. Don't call us, we'll call you. He knew that, but had he overstepped the mark by making a fuss about Oli's bullying? He shifted uneasily in the chair. Now here he was sitting in a damn five star woefully unprepared.

The news coverage continued.

'The conference on acid attacks, which Ms Parkhurst had been organising, will still go ahead. Victims are flying in from several countries to take part.'

The iPhone again. Simon King would be there in five.

Suddenly Miller wanted to visit the toilet. Real fear had overtaken him now. The next thirty minutes would determine his political future, a meeting with a high-level Party official, and he wasn't even wearing as much as a shirt and tie.

CHAPTER 5

One thing you couldn't avoid noticing with Simon King was his immense body mass. Regular lunches with Members of Parliament at the Buckingham Hotel were a contributor to this. Added to this a natural arrogance fitted well with his obesity and gave real substance to his dominating personality. As the longest-serving member of the board of the most successful political party in the country, no one dared challenge his authority.

During the war, the five-star hotel had been the gathering place for lobbyists and civil servants, and somewhere for industry representatives to make their case. Rationing had affected companies and mingling with those in government gave an opportunity to influence things. It meant they had one ear to the heart of Westminster. And nothing much had changed. It was still a favourite with those who wanted to be physically near to the seat of power.

'How are you doing today?' King greeted the concierge he knew well as he skirted around for familiar faces.

'Very good indeed, sir,' he heard back.

The Buckingham's other attraction and why it was popular amongst the Westminster set was because it had a House of Commons Division Bell. When this sounded it was a signal the Speaker had cleared the chamber and there were only eight minutes remaining for MPs to return to Parliament. The windowless restaurant, black banquette seating and dark-wood furniture gave it a snug intimacy. Ideal for gossip and intrigue.

Saturated with political history, the Buckingham was King's choice of location for his meeting with Robin Miller. And even the lobby would be just fine for what he had in mind.

Party loyalty was Simon's big thing, and this was the issue he had with Miller. He was due for a right bollocking. You could only serve one master and the master here was the Party. Every activist, wannabe candidate or MP was indoctrinated with the consequences of disloyalty. They had to be. The only way to run things. But it rarely involved Simon King directly.

So what was he doing here himself? Why did he have to spell out to this arrogant young man what was usually done on his behalf by those much lower down the food chain? The expected conduct. What you do or, in this case, don't do, was passed on member to member. Full dedication was assumed. Or you're out, buster. It was shrugged off with the phrase 'sharp learning curve'. The ambiguity was intentional. No one received praise for their efforts. It didn't need to work like that. More the reverse. If you stuffed up on something you'd know damn quick!

The Conservative Party was not only one of the five major political parties in the country. It was tops. Through history the Tories were accustomed to power, controlling government and passing laws. Every activist after a career in politics learned that lesson quickly enough. Don't buck the system. How the party operated, functioned on a daily basis, was something you didn't question.

Donations, advancement, perks, liaisons and most especially conduct. To go against the party line was plain stupid for anyone who sought the Holy Grail—a place on the Approved Candidates List. No one dared breathe a word about how matters really worked. They might disagree on policy rights and wrongs, but the Party was God and God set the rules.

There were serious consequences for anyone who didn't knuckle under. They were made examples of, disciplined and distanced. That way, activists were kept in their place. They considered themselves privileged to even belong. Wives, husbands, sons and daughters, all expected to have to trade their weekends if the Party wanted them to do so.

Many of the party faithful had benefitted from a private education. They were seen by the public as clannish and elitist socialising remote from mainstream society. Their lives revolved around Tory events which happened daily, weekly, annually. And often they courted and married other party activists. No one questioned who pulled strings at the top of the structure. If anyone stepped out of line, the system closed against them. They were all of a sudden no longer on the 'in'.

As he approached the distinguished building across the street from St. James's Park tube station, Simon King was thinking Miller had now put himself in that category. Entering the foyer he picked out the red-haired activist straight away from his picture on social media. He'd seen him often enough before. Remembered Miller telephone canvassing at headquarters.

Robin sat in a beige suede chair. His colourful sweatshirt, corduroys and casual shoes would have been more fitting for the pub next door. King used that place too for these sorts of interviews. But it stank of vinegar and stale beer and hadn't been quite right for what he had in mind.

Nor the other nearby political drinking hole, the Westminster Arms. That was far too public. He wanted to intimidate the young party member. The more imposing the setting the better.

Miller rose as King approached, knocking over his seat.

A good start. The guy's petrified.

King prided himself on reading people well. He knew everyone of note in the party and most junior activists like Miller by sight if nothing else. He could work out what each one of them needed within a second of meeting.

King crushed the young man's hand in a vigorous shake noting with satisfaction the wince of pain.

'Sorry I'm late. We haven't met before have we?' This was to be a breeze. 'Seen you about, of course.' By now, it must have dawned how much trouble he was in. Not that he wasn't a bloody good activist, apparently. But by having the audacity to complain about bullying in the party he'd well and truly overstepped the mark.

'I appreciate the meeting,' Miller said in even tones.

There was a five-second silence.

'You went on the campaign bus, didn't you?'

'I thought the Party should know what was going on.' Robin looked the director straight in the eye.

The party director stared back.

'One of the most successful initiatives we've ever had.'

'Yes. It got the vote out.'

'It certainly did, which was the whole point.'

'There was drug taking on the bus. Did you know that?'

Miller was far cockier than King had expected. So he gave him a patronising look and said, 'You'd have to substantiate this.'

Who does this upstart think he is?

'I believe I'm not the first to complain about Mr Harrington's behaviour,' he said. Unfazed.

Simon King remained deadpan as his blood pressure rose. It was obvious Miller had no clue on how political parties worked top down. Membership had fallen before the last election. Deliverers, leaflet stuffers, door knockers and canvassers were on the decline. Harrington had come up with a great idea to rebuild the base. Bus students around the country to shore up support and give the party a new dynamic. The booze, crisps and free nights was all part of it. And always with a good chance of sex thrown in.

'Were you aware how much it helped win the election?'

'The fish and chip suppers were very well received.'

Simon leant back in his chair. 'You complained about bullying behaviour?'

'Yes.'

'The Party takes allegations of bullying very seriously. Most activists accept working in a pressured environment.'

Was this guy for real? Oh, God. Sometimes, but rarely, Simon King had to spell out the bleeding obvious. Only once in a blue moon did he have to resort to this level of sarcasm. Listen, you five foot nothing, don't you get who I *am*? Know I can rain big time on your parade? Destroy your whole bloody career, make your life a misery, and kick you out of the party. Wake up to yourself. Bullying is nothing. Politics is all about intimidation and control.

'I was hoping to have a meeting with you before now,' said Miller.

'How often did you go on the campaign bus?'

'On three occasions.'

'The bus made a huge difference to the election. Some constituencies had only a handful of members to support their candidates. It provided the extra help.'

'I know. But it could have delivered even more. It often left people behind. It was supposed to go at nine from central London. Mr Harrington wouldn't wait for a second even if he knew someone had been held up in traffic trying to get there.'

'You didn't put that in your report.' His message wasn't getting through. Maybe this idiot was autistic or something. Perhaps just thick.

'No. I didn't put that in. You're right.'

'Most activists who want to get on are bullied from time to time. It's not a kindergarten you know. You can't expect to be mollycoddled. If you can take all that's thrown at you, you'll be able to cope with politics. If not, you won't. What is key is loyalty. Loyalty to The Party and its policies.'

'I am a very loyal person.'

'Everyone is expected to do their bit. It means taking orders. And other party members don't take to anyone who bucks the system. That's not how it works. Most activists have pride in their loyalty. The ultimate prize is getting into the House of Commons. For that you are expected to turn a blind eye to certain things.'

'I was not referring to the odd swear word here and there. I'm talking about blackmail, cyberbullying, posting lurid sex videos, even using coke openly.'

'University doesn't prepare you for everything in life.'

'All organisations should have a bullying policy.'

King looked away in irritation. 'You may make a formal complaint if that's what you want to do.' It was time to

31

deliver the killer blow. 'You mentioned you wanted to become an MP. Have you considered applying for the parliamentary list?'

Thousands queued up to get on the list. The process long-winded and demanding. But the essential first step to getting selected for a seat.

'Maybe in two years. When I've got more experience.'

'How are you planning that?'

'I am standing for the local council. I'm next in line for Churchill Ward in my constituency. The association members have interviewed me. It's opposition-held but I know I can win it. I'd be one of the youngest councillors in the country.'

'Then strict conformity to Party rules and behaviour norms is essential.'

'Did Oli do that? Is groping acceptable behaviour?'

Simon's pulse quickened. This peasant was annoying him.

'Can you tell me where you envisage this going?'

'I'm reporting this because Mr Harrington is threatening to have me kicked out of the Party. His father is an MP. Together they could make that happen'

'James Harrington is well respected. True. But you're talking about his son.'

'The Tories are my family. I spend more time with Party friends than my own parents. It means that much to me.' As if to swing the balance, he pulled out a handful of canvassing leaflets from his sack, which was by now on the floor of the lobby.

'I'm a loyal supporter. Why would I do anything to embarrass the Party? That's what Oli is doing. Not me.'

Simon King ground his back teeth together. Was this clown for real? During the following fifteen minutes King listened in silence to minute details of words which caused offence and how Harrington's sex pestering had driven one girl on the bus to attempt suicide.

'He never stopped. He used disgusting vulgar offensive language even about the dead, such as this feminist campaigner.' Miller looked over at the news screen replaying the Alesha Parkhurst story as if to stress his point. 'I put that in my report. Good manners aside, the party stands for diversity.'

Girls cutting themselves. Alesha Parkhurst. Threatening conduct. So this sensitive issue hadn't gone away as it should have done weeks ago. The report needed clever handling, or it would rake up a whole load of matters which Simon King really didn't need resurrecting.

King lied smooth as silk. He reassured Miller his activism had been noticed and everything in the report he'd sent in taken into consideration. 'To protect the party, we will have to keep things confidential for the time being. Thank you for giving us the heads up on it all'

'I am only doing what is good for the Party.'

King stroked his upper lip. Coke, a sex pest. Loose talk. Yes, Harrington was way out of line. 'Step one, we've met. Step two, you'll need a witness statement.'

'I can provide that easily enough.' Robin Miller was super confident on that score.

'Good. Send it on and I'll see to it we advance the matter.'

Robin Miller thanked him and left first. As he departed the building, he beamed because he'd been overly reassured.

The name he'd built for himself would remain intact. Tick. All the hard work, his social enterprise achievements, the fundraising, thousands of hours of leafleting, knocking up, street stalls, and volunteer recruitment noticed. Tick. He'd not wasted his efforts.

King watched him go and marvelled at how easily he could manipulate activists if it suited him to do so. As King climbed into his black cab, a different thought entirely was running through his head.

Miller was finished in the Party. Why couldn't he see that?

CHAPTER 6

The phone snapped her out of sleep. Who was it? An unrecognised number from a UK mobile, so not her uncle from Australia, the only person who'd have a legit excuse to ring at ten past six.

'Karen Andersen?'

'Yes.'

'Oh good. You're up, are you? Expecting to leave a message.' He trailed off. 'Detective Inspector Donald Partridge here. We've met. Well, sort of.'

'We were on the BBC yesterday.' She'd recognised his voice straight away.

'Thought I'd call. Welsh TV asked me on their show this morning, would you believe? We were discussing the same case. Alesha Parkhurst.' He cleared his throat. It'd been a six o'clock broadcast, he explained, and they'd wanted him because she'd died in Wales. 'My next interview isn't until seven o'clock, so I've been told.' He apologised again for the disturbance.

'That's fine. I got up ages ago,' she lied smoothly.

'I listened to what you had to say on the program. It was good. Not that I agree, mind. Also, you rambled on a tad, rushed it.'

God, he could be blunt. If Karen had written his profile, it would have read dedicated, principled, intelligent, *and unsubtle.* The remarks stung because she wondered how she'd gone and that was not too great by the sounds of it. She swallowed hard.

'Could do with an opinion on something,' he said, filling the silence that followed. 'It's right up your alley.'

They agreed to meet at midday at the coffee shop across from her flat. The street was wall to wall cafés.

'Would there be somewhere to leave a vehicle nearby?'

'There are a few meters on Devonshire Road.'

'You don't by any chance have a resident guest parking ticket? Saturday can be a trifle difficult down your way.'

Karen didn't. She'd not yet applied. But this introduced the idea maybe she should get herself another motorbike. Having said it was too early to talk shop, Quacker did just that. He started up on Alesha Parkhurst and the view the investigation into her death had been a complete and utter cock up. Total shambles. Realising it was likely to be a long call, Karen struggled one-handed into her kimono. It was a faux satin affair she'd got from the local market. At least it felt cool against her skin. She was burning up with low blood sugar.

She carried an envelope into the kitchen to take notes while Quacker rambled on. The kettle had a three-quarters full feel. Fumbling for the switch in the half-light she sent an unpacked box of crockery crashing.

She hobbled around, sidestepping broken china which could cut worse than glass. By the time she'd made tea he'd been speaking for ten minutes in a steady stream. There was nothing stopping him.

A heavy knocking on the party wall was a sign to end the noise. The neighbour she hadn't yet met was sending her signals. Provided that D I Partridge would pull her in on this case, looking at why Alesha Parkhurst had killed herself, Karen would stick with the call through thick and thin. So she ignored the hammering.

In the centre of the table were articles on Alesha Parkhurst she'd run out the day before to prepare for the BBC. She chucked the illegible scrawl on cyberbullying she'd written in a recycling box. She wouldn't show that. It would give the wrong impression. It was important for Karen to demonstrate she could structure a proper investigation. Best to print stuff out.

Someone telling Quacker they needed him back in the studio forced an end to the call.

'Well, got to dash,' he said. 'I'll see you later then, shall I?'

'Absolutely,' she whispered, still trying to keep her voice down and not to disturb the neighbour.

Due to the unexpected offer of work, her mood lifted and kept soaring, too high. Outside the window, Chiswick was stirring. Inside her sleep-deprived brain, her mind was once again whirling out of control, teeming with too many ideas at once. Home decorating. Where the Alesha Parkhurst case could lead me on to next. Maybe MI5? Plus what her moving-in party planned for later that night would do for her flagging social life.

Dressed in running gear and backpack, Karen put 'Fly Me to the Moon' on the iPod and left the flat. Turning into Devonshire Road she broke into a fast jog. The fresh clear air cooled her face. But she was so hyped up she hardly felt it. She lengthened her stride, settling into a run. The area was all terraced houses and small front gardens with orange and citrus blossom. Despite this, everything was a grey blur. As she jogged on in the Hammersmith direction nothing more mattered. The beat of her feet, the rhythm it made, was her only focus.

Two kilometres on she'd exhausted herself. She leant back against a wall realising she was streaming with tears and let the sun warm her face and dry them. Shit, why cry? What was the matter with her?

An hour later Karen was heading home from the express supermarket. She'd stuffed the rucksack with free-range chickens, onions and garlic. In each hand, she had a bottle of Cabernet Sauvignon because she was too stingy to buy an extra reusable bag when she owned heaps which were stuffed under the sink. Despite her earlier breakdown, she now couldn't wipe the smile off her face. How fast her mood could shift! The medical diagnosis was cyclothymia. She called it madness.

How had she got so lucky? Even if Quacker had been off beam with his murder theory, working on the Alesha Parkhurst case was a dream come true. The spirits had intervened at last. She was so into thanking those above she barely took in what was right in front of her. An ambulance parked outside her door.

CHAPTER 7

Karen Andersen spent her early days in Little Hallingbury. It's a small village with a pretty church not too far from London. She should have maybe married a local solicitor and by this time been working as a publishing assistant. That's what her parents would have been happy with. Instead, she moved to the city in search of a spicier deal. In fairness to herself, mundane jobs didn't suit her temperament.

She blamed her maternal grandfather for the path she took. His name was Neil Masters, and he worked in the Middle East after the War in a desk job as chief health officer of an oil company. He'd met Ian Fleming, was a gun enthusiast and his adventures were epic. In Karen's mind he was James Bond, and she was Modesty Blaise.

His life absorbed her. She was thrilled by accounts of his hawking expeditions into the desert and visits to Bedouin camps. She begged to hear over and over the small details. How even though his first home in Kuwait had been only a tent but management had still insisted on formal dress for dinner. The kids at school said she lived in the past which hurt. They accused Karen of making up stories about him. This, coupled with being over anxious made it difficult for her to make friends.

Karen's very earliest memory of her grandfather was him driving her somewhere and being struck dumb because he was so tall and impressive. To get her to talk, he'd asked her, were they being followed? So that's probably where her interest in everything espionage related all began. He told her if ever she was bored, she'd only to imagine the car behind had a foreign spy in it. And you had to lose them or else. How did he know all this fun stuff? It was only when she was older her mother told her that he worked for MI6 in the nineteen sixties when Kuwait was approaching independence.

So instead of a settling for a regular nine to five, Karen set her sights on being a private investigator. In reality, what she did was routine. No high-speed car chases throwing Russian spies off the trail or shooting guns at people in the street. There was a fair bit of ducking behind parked vans, but mostly to check position on Google Maps. However, the job required at the very least a person who didn't take fright at the sight of an ambulance squared up outside their door. And this was Karen that morning. Pathetic.

What was going on? Cars forced to manoeuvre around the emergency services meant the traffic backed up Devonshire as far as the Chiswick High Road. It was causing quite a stir. Plus, nosy shoppers to have a pry into the communal hall space.

The driver had by now closed his back doors, and the ambulance looked ready to roll. But seeing she lived there, the medic in charge was interested in quizzing her. Mostly about why she'd ignored her neighbour's call for help.

'Mrs Cochrane knocked on the wall for ages, apparently.'

Oh dear, so that's why she was banging!

She climbed the stairs, guilty as hell about misreading the thumps. The shopping unpacked, she took a shower to calm down. She fried shallots, chopped garlic, browned the chicken like a fiend. She was hours behind with the evening's prep. But being manic has certain advantages in that people like Karen are willing to take shortcuts at speed rather than run late. So she knew she'd be ready on time.

It was an easy choice what to wear for her meeting. All black was Karen's usual work outfit. If it was raining, which it was by then, she would go for the investigator's classic, a beige trench coat. Despite its frumpy image, it had become high street fashion. Quacker was wearing the same blue suit and tie from TV. He looked overdressed for a Saturday in casual Chiswick.

'You've got your belt twisted,' he told her. 'Lived here long, have you?'

'Two weeks. My neighbour's just been taken to the hospital,' she blurted out for no reason. 'She's ok though.'

'So what's your real take on it?' he asked. 'The Alesha Parkhurst case? I put your name forward to the producer and suggested if they were still interested in pursuing the cyberbullying angle to contact you.'

'If?' She started and stopped, not wanting to challenge him too much at this stage. He could be her next boss. 'You mean, what someone should do if they're being cyberbullied?' She was already getting into her new role as a TV expert. Magazine interviews soon, no doubt.

'Yes. Best thing, get off Twitter and Facebook,' he answered for her.

'It's not always that simple.' she said.

'I don't engage in this social media herself. My children do. On the internet all the time.'

Karen told him about the abuse. How it had carried on after Alesha Parkhurst had died. 'Alesha never deserved what she got. She just thought that some Muslims treated their wives like -'

'Like many Western blokes do no doubt!' He laughed at his own joke, then turned serious again. 'So who was tweeting this, do you recall?' He took out his phone ready to tap in some notes but put it away in favour of a pad and biro. Far more his style.

'Mostly other women.'

He raised his eyebrows. 'So much for feminism!'

'Trolls and bullies can be men or women. They're all sick in my opinion.'

'Can you ever do anything to stop bullying, do you think?'

'Yes, I believe it's possible,' she replied, despite her school days and hiding in cupboards flashing into her mind.

'How many of your cases are successful? For example, someone working for a crowd or a firm reports an issue. Then what happens? They get a report on the file and told to lay off. But will that fix the problem?'

'It would be nice if it did,' she answered. He adopted a knowing expression. 'Most companies farm their complaints out to consultants who do anything they are told so long as they get paid.'

'So they cover it up?'

'Not all. I wouldn't.'

'You apart, though.'

'In a word, yes. The company labels them a troublemaker. Maybe there's a payoff, but they find a reason to get rid of them either way. Short term, office policy is rewritten. It helps stop the bullying for a bit, but it often resurfaces. You can't change human nature, can you?'

'You ever worked with a political party?'

'No.' She hadn't.

Quacker sipped his coffee and reflected on what Karen had said. She was wondering when he'd bring up the case. Why she was there. He wasn't moving on the issue, so she raised it herself.

'You still reckon she was murdered? Alesha Parkhurst?'

'Well. Can't imagine a strong woman like her being pushed to take her own life over a few nutters on the net!'

Karen glared at him.

'You don't agree.'

Her body language must have said it all. She crossed her arms but then uncrossed them almost straight away. It was necessary to have a viewpoint. Equally important, she didn't want to appear too difficult to work with. It was essential to take in all scenarios and expand thinking. She'd been accused of jumping the gun more than once. So she sat still and listened.

Quacker believed vital clues were missed. Alesha Parkhurst had been high profile on matters other than sharia law, such as sex slavery from Eastern Europe and acid attacks. So much so, she'd been planning to fly women to the UK from Africa to speak about their abuse and other trafficking issues at a conference she was arranging. There'd be plenty of crims who'd want to silence her on that point alone! Perhaps one had killed her and covered it up.

Karen clenched teeth until she finally had the chance to put her bit in. It came out in a matter-of-fact tone, or so she thought at the time. Didn't he know how much pressure Alesha Parkhurst was under? Hounded day and night over the internet?

Of course it was anything but. Having bottled it as long as she had, it came bursting out in a torrent. It was a pet hate, how some people couldn't imagine suicidal thoughts if they'd never experienced them. She felt herself sway with anger.

'You'd think someone would learn to deal with all that though,' Quacker said. She assumed he was still speaking of Alesha Parkhurst.

'Sleepless nights, panic attacks. Victims are up to nine times more likely to contemplate ending their lives.' She stared at him. 'She killed herself.'

'Erm, well you seem convinced about this scenario.'

Karen's hands shook with adrenaline. She'd been woken at six, talked at for three-quarters of an hour on the phone and now was being challenged on an issue that was quite close to her. 'I have a different opinion on the consequences of bullying,' she said preparing to leave.

Plus it was Saturday. And if she wasn't going to get any work out of this meeting she needed to get her party prepared. She had to go.

'As I mentioned earlier, I have a small matter for you,' he said over the scraping chair.

Hearing this, she stopped at half stance. Wasn't this what she had come for after all? She sat to hear what he was proposing for her as an assignment.

It was not the Alesha Parkhurst investigation. Despite everything she'd been led to assume, the death of the feminist didn't feature and a lot of Karen's preparation had been in vain. But it was a case all the same, a missing person case and a sensitive one. It involved the Conservative party. A young man had disappeared after he'd attended a private meeting with an official at a top London hotel. This was only the day before. The boy's father, someone Quacker had met by the swimming pool while on holiday in Goa, had rung him out of the blue for a spot of advice.

'Not an easy case. Twenty-one-year-old goes AWOL overnight in the big city. His parents are worried sick.' He paused.

Karen wondered at first whether he was kidding. *Missing since yesterday?*

'What is a mite unusual about this, which is where you come in, is his backstory.'

'Which is?'

'He's a Tory activist who reckons he's been bullied by some older party members for starters.'

It seemed she'd become a fully-fledged cyberbullying expert after her one TV appearance.

Robin Miller had only told his mother about this bullying side of things the day before the meeting, and how he'd complained to Party headquarters weeks back and heard nothing. But then he'd been summoned finally to discuss things. Their problem was they'd not had a call from him since. Very unusual and out of character. No wonder the parents were in a state of concern.

The Millers had recognised Quacker on TV from their holiday. Then Karen had come on air. Her appearance warning about how many young people take their lives after they'd been bullied had struck a nerve with them. She'd used a term they hadn't recognised.

'Bullycide,' she said.

CHAPTER 8

Karen broke off eye contact with Quacker. Because of the way he'd built it up on the phone, by discussing Alesha Parkhurst for hours on end, her hopes of working on the case of someone she'd by now promoted to the category of a close friend, were dashed. It was disappointing.

However, a young guy was missing. It was a serious worry to the parents or she wouldn't have been sitting there at all. They'd mentioned her by name having seen her on the TV. And on the upside, Robin Miller's bedsit on the middle floor of a Victorian conversion in Maida Vale wasn't a million miles away. With other cases, she'd been sent all over the country.

Quacker had paid a visit to the place on his way through. 'All shut up like Fort Knox, it was' he said, looking around him as if half expecting the missing bloke to be sitting right behind in the coffee shop. Anyway, it'll probably all be clarified shortly. With your expert help. So how would you go about this to start, do you think?'

'You told me Robin's phone was off. Dead?'

'Yeah. Before mobiles, nobody would have noticed anything wrong, would they? Now if it doesn't answer straightaway we immediately jump to the worst conclusions.'

'But sometimes you have to,' she said.

'Of course you do. However, he may well turn up having had one or two jars too many and we'll all call it a day. Let's hope so.'

'I could cancel my thing tonight. Happy to do that. I'm holding a party.' Even if the young guy's disappearance turned out to be a false alarm, a missing person case took priority over socialising.

'Oh, no need,' he said. She appreciated that. His face softened as if he was now thinking red wine and popcorn. 'Got many coming?' He prodded at his phone.

'Just a few.'

Then they discussed how you're not officially classified missing for twenty-four hours. But of course there was plenty for her to do in the interim. Like check out social media.

Even that had to be done discreetly. She doubted Robin Miller would welcome too much fuss unless something serious had happened to him.

'You're right there.' He agreed. 'The dad doesn't need to go down that route yet. His lad is probably staying over with friends. Doubt he'd welcome hobnail boots showing up at his door because he hasn't called his mum.'

But they also agreed, start *somewhere*, just in case. Even though it was way too early for the full Police National Computer.

'Have the parents checked the hospitals?' If Robin had been in an accident or collapsed on the street, it was next to try. Phone dead or lost, no ID, unable to make contact.

'Much doubt they've contacted London A&Es. Perhaps start on those if you can?' Quacker then placed his three-inch serviette on the wooden bench which served as a table top. From the looks of it, she'd got the job tracking down the activist.

He finished with, 'I'd better let you go. Parties need a lot

47

of organisation, don't they? Do what you can about Robin Miller, anyway.'

Back at the flat, the chicken dish had burnt dry and an acrid odour filled the room. In addition, Karen had three missed calls. First she checked a text which had come in during her briefing with Quacker. Three people couldn't come. It meant the flat warming guest list had dropped from thirteen to ten. Probably not a bad thing, judging by the state of the food. And the unexpected extra work load.

Karen's contacts book held a list of every hospital in the UK. But first off she called the Chelsea and Westminster. The person who deals with this enquiry is usually the one in charge of Emergency Room Admissions. Robin Miller? It drew a blank. Next she rang the St Thomas' Hospital, after that the Charing Cross, working through each one in order.

The afternoon was moving apace. Karen bounded about double-jobbing and swearing at herself for not having done more the day before. She put her phone on speaker and scraped away like billy-o at the chicken dish which by now had stuck to the bottom of the pot like the proverbial to a blanket. It was ok, just, but by now looked lean on volume.

It's always when you're under pressure you find yourself short of the random items. Like having enough washing up liquid. So Karen raced up the road to the supermarket, the mobile now wired in to her ears. Back home, the frying pan needed scrubbing, the floor was swimming in oil and the extra plates for this mammoth event were still at the bottom of a packing box. She was struggling to get on top of the tasks, but at least keeping up with what was on her urgent list.

Then a calendar prompt to herself. 'PARTY 8 PM.' As

she hung up from the sixth hospital, there was a WhatsApp message from a girl who always cancelled invitations last minute. It read, 'Did you get earlier text I left? Sorry. Can't come.'

After this, her phone vibrated continually with a stream of the same. More lame excuses and dropouts. Eventually Karen was down to four with one 'maybe'. There was the last-ditch option of trying for standbys if she could think of anybody willing to stand in for a drop out. But she couldn't.

At five o'clock the party, or what was left of it, was under control in that she'd set up the buffet area for *eleven.* She hadn't the heart to set it for less. Candles out. Glasses polished, dress ironed, bed made, dirty towels replaced, bath hosed down.

Also, she'd made a darn good start on her missing person enquiry.

She fired up the laptop, brought up Google, typed 'Robin Miller' and pressed enter. What bounced straight back was 'unable to connect to the internet.' Shit. But by the time she'd taken a second pre-party shower and got glammed up, the net was up again.

Robin Miller is a fairly common name so a standard internet search provided several profiles. Twenty-five on LinkedIn, the same number on Facebook, half a dozen on Twitter. Through a process of elimination, she established which profile was his. It was easy enough. The distinctive ginger hair, London location and Tory party credentials brought him up straight away.

LinkedIn wasn't much help. Nor his Facebook account, which hadn't been updated in ages. But he was a super active user on Twitter. At least super active until the last twenty-four hours, which fitted with the information she'd been given about the time of his disappearance.

Karen looked at what he'd put online. He mostly retweeted political news and memes, but he'd also put up how he was being bullied and used the hashtag #bullying to promote the posts. Several spelling errors made her think he'd not checked carefully enough before pressing 'tweet'. Such as one of his last posts which read, 'Som nsty people out there. #bullying #beingbullied'. Karen knew this was like a red rag to a bull for trolls and thrill seekers. One said, 'Kill yourself you creep'. *Shades of Alesha Parkhurst.* Unfortunately it'd been 'liked' twenty-two times.

At this she felt a massive surge of sympathy. From the tone of what he wrote online Robin Miller was someone decent enough if a little too open for his own good. People had exploited him, without a doubt. He was the sensitive type, the kind who'd throw a party and no one would show and he'd be deeply upset by it. Looking at the table set for eleven Karen could relate to him.

Given all this, she was 'DEFFO' on his trail to help him if needed.

CHAPTER 9

When Zinah al-Rashid wanted to block out a bad memory, she didn't grit her teeth and will the vision away; she went shopping. It generally did the trick.

That Saturday morning was like that. She performed *salat.* After the ritual prayer, she studied the Koran. But despite all this, her head still replayed an evil scene repeatedly without stopping. She couldn't function this way. The agitation wouldn't abate. Most days she was bursting with ideas, but today nothing came. So she was seeking the inspirations and mood shift only a luxury store could provide.

For the past four years, Zinah had been content to support her father's direct action as her sole mission. How revered he'd been by the true believers! First was her conversion to Islam, then wearing the burka. Fundraising for the cause had been scarily exciting. It gave Zinah status because she'd stood out as exceptional in Syria. Since Cardiff, twenty extra girls were saving their money to cross to the Caliphate. But then her *abu* was murdered and everything changed. That was when Zinah's sense of self-importance collapsed. Who was she now? Nobody special.

What made it worse was how the British people cheered at his murder. They hated her father almost as much as she loathed the Tory MP who'd abused her as a seven-year-old. Or her stepfather who'd been responsible for leaving her with him in the first place. No wonder the last twenty-four hours were the worst of her life. Since then, getting on the list of martyrs and performing 'lesser Jihad' was all at once paramount. Zinah al-Rashid, she asked herself, are you ready for this harder task? *Inshallah.* God willing.

She needed the approval of the Brotherhood, and quickly. But why so fast? Was she suffering FOMO, fear of missing out?

Also the TV news was full of stories of historic sex abuse. Ten percent of victims named prominent people. She was itching to do so too. It was driving her crazy. But it would compromise her double identity.

Sit on your hands! Your time will come! *Allahu Akbar.* God is greater!

No she couldn't afford too fast a move. She had to keep who she was concealed for longer. It would bring an untold opportunity to perform Jihad.

When Zinah entered the upmarket department store, she was hoping for a massive pick-me-up to calm her racing mind and remove the dark thoughts and bitterness. And she got what she hoped for.

This familiar foray into the self-indulgent world of the rich worked like magic once again. She felt renewed by the sweet smell of a hundred perfumes which filled the air. A happy-giddy moment. Was it dangerous to be this overconfident? So at ease was she with the guise, the full black cloak, facial covering, plain spectacles, she almost burst into the *nasheed* or jihadi song, '*My Ummah, Dawn Has Appeared*'. My community, Dawn Has Appeared.

Zinah allowed her mind to sweetly drift as she toured the elaborate marble floors and let the pleasant sensation take over. The obsession with dressing in full Islamic robes had been with her for years. Ever since her stepfather had referred to women who dressed that way as 'bags of soot'. Little wonder it was now her favourite attire. She'd perfected the role. Oscar-winning performance no less. The whole thing gave her the greatest adrenaline rush in the world, but she had to keep strict self-control. Or she'd be found out. He was hypocritical, stingy, and corrupt. However much she wanted to shout it from the rooftops, no one could know how much this creep, this well-known creep, had shaped her views on the West. At least not yet.

No way can anyone in here pick me as the person I was before conversion.

Time flashed past, and soon it was approaching four in the afternoon, rush hour. This was when most Arab customers arrived and wandered in twos and threes, dripping in twenty-two carat gold from wrists and fingers. But solitary Zinah was superior to them all because she needed no show of wealth any longer. Not anymore. And nor should they, not if they were true Muslims.

Zinah could write a thesis on how these wealthy women shopped late, ate late, and slept late. About how opening hours and staff numbers revolved around these high-value shoppers. Having once worked there herself she knew more than anyone about the store's VIP rhythms. So much so she'd even once won Employee of the Year.

Nobody would recognise Zinah now though, would they? It was ten years ago. Then, at twenty-two, the store management marvelled at her flexibility, adaptability. One minute a tall, elegant mannequin and next, the nerd in the accounts department with black-rimmed spectacles and flat shoes. She'd been the ultimate team player. She still was. Today same player, different team.

Maximum ability for change was the sign of leadership and she was proud of this adaptability. *But it was now time to trial these skills.*

She ambled slower through jewellery, her favourite sector, killing minutes, soaking up the opulence. The polished display cases gleamed with the expensive brands Zinah once craved but Zinah could never afford. For instance, the Hublot watch the pot-bellied bloke was trying on was at least £15,000.

How good she no longer wanted these things.

'Can I help you?'

Zinah lowered her head to avoid direct eye contact, and she didn't reply as this might give the game away. Voice recognition. Instead, she angled towards the far side of the showcase and pointed to a diamond-studded Piaget. Would the 'watch girl' recognise her? She didn't. Not a bloody clue who she was serving! In fact the girl she'd once downed pints with just fished the piece out of the cabinet for Zinah to try without even batting an eye.

We used to work together. I trained you, Miss Stupidity!

The twenty-thousand-pound timepiece twinkled under the bright lights and for at least five minutes, Zinah played with its sparkle. It was fun teasing her!

London was still full of Saudis and Kuwaitis who'd come to enjoy the warmth of the city summer and Ramadan was well and truly over. During that month everyone had been fasting, Zinah included. And it was ok to indulge afterwards, but a bit. Not to such excess. It disgusted her. If this pillar of the religion was all about self-control and moderation, the aftermath display of greed was the opposite. *Not what it's about.*

Dressed as she was, it was simple to fit in because the shop was a sea of the same. Flowing black silk. Since the burka had been banned in France, there were twice as many on show in Harrods. Probably worn as a sign of defiance.

During her browse, and even though it was against her own rules of relaxing, Zinah never stopped going over her latest plan. She couldn't stop running through her ambitious new idea. It involved raising more money, yes. But why not? Look around at so much of it foolishly spent! Thousands of pounds wasted. For example, what's with the robed and veiled woman handing a gold Amex card for two identical handbags in different colours. *Tell me the point.*

The teenagers with her, so young they were still at the squealing and prodding stage, were no better. They'd already become fixated on useless fashion. One had a denim-studded shoulder bag and the other a quilted clutch the colour of bubble-gum. They held them up against the jet black cloaks to check the colours matched. Didn't they understand how ridiculous that looked?

It was obscene how much these young girls had at their disposal. Senseless, when back home they weren't even allowed to leave the house. What was the point loading up on expensive leather ware and labelled leggings at ninety quid a pop just to show off to their friends in Riyadh?

Why did parents allow their teenagers to spend on trivia instead of the hungry in Syria?

It was a waste. Therefore Zinah willed the girls to walk off and leave the packages behind with all her might. *Drink your coke, then go.* That way she could have scooped them up under her cloak before they had a chance to miss them. They would have fetched big time on the net.

Although this didn't happen, the next best did. Here she was walking through a world of consumer excess and not a stirring. She felt no yearning. None whatsoever. It had gone, gone, gone. *Inshallah*, if Allah wills it, Zinah's faith was now all consuming. *Alhamdulillah.* Thank God!

She toured the first floor to check out clothing.

Why were these young girls so fixated on the latest western trend? Had she been as impressionable at thirteen or whatever age they were? And what's with this swimming lark? Arabs hated splashing about in the water as far as she knew. Today they bought burkinis in bright colours to parade around in on the beach and draw attention to themselves.

The Saudi women in particular made Zinah seethe. They'd turned their back on the Syrians, despite it being right on their physical doorstep. It left it up to true warriors like her father to do their duty for them. Instead, here they were, Saudi sirens, stocking up on perfumes, buying a surplus of everything they didn't need or couldn't get in the Middle East.

Crazy. Even the Harley Street Clinic was all booked out. Muslim women could take nothing into the body during the Holy Period. So they stampeded in to order injectables and Botox the minute Ramadan was over!

The boys were no better. Look at the spoilt brats in Gucci and Louis Vuitton getting a shoe shine when they should be at prayers.

At five Zinah made her way to the store's French cafe. The new girl called Fatima, a potential bride recruit, sounded promising, but then they all did at the start. This one had been brought up accustomed to wealth and privilege, or so she said. Which was why Zinah chose Harrods this day for their initial rendezvous. Also hadn't she described herself as empty and seeking 'different values'?

Ok, so Zinah would test her. Was Fatima ready to give up all these heady temptations to serve Allah?

When she got there, the typical Arab guys had packed onto outdoor tables, waiting for a money-grabbing western girl, no doubt. But the inside area with its ornate decor was quieter, which she preferred. She was bang on time.

No sooner was she seated than Fatima approached. Around eighteen, petite, dressed in cheap fashionable clothes. Full European, but all topped off with a black hijab.

'Zinah?' A super high-pitched voice more like a canary's.

'Fatima?' She raised a hand, but not the face covering. It was important to set an example right from the start. Westernised applicants had to know what they would have to take on. Zinah's position with the Isis Brotherhood depended on her immaculate performance instilling these ideals.

From then on, the two women communicated in the agreed coded language mixed with plain English and a smattering of Arabic. It was the first test of many. Fatima's delivery was super quick, but she had a squeaky voice. As she chirped and cheeped about education and hobbies, Zinah made her assessment. Would this eighteen-year-old schoolgirl pass as suitable as the future bride of a proud jihadi warrior?

But what was with the high pitch? Should she ask?

Possibly Fatima had suffered an injury which affected her vocal chords. The reason for Zinah's concern was real. She hoped the voice wouldn't put off a fighter when he came to meet her. They could be so particular. But then Fatima was pretty. So, if she was prepared to risk the trip, then her soldier match would no doubt accept her.

Generally, Zinah was impressed. The first twenty minutes passed quickly which was a good sign. And the teenager's enthusiasm for the Caliphate was impressive. By five thirty Zinah al-Rashid was as high as a kite again about her life.

CHAPTER 10

The phone went. 'Did you get what I emailed you?' It was Uncle Bob from Australia at three in the morning Oz time. He'd been checking up on Karen since her parents had died.

'I'm about to read it. After I finish what I'm doing. 'This was adding last minute herbs to disguise the unmistakable aroma of the burnt bird.

'Yes. I came across this and thought you'd be interested. Right up your alley.'

At ten past eight and with no guests arrived, Karen opened the email.

Isolation

The aborigines have a tribal practice called Pointing the Bone. This is a method of execution which leaves no trace and rarely fails to kill its victim.

The bone can be from a kangaroo or an emu and its shape varies from tribe to tribe. It is from six to nine inches with one rounded end through which a hole is bored and tapers to a point as sharp as a needle. A piece of hair is threaded through the hole and glued into place with a gummy resin from the spinifex bush.

Before it can be used, the bone or Kundela is charged in a secret ritual performed by priests. It is then handed to Kurdaitcha, who are the tribe's ritual killers. Their task is to hunt down the condemned.

The name Kurdaitcha comes from the special slippers the aborigines wear on their quest. Made from cockatoo or emu feathers and human hair they leave no footprints.

The Kurdaitcha who hunt in twos or threes, wear feathered masks and stick kangaroo hair to their bodies with human blood. They will pursue a quarry for years never giving up until the curse is delivered.

Once found one priest goes down on to one knee and points the Kundela. The victim is frozen with fear as the Kurdaitcha chant the short piercing mantra then return to their village where the bone is ritually burnt.

From that moment on the condemned is banished from their village forever. No one may speak to him or associate with him. If they do, then they too are punished and sent into isolation.

For most tribal members, having the bone pointed is a sentence of death. Waiting for the inevitable, coupled with the shame and isolation, often forces the victim to suicide.

Had someone pointed the bone at Robin Miller? Is this why he'd disappeared?

CHAPTER 11

I don't want to be here. The District Line train pulled into Turnham Green. Haruto Fraser, freelance photojournalist, and very reluctant party goer, stepped off the tube onto the platform. Pushing ten o'clock, he'd far rather have been in the Coach and Horses in Soho closer to home.

He exited the station and turned left onto Turnham Green Terrace. A young homeless guy sat cross-legged on the pavement under the overhead tracks, head in a book, reading, helped by a torch in the dim light. Haruto stopped and felt in his pocket. Give him something. Dropping a gleaming coin into the begging bowl he noticed with amazement the book was not only poetry, but poetry by Robert Burns.

'I see you're reading a favourite of mine. My Dad is from Edinburgh.' With no reaction, he walked on, but now reflecting with pride on his genetic heritage. A strong sense of independence and self-belief coupled with an inner toughness which his profession rarely required him to draw on. He'd also picked up the wry humour typical of a Scot. *That could come in handy tonight.*

An uneasy feeling in the gut told Haruto trouble lay ahead. He was in Chiswick well and truly under sufferance. Hailey had given him hell to force him to come. Other than the hostess, he would know no one at the party and he hated parties, anyway. And she only wanted him there to show they were still an item. Which they weren't. Their relationship, as far as he was concerned, was over. And her game playing was one of the many reasons it would never have worked in the first place. Take tonight. Even though he'd agreed to turn up, she was still sulking. When he'd texted to say he was running late, she'd not even bothered to respond.

Her jealousy was a big, big problem.

From his father, Haruto had got broad shoulders and a well-built physique which women found attractive. Likewise his hard to read eyes were as angular as they were green which made women want to look deep into them.

Despite not wanting to attend this party, he'd at least made an effort. Tonight he wore a dress shirt, waistcoat, a blazer and a scarf. Depending on how he dressed, Haruto Fraser could pass as either Japanese or Scottish. He had two looks which separated the two. A red and black tartan kilt for formals. Then a quirky, loose layered way of putting clothes together which was distinctly Tokyo creative.

It was a beautiful evening, a photographer's dream. Semi-dark. More satisfying than sunrises or sunsets, which were trite, too easy and pat, the full night sky was a real challenge. So as a great moon rose and hovered over Chiswick Common he diverted off into the park.

He chose a manual mode with a wide aperture and high ISO, braced the camera on a stand, pointing up, Haruto clicked. Set at 30-second shutter speed for each one, the series of pictures took ten minutes.

The iPhone theme chord jolted him back to reality. It was his mother calling from Tokyo. Even though he was twenty-six, she still spoke to him like he was twelve, which could be endearing, sometimes. He could have avoided it, but he didn't. Anything to arrive late to this wretched party.

But wafting across the common from one of the restaurants he picked up the pleasing smell of garlic and onion. It reminded him he hadn't eaten all day. Hitching the heavy camera bag high over his shoulder he quickened pace towards Devonshire Road. He could delay no longer! When he was outside the address, resigned to his fate, he pressed the bell.

'Oh, Hi. How are you? 'Karen Andersen, party-ready was dressed in a blue mini dress and seemed more surprised than she should have been to see him standing on her doorstep. Haruto took a quick glance at the deep cut top covering her nipples. *Nice.* They'd met briefly and only once before, but he couldn't remember fancying her as much back then as he did right now. 'Isn't Hailey with you?' she asked.

'Nooo. The plan was to meet up here. I thought she'd have been here already. If it's awkward, I can leave. Not a problem.' Haruto saw right then the perfect opportunity to duck out of three hours of nothing talk to people with whom he hadn't one sensible thing to share.

'Oh.'

Haruto could have made his getaway then without causing too much offence because he'd been invited as part of a couple. Perhaps her small breasts and bare feet had something to do with it. Or the fact that by now he was half starved. Also, by now, as if coaxing him in, Karen had turned and was already halfway up the stairs. So he was snookered.

Haruto followed on up with a heavy heart wondering where all this would lead. In the flat Randy Crawford was playing 'One Day I'll Fly Away' which was apt. *If only I could right now.*

The main room appeared smaller still, being crammed with unpacked boxes. It was the scene of a total party disaster, over-catered, heaps of unopened wine. The food of sorts sat drying out, shrivelling up on the sideboard.

'Hailey's not been answering me. But I've left a message,' he said not knowing what else to add because the night looked like it had been a complete and utter shambles. *It was too awkward.*

On a late summer evening, the small red candles didn't seem too out of place. They gave the untidy flat an intimacy which appealed at a deeper level.

But now what? As he stroked his wispy beard, he wondered how he should extract himself from the situation. It looked as if Karen had even begun packing away. Her eyes were full of hurt pride, so obviously he hadn't misread the scene. No guests. She held her hands together in front of her as she asked. 'Would you like a drink?'

Haruto had been on the point of leaving. Then he had a change of heart. He divested of the camera gear, tucked it away in the corner alongside an ageing laser printer, and struck an upright pose. 'I'd love one. Thank you.'

Maybe turning up to a dead party was better than entering a room full of luvvies, druggies, or London socialites blotto on designer gin. And by the look of the stack of clean plates remaining, more guests might show after pub closing hours.

Anyway, aside from all that, he was famished. And there was plenty to eat.

CHAPTER 12

Karen got up to clear the plates which hadn't been used. The night had been a prime bloody disaster. Her party was supposed to have started at eight. Only one couple had shown, and even they'd left early saying they had to go on somewhere else.

She decided to put the event behind her and go to bed. Start over fresh the following morning. But the damn doorbell went. An unexpected, brutal tone which jogged her out of her sense of isolation. She couldn't ignore it.

The time was ten twenty when she checked her watch. By then you're past pretending to be pleased to see new people unless of course you've already got a full house. Which for Karen was certainly not the case. But she had no option but to open the door, and quickly. Or risk another loud blast of the bell. Mrs Cochrane, her neighbour, back from hospital, was in bed and probably sleeping. Karen didn't want a repeat of that morning's drama.

When Hailey's flatmate was stood there, Karen assumed Hailey would be somewhere behind him. Late or not, that would have been ok because it would have brought the numbers up to four. Still grim, but acceptable.

'Hi. Remember me? Haruto. Is Hailey here?'

'No, she's not.'

While Haruto was an interesting guy, Karen hadn't invited him to the party herself. He was going out with Hailey, and she was coming, wasn't she? She'd expected them together. They were, at least according to Hailey, inseparable.

So Karen asked, 'Isn't she with you?'

He shrugged. 'We were supposed to meet here. Thought she'd have arrived by now.'

She remembered at that moment that she quite liked him. And sensing he'd leave if she didn't invite him up, she turned and led the way up the stairs. 'Come in, anyhow.' As she did, she went over in her mind the history between them.

He flatted with Hailey as Karen had done herself for a brief period waiting for the Devonshire Road transaction to complete. When Karen had moved out, Haruto had moved in. Then they'd met again fleetingly when Karen had been collecting a heap of crud she'd left behind. Hailey had been in such a hurry to get her out the door, they had both overlooked a further packing case. It was a pain in the backside, and Karen had been on to her about it, on and on, trying to clear the load. But each time there was a problem at the Hailey end. Karen reckoned it had something to do with this new, blossoming relationship.

'You had a good party?'

The stairs up to her flat were steep so Karen was too breathless by the top to answer. But she needn't have bothered. The empty candle-lit room said it all.

'Red or white?' She pointed to the two nearly depleted bottles, but he still took in the eight full ones lined up unopened. She felt herself flush pink.

Haruto looked down to the new carpet, up to his phone screen, then around the deserted room. Finally, straight in the eye, smiled. 'I'm sorry. I should have brought a bottle.'

'It's ok. I've got plenty.'

At this, they were both grinning.

He still had his backpack on when he tapped out some numbers, like undecided whether he was going to stay or not. 'Calling her now.' Then locking her gaze with a playful grin he answered, 'Red, please.'

Karen slopped some Cab Sav in a glass, relieved he appeared to be in no hurry to go, and, at that moment she understood what Hailey saw in him. He was very dry. And a sense of humour was what she needed right then.

Haruto left a message on Hailey's phone.

'I'm at Karen's dinner party. Can you call back? We were wondering what's happened to you. Hope you're ok.'

He removed a grey Wolfeepack from his shoulder and plonked it down on the floor. As he did so, he relaxed. His face brightened like the sun through clouds. They talked about the great location, her framed pictures of London in the fifties and the best times to go to Portobello Market where she'd got them from.

'Ignore the mess,' she said, rather late.

They stood by the kitchen bar waiting for the call back from Hailey, wondering if it would ever come.

He raised a glass to her new home. 'Cheers.'

'Cheers.'

'I can't understand why Hailey's not here. She was supposed to be. I know that. Have you heard from her at all?'

'No.' The absence of explanation was a sore point for Karen. She'd been expecting her with or without this guy. She thought their friendship extended that far at least. 'I hope she's ok,' she said to affect concern knowing only too well there would be another reason for her no-show.

In a matter of seconds, because the call was from Haruto's and not her number, she rang back. What was he doing there, she overheard? It didn't sound to Karen as if Hailey had ever planned to come.

Wiping with a dry cloth, she busied herself in the kitchen, so as not to let him think she was listening. But of course she was. Haruto was being diplomatic, speaking in mumbles. She picked out the words 'rude' and 'you can't do that' and felt a twinge of hurt. The call over, he placed his phone face down on the granite counter.

'Is she on her way?' she asked, pretending not to be too bothered in any case. But it didn't fool Haruto. He could tell she was unimpressed.

'Nope. She said she'd already called you to explain why.'

Karen unlocked her iPhone and went through the charade of checking messages. But it was a charade. She knew every one by heart, having kept a look out all afternoon. There'd definitely been none from Hailey.

He shrugged it off. 'I wasn't supposed to be here either, apparently. But she was coming. She said she was. I even wrote down your address.' He took out of his wallet a Café Nero's loyalty card with Karen's flat number and street scribbled on the reverse to prove his point.

His phone went, and it was Hailey again. This time she adopted a more conciliatory tone. She'd had a couple of minutes to make up an excuse. She was not feeling well and there was some fabricated history to shore this up. Next, Karen heard Hailey ask Haruto when he planned to be back. And could it be soon? Out of the blue, he said, 'Do you want to speak to Karen?' and without waiting for her reaction, passed the call over in her direction. Karen had no option but to take it.

'Hi, Hailey.'

'Karen,' she cooed, trying quickly to cover not wanting to talk to her. 'How is it? I bet you're having great fun. Is it wonderful?'

'Erm.'

'Sorry I'm not there.' She gave a little cough. 'I thought I'd called you about it. Or maybe I didn't.' She petered out. 'Oh God, Karen. I think I'm coming down with something nasty. What have you been up to, anyway?'

'Erm.'

'Yup. If I forgot to message you, I really meant to do so.' *Face saving.* 'Must have fallen asleep because I feel so bloody lousy. What's the time?' She gave a noisy yawn as if to stress the point. 'Oh, dear. Erm. How many are there? I bet you've got scores.'

'Only Haruto and me.' There was a protracted silence. 'I mean, the others have left.' Another nothing. 'Hailey, I need to collect the rest of my belongings at some stage. Would that be all right?'

Typically, not wanting to commit to a precise time which she'd then be forced to cancel, she avoided once again the issue of Karen collecting her stuff. Instead, she brought the conversation around to Haruto. When she did her tone hardened. 'Can you put me back on to him please?' It was well curt.

Haruto took the phone and winked at her, which made Karen's stomach flutter. Then he walked away with it so she couldn't overhear, rotating the wine in his glass. Karen expected him to leave any second, so she poured herself more white and sat on the sofa. She'd stop work until he left.

Finally the call ended, and he turned and put down the drink, then threw himself down alongside.

'What's happening?' she asked him.

'Not a lot.' He leaned forward towards the table and slid the phone across it. He stretched his arms high above his head and yawned. 'Is that food still in the offing?'

The chicken was passable. It had improved from being off the hob and sitting on a plate warmer for close to three hours. Karen hadn't eaten either, due to nerves. But soon they were both wolfing it down as if it was the Last Supper.

Despite the awkward introduction, they chatted on like old friends. When she next looked it was four in the morning and time had flashed by.

The best evening ever. Doing the washing up and placating Hailey could wait for another day.

CHAPTER 13

When DI Partridge first woke, he checked his watch. Normally at seven he'd be up and at 'em Atom Ant doing whatever needed doing. Hard at work on something useful, at least by the time wife Chris returned from night duty. Instead, he took two aspirin and snoozed on. The left side of his body throbbed like hell.

A hip replacement involving a spree in hospital was a matter he'd usually avoid. Keep away from that knife, was his motto. But if it meant trim nurses and relief from gnawing pain, he'd take it happily. Get it over with fast now Junior Doctors were threatening more strike action.

His presence wasn't required at the station today. But he hated staying in bed on a day off so he finally gave up trying to grab more sleep.

Home for the past twenty years had been a suburban semi in Acton. Nothing flash, two up and two down. They'd modernised the kitchen and added a marble-topped bathroom and a conservatory which faced west. But there were always scores of other jobs waiting for weekends.

Quacker showered and dressed in a blue and white check shirt and khaki shorts. There was another reason he'd didn't want wife Chris to find him still in the sack. She'd only recently delayed a planned trip away with her sister. Though she denied it, Quacker was concerned it was because of his hip playing up more than normal. He didn't want to stop Chris going off and having fun on account of him.

The kitchen was much as he'd left it the night before, so

he cleared that up briskly before dropping sliced wholemeal in the toaster. Brown bread was Quacker's only concession to a healthy diet. As he searched for the marmalade, he reflected on his TV work, specifically the Alesha Parkhurst story. As one of the country's top rape and murder experts, Quacker was doing far more media than he used to.

Being on the television meant he was still the butt of jokes with the lads. The clean-cut look, white shirt and tie appealed to women who iron, they would say.

Want my autograph next, I don't think.

Bloody internet. Call it progress? Stalking cases tripled because of Facebook.

The back door opened. Chris entered, laden up with the picnic clobber Quacker had left in her car after the past weekend's outing to Windsor Great Park.

'Hi, dear. Any news on the boy?' She was referring to Robin Miller as she was very much in on this. Quacker and Chris had palled up with the parents on their last holiday to Goa where they'd shared nightly drinks by the hotel pool.

Chris wore a loose-fitting top, dark trousers, and comfy shoes. But she'd recently gone on a crash diet to prepare for a black bikini and the weight loss was working well. Not bad for forty-eight, he thought.

'Not a sausage.'

Chris pulled a sympathetic face. 'Don't half fancy a tea. A hell of a shift.' She scraped her hair back into a tight pony tail, less flattering than loose. Casting around and taking in what they were short of, like everything, she next dived into her bag and searched out car keys.

Despite night shifts, Quacker's wife rarely slept long in the day. Put him to shame on that score. She was far too

72

active for that, which was one of her many redeeming features. Another was listening to him. Ha, ha.

'You off so soon? You've just come in, love.'

Chris tucked the flimsy blouse into her waistband, wrapped a red jacket around her shoulders. 'But we're out of milk. Can't have a cuppa without milk, can we?'

Quacker lifted the empty carton. 'Sorry, love. Thought there was another one in the fridge.'

'Nope. No problem. TV appearance went all right yesterday?'

'Yes, I think so. This Alesha Parkhurst case should be for the murder team, as I was saying on the Box...' But Chris was already out the door. 'Talking to myself again, am I?'

She always was on the go with at least ten things at one time as if multi-tasking was her passion, he was sure of that. But they enjoyed the perfect marriage. There were never any dramas or unreasonable demands from her. Plus, he could describe a corpse without her turning green. Being a nurse, she had a strong stomach. Not only that, she often had something half sensible to add.

Quacker picked up a postcard from another of Chris's friends who'd visited Goa. The only blot on the horizon was just that. Her being dead set on buying a place in Calangute when Quacker retired. What to do about it!

At eleven o'clock his iPhone vibrated. When the name flashed up on the screen as Drew Evans, the Kiwi who managed the local hockey club, he brightened up. Excited to be called, Quacker forgot the pain in his side. 'Can't do without me then?'

Quacker knew they training staff would only ring like this if they needed an extra coach. The sport had picked up big time. It wasn't any way as popular as football or the gym. But after the Brits won gold at the Brazil Games, young and old and everyone in-between yearned to pick up a hockey stick again.

'You got a spare set of keys for the second field, Quacker? We've a problem here.' The original bunch had gone missing from Reception

'In a word, no.'

Then they may need a bolt cutter, he was told.

'I don't actually have one of those about my person right now.'

They had a big lesson starting, so this was no time for banter. Quacker knew what Drew meant. 'Very embarrassing to be holding a beginner's session when you've got a heap expected and can't unlock the bloody gate.'

The key for the field hut was included in the missing set. 'The keys gone means you can't get into the hut to use the lockers either I suppose? Any idea who took them?'

'No one knows. Obviously not a club member then. It's time we tightened up on our security.'

'Strange.' said Quacker, thinking to himself, why would anyone want to steal a bunch of Velcro aprons?

'Have many arrived?'

'We've got people waiting already and they can't even warm up. Or leave their kit.'

'Tad embarrassing.'

'Big time. As a matter of fact two England stars said they'd drop by later and give a pep talk seeing as there's a good crowd expected.'

Everything and everyone were missing. Pints of milk. Twenty-one-year-old activists. Sports club keys. Anyway, none of that would help solve the problem. A solution had to be found.

'Looks like you need a bolt cutter, as you say. I know where I can get hold of one sharpish. Leave it with me.'

Minutes later a squad car was hurtling toward the West London Hockey Club, lights blazing. On board was the exact right equipment to break open a hefty padlock. Quacker hobbled to his Ford Fiesta, turned the ignition. Johnny Cash started up, singing his signature tune. He was still 'walking the line'.

He drove towards the sports field thinking how he'd better get on to Karen Andersen and the Millers. Had there been any more news on the son? Emergency systems alerted. Probably when they'd cut through the lock at the gates and made a hell of a mess, the keys would reappear. Most likely the same would happen with Robin Miller.

CHAPTER 14

Karen woke this dawn on a high, too early, trembling from lack of sleep. Instead of going back to bed, she went for a brief jog, not able to stop smiling. The reason was Haruto. The party had been a flop in one sense of the word. But it'd meant they'd hung out together long into the wee hours and those had passed in a flash.

When Karen returned from the run, nausea overcame her enthusiasm for work and bed called. It was a quarter past nine when she resurfaced and guilt got the better of her.

Coffee in hand, she brought up Robin Miller's social media feed because his phone was still not reacting. Karen's ingenious plan, or she thought, was to drop round to the bedsit next thing. So looking at Twitter was just a random act. *What she saw was like a bolt.*

There was a fresh post on social media. It read: 'Join us at #Churchill War Rooms. SW1A 2AQ. Beer in pub after.'

The tweet had been up for over two hours and already 'liked' by the Twitter account of the Imperial War Museum. But these War Rooms were not close. So, in seconds Karen was out of the door still dressed in sports kit and running shoes.

It took seven minutes to make the local underground. But when the District Line rocked up straight away with Upminster on the front, hope sprang eternal. At five to ten she got to the location.

The bunker is every bit *espionage* as it's where the

government command plotted battles in the Second World War. So Karen had expected the museum to be busy and for Robin Miller to be waiting there with a clutch of Party faithful. That morning neither was the case.

Karen stood outside the entrance unprepared, dressed in too little for the changing weather. The sky turned an ominous elephant grey colour. A slow thudding robbed her of too much inspiration, caused by exceeding the wine limit the night before. Two groups passed by but didn't appear to fit what she'd expected a bunch of Tory activists to look like.

At ten a Chinese guy approached, early twenties, glasses and jeans, smart. He crossed to where Karen was standing and, taking in her sporty attire, seemed to change his mind. Instead, he backed up to his original spot and checked his phone. But after a minute or two, when no one else showed, wondering about her, he looked over and made a light attempt at conversation.

'Hi.'

Karen walked over to him and they stood together in silence for a few beats before her raising the subject of Miller.

'I'm waiting for him too. William, William Wan.'

'Karen.'

'Robin should be along real soon. Don't know why he's late. Have you been here long?'

'Five minutes.' They waited on, not speaking. She played with her thumbs in her pockets while he continually checked his iPhone for updates.

William Wan pushed a pair of glasses back on his nose. 'I guess not everyone in the party's as crazy about Churchill as we are. Then most guys have been here before. You?'

Karen pretended not to have done, otherwise out would come the whole story of Miller's disappearance. Maybe not too wise under the circumstances. All the same, the dehydration and standing waiting was making her irritable and also she'd fallen into a trap of her own stupidity. Now he was suggesting she do the War Rooms tour on her own.

'Is Robin always this unreliable?'

'If anything, he's the opposite and arrives an hour early.' He tried Miller's number for the umpteenth time. 'Can't think what's happened to him.'

Aware of her fast-failing phone battery Karen brought up the Twitter feed while there was an iota of juice left. There'd be one retweet since last looking by someone called Wills.

'That's me.' He grinned. 'Everyone calls me Wills.'

The profile picture bore this out.

'Robin, where are you? Come on, man.' Wills let out another sigh of disapproval. 'How did you hear about this, anyway? You a Party supporter?'

'I read it on his Twitter feed.'

'Oh!' he smiled. 'At least someone reads them.'

'But it seems odd though. Why would he write this if he wasn't planning to join the group himself? Doesn't seem right, does it?'

'Robin didn't post it. I did.'

What was going on? The announcement was on Miller's account.

'When the details weren't up this morning, I thought he'd forgotten to do it. That's why I put it up for him.'

'But they were on Robin's Twitter feed?'

'Yeah. But I know the log in, like he knows mine. Thatcher345.' He coloured when he realised he'd been indiscreet. 'Maggie Thatcher. She was the greatest. No surprises we are fans.'

'But I assumed this was a personal account. Isn't it?'

'Yeah.' He was looking through the feed at pictures of the two of them together canvassing. 'I am his social media agent!' He laughed and scrolled through the messages, even those with the bullying hashtag.

'Robin puts other stuff on it too,' she said, hoping by now Wills would open up on the issue which may have resulted in his doing a vanishing act.

'Sometimes.' His mood darkened. 'This is not like him at all. He's probably lost his phone and that's such a load of crap if it happens. Or maybe gone home because the family are real close.'

It hit her. William Wan hasn't a clue about the disappearance. Robin Miller is still AWOL. Now where to go with this?

'Did you know Robin has been reported missing?' At this, he gave Karen a dazed look. He stared at her aghast, and she wouldn't have blamed him if he'd thought she'd made everything up on the spot. 'That's why I'm here, to see if he showed up.' Karen knew she was coming across really badly. More unsure of her facts by the second.

The whole thing sounded lame, which Quacker had warned her about. Even the fact she was an investigator didn't ring true, dressed as she was and with no proof of identity to back it up. Not to mention the lack of battery on the phone. She could have been insane, the way he gaped when she told him.

'PI? That's cool.' He nodded with approval. 'Did you know Robin was being bullied?'

'Can you tell me more about it?'

William wrinkled up his brow and his expression changed. He rubbed his face as if he was nervous, shook his head as if he was uncomfortable about saying too much more. 'Maybe he should do that himself. How long has it been since his parents heard from him?'

'Friday afternoon was the last message.'

He was mentally counting back. No, not that great an amount of time after all and Wills was certain he'd show up soon. He tapped Karen's mobile number into his list of contacts and they made their farewells after agreeing it was unnecessary to go underground in the circumstances.

'Who knows? I might have news for you later this afternoon,' Wan said over his shoulder as he walked away.

CHAPTER 15

At a little past eleven that morning Wills got back home to Camden. His uncle was out, which suited fine. Eric always took a swipe at William's politics if he was wearing his Tory tee shirt or knew he'd been out canvassing.

Wills had good reason for joining the party and a more pragmatic one than he could explain to his relative without causing offence. Eric Wan, a retired shop owner from Soho's Chinatown was very pro-Chinese. But the twenty-five-year-old UCL graduate was different. He didn't want that and to be just another British Asian with a maths degree. Wills thought somehow the Conservative social set would define and help his artistic ambitions. Nothing too right-wing about it at all.

While he and his uncle were chalk and cheese, Wills was indebted to him all the same. Free board in a substantial detached property with elaborate Chinese décor was not what everyone of his age enjoyed. Five bedrooms, three baths, only two used. Plus, he could do whatever he liked within reason. And a landscaped, fully maintained garden to go with it. But more than that, he and his uncle shared a good laugh together.

First off, Miller got him in with the Tories. Both Robin and Wan had networking ambitions. While Robin wanted to become PM, Wills was an aspirant producer on the lookout for wealthy Tories who might invest in his arty movies.

The living room or salon as Uncle Eric referred to it was

where Wills stretched out to absorb the oriental vibes of the curtains and cushions. Wills, a cool head in a crisis was now racking his brain. And the Buddha statue and priceless artefacts didn't exude their usual calming effect. Nor the photo of his Grandfather which gazed down at him.

Where was Robin Miller?

Why did his phone go straight to voicemail? What could have happened to him?

When Wills was upset, which he was now, he used coke. *Not today.* He'd had kicked the habit, well mostly. Plus, today required crystal clear thinking. Instead of reaching for a line of the white powder, he buried his head in his hands.

A missing person? Was it true?

Had Robin disappeared? Was it linked to the bullying? If it was, it'd maybe been William's fault things had got quite as bad as they'd become. Unknown to everyone else, Wills had been the instigator of the official report and he'd been the one who'd urged reluctant Robin to write in to CCHQ. After all, Robin couldn't have compiled the document by himself.

In fact, Robin had been dead set against it. Unlike Wills, Robin had always shot to the defence of the Party no matter what it did. The guy was blinkered to its manipulation of lists and favouritism practices. He was a bit naïve that way. Unlike Wills and his uncle, who recognised cultish behaviour straight away when they saw it. If anyone knew about closed societies, it was the Chinese.

Robin was the type who avoided confrontation if there was any other way at all to achieve his aims. But Robin could also be strong, almost too much so, almost bordering on arrogance.

When things deteriorated, it'd been William Wan who'd said to him, 'You have got to put this shit down on paper. Otherwise, it won't stop, man.' Robin had done what Wills had told him. But then there'd been the repercussions. Despite the fact Robin heard zippo back from the party in acknowledgement, he'd still been cold-shouldered by other activists. Everyone sensed something was going on, that Robin was to be avoided.

The other campaigners kept low profiles since the bullying issues became public, not wanting to get involved in case it was them to be next in the firing line. Bystanders were like that. Instead of backing him, they'd backed off!

And then that video had appeared.

Robin had been distraught at the film when he'd seen it. The guy hadn't deserved that. Had an activist posted the sex tape on the net as revenge for his complaining about them? Robin saw this as a sign of things getting way, way, way out of control. *Still no word back from CCHQ.*

'I have to speak to the Party again. I know they'll help.'

'They haven't answered until now.'

'Probably too busy at the moment, mate.'

'Might be trying to duck-shove the issue.'

'Doubt it for one minute, Wills. Why would they do that?'

'They'll never talk to you, man. You have to hit them again.'

So nobody was more surprised than Wills or delighted than Robin when Simon King wanted to meet up with him there and then. When he'd read the message on his WhatsApp, Wills, at a party and high as a kite, had not replied.

And now Robin was missing? Maybe the meeting had turned bad? As his only friend, it was up to Wills to find out.

Robin's bedsit was a dark and dingy tip, with no cooker or fridge, which was enough to send anyone downhill. But it was in the Westminster West constituency and Robin needed to live there to get on the council list. When Wills had gone over to discuss the sex tape, getting it off the internet, they'd even had to drink warm beer. How bad was that?

William surfed the net on the phone.

What? Despite their efforts, the video was still bloody showing. Was it that impossible to remove?

Like the many-headed Hydra, chop one off and another grows. Robin was the shy type and the sort his uncle took the piss out of, which Wills hated. Because this was no laughing matter.

Damn film.

Once it's uploaded to the net, porn propagates in nanoseconds and there's no stopping it. Other servers pick it up, then the PCs of web browsers, and the next thing you know it is being watched in Starbucks, Mumbai.

But *who'd* made and posted the tape wasn't half as important to Robin as preventing his family seeing it. Or also what it could spell out for his long-term political ambitions. Because mud sticks.

Was Robin depressed over the whole thing? Where was he? Why didn't he get in touch?

Wills knew he had to remove the film. He googled 'How to delete sex tape from net' as he'd done so often before. The same sites appeared featuring a list of providers who reckoned they could do it for a fee, a massive fee at that. *No way!*

A story flagged by Google was of a girl of fourteen who'd taken her life over a sex video like this gone viral.

All this online abuse hurt. It drove victims of all ages to kill themselves, not just teenagers. What about Alesha Parkhurst? Even if Wills didn't believe the suicide story, she'd still suffered, hadn't she? Alesha had a sister who lived next door to the Wans and had had this to say: 'Makes no difference, suicide or murder. She went through hell online and all because she was a feminist.'

Cyberbullying was lethal stuff.

Wills logged into Robin's Twitter account and picked up the stream of responses to his #bullying hashtag tweets which included trolls urging him to 'top himself'. Last time Robin and Wills had met up, he'd seemed cool about all this. But what'd happened since then?

The more William thought about it, the worse it got.

Maybe he's now feeling like shit wherever he was.

Wills decided when he tracked him down, how about he do something practical to help with the guy's living situation? Uncle Eric might put Robin up in the house for free. Maybe that way Robin could still keep the Westminster West address. Failing that, Wills and Robin could get a flat together. If this meant Wills paying a higher share of the bills, that was ok with him. He was cool with that.

Imagining this happy ending, he hightailed it to the kitchen. Pulling the cap off a *cold* Coors Light a good outcome was now a certainty in his mind.

Where was he scheduled to meet up with Robin next?

Wills would allow no more flash images of Robin lying numb, unconscious, and maybe even dead. That was all rubbish, man.

He scoffed a lump of cheese straight from the fridge in celebration.

CHAPTER 16

At nine o'clock that morning Bea Harrington kicked off on one of her *Political Women* training sessions at Party headquarters. This London course was always well attended. The girls had travelled in a fair old way. The ex-army bomb disposal expert in the back row was from Loughborough. Another from Cornwall.

'Welcome everyone!' Bea, the second wife of James Harrington MP was petite, lively, pretty. She loved giving these presentations, which were her version of The Apprentice. The work was unpaid at least in monetary terms. Possible compensation could be a seat in the House of Lords someday, which would fit her nicely.

As part of a nationwide programme to recruit more women, Bea swore by the need to attract complete newcomers. So twice a month she gathered a merry band of helpers, bods from both the voluntary and elected party, to give a talk. Hands-on insider info. It was useful for up-and-coming candidates to hear direct from those in Parliament about how they'd made it. These deified advisers, ex-Board members and politicians, even included a male MP who'd come damn close to losing his seat over a sexting scandal. But today Bea was there single-handed.

'We must get more females into politics' was her soundbite.

It was not only a feminist issue but also prudent. The Party needed more women, more female candidates, more committed activists to be deployed. Less trouble than the boys, the girls were far easier to cajole. Plus, they came with ready-made support groups; their families, who delivered in all weathers and rallied round their mother or wife or daughter without putting up a squeak. They were diligent, smart, proactive. Frankly, the girls did more, full stop.

Also, women didn't sit there like the guys, hands around the back of chairs, fantasising about becoming PM in five minutes flat. What the party needed were foot soldiers, ambitious ones, but foot soldiers all the same. Grassroots people. Of course she never told wannabe candidates that in so many words.

The classic motivator, Bea emphasised instead what was in it for *them*. How the Party needed their unique skills and experience and their personal style. Their different backgrounds. That they'd had City jobs, or farmed sheep, or sat on the School Board was so, so important. No wonder the ladies lapped it up. 'Women make up half the population. They protect women's rights. For far too long we've taken a back seat.'

Bea could rattle these sentences out in less than five seconds. Not that she didn't believe what she delivered, but she'd rolled the words out so often her delivery was flawless. Bea was not only an avid feminist, but she was a realist with it. 'Women are the bulk of low-wage earners and heads of households. Health issues and child care are handled more by us. We make better MPs, listen more. Trouble is the ladies don't know how to promote themselves.'

The course was working! There were far more female members of Parliament now than Bea could ever have dreamed of ten years ago.

That morning Bea couldn't take her eyes off a woman in

the front row. Who was she? Wasn't she *already* a candidate? She'd been around for one parliamentary term she was sure, though maybe not yet tested a seat. It was a trifle surprising the girl was attending her course because it was mostly, but not *exclusively*, for beginners.

The woman bugged her. For instance, Bea would usually touch on her husband being a sitting MP at some point during the day, but she never dwelled on it. The training was for and about female MPs. But it seemed today, at every blasted opportunity, this girl brought him up.

Who cared a monkey's which committee James sat on?

Never mind her husband! Bea had been a parliamentary candidate herself in the nineteen-eighties, back when women barely featured. She didn't need to ask James Harrington MP to know what she was talking about.

'Been there. Got the tee shirt.'

Another thing was Bea's personal details. If she felt the necessity to mention her past, it was only ever a fleeting reference to it. She might tell the group she ran a successful interior design shop yonks ago in the Kings Road, BP, before politics. But that was about it. Nobody pursued the subject or was remotely interested in what Bea Harrington used to do. This morning, however, one of the attendees wanted to know her background. 'Can't remember,' she joked. 'Too far back.'

But the woman in the front row, who had introduced herself to the class as Tammy, answered not only straightaway but with the correct details. 'Number four three three. Sold Osborne and Little fabrics.'

Bea took a beat at this. How the hell did she know all

that? She glossed over it with, 'Anyway, this course is not about me and my past. It's about you and your futures.'

The Party was Bea's passion and it should be theirs, she told them. What opportunities were available? How could they become an MP? She ran through what they would earn, the two offices, number of staff. But, first off, what they needed to know. What was it? *Getting-on-the-all-important-parliamentary-list.*

'That's the initial hurdle. Next, you must get selected, and then elected. And after that rise to Ministerial office.'

What was the best decision they had made today?

'By joining Political Women' someone shouted from the back bringing on a ripple of polite laughter. *It worked every time.*

'Right. Everyone involve yourself and get bloody stuck in as soon as you can. This morning you are already well on the fast track to the green benches and that's vernacular for the House of Commons if anyone didn't know it.' Another chuckle. This way, they would learn what was expected of them.

For one, they'd need to be determined. For two, those going through the process would have to recruit other Party members, particularly other female talent. 'There aren't enough younger ones in the pipeline.'

'Come on girls, we must have more women. What must we have?'

'More women!'

This got them animated. 'Getting involved is the way through. Distributing pamphlets in the rain is the minimum. Whether it's tedious as hell stuffing envelopes or not was all part of being in the family. And the party is a family. Like a family.'

Party life revolved around local associations. The grassroots campaigners were the meat and potatoes of support. Westminster was a different ball game.

'Getting selected, being noticed, getting on, being promoted, that's what you have to do. Not doing your stint, like telephone campaigning will side-line you. Dodging your bit is a no-no.' At this, they looked worried. That is except for front row 'goody two shoes' who was no doubt on the phone every bloody evening.

'But?'

She anticipated the 'what if?' question with her own, 'What if you've got a shit of a husband or boyfriend who doesn't support? Get rid of him.' They burst out laughing. 'What happens if a by-election is called and the party needs you as back up and you're in the finals at the local tennis club? Miss the match.'

Canvassing was more important than their personal lives. 'It's not about just you, either. You've got to rally around the others standing because that's how it goes. If you can't help out, then say you're working. Always working. Never on holiday, or say you've booked a holiday. You're expected to drop everything, even your mother's funeral, if there's an election. When it's your turn to run, others will show up for you. That's how the system works.'

You will be dropped or deselected or hammered out of the Party on the spot for disloyalty, she went on with. Complaining about bullying, and all that rubbish. Embarrassment stuff particularly.

You could hear a pin drop. They were thinking, what did that all mean for me?

As she delivered this out loud, she was mulling inside over Robin Miller who'd complained about her bloody stepson Oli. This Miller character had rung her husband James once about it, which was ok. But then there were calls all hours of the damn night which Bea assumed were also from him. He'd gone too far, over the top. Big time.

'What this means is you will be asked to sign a form declaring if you know of any reason you could embarrass the party.'

They all looked nonplussed.

'I doubt if that would apply to any of you here today. Women don't bring shame on the party but blokes do. They're often caught with their trousers down being videoed doing what they shouldn't.'

This lot would be ok. They were as bloody dull as ditch water.

But have no illusions either. This is not a cake walk, she told them.

They were all eager, notebooks poised, ready for Bea's inside wisdom. A babble of chatter filled the room. Yes, every one of them wanted to progress and every one of them needed all the help they could get, they murmured. They'd heard the whole selection process was deadly.

Once you were on the List, and even before, the best thing was to set aside forty hours a week at least during elections. The more you raised your profile, the further you climbed. But, Bea told them, they shouldn't look so worried at this because if they were truly committed it wouldn't be a problem at all!

'Who plays golf? Sails? Gardening?'

Politics is a hell of a lot of fun and no different to any

hobby was when you came to think of it. *She had to get that across.*

'Be prepared to move house if you get to stand for a half -decent seat. Take the kids out of school. Give up your business, Christmas, that sort of stuff.' They would be constantly monitored, reports made, watched, snooped on. 'You know all this anyway, don't you?'

The more you commit to the party, the further you go.

Does anyone here have a double-barrelled name?

The girl at the front raised a finger. 'I'm Smythe-Kell,' she said.

'Best to drop part of it in that case.' Long names not only smacked of privilege they also didn't fit on the ballot paper.

Bea then covered the fundraising issue and the party conference they must attend.

The class livened up at the sound of a future grooming training session, eager for something lighter, learning how they could change their look. Things like, why did they need a dress diary? Bea told them women had to avoid too many photos in the same jacket.

'You have to know stuff like how to handle flyaway hair in a shot up a windy hill to promote the green belt. On a farm. Oh, and skirts not too short. Remember most podiums are up a level and they ride up as you sit down.'

Bea looked at her watch. Nearly over.

She told them who'd be joining next time to coach on public speaking. The guy coming would quiz them each in turn, so it was best to arrive prepared. Important to have an answer to hand because whoever it was would toss *any* personal or political question they wanted to catch them on the hop. That was politics for you.

She glanced at her notes for examples. How did you vote on the Referendum? No, a bit late for that!

Why do you think you'd make a good MP? What would be your private members bill? Give me your views on Assisted Dying. How would you fundraise for your campaign?

'Anyone want to ask anything?

'Yes. Bea, how do we hear of seat vacancies?'

On the List, they could apply for seats. So that was why passing the parliamentary Assessment Board known as the PAB was paramount. But no doubt they would all swim through that no problems. Next week, she'd cover how to fill in application forms. Questions anyone?

Bomb Disposal, having had a run-in with her Association Chair because she'd refused to canvass on her own, wanted to talk about whether it was dangerous or not going out alone.

'Better to go off in pairs.' Bea backed her up.

'That's not always possible,' said Ms Penzance to the army girl. 'I stood in an opposition seat once with zero support. No one came out delivering with me. And I had to do fundraising too.'

Smythe-Kell, who'd remained quiet most of the time, raised a red-lacquered nail. 'Tammy Kell.'

She'd dropped the middle part of the name already. Impressive.

'How much money would we be expected to raise?'

How long was a piece of string? But generally speaking, a few thousand was the target. She told them how candidates put on speaker events or got volunteers to hold coffee mornings. But not to worry their cotton socks over this. She would run another course to cover finance, accounting, and election law.

'I have to flee,' Bea said and rushed away. She was a busy woman, but a happy one.

CHAPTER 17

By midday, Karen was back at her flat staring at the stack of unused plates from the night before and feeling wretched. The party had been a catastrophe, wasted effort. But then Haruto had shown. Or had he? Had she imagined it all? The great time they'd had. The mind plays bloody tricks. She was seeing failure in herself at every turn.

Like how she'd squandered hours at the Bunker with nothing achieved at all while a fragile bullying victim was still missing and probably growing more suicidal by the minute. Then to make matters worse, though Karen's commission was to solve the mystery of Robin Miller, ever since the TV interview she'd become obsessed with the death of Alesha Parkhurst. So much so, Karen couldn't get the last conversation with Alesha out of her mind. It was proving too much of a distraction.

She sat on the bed for ten minutes entertaining doom and negativity, unable to budge enough to stand on her two legs. Were her feet superglued to the floor? What was in those packing boxes? Why couldn't she damn well get on with things? In seconds she was tumbling into dejection and self-sympathy. She would never ever, ever, amount to anything, marry anyone, have children, be in love, fall in love, win the Lottery, go on holiday, leave the flat. *Ever again.*

And, more to the point. When would this hangover lift?

The best way to deal with investigators' block is to Google like mad on a subject, any subject no matter what.

So within minutes she'd overcome her state of inertia and drive was back. From barely balancing on a bike, she was now whizzing downhill on with no brakes, mentally speaking.

Two hours later, Quacker rang. There was a twang of stick hitting stick in the background. 'I'm at the sports club,' he said. 'How are you doing, anyway?'

'Really well.' Karen said almost automatically.

'Have you had any news on Robin?' he asked.

Karen recounted the work done on his behalf. How she'd not found him on the hospital search, which was a positive. In reality, she hadn't stopped since they'd met up at the coffee shop. Even Haruto had joined in looking for him, which was one reason he'd stayed on so late. Of course, Karen didn't tell Quacker that bit. Instead, she prattled on about the Twitter announcement, the Churchill War Rooms and how she'd established Robin was acting out of character. Also about the visit made to the outside of his bedsit property but, like Quacker, hadn't been able to get in. Her stream of facts ended with, 'Nothing too much so far.'

'Well done, well done.' He was trying to be chatty and encouraging as if he could sense Karen was low and needed cheering. 'Would you believe it? We had a key theft here a few days ago. This goes to explain why I'm now standing on the side of a pitch shouting out to twenty adults in gym shorts with a bolt cutter in my hands. Strange about that Twitter announcement, isn't it? You must enlighten me on this posting sometime. How was your party?'

'Well, I think.' It was the second time she'd avoided the truth and wondered if he could tell.

'On Miller, best next if you speak to his family. Maybe

get more leads from them. The Dad's been contacting me quite often.'

'Sorry about that.'

'Well, they are understandably anxious. He could show up at any minute and let's hope he does for everyone's sake. But what I will need, if it's ok, is this information you've discovered so far put down on paper? A report.'

This is standard practice. So, as soon as the call was over, Karen set to writing it up. As she was doing so, a WhatsApp message came in from Haruto. He was the last person, other than Robin Miller, she expected to hear from at that moment.

'Are you in?'

She replied straight away with a yes.

'Thought I'd drop by and give you a hand with the clearing up.' he said. 'I'm almost outside.'

He was dressed in jeans and a white sweatshirt and orange tennis shoes. Karen remembered he'd worn this mishmash when they'd first met. Why was he here? 'How's Hailey?' she asked. It was a loaded question.

He grinned. 'Not happy.'

'She's quite keen on you.'

'I know,' he said, 'And that is what my problem is.'

Hailey's calls to Karen up until the party had been all about how totally into him she was. Hailey seemed besotted. So Karen thought it best to change the subject with Haruto, not get involved, if she wasn't already.

'I had a hangover this morning.' Karen said, waiting for the kettle, wondering like the night before when Haruto would leave again and she could get back to writing up Quacker's report. Not too soon, she hoped.

'Me too. But an English fry-up helped.'

Haruto picked up the morning's newspaper she'd grabbed on her way out of the Tube station returning from Central. 'Anything in here on your guy?'

'No. Chinese hack-proof computer networks, electric bikes breaking the speed limit, Russian students sent as spies. Nothing on a missing British political activist.'

'I suppose is not that surprising?' Haruto added.

Karen sat on the sofa beside him, wondering how her mood could have about turned and soared so high in five minutes flat and whether that was a good thing or not. 'An average of seventy children under eighteen disappear every day and Robin Miller's not even in that age group. Nor is he famous.'

'And have we got a trace on his phone?' Haruto had involved himself in the operation obviously.

'His phone's still dead.' she said.

'You never know. He might switch it on.' He closed the paper. 'So what are you going to do on it next?'

Karen's silence said it all. She didn't have a clue right then. 'Not too sure.'

'I offered to look at your laptop,' he said. 'It was stop-starting a bit.'

He hadn't forgotten, but she had. Wow.

'Thank you. I'd appreciate that.' Her reluctance to have it fixed outside was based on security because her computer handled sensitive data. Fraud investigations and personnel checks meant Karen had access to private records, which falling into the wrong hands could be used for blackmail.

Haruto fiddled with her machine as Karen continued making coffee.

'Maybe nothing in the papers,' he said as he turned the screen in her direction. 'Plenty on Twitter.'

Plunging a newly boiled cafetière of Columbian was not the best time to hear that. The coffee exploded over the top and she grabbed her iPhone to save it from either splashes or total ruin.

'What's that?' Karen had not checked the net since talking to Quacker.

He was right. Twittersphere had a hashtag #missing #RobinMiller. It was full of news of his disappearance.

Haruto looked at Karen like she'd arrived two hours late for the office. How could she miss this? She should have known about the media update on Robin Miller. That was her job.

'So what have you been doing all this time?' he teased.

What Karen had been doing other than thinking nonstop of Haruto was googling everything she could *on Alesha Parkhurst*. The backstory, the hanging, the cyber abuse. Karen had scrolled through all the threatening messages. Few feminists criticise Islam, like Alesha did. Mostly they are too chicken, or, as some would see it, too sensible. Too scared of the type of vitriol she'd received. Islamic extremists considered what Alesha Parkhurst was campaigning about was *hate speech*. And some had threatened to stone her for it.

Karen had even discovered there'd been a woman, wearing a full burka, sighted around the Cardiff Hotel the night Alesha Parkhurst died. She could have done it. Karen already had a lead on this because the woman's name had cross matched with another case she was working on. It was Zinah al-Rashid.

CHAPTER 18

The upper portion of Ann Bishop's crumbling Victorian mansion in Acton Vale was different to the bit beneath. Upstairs was decorated much as you'd expect for a wealthy lady type who'd downsized in the 1960s. Traditional sofas, floral carpets and Laura Ashley curtains. But while the rooms above ground gave the impression of conservative comfort and security, the basement below evoked the set of a low budget horror movie.

Thirty years previously, when first bequeathed the property from an older husband, Ann Bishop had let it out to a geography teacher with a mild hoarding disorder. He'd then become a long-term tenant. After the old teacher had been admitted to a nursing home, the underground flat had needed a serious clear-out. But it never happened. Instead, the place remained as was, a blast from the past, down to the flower power wallpaper and orange cushions. Out of deference to her former lodger and occasional lover, the retired Wren wanted things left as they were.

For Ann's granddaughter Zinah al-Rashid, self-styled that way after her conversion to Islam, the basement was prime for her covert operations. Perfect. Because of an encroaching Alzheimer's condition, Ann Bishop hadn't been down there for years.

As for Zinah, it was a shit hole, a hellhole, a bloody khazi. Mountains of junk, mildew on the walls and a heavy smell of damp. But it was also rent free and had half-decent Wi-Fi. Plus, the overflowing dustbins kept outside were efficient in deterring unwanted visitors. The moss-covered stairs leading down were nothing short of a death trap when it rained.

A lot of the kitchen equipment was broken to bits, but the stove and sparky microwave at least worked. As did the old-fashioned chest freezer, set hard back against the rear wall where it had been for forty years. And the toilet was passable.

Space was the biggest problem of all. Zinah had brought in a sewing machine, and all the other essentials required for a working office such as a computer, printer, and so forth. But crowded out with the former teacher's furniture, it was hard to manage. She needed more room for the piles of leaflets and boxes of laminated paper for the job she did. Zinah and Ann Bishop, however, had struck a deal. What went on *down there* was her granddaughter's business. 'I won't interfere, my dear. Do whatever you like, but change nothing. Not a thing.'

Any slightest hint or suggestion of clearing contents would send her grandmother doolally. *Don't touch! Leave things as is!* So Zinah left them alone. She knew a good deal when she had one. Bugger the lack of space. It wasn't worth risking conflict by altering the place and having Ann discover what she'd done on a surprise visit.

That way everyone was kept happy. It was not as if her granddaughter slept there, was it? On the nights that 'Miriam's girl' stayed over, there was a small bedroom at the front of the ground floor which served perfectly. But what the old lady would have been horrified to learn was how letting Zinah use the basement she was aiding and abetting terrorist activity. Finding this out would have killed her.

Learning what was really going on in her below ground apartment, a slick operation involving fundraising and recruitment, would have put her six feet under.

Zinah had been trained in financial fraud by a hacker in Enfield who was a pure whizz. What she made was drafted straight into the coffers of the Islamic State. The spam emails always went from public servers to avoid detection, particularly the one that read 'Your PayPal account has been compromised'. She mostly worked from different coffee bars and libraries. But today she was running very short of time. She was also growing bored. While the scamming returned great results, she was fast tiring of it. *Only one more batch.*

Zinah fired up her Dell, opened the mail client. The template she'd created and used before read 'Customer Survey–Get £50 Reward.'

'The Wells Online department kindly asks you to take part in our quick and easy 5 question survey. In return we will credit £50.00 to your account–for your time!'

'To credit your £50 reward, we need your Wells User ID and password, and your Wells credit card number, expiration date, three-digit security number, postal code. Mother's maiden name and email.'

She keyed in the database of addresses bought off the internet and pressed send. The emails streamed out. Now it was a case of sit back and wait for the replies to roll in.

Zinah opened the drawer which she kept ajar because the knob was missing. She tossed in the ring of keys Fatima had given her at the Harrods coffee shop, which belonged to some hockey club close by. What was this sister thinking of? Was she bonkers or just plain showing off?

Zinah mulled over what had happened during the interview, how at first they'd talked nonstop about the cause and commitment to it. Most of the conversation was in code. So Syria was 'Southend'. Fighters were 'executives'. A bride was a 'winner'. This was standard practice designed to test an applicant and see how well they performed under stress in public. The first meet up was always in person. Later they would Skype and WhatsApp.

Zinah had assessed Fatima first off as a trifle young, dressed slutty. That would all change of course if the girl was to go over and above for the faith, to prove her willingness to serve Allah above all else. Zinah stressed this. Fatima would need every ounce of determination if she was to marry one of the top 'executives'.

Satisfied Fatima would pass the test to become a potential jihadi bride, they'd then exchanged addresses for further contact. But would the young woman stay the course? From the first ten minutes you could mostly pick whether they would or not, but Fatima had proved a hard character to judge. So Zinah had asked her as much.

This question had prompted an extraordinary but delighted reaction. As if to prove her devotion, the kid had suddenly dived into her fashion rucksack and pulled out a fist of keys.

'What are those?'

Swinging them back-and-forth, Fatima, forgetting she was in a busy tea lounge and on show, had then boasted she'd stolen them from a hockey club and how easy it was to do. Simple. The girl at reception had just passed them over, no questions asked. Wasn't it cool? Don't worry, no one knew her there. They'd never trace her.

With that distinctive voice? Was she living in cloud cuckoo land?

'How did you know this place?'

'My friend used to train in hockey and play there. She took me along once.'

With that she'd scratched around inside the sack again and fished out a small plastic bag. Within that was what looked like an old mobile wrapped in bubble-lined padding and folded into a pair of knickers.

What was it exactly?

'I don't know yet if it works.'

With those words, a hit of adrenaline entered Zinah's blood supply.

Works? Is that a bomb? *Act normal.*

Fatima laughed at the reaction she got from Zinah whose eyes darted round the café at once. At the other tables, deep in conversation, oblivious. Customers blissfully unaware that what the two women were looking at was not a purchase of silk knickers but the scraped together rudiments of an improvised explosive device. *This girl was a loose cannon. A hot head.*

'It's ok,' Fatima said brightly, slipping it back into her bag. 'It doesn't work yet.'

'You're sure?'

'Yes.'

'Can I have it? Will you give it to me?'

At first she didn't want to hand it over.

Zinah had gone further to get her to comply. 'But I see now you are committed.'

Zinah was on the point of asking why Fatima had taken the keys. But she didn't need to. It was obvious. Bombing lockers was almost a standard teenage trick and nothing new. Better still if they were located within a middle-class sports club where no one would be expecting an explosion. It made an easy target, a piece of piss.

'I can tell you are ready to serve Allah.'

With that, the girl handed over her bundle of bubble wrap, but she took a while to recover her bubbly personality. She'd felt ticked off.

Zinah was aware it was pretty easy to make a phone bomb. Not that she'd done one herself. But she knew the theory. Incorporated into the explosive material, the mobile's electrical current is enough to jolt the charge to set it off. Making a mobile incendiary is so simple, the only reason kids didn't do more of it was the cost of phone replacement. But if you had an old phone you were happy to lose, then that solved that problem, didn't it?

Whether or not the stolen keys and half-made explosive device sparked an idea for Zinah, it certainly changed her appraisal of Fatima. This was a sister who she'd have to monitor closely. Reckless and silly schemes like the locker bombing Fatima had dreamt up could mean big operations such as the one Zinah was planning being compromised.

However, thinking about the bomb farce and the successful way Zinah had diffused the awkward situation, got the gadget off the girl, she was by now herself firing on all cylinders. So much so that when the overhead light flickered and failed, she didn't curse as she usually would have done. She was cool.

She had in her hand a ready-made explosive kit. There was another mobile phone she needed to dispose of pretty soon. This was meant to be. Why not strap the two together?

Thank you, Fatima.

Looking at herself in the cracked mirror, scrutinising every detail, admiring her skill at recreation, reinvention, maybe bombing, she was now itching to go.

Zinah applied her thick heavy eye liner. It was a shame much of the Sophia Loren effect was lost under the plain spectacles.

The transformation from Western woman to devout Muslim was rapid. When she left the basement an hour later, she merged seamlessly with the other Arab women who thronged the high street. *She looked great.*

CHAPTER 19

At the time of the Alesha Parkhurst story Karen had also been working on a grooming case. It involved a teenager being turned against her parents by someone she'd met online. Her name was Tessa Clark.

'She went to bed one night as a normal girl and came down the next morning completely different,' the parents had said. This was eight months previously. Since that time she'd adopted the headscarf and claimed to have converted to Islam. Having changed her name, she now only answered to Amirah. The family assumed she was meeting up with a Muslim boy. But they didn't know for certain because their daughter had shunned them ever since.

So while Quacker was whizzing into Paddington from his TV interview the morning of her failed house warming party, Karen had been on a hired motorbike going in the opposite direction to see the girl's mother, Linda Clark. Karen always crammed things.

All Karen Andersen wanted to do was to meet her in person and deliver the mother good news. That her teenage daughter was meeting a nice boy from a decent home who took her bowling and he wasn't a married man or a sex pervert. But unfortunately for Karen she couldn't do that.

Linda Clark sat by herself on a high bench with a cardboard cup of machine coffee. She wore jeans, a shirt and hiking boots. She was around forty with cropped brown hair, worked in a library and her husband was a landscape gardener.

'We have photographs for you,' Karen said. One of her colleagues had helped out. They'd put a trace on the daughter to find out who she was meeting up with outside school.

Linda Clark now looked worried because reading her face Karen was retransmitting the mother's deep concern. 'Have you found something? What? You have and you don't want to show me, do you?'

Karen spread the pictures out in front of her. They showed her daughter and a woman in full Islamic dress engaged in what looked like an intense conversation. 'Do you know this woman?'

'No, but she is learning Arabic, she tells us. So it could be her teacher.' Her hands shook as she looked at the black and white print outs, her vulnerability on show like any parent who feels powerless to save their child from harm.

'Why did you think she was meeting a man?'

'Because she's been speaking to her friends about getting married.'

'Has she said who?'

The tears flowed down her face and they confirmed her fear. 'No. I'm scared.'

Karen was sad for her. 'Why?'

'Because she has been talking about wearing the burka. I have nothing against women expressing themselves how they want, you understand. But it is the way she's behaving that's frightening. Her determination to shut us out.'

'How does your husband feel about her converting to Islam?'

'We're not against Islam. We have many friends who are Muslims and refugees. It's more we don't *understand* it. We brought her up to be so independent. Also neither of us are religious.' She welled up. 'We love her very much and we don't want to lose her. It's just we worry she'll come to harm. I even went to a feminist conference in Cardiff about all this stuff.'

'Was that the one given by Alesha Parkhurst?'

'Yes, it was. You were on the TV yesterday about her, weren't you?'

I flushed. 'Did your daughter attend the event?'

'No. A year ago she would have done! But that evening she was meeting up with someone from school, or so we thought. Alesha Parkhurst committed suicide, didn't she?'

'What was she speaking on at the conference?'

'How teenagers were being groomed over the internet.' She shot me a terrified look. 'Do you think that's happening to Tessa?'

'How did Tessa react when she heard of Alesha's death?'

'She said she deserved it because she was an infidel spreading lies about Islam.'

They both knew what that meant. But Karen confirmed it.

'Then yes, Linda. There's a good chance Tessa is being radicalised. If so, she may plan to leave the country.' She didn't need to say any more. Linda Clark was in the picture. How maybe Tessa was being groomed to be a jihadi bride.

'If you were me, Karen, what would you do?'

Over the next ten minutes Karen Andersen gave Linda Clark a whole set of instructions. She outlined what she needed her to do. To search Tessa's bedroom when she was at school and to somehow get hold of the security code for her daughter's phone. Had she ever got into Tessa's computer? Who were Tessa's friends in class and could Linda trust them? It was a lot to do. But Karen warned her Tessa was almost certainly planning to travel to join the Islamic State. If they didn't work to stop her, then Linda may never see her again.

This was far more serious an issue than the Clarks had expected it to be when they'd started out on the investigation.

During this conversation Karen also learned whoever had met up with Tessa and was radicalising her had travelled to Cardiff. She'd been there on the night Alesha Parkhurst died.

Linda Clark was a speedy worker. By the time Karen had returned to London she'd got into her daughter's phone and succeeded. She'd pulled a name. In return Karen promised Linda she would do everything in her power to save her daughter from making the biggest mistake of her life. Even if it meant going undercover to confront Zinah Al-Rashid in order to do so.

CHAPTER 20

Simon King, sitting feeling maudlin in CCHQ, was heartbroken, he told himself. He must be. Men don't take rejection well either even though they're expected to cope with it better than women.

She was haunting him.

He kept thinking of the petite frame and appealing eyes.

Had it only worked out differently, life would have been wonderful.

Today he could not concentrate on anything else but her and how it had all started. An unlikely infatuation in the first place, but one which had rapidly grown out of control. So much so, it got to the point he'd stalked her every step.

A desperate urge came over him. He craved taking her once again in his arms to tell her how beautiful she was and how sorry, very sorry, in fact, if he'd got things back to front. There was no way to turn the clock back. They would never be an item. He had to move on, put it behind him, change his thinking.

Even the trip to the kitchenette provided no distraction from the subject of attractive women. He made a cup of instant, fine. But then one of the Sloane style girls had come in to disturb his peace, looking for an excuse to break from telephone canvassing.

'Can I make you a coffee?' He offered.

She'd seemed surprised. King wasn't known for his sociability. 'Wouldn't say no.' But then, 'Be back in a tick,' and ducked away, out to grab someone as they passed in the corridor. When the girl finally returned, she stood with her rear against the counter and arms folded, lost in thought.

'How's it going?' King was hoping to open up a conversation

'No one's in today. I'm sick of making calls to an answering machine.'

Simon King cleaned up the countertop and replaced milk in the fridge as an excuse to stick around. He even washed two mugs someone else had used and left dirty. They slotted perfectly into a small space remaining in the cupboard. He didn't leave.

King knew the younger crowd saw him as a killjoy because of his tendency to patronise. Maybe the girl was one who shared this opinion. If so, this was the price he had to pay. His banter was only meant in fun. Making her a cup of coffee was a gesture and an attempt to put that right. So when she didn't engage, it irritated profusely. After ignoring him in favour of surfing her phone, she'd collected up the cup and rushed away without further comment. Barely a thanks.

No, he could pass on the modern woman and this was one example why. But all the same, she was pretty.

The casual flirtation was supposed to ease King's thinking, not start it rolling again. Was he that unattractive?

So once again disturbing images and judgements were flowing like a river and he couldn't stop it. So that didn't work.

Coffee in hand, King returned to his cubbyhole and files. He clicked on the outlook programme. Paperwork was piling up. All this Miller business was to blame. It'd churned things up right enough, causing Simon King all the ripples of self-examination which led to sleepless nights.

Also, not getting back to where he lived since the Tuesday before but instead staying on in London where he could think matters through, added an extra domestic toll. He was out of socks.

Bullying issues were not that uncommon. Simon King was used to hearing a whole heap of tittle-tattle daily. It was usually put down to the rivalry between activists and candidates because competition for seats was so intense. All this suited the Party fine because rarely did it reach the official report stage. Mostly because no one dared!

The younger Harrington was out of line. He was born intimidating, a bully, a boisterous child no doubt. Then he was raised in a political household, wasn't he? Perhaps Oli needed a chivvy on his aggressive manner and lack of subtlety. But Robin Miller was not blameless. From the way he'd conducted himself at The Buckingham it was clear Miller had also grown far too big for his boots. Yes, he'd had brought a bucket of trouble on himself from not heeding the warning being given. Fault on both sides.

King fumbled with a few paperclips so to anyone passing he appeared to being doing nothing out of the ordinary. But he was busy scheming what came next. Then rather than staring vacantly at the party posters covering every inch of the wall in front, he doodled on a discarded envelope. He sketched a tree with no roots or leaves. A therapist might have suggested it reflected inner storms leading to isolation. Typical of a man who'd lost his family. And that was Simon King.

He worked on a bit, alternating between non-urgent phone calls and another known diversion from heavy matters. That was updating his official Twitter account. Networking online wasn't Simon's pet activity. He preferred face-to-face contact. But social media was a damned useful device to spy on campaigners, what they wrote, or hash tagged, and whether they were being indiscreet. Compromising the party rhetoric.

From time to time, Simon King wrote some original political tweets. But if he indulged in creative posting, it was more likely to be on a different stream. His false 'King Si' account.

Under the name of John King. This was an outlet he used to vent his personal views, like his support for Justice for Rape Lies. Of course it had to be incognito. It certainly wouldn't do for a director of the party to be feminist intolerant in this modern age. So @KingSi77 was where he went to have a rant without impact on his public image.

For someone wanting to change focus, this provided King that day with some light amusement, but it did little to improve his overall mood. In fact it made matters even worse.

He read posts under the hashtag #NameAGirlsFavoriteLie. Sometimes these were droll observations, other times far more cutting. Today a guy who'd been stitched up by a woman had written, 'Lies spread during child custody fights "He abused me!" Too many husbands falsely accused of violence.'

He liked this post and retweeted it. Forty-two random followers on the John King account weren't a lot, but so what? The odd sign of solidarity with the men's rights movement didn't harm, and it made him feel better about himself.

King would not have considered himself anti-women in the slightest. He saw himself instead as an old-fashioned bloke, protective, the sort who opens a door for a lady and pulls out a chair for her. He hated the call-out culture and the hardened feminists who raved on about male abuse without giving a thought to the fact women too could be violent. These were the girls who ganged up. The ladies who lied. What about them?

King was divorced, and he and his ex-wife were no longer friends. He referred to his ex as 'the Rottweiler' and this was because of her temper, not his. The unfairness of it all. Home for Simon King these days was a small terrace on an estate outside Bishop's Stortford. Meanwhile the ex-Mrs King languished in a four-bedroom house in the leafy Surrey countryside.

'She's got two men to pay her bills now,' King would tell friends. Or 'Wait until he discovers the brimstone and fire side of her personality!'

Zero loyalty to anyone but herself and her bank account.

After they'd split she kept the kids, the property, and even his war medals. Whatever would she want with those, he'd told friends? To remind her of our battles? But King's flippancy barely covered his inner bitterness.

He'd never fully recovered from the acrimonious divorce mostly because of the custody issue. His former wife had played the abuse card and got away with it.

He'd not seen it coming. How could he have done when she'd made it all up?

'Did you abuse your wife?'

'No.'

'Can you prove you didn't?'

'No.'

'Did you drink to excess?'

'Who wouldn't drink to excess living with the Rottweiler?'

The court takes these things seriously. It's no time for sarcasm. When he'd acknowledged he had indeed come in drunk a few times, and who wouldn't, they'd not seen the funny side. Then King had been too upfront and honest about how once he'd staggered in and fallen against the Christmas tree and it had collapsed. And yes, he'd come bloody close to belting Mrs K, but close didn't mean he'd actually done it.

According to King, the Rottweiler had seized on this to completely embellish her story and after that all hell let loose. She'd gone on to tell the court a series of made-up stories. These included assault, rape, and the attempted sexual abuse of his five-year-old daughter.

After that pack of lies, he'd had no further contact whatsoever with his two children.

Men got a bloody poor deal today, bloody poor deal.

King was in a fix. There was not just one problem with Miller's bullying statement but several. The sex abuse allegations in it had sent him into a rage the first moment he'd read them. But were they true? King had been through that horror himself. Bogus rape claims destroyed lives because the finger pointing lasted years. You could never clear your name or prove your innocence. Historical allegations were even worse. And what about the party reputation? The complete breakdown of his own family life over lies and false stories was why the Conservative Party meant so much to him. He'd do anything to protect it. It'd filled the chasm his divorce had left and replaced the gaping hole with at least a purpose in life.

The longer he stared at Miller's report, the more it made him seethe. All that and added to it the extra stuff he was reading on the web incensed him. Feminist claptrap. Divorce pay-outs. Male privilege. Suicide. Alesha Parkhurst. Bullying. Damned Battle bus overspending consequences.

The report was toxic. There were serious implications for him and the smooth running of the party as a whole. The potential for embarrassment and a vote of no confidence surfaced daily as it was. Wouldn't the press love tittle-tattle like this?

Four other personnel files littered the desk. He stacked and moved them to one side. It was time to clear space and action something. But what?

The hour was pressing. Decisions had to be made.

He deleted all Miller's emails which had arrived into his account. Gone! Then he slid the statement in front of him back into its hand-addressed envelope and secreted it right at the bottom of his briefcase. He'd bury the complaint once and for all.

CHAPTER 21

At ten past 6 that afternoon, Simon King arrived at the Westminster West constituency office. The layout of the place was similar to hundreds of other local party headquarters dotted around the country. Too small for purpose. An over crammed room with a picture of Thatcher in her heyday, another one for the printer and just enough standing space in the hallway to hold twenty or so canvassers before a Super Saturday.

Fit and trim for his seventy-four years, Chairman John Toady sprang up and greeted King like royalty. Having been with the party for half a century at least, Toady knew this unexpected drop-in from someone from HQ signalled something brewing.

So what was the reason for his esteemed visit, he joked?

Simon King had to avoid going too soon on to the subject of Robin Miller. It was vital to take his time and conceal any personal reasons for the request he was about to make. Otherwise, it'd smack as a petty vendetta.

Toady, seated across the desk, was spouting forth on campaigning shortfalls and the need to involve more ambitious youngsters at the grassroots level. 'We had two councillors die on us last year,' he said. 'Grim stuff.'

'Inevitable.'

They were short of campaigners like Robin Miller.

'Old age creeps up doesn't it?' King said, biding his time.

'The Party knows of the problem, Simon. Not enough members. And with the dwindling numbers, a hundred and thirty thousand, seventy percent men and half of those over sixty, councillors popping their clogs is unsurprising. Good Lord. Our membership equals the population of a small city after all, doesn't it?'

'I'm aware you need more council candidates,' said King. *As if Toady was bloody psychic.* Not the best conversation to raise the subject of Miller, but it had to be done.

'Need more of everything, funds, office space, footsloggers. The younger kids can be trained whereas some of the old codgers want to help but they don't have the faintest idea what canvassing is all about, Simon. Take Monty. You know him, don't you? Classic. He loses us more than he gains. They're the type who thinks they will change someone's mind by haranguing them on their doorstep for half an hour which does the damn opposite.' Toady gripped the arms of his chair and his face shone with good humour. 'He'll bloody argue till the cows come home, will Monty.'

It was futile to disagree on the need for more activists like Miller. Fruitless to stop Toady in mid flow because he was enjoying himself. Spilling out the hackneyed slogans, talking on about his pet subjects. Potholes, fly tipping and speed bumps.

He can hammer on about this forever.

'Yup, you do.' Give him ten minutes more, Simon thought. It was all part of the softening up process.

Toady would rather talk the talk than walk the walk out on the canvass trail himself.

So they agreed ten times over how vital it was for the party to have canvassers and twenty-year-old enthusiastic newcomers on board to get the pledges out and why.

Research, that was why. 'Hours spent on reconnaissance is never wasted,' said King.

'Of course, Simon. Not teaching you to suck eggs. Being in the Army and all that.'

When Toady was ready at last to hear what a party director was doing there, King told him he wanted Robin Miller dropped from the council list.

Today reacted, as expected, badly. He turned red in the face and his nostrils flared. 'Deselected? One of the best activists we've got? And he's up next for Churchill Ward.'

'I thought he was.'

'And I suppose you want me to do the dirty, not you do it. Is that it?'

Simon didn't answer.

'Can't see why deselection is necessary, Simon' Toady was still protesting.

'Head Office reasons.'

Toady cracked his knuckles. 'And that's it? CCHQ orders?'

'Well, if he's so good on the doorstep, you could still use him for a spot of delivering, couldn't you?'

The Chairman's tone turned sarcastic. 'Oh absolutely. He'll be delighted with that, thrilled in fact.'

They glared at each other. Both were aware that was how the party operated when it wanted to dump someone. But only one, namely Simon King, knew this was not a party committee decision but one taken by him on its behalf. Hopefully Toady wouldn't work that out. And King betted Toady would comply because the Chairman was after an honour. He wouldn't risk losing the chance of a 'gong' for fifty years' service over a five-minute wonder like Robin

Miller.

Deed done, Simon King picked up a bunch of flyers and the canvass sheet attached. 'Need these delivered?'

Toady jerked in his chair, still incensed. Then he slapped the table, sighed with weary resignation. It was not worth arguing with King over this. He was a ruthless bastard if he needed to be. Nothing Toady could do about it.

King had offered to stick a few leaflets through doors. So Toady picked out an area around the Lisson Green Estate with the point of his pencil. 'You could get rid of that stack for me. Perhaps you'll meet up with Miller's friend William Wan out there. I believe he was expecting Robin to join him there though I don't know whether the lad has showed up yet.' He muttered something. 'Aha. On second thoughts, you'll no doubt want to steer clear of those two, now, won't you?'

'Not a bad idea to avoid them under the circumstances.'

King handed the flyers back and in such a way it emphasised he was deadly serious about the demotion. There'd be consequences for Toady if his order wasn't carried out. 'At least not until after you've had a chance to deal with things properly.'

Knowing he had lost the fight to save Robin Miller's council career, Toady swivelled in the chair to swop the first bundle he'd given King for a stack of feedback surveys. 'Well, kind Sir, if you would like to make yourself useful, you might get a few of these distributed round Bell Street.'

Miller being dropped from the council list would be a load off Simon's shoulders. It would be the last he would have to hear about bullying issues. Doing a bit of foot slogging for Toady was a tiny price to pay in comparison. He was sure of that.

CHAPTER 22

Zinah caught her reflection in the glass doors of the bus before they sprang open. Full Islamic dress, burka, covered head to toe. She raised her skirt slightly to avoid tripping and clambered aboard. Usually it was fun playing this role, but today she was too much on edge. Prickly. Her oyster card beeped and made her jump.

As the driver swung out into the traffic, she was thrown off balance. Sideways glances came from both sides of the narrow aisle dividing the seats. That was usual. Western people often stared at her. The look they had on their faces when they did so screamed, 'Why don't you show your bloody face? What are you hiding?'

Women wearing the full-face mask in Britain weren't welcome. They were associated with one thing and one thing only. *Terrorism.*

The only concession to western values was Zinah's large chocolate coloured leather bag by her side.

Want me to hold it up? Do you recognise the label? Does this impress you?

Clothes mattered and the brown Birger was a perfect prop. With a designer accessory Zinah could blend in with the elite in Harrods, no questions asked. And despite the snubs, being away from the stifling basement and mingling with the public on the bus usually lifted her mood.

Zinah's phone sounded, and as it did she shuffled to free the string of her headphones. It was Ahmed. '*as-Salaam-Alaikum*'. Peace be unto you.

The whoosh of the air brakes signalled a stop as she answered back 'Alaikum Salaam' while watching a woman carrying a folded pushchair struggle aboard with two kids in tow.

'I am sorry to hear about your father. He is a martyr,' said Ahmed above the racket caused by the bottom deck now filled with squealing children.

'*Shokran,* Ahmed.' Thank you.

Zinah listened carefully as Ahmed set a time for the next coffee rendezvous. His English had a strong Birmingham twang. The arrangement was supposed to sound like a romantic date if security was listening. She hoped they weren't if only because Ahmed was a complete creep. *A date with him!* But Ahmed was a vital part of the team around her, supporting her intent to avenge the Prophet. She had to put up with him.

Ahmed made the orders, or that's what he liked to think. In his arrogance. Now with her father dead, Zinah and Ahmed had to be in more direct contact which was a complete and utter pain.

Meanwhile, the 207 trundled on, regardless.

Zinah rang off. She turned from the window to stare into the pale grey eyes of a three-year-old, clearly fascinated by her dress. It made her uncomfortable, so Zinah looked away, back to the passing traffic.

'To perform jihad you have to stop obsessing about kids,' she'd been told. 'Look, we've all got sons and daughters. What do the non-believers care about ours? They bomb them without giving it a moment's thought.'

This morning the child's mother squeezed her large frame into the seat alongside and lifted the said child onto

125

her lap so there was no avoiding the anxiety. Zinah felt a light trickling under her arms. *Could a kid this young read her mind?*

How would the woman react if she knew how much Zinah despised not the two of them in person but what they both stood for? Her lips tightened, and she had a sinking sensation. But should Zinah al-Rashid feel this guilty about these people when they felt exactly the same about her? Didn't they know none of society is blameless? And, even if they didn't, so what? Zinah wasn't the only convert to the cause. There were literally hundreds of Zinahs. Thousands.

The bus dropped off and picked up at Second Avenue, then First Avenue and each time a fresh group of shoppers boarded. There was a rustling of plastic bags and then the strong aroma of fried chicken. When she was this engrossed in her work, she often forgot to eat.

As they stopped and started in the London traffic and the greasy smell permeated the air, a grey mist descended over her eyes. Maybe a lack of blood sugar? Her stomach gnawed feeling raw and a shot of bitter bile rose up into her throat. But it passed as quickly as it'd come on. Perhaps she'd buy something to eat later. But her heart and not her gut was the most important thing right now! Surely.

Vengeance for her father's murder?

Since meeting Fatima two days ago Zinah saw herself differently. She was no longer someone happy to administrate for the cause in a minor way. She was a brave soldier of the Caliphate ready to serve. Someone who didn't need reminding by an eighteen-year-old of the final objective. Zinah had transformed into a renewed and strengthened warrior who would no longer let teenagers undermine her self-confidence. Zinah was the one with the talent. Not Fatima. Otherwise, how had Zinah managed to stay under the radar, to avoid falling into the obvious traps set by the enemy?

Traps like moving too quickly before you are prepared, traps which would blow your precious cover. Traps such as not knowing bomb targets had to be selected with great discretion or else it was the total undoing of years and years of careful planning.

Despite all this controlled thinking and affirmations to remain patient and calm, by the time she reached Shepherds Bush station Zinah was burning up with ambition.

I want to do something. *Now.*

At White City the woman beside her pressed the bell. A group were already up and waiting to get off as the bus rocked back-and-forth nearing the stop.

The moment the bus stopped a crowd of noisy teens clustered around the exit were first off. Behind them, an orderly queue shuffled forward one by one to leave.

Just as Zinah was ready to step down, a man with a dirty backpack who'd been behind her pushed in front. As he did so he landed a sideways blow against her shoulder.

'Hey, what you think you're doing?' screamed the woman who'd sat beside her. 'Racist pig. That was deliberate that was.'

Everyone else now pulled back to give Zinah space.

The queue jumper took no notice, but charged ahead down the street, tossing his copy of *Metro* on the ground as he went. Zinah lifted her cloak and stepped off.

As she did, she caught sight of the discarded newspaper. The headline was 'British girls lured to Syria to become jihadi brides'.

So that was his problem. She promised herself a full read of the story later.

CHAPTER 23

As much as she'd wanted to, Zinah didn't stop and scoop up the castoff newspaper. There were too many eyes watching. But White City tube station had plenty of copies.

On top of the Fatima incident, the headline story was another slap in her face to remind her she wasn't getting enough recognition. That day the *Metro* ran a half-page photo of a topless blonde with hair extensions and next to it a small insert of the very same girl in full Islamic dress. The article highlighted the number of white girls being radicalised online. A hundred, maybe more, had made the journey from Britain to Syria. The draw of high adventure and attention seeking were proving a heady mix for so many young girls.

As she read on, Zinah had a hardening in the pit of her stomach. *A hundred? A lot more than that! Ask me, I know. I send them.* 'It's the women who've stepped up and into the shoes of the males to fulfil the command of jihad.' A burning sensation in her throat. *Why write just about white girls as if being brown doesn't count as much?*

She walked quickly weaving through the crowded pavement. Jealousy has that effect. Zinah was slowing for no one! Several people had to step aside to avoid her. Ok, so Zinah wasn't the first female convert to the cause and nor was she a jihadi bride, she knew that. But as a facilitator, she was the person taking the most risk, wasn't she? It was hard to accept when a nobody like this girl in the paper took what should have been Zinah's publicity. Small wonder she was seething with bitterness.

What calmed her down eventually was something spiritual. An awareness of her destiny came over her as she slowed her steps. Sure it seemed unjust 'to have someone pipping you at the post' as Ahmed would say in his Brummy-Paki way. But there was Zinah's master to concentrate on, the Big One. She just had to keep her eye on the ball. With her unique talent, her adaptability, her all-encompassing brilliance Zinah al-Rashid would soon be the best-known woman jihadist in London and across Europe.

So far many of the women who'd tried for that mantle had mucked it up. There'd been the mother-of-four who'd become the first prisoner of France's all-female Isis cell by plotting to blow up the Eiffel Tower. She'd been put on trial for attempted murder and involvement with a criminal gang preparing a terrorist act. But so what? What was that if not a failure? Zinah was better than them. These cheap publicity tricks were typical of fame-hungry pretenders, the Page Three girl, the French woman, Fatima.

She tossed the paper aside before arriving at Westfield. As soon as she entered the enormous complex, the bright signs perked her up. They always did. The food courts zinged with activity.

The soothing store music, the murmuring water fountains, all put her at peace. Once again Zinah was back in the flow. She was still anonymous. There was a time to go public and get her face in the paper. But not yet, anyway. *Be patient.*

She recited to herself the instruction she had learnt by heart from the pro-Isis Zura Foundation.

'If a woman is raided in her house, she may defend

herself with weapons and if she has a suicide belt with her, she can detonate it without the permission of others.'

Also, 'Martyrdom operations are permissible for women but only if the Amir has permitted it and it is for the public good.'

Zinah al-Rashid would be a martyr. One day. That's how she'd make her personal mark on Westminster and how she would enter the history books.

Chatting on skype or messaging over the net was one thing. But not in the same league as planting explosives. Because CCTV cameras covered the city, it was far riskier. But the problem was, if she couldn't do that, test herself, would she ever be able to face the ultimate challenge which still lay ahead?

CHAPTER 24

When Haruto left Karen's place to do whatever he had to do, she felt flat. First off, her job was tackling the report on Miller, which she did. But the blues returned and his leaving without saying when he'd see her again made Karen feel even worse. *What did all that mean?*

Karen's idea of depression-beating exercise was swiping out at an imaginary opponent with a fencing foil or swimming a length of crooked backstroke. There was a community centre close by with a decent sized indoor pool so her plan was to go for a swim.

By this point, however, there was a stench coming from somewhere under the kitchen units and this time it was not the leftover chicken. A dead mouse maybe? She couldn't ignore it but neither could she track the smell. The warped plinth was a bugger to remove. When she finally managed it, she found no carcass, only a heap of crud. But it gave Karen an incentive for the in-depth clean overlooked when she'd moved in.

Scrubbing away made Karen stew over the morning's happenings. She was cross with Haruto but she blamed this on Robin Miller. Why wouldn't this elusive chap use someone else's phone if need be and contact his family at least? Put all their minds at rest.

Having slopped the floor and the underneath of the cooker, Karen was now sick of water. Instead of the local swimming baths, she decided to head for the nearby Westfield shopping Centre, and she did so by public transport because she'd returned the hired bike. Anyway, she figured, what could be better than watching life roll by from the front seat of the top deck of a London bus? Nothing.

Quacker had wanted Karen to contact Robin's father, David Miller, directly. So she called him from her throne on the 237. The traffic outside was crowding every inch of the lanes beneath while above there wasn't a cloud in the sky.

A nice guy, she spoke for enough time to sympathise with him over his son and suggest where and when to meet. This was to be at Robin's bedsit in Bradiston Road. Then, she directed, if it was required, they could initiate an official missing person's report.

Karen's next call was to William Wan as a follow-up from their talk outside the Churchill War Rooms. Wills was out on the streets delivering political leaflets when he answered.

Hadn't he mumbled something about campaigning on leaving Karen earlier that morning?

Now it was clearer why. He and Robin had been planning to leaflet Church Road Ward together in the afternoon after the Bunker visit.

'But no Robin as yet?'

'No Robin.' He repeated his surprise his friend not showing. 'I don't understand it. I can't work it out. It's not like him at all.'

While Westfield is foremost a monument to consumerism, it's also got a great range of what's today called easy dining. It was as Karen was walking towards the fast food area she answered a call from Haruto. 'Where are you?'

'Westfield.'

'Karen, Robin Miller is close by.'

His phone was emitting a signal. It was a long way from where Wills Wan was expecting him to be out canvassing in North Westminster but, as happened, a very short distance from Karen.

'It's somewhere in your vicinity and maybe even the shopping centre itself.'

Westfield is not the best place to buy everyday items like a mouse trap or a can of Haze freshener. Nor the easiest location to find someone because of its vastness but Karen called his number all the same. Perhaps he'd agree to meet up as she was there. The phone rang twice and then dropped out dead.

She went to call Haruto back to get a better fix to track the signal when an announcement came over the speaker. *Clear the shopping centre immediately. This is not a fire drill. Leave the shopping centre now by the nearest exit.*

Karen asked another shopper if she'd heard what was said and what they had to do. No one seemed to know exactly. Frightened shoppers looked over their shoulders. Leave yes, but, which way to go? Then fear spread and in a matter of moments people began moving ever faster to the exits. *Could it be another terrorist attack?*

When some ran, others copied.

'I think it was an explosion,' said a bearded man in his twenties. 'Don't go that way. That's where it came from.'

The word 'explosion' took root. Bad news travels fast. Panic stricken crowds, many screaming, ran for their lives.

For Karen, time was in slow motion. But that didn't last long. Fear gripped her. If it was a terrorist attack, then she had to move. But she was rooted to the spot with indecision. Heart pounding, she forced herself to get a grip. Her mouth was dry and her legs felt weak. Perhaps there were others due to explode.

Are we trapped and all going to be slaughtered Kalashnikovs?

I have to get out!

Not knowing whether the direction was right or not she joined the stampede. Pairs of security guards, each with a wildly barking Alsatian rushed past in the opposite direction.

I must be on the right track.

Crying babies, screaming shoppers all added to the sense of terror. A green exit light ahead gave her a target. Dozens of frantic people swept Karen out into the sunlight.

The air filled with the wail of sirens as armed police units pulled up at the House of Fraser entrance.

The shopping centre was now in lockdown. Erected cordons fenced off the stores and nobody could get in other than the emergency services.

Security barked orders to keep moving. At the heart of a mini human charge, the epicentre, Karen had little option anyway.

All anyone knew was there'd been an explosion. She called Haruto when she could stop her hands shaking.

'A bomb? Are you kidding me?'

'I called Robin Miller.'

'Never mind about that now. You'd better get out of there and head back to the flat.'

Apart from an elderly lady who'd tripped in the crush Karen couldn't see any obvious casualties.

Karen immediately phoned Quacker to tell him about it. 'I'm at Westfield and there's been a bombing. I was caught up in it.'

He was picking up accounts of the blast from his own sources when she rang.

'That's very interesting. Thank you for alerting me to that fact. Ah, yes, I can hear the ambulances in the background. You ok, are you?'

Her heart was in her mouth. 'I think so.'

Quacker was in full police mode. 'Reports are coming through now. Fancy that, you caught up in it? A locker explosion by the sounds of it. Best be on your way out of there if you can do so.'

He stayed on the line, which she appreciated, monitoring simultaneously what was being updated via the office or picked up on social media.

Karen reached the perimeter road where the buses pull in. 'It's upsetting, this type of thing, isn't it?' said Quacker as she puffed away, still half-winded. 'First accounts, the explosion was a device left in a phone charging point. Could have been a battery exploding even. They've done that once or twice.'

Karen crossed the tarmac and headed toward the growing queue for buses. 'Do they know for sure that's what it was?'

'It is sounding that way. Those charging lockers are very useful, aren't they? Tried one out myself last weekend when my phone died. It'll probably mean that many shops will take them out now if they can be used to plant IEDs.'

The bus stop was as busy as Piccadilly Circus on a Friday night with people six deep. Mayhem.

'My 237 is coming.'

Quaker carried on regardless. 'I remember when the IRA was bombing London in the 70s. You couldn't get a left luggage locker at the station for love or money, which was very inconvenient for everyone. Are you on the bus yet?'

Even if there was one standing in front of me, or coming along shortly, Karen would not have got on it.

'You'll find him quite affable, Robin's father. Have you spoken to him at all?'

Karen told him about the meeting they'd arranged, but not about the phone trace on Robin's mobile. That was between her and Haruto.

CHAPTER 25

Eventually Karen picked up a 237 and could check the coverage of the Westfield explosion on social media which was already showing pictures. The roads clogged as the traffic slowed to let police cars through and also ambulances which, as it turned out, weren't required.

It was uncanny. Outside the bus were all blue flashing lights and squealing sirens while inside no one said a thing to each other. A complete disconnect. It was as if no passenger aboard had the foggiest what was going on further up the road. Or cared.

For Karen the sheer horror of what *might* have been, hit her around ten minutes later. When it did, she craved familiarity and to offload to someone. So it was unsurprising she overreacted when she saw Haruto standing outside Chiswick Police Station where the bus stops.

'I knew you'd be on one of these,' he said, reaching out not to take her hand but her backpack.

'Thank you for meeting me.'

'Sounds like an incendiary device left in an iPhone charging point. You must have been close to it.'

Her stomach still heaved but the last thing she needed was food. However, she happily let him to guide her to Zizzi's and to have somewhere to sit and vent. It was a clattery place perfect for Karen's emotional recovery.

'Haven't you've eaten already?' She hinted.

'That was hours ago.'

'Robin Miller's phone? Is it still giving a signal?'

He shook his head. 'Not anymore. Maybe the blast interfered with it.'

William Wan's phone was also not responding. Calls went straight to voicemail.

'Modern technology isn't all it's cracked up to be,' Haruto said. 'Despite all the communication, when you want to get hold of someone, you still can't. Then when there's someone you don't want to hear from, you have no excuse not to answer.'

With all the forced excitement Karen had not given Hailey another minute's thought. But Haruto had been getting a constant stream of WhatsApp messages from her. He shook his head and sighed. 'There's a new snap chat thing which is cool' he said trying to be jokey again.

Haruto took a selfie of them then played around with an app which added funny hats and distorted faces. Laughter is the best tonic. Pasting pig's ears on your head can be therapeutic. So the following hour they spent buried in mobiles amusing themselves in a juvenile manner.

However, Karen hadn't considered the repercussions. When Hailey saw the postings, she came back straight away with a WhatsApp message. 'Thanks a lot for stealing my boyfriend.'

Haruto glanced over, read it and raised his eyebrows. 'Passive-aggressive,' he said.

Karen felt herself grow hot. Was Haruto a boyfriend? More like a brother figure, sadly, or a crush.

Haruto hadn't missed her awkwardness. 'I've had eight missed calls so far.' He held up as many fingers and then stroked his goatee beard.

'Shouldn't you call her back?' Karen's voice, dried and

croaky after the incident, had reduced to a mere whisper. Hailey was having a total meltdown. Her mind was not only on the moral side of all this, or losing a friendship, but on implications of the gathering storm between them. She was still storing Karen's personal possessions. Some had sentimental value. Karen could see them ending up in the dustbin.

'No. She's driving me nuts.' Haruto continued smiling into his phone. He was enjoying himself and receiving plenty of positive feedback from his friends on his Viking ear posting. 'Hailey's a psycho. You know that.'

Karen couldn't argue with this. The glamorous girl she'd schooled with and then rerun into during a stint in an office five years back definitely had a strong narcissist bent. Hailey had used Karen ever since as a sounding board for her relationship dramas, of which there'd been plenty. Haruto was just the latest in a long chain of them. But this didn't make things any less awkward. Hailey called Haruto by the name of Harry. It was Harry this and Harry that. And Karen recalled how several times Hailey had rung her to say that she'd 'had it up to there with Harry' because of his commitment phobia.

The next Hailey WhatsApp read 'Can't believe you've shafted me like this. You know what Harry means. The WORLD.'

Karen didn't reply.

The following ones continued in the same vein, one after another, seconds apart.

'Block her,' said Haruto as their orders were placed on the table.

'I can't do that. Nor should you.'

'I haven't. Yet.'

'Marriages have broken up over WhatsApp' Karen said, wondering whether Hailey and Haruto's on-again off-again relationship would survive or indeed go the same way. She sipped her Pinot Grigio not knowing if she really wanted them to patch it up or not.

'It's too invasive,' said Haruto as his fat pizza arrived, so thick she wondered how he would fit it all in.

'You're right,' she agreed.

WhatsApp is the worst. It has three ticks involved with sending a message. A green one shows that it's been sent but not received. Two means it has arrived, but the recipient hasn't opened it. When you get a couple of blue ticks, the message has been read. Karen closed it down before she got herself into more trouble. Haruto swigged a cold Peroni from the bottle, unaffected by the girly drama.

There was nothing wrong with the chicken, but when she swallowed, bits stuck in Karen's throat and tears filled her eyes. She didn't like conflict with friends.

They tried to recapture their light mood, but it was impossible.

'Have you heard of Face Swop?' he asked as she was battling a running nose.

Haruto took another selfie of the two of them and used an online compositor to superimpose one face on the other. It was then Haruto's bad idea to send this picture through to Hailey.

After they'd eaten, Haruto walked her back to the flat. He thought they needed to knock heads together on Robin Miller. And he was concerned about Karen's mental state after the Westfield experience. Could he stay over on the couch? Karen read this as more to avoid Hailey than to help with her PTSD.

'If you want. Actually that would be nice. Thank you.'

Haruto told her she shouldn't worry because Hailey had told her she was gay. He watched her startled reaction, with growing amusement.

'I didn't think as much,' Haruto said and shook his head and raised his eyes as if to say 'women!'

The Face Swop, as expected, was the last straw for Hailey and Karen's friendship that evening. But she didn't dwell on it too much. She was far too excited about the prospect of having Haruto as her new partner in crime.

CHAPTER 26

Karen woke with bright morning light shining into her eyes, nauseous and the room turning. She lifted her head, which only made it worse.

Rolling over on her stomach, she waited for the sickness to pass before crawling up into a ball. In time she got herself together enough to get dressed. First things first. Search the latest update on the Westfield explosion. *There wasn't any.* In her state of post-traumatic mistrust, she imagined this was all part of a deliberate government conspiracy to keep the news from the public.

As far as attacks go measured on a scale of minor to major, Westfield didn't even feature. It was inconsequential. Counter Terrorism Command was still digging into it, but no one had been detained or was even under suspicion. Their take on it was perhaps an exploding battery in a mobile phone or, at the worst, a prank. Karen felt cheated.

So life in West London continued on that morning unaffected, and her's would have done so too if not for the get-together with a girl called Fatima. Karen was already regretting it.

She'd been forwarded Fatima's details by Linda Clark who, since their meeting about her daughter possibly being radicalised, had followed Karen's suggestions to a tee.

Not only had Linda managed to get into Tessa's mobile but also read all the messages on the WhatsApp group her daughter had received. The worried mother passed Karen everything. Karen then messaged Fatima posing as Tessa's friend. She succeeded in convincing her she was a fellow convert.

Fatima then agreed to introduce this new girl to their network, and that's how Karen came to be added on under the Arabic name of Basilah. All the young women in the WhatsApp group were preparing to travel to the Caliphate. The deal was Karen would first meet Fatima who lived in Acton.

Armed with all this knowledge and a convincing backstory Karen met her contact as instructed, in the rubbish strewn back alley behind Fatima's house.

By then, Karen was thinking on a minute by minute basis about how Zinah al-Rashid was a danger to not just Tessa, but so many other teenage girls. Zinah was active on social media and hadn't she also been instrumental in sending hate messages to Alesha Parkhurst? If Karen could get to meet Zinah al-Rashid through the underground bridal recruitment system, her objectives would become clear. But to do so Karen also realised she needed to pass herself off as an authentic convert to Islam and a potential jihadi concubine.

As if.

Fatima, who spoke in one of the highest voices Karen had ever heard, was super cautious to begin with. She'd not completely bought the story on Amirah being still on board because someone had told her she had stopped wearing her hijab to school.

'Amirah's got cold feet. She's dropped bloody out, hasn't she? It's because she's got a bad mum.'

Karen, posing as Basilah, talked with Fatima for over half an hour before persuading her she was legit and wouldn't shilly shally around like Amirah. Could Fatima perhaps give her a heads up on what would be expected of her at the interview? Basilah could pass as younger than her real age, didn't she think? The most important thing was being devout and committed.

Unlike someone they knew.

When Basilah and Fatima were chatting away like old friends, in five minutes flat Karen learnt about the coded language girls had to use to get on the wedding list. It was essential to be smooth as silk with the lingo. But even so, it was harder to arrange to see Zinah al-Rashid in person than win an audition with Simon Cowell.

'It's about commitment, yeah? You got to show that.'

That's when Fatima told Basilah what lengths she'd gone to to demonstrate how prepared she was to serve Allah. She'd only done so on condition that Basilah promised not to tell anyone. Particularly Amirah. Definitely not Amirah! Fatima didn't trust Amirah's mum. She might read her phone or something.

Fatima had stolen the keys to a West London hockey club nearby. She'd gone on the net and found how to make a bomb and done it. If she hadn't been talked into handing this over to Zinah al-Rashid in Harrods, Fatima would've broken into a sports hut and blown out one locker.

Karen's ears nearly flapped.

'But guess what, Basilah?' she'd gone on excitedly. It'd worked out much bigger than that, so it was okay. Zinah al-Rashid had only detonated Fatima's device in bloody Westfield, hadn't she? And the bomb she'd made had worked. *Wasn't that cool?*

CHAPTER 27

What was the world coming to? When Quacker first heard not one but several police forces wanted to make misogyny a hate crime, he blew a proverbial gasket there and then in the office. What next? Had people got their priorities in order? It was a good thing there were still bods left after all this PC stuff they had to deal with. Barely enough resource for the real crimes, the stabbings, rapes, burglaries and terrorism, seeing it was the day after Westfield. Everything serious seemed to take second place to offence politics.

'It's taking all the fun out of life.' He knew he was extending it when he went on with, 'A bloke can't look down a girl's front today without being arrested for it.'

'I'll ignore that comment,' said the officer. 'Bloody good thing too, in my book.'

'Looking down someone's dress doesn't mean you will leap on top of them.'

'Not with your hip in the state that's in,' she'd fired back at him.

This sexist banter was commonplace and delivered without malice every single day of the week. But Quacker was more than a bit cynical about the proposed misogyny regulation. The fact was, the political conference season was fast approaching and the cops were stretched to buggery as it was. New laws like this just added needless extra strain.

'If you read some of the stuff on the internet that I do, you'd be more bloody sympathetic.'

'I very much doubt it, Christine.'

'But this new law might stop the gropers.'

'Oh yes? And how will that help?'

'Well it's mostly Asians doing it, isn't it? Different cultures and all that. And no one can touch them folks for fear of being called racist?' Christine Suri herself was a British Asian and knew most of what was going on in the immigrant community at any moment so she was someone to listen to. But, all the same, the whole misogyny matter needed some perspective. Quacker had had too many hands-on experiences wrestling chavs on a Saturday night to not think some of these girls didn't bring it on just a bit themselves with their drink to destruction approach.

'Yes, but this sexual grooming has got pretty bad. Need to arrest those blokes.'

'But isn't all the stuff that goes on between men and women sexual grooming? Him trying to get his leg across and all that?'

Quacker took a gulp of his coffee and thought back to the days when he played guitar in a band. Had he told Christine about that? Yes, he had. Remember those photographs of screaming teenage girls throwing their underwear up on stage at pop concerts? None of that happened to Quacker's group, worse luck.

'Maybe you just weren't cool enough.' She winked.

'They called it 'hot' back then, Christine. And I was eighteen at the time.'

'You got any pics we can have a laugh at?'

'Somewhere I have. I'll bring them in to show you. More innocent days they were. For me, anyway.'

'How've we gone and changed the subject from Westfield to talking about this?' She leant her face on her arm.

The Westfield locker explosion had somehow led on to debating all society's ills. Why'd it happened? These conversations always reverted to a topic like sex, the changes in attitudes to it over the years and how that affected offence rates. There was a connection. Somewhere.

Quacker said 'But I've got a point, don't you think? Current trends are all very well in having a go at traditional society. It's too staid and all that jazz. But these modern values aren't helping with our police work because no one knows the rules anymore. Men can't be all criminals just because they've got a set of balls. Small wonder we were born at all if having a sex drive is so bad?'

'But then why are our six-year-olds who should be learning to read and write being taught about paedophiles? We do have a problem,' Christine countered.

Then the talk went from the sixties to the toll caused by sexual frustration, the link between that and terrorists being promised seventy-two virgins in paradise. Explosives being placed beneath tables of outdoor cafés under beach umbrellas in the South of France. Christine had it summed. 'All perverts, these extremists. They want to troll the beaches and spy on girls in bikinis.'

The spate of small bombs, like the one at Westfield, whether it was a prank or not, was worrying. They both agreed on that one. These minor episodes were harder to stop than the more serious plots because of their random nature. And the next one might be lethal. How could they all best get ready for it? What more could be done to prepare for a full-scale terrorist attack?

The thought triggered a connection. Quacker selected

Karen's number on his phone from a list on speed dial thinking he'd better check up to see if she was okay. But before he could do so, he received a call in from the main switchboard.

The lifeless body of a young man had been found in the corner of a plant room on the Lisson Green Estate, which was a well-known haunt for drug takers. He'd apparently been dead for some hours. If someone died of an overdose somewhere like that, they'd not be discovered straight off. It had happened before. The only difference this time was the body appeared to belong to a junkie with right-wing connections. When the police had been called, they'd found the victim lying next to a heap of conservative party-political leaflets.

This had to be Robin Miller.

At least the mystery of his disappearance was at an end.

CHAPTER 28

What to do next? Was there any more news on Robin Miller? No, not a dickie bird. Was he alive or dead? No idea. But as for Tessa Clark, there was plenty for Karen to investigate and it all centred around Zinah al-Rashid.

As a jihadi recruiter, she had been very effective and persuaded scores of schoolgirls to drop out of A levels and travel overseas to join the Caliphate to become chattels of terrorist fighters. From what Karen, posing as Basilah, had learned from Fatima, Zinah al-Rashid was also a scammer, a shoplifter and now perhaps a bloody bomber.

Zinah al-Rashid had even crept onto Karen's list of suspects over the death of Alesha Parkhurst. Hadn't Linda Clark told Karen Zinah al-Rashid was in Cardiff at the time of the feminist's conference? Maybe staying at the same hotel? It made some sense.

Karen's other case, which was the search for Robin Miller, frustrated her. Nothing was moving on it at all. His phone was dead now and she and Haruto had given up trying it. The stress of not coming up with anything concrete to report played tricks with her mind. Without any rational basis she got the sense somehow the two cases were linked. Mostly because she couldn't separate them in her brain.

By now it was conjuring up disturbing and bizarre scenarios.

Robin Miller was in a ditch somewhere trying to claw his way out, suffocating. It was black and hot.

Miller was floating down the Thames.

Karen was floating down the Thames.

After a while, she lost track of how many laps she'd done round and round the water feature in Chiswick House gardens. None of it helped.

Robin Miller abducted and tied up in the boot of a car. Karen trussed up in bondage in a Syrian desert jihadist camp. Robin Miller asleep in a recycle bin. Umpteen unlikely possibilities chased one another through Karen's brain.

Her personal life was no less soothing. Hailey's messages had unsettled her. Karen knew she needed to break ties if they hadn't already been severed, but not before she'd removed her storage carton from Hailey's flat in Knightsbridge. She'd been wary of leaving it there too long, but not counted on anything quite as odd as the falling-out they'd had.

She sprinted the length of the Chiswick House wood and back, but it didn't help her sort out her options. Haruto was the real issue between the two of them.

She went over what happened again and again. Perhaps it was her fault for asking him up the stairs that night of her party when she could easily enough have told him everyone had already left. Why had she done that? Did she fancy him? Was Haruto her future? Wow. Or maybe just an opportunist as Hailey had suggested? Perhaps staying in Karen's flat was simply convenient for him until he broke up with Hailey and then he'd be off. Probably.

If so she should ask him to leave the second she got home.

But.

Big but.

Haruto was helping Karen with the Miller case. It was vital she solve it and for that Karen needed his support.

Also, there was more to unload.

Maybe she should let him in on the investigation into grooming and Zinah al-Rashid. Who else could she tell about her meetings with Linda Clark and recently with Fatima?

So what's the problem?

It was something else. It was how she felt about him. Should she indeed be working with him at all? Her physical attraction to him was scarier than the impending journey to Syria.

What if Haruto didn't feel the same about her?

She feared what rejection might do to her fragile state. She'd be a total mess.

Everything to do with the past few days, once so exciting now sent Karen into meltdown. The hefty mortgage to pay, her disastrous social life, dangerous shopping centres and even the world of women in burkas.

She was in a turmoil of indecision. So much so the jogging had slowed to a snail's pace with hunched shoulders and dragging feet.

Karen remembered a lady called Alexia, living round the corner in Binns Road. Diagnosed with diabetes at sixteen her eyesight rapidly deteriorated with the disease. A rare case. But at twenty-five she was now ninety per cent sight impaired.

Alexis believed in the power of the universe to help make choices.

But that morning Karen was ready to give anything a

try. Along with almanacs, star signs, tea leaves and voodoo spells.

For Karen, Alexia was a fine example of perseverance and positively and she had told her, 'It's all to do with sensations. One choice feels good and the other bad. You just have to ask.'

So Karen asked the universe, the trees, or even the light rain drops, should I chuck in this job? A nine to five was starting to appeal.

She marched on listening, craning her neck this way and that, but hearing nothing from above. No, it felt no better at all. It was a load of rubbish and she had to make her own decisions after all. Then, just as Karen was resolved to this and wondering how she'd become so sloppy and uncertain about everything, there was a faint stirring.

'Some think the heart is mushy and sentimental, but it's not. It's the source of karma.' Alexia had told her.

Like tapping into a cosmic internet, visions flooded in. An intensive rushing noise filled her ears. Peace descended, and all around was quiet.

Louis Armstrong's rendition of the immortal 'What a wonderful world' ran through her head. *Yes, it was a wonderful world.* A rather manic mood returned. A surge of adrenalin revitalised her.

It was ok having a downer if you can recover afterwards, she told herself. It was all part of the 'keeping going' philosophy.

All of a sudden she couldn't get home quick enough.

Everything she had doubted a few minutes earlier was suddenly crystal clear. She'd become distracted!

She'd been completely taken over by the mystery

surrounding Alesha Parkhurst as well as the welfare of Tessa Clark. But the Clark girl was now safe and had stopped wearing her hijab. She'd heard as much from Fatima and the same in a text from Linda, her mother.

The only matter she should be focussing on right then was the Robin Miller situation. And if Haruto Fraser could add his clever brain to that he could stay on as long as he damn well liked. Hailey, with all her mind games, could take a running jump. Karen had important work to do, and she had to get on with it. Every single second was precious.

While she was delighted to see Haruto back at the flat in his pet place on the sofa, she was less so to hear what he had to tell her.

'Your job's over, Karen. They've just found Robin Miller.'

He turned his laptop round towards her and she crouched down to read a breaking news headline. 'Body of political activist discovered on Lisson Green Estate.'

Karen thought her eyes would pop.

They glanced at one another.

Robin. Dead?

She stabbed at her phone beside Quacker's name without taking a breath or composing herself.

Quacker was already at the City morgue. But what he then had to say to her made her ears ring in disbelief. It wasn't Robin's body they'd found, but someone else's.

'So not too much for you to worry about,' he assured her. 'Papers often get it wrong.'

It was a different person entirely, Quacker told her, and by the unusual name of William Wan.

They weren't sure of the cause of death, he was saying,

not letting her slip a word in, and it could well have been self-inflicted from a drug overdose.

But foul play hadn't been ruled out.

CHAPTER 29

Bea Harrington cried without making a sound. Her iPhone lit up under the sheets as she scrolled through messages. She was trying to distract herself with rereading what'd been put on a WhatsApp group she belonged to and even write a long and silly reply. The fact her husband was feigning sleep again upset her. Should she say something? Or once again ignore the issue.

Maybe his reluctance for sex was an age thing. It could be he was drinking too much or working too hard, the reason he couldn't 'get it up'. These things happened. Not that she wanted to suggest he involve with Viagra and all the drug taking nonsense. But what if it was something medical like kidneys, diabetes, even cancer? If so, she should urge him to seek help and straight away because time was always of an essence.

Then there was another possibility.

He doesn't fancy me anymore, and he's got someone on the side.

This was bugging like hell and she knew she should ask him if there was a younger woman, but she couldn't bring herself to do so. What if he said there was?

James was her everything. Their lives together were so interlocked that the thought of separation was unimaginable to Bea. She'd never even considered them breaking up. It was a ridiculous, far-fetched idea, completely out of whack.

But once she'd begun on this mental tack, she couldn't

reverse her thoughts and soon she was obsessing and obsessing about other women. Who could it be? When could it have happened? Who was the blonde someone saw him with in the bar last Wednesday?

The retirement issue had caused a rift. He'd announced one day a few months ago he was thinking of giving up his parliamentary seat because he was fed up to the back teeth with opening fetes. How ridiculous! Everyone knew James loved that part more than anything else.

The timing didn't fit either particularly after the Referendum result with the UK leaving the EU. They both were aware Brexit meant higher office was on the cards. Prestige, pay and all the authority James had craved for years, which had up to the Yes No vote passed him by, was once again within reach. Mad to leave now. After all this investment of time.

They'd quarrelled about it. But was this the reason for his shift in mood? Was this the cause of this impotence thing, which was making him irritable and thoroughly unpleasant towards her?

'You've got to keep it together,' she said into the pillow. She'd meant it to sound soothing and encouraging, but it had come out all wrong as these things often do. 'I mean, you're right in the running for Ministerial Office. You know that.'

Then, despite the muffling of the bed linen, she'd heard, 'Not that again, please.' At which point Bea froze, felt her temperature rise. 'What are you going on about, not that again?' Should have let it go. Too late now.

He gave a heavy sigh, and she knew he'd turn over towards her. 'At sixty?'

'That's nothing. Even Jeremy Corbyn resurrected himself from the dead.' That sounded bad. 'He's become a rock star. You could do the same.'

'What's the time?'

'Quarter past one.'

'Is it? God, I must get sleep. Full day tomorrow.'

'Me too,' she said but didn't mean it. By now she'd worked herself into an upset situation.

Bea got out of bed and padded to the bathroom. When she returned he'd rerolled over and was ignoring her again. She flung the corner of the duvet off her legs to cool down but her hot head was still spinning.

James was a keen canoeist, six foot two and slim as a dart. He looked brilliant, more forty-five than his proper age. But despite good looks and oodles of charm, his weakness wasn't women. If anything it was the gee-gees. Or was he playing the tables again? Could that be causing these problems? The money trouble was all in the past, but just to be sure Bea would check their bank statements in the morning.

Having worked in the casino business, the cause of his stress could be a betting thing. James served on a cross-party committee. The gambling lobby in Gibraltar wasn't too thrilled about the Referendum result as it would mean the country would leave the EU. Most of their staff travelled in daily from Spain. So this crowd were giving James plenty of stick for his vote in favour of Brexit. But they'd talked about that often enough between them. Couldn't be the gaming bunch.

So if not that, what? Hot then cold, she covered up again with the duvet. 'It's because I'm not your fantasy anymore.'

This tumbled out. Having willed herself not to say

anything like it, she'd done so. She regretted it.

He'd be on the verge of nodding off but this brought another sigh and the words, spoken slowly, 'Don't be silly.'

'It's ok. It doesn't matter.'

'No it's not. I'm sorry.'

She said nothing.

'I've had a lot on my mind, you know,' he added.

Well, what is it then? Their lives were super busy, true. And the thought of him not loving her anymore was mad, wasn't it? But despite what he said, and her believing what he said, she was just not letting it drop. Couldn't she switch herself off? She sensed he felt wretched, so why was she still allowing something to develop that needn't have done? So the man she'd married fifteen years back, with a prick the size of a donkey's, sustained no erection with her any longer. So what? Leave it.

But instead, she did the opposite. She asked 'Is it me?'

'You know it's not you,' he said. His tone softened.

The relief washed over her with such pleasure she wanted it to sink in and last forever.

He rolled over again and moved toward hers, nuzzling up, closing in. She snuggled into the warmth, wanting to be comforted, but then he continued to press against her. This action of him moving up behind her a little too close gave her a sudden ripple of discomfort.

He wrapped his arms around her. 'You know you're the only girl for me?' But his tone had an icy edge to it. She shuddered, and a coldness ran over the stomach.

She wriggled to free herself an inch, but somehow couldn't. This wasn't normal. When he didn't react or relax the hold, she talked about work matters, about the EU, the

Referendum. But he still didn't loosen the grip.

More inane chat. How Bea had got the double room she'd booked them for the upcoming Party conference swapped for a bigger one a floor higher up and twice the size. How she'd had a struggle to get that agreed by the hotel. Had she told him that?

He ignored the question. Instead, he grasped her around the stomach area tighter. She moved the chat on to the subject of Simon King. Anything to connect. James had met the party director for dinner that night. Bea had not been able to join them both until dessert. She'd interrupted quite an intense conversation between them.

'Did you have a good evening? Did you tell him about that Robin Miller ringing here?'

'I did.' Nothing more. Now his arms were wrapping her even tighter.

'What was he saying?' She spluttered, 'I can't breathe, James,' so he released his hold. 'Did I interrupt anything important? He looked down when I walked in.'

'Did he?'

Bea's impression of Simon King was like everybody else's in the Tories. A gentle giant who wouldn't upset a fly, loyal to a fault, in particular to old friends in the party 'Feel sorry for him. A lonely guy.'

James pulled back. 'Sorry for him?' A funny tone. Was he mocking her?

She experienced a hurt feeling. She froze in the sheets.

Then he moved up to press against her again and squeezed so hard she gasped.

'Go on. Tell me what you think of King. Do you fancy him?' He was suddenly talking like a teenager at a school disco.

Her heart thumped. Why was he behaving this way? 'No. Of course not,' she said and kept deadly still.

'Well, he wasn't always that size. He wasn't always that nice either.'

He took a finger and prodded her in the back.

The hair lifted on her neck and her armpits were clammy. But the way her stomach reacted was as if she'd been punched. A flying sensation. It was not like James ever to act in this manner towards her.

'He was a bully in the Army,' he said. 'Brilliant at concealing it, though.'

She remained silent.

'Part of service training.' He ran a hand up and down her arm. 'Not obeying orders can be deadly so they turned a blind eye to his methods back then.'

'They did,' she said, agreeing.

'Now you've got damn politicians pontificating how institutional bullying costs the country billions. All that rubbish. Different story if your life depended on it.'

Bea's eyes smarted. She didn't know where this was all leading, but at least they were now talking smoothly. 'Would have lost the war without it.'

She mumbled in agreement again, but mostly because she was thinking about her personal situation. Act normal and keep the conversation going. But she was fine with the sentiment and his viewpoint that in the services men took bullying with a pinch of salt because they had to for Queen and country.

Let's change this dialogue. It doesn't feel right.

But now James couldn't be stopped. He talked about the

no-nonsense side of army life and how it wasn't the cocky lads or the best soldiers who were treated like shit but the ones who wanted to leave because they unsettled the rest. As he did, he was growing angrier and nastier.

'You didn't drop out, you didn't quit.' The beastings and bollockings were used to instil discipline. And King was the worst of the lot. Didn't she know?

'I think you'd have fancied Simon back then,' he whispered. When he did so, it was so close to her left ear she recoiled and her heart quickened.

Sweat trickled down her face. She attempted to pull out of the clinch, to breakaway, to send a message 'That's it, let's go to sleep now.' But his hands wouldn't allow it. He wouldn't release their grip.

'Simon made this recruit's life hell. He was super fit back then. Did I ever tell you about it? Everywhere this wretched bastard ran, Simon outpaced him.'

'Poor guy.'

'This chap couldn't keep up. He was bloody shattered.' He ran his finger up her spine to stress the point. She felt him harden at the same time.

'Shattered, shattered.' He was blowing into the same ear.

Pins and needles crept up her back. When she opened her mouth to resist, nothing came out.

'King loved it.' The erect penis was now hard against her bottom. He pulled on her hair. Electrical impulses gave a tingling sensation. 'Simon King got off on it. The bullying turned him on. He drove and drove him until he collapsed.' He was silent for two beats. 'The guy died three days later.'

Bea was dripping wet with sweat. 'James, I need the toilet.'

His hands had found their way between her legs. 'That's what the girlies like though. Hard, haaaaard men. Isn't it?'

'No, no. It's not.' She was inaudible. Her heart was pounding fast enough to burst.

He tugged on her shoulder to turn her over. When she resisted, he yanked, and she cried out.

'No.' Was this her husband? James? The man she married?

In one clear move, he was on top of her, the erection forcing inside in a quick thrust. His hands were around her neck. Her eyes grew larger until she thought they would explode. It forced her lips apart. His face was above hers, a familiar face, but the expression was one she didn't recognise. *It wasn't him, surely.*

What was he doing? He was raping her.

Her husband released the squeeze on her throat, but by now he was well in the zone, smothering her small form beneath him. He climaxed in seconds, ejaculated, rolled off her.

It was over.

CHAPTER 30

The day after she'd hit Westfield by placing a phone bomb in the charging locker, Zinah al-Rashid scoured every newspaper.

Things had worked out well as far as causing a crowd reaction, a mini-stampede, and her making a smooth get away undetected had been concerned. But not for anything else. The press coverage the event received was minimal. Why wasn't there more?

Her hands trembled with disappointment as she turned the pages. The incident featured as fifty words on page five of the *Daily Mail*. Same in most of the other dailies. A fuller account by local online news channel *Get West London* and a tiny section in the *Metro*, but she hadn't seen that yet.

The stories were the same in each case. How a small home-made device had exploded in a phone charging unit in Westfield. One minor injury caused by the panic only. The event, at this stage, was not being treated as terror-related.

So when Ahmed called from his restaurant kitchen in Edgbaston frothing at the mouth, she didn't know whether to be pleased with herself or not. How'd *he* picked up the news when to everybody else it was no big deal? But then there's a crowd in Hagley Road who will comb through constantly for any radical activity whatsoever or even anything which could be claimed as extremist-linked. There's been an explosion? Sure, it was Isis. So tell Ahmed about it.

Ahmed of course wanted to know from Zinah. Had she

heard about Westfield. It happened near her, so she must have done. She must know who was responsible for this foolish act, he was screaming down the phone. Could she name anyone who could have done it? The culprit had to be a sister. Everyone was calling it a hoax.

A hoax! Is that how he viewed it?

Ahmed was livid. Whoever it was who'd done this ridiculous thing had stepped way out of line. And he was determined to get to the bottom of who'd done it.

Zinah took a sip of black tea and lied about how she'd read about it on the net but didn't have the foggiest who'd planted the explosive. She'd investigate. Of course she would. She agreed with Ahmed this sort of thing risked upsetting serious plans and exposing the networks of brave warriors.

'You must tell these girls to study the Koran. Tell these girls to stay indoors. Tell these girls to support the jihadist fighters. Nothing more.'

By agreeing with him, or being forced to, Zinah al-Rashid was growing to loathe Ahmed. Who did he think he was? A bully boy, pushing his weight around and a damn nag too. He wouldn't let the matter drop. Did Ahmed suspect she'd planted it herself and if so, was this his way of undermining her? She wasn't sure.

The computer pinged.

'Congratulations! Your item has been sold.' Etsy had come good again. Zinah's online shop was a perfect setup to rid her of unwanted luxury accessories such as her Michael Kors mini bag. She sniffed it again. The leather smelt like every pleasurable experience ever! But designer goods went well over the net particularly if they were the top labels.

When she sold the next items, she resolved the money would not go to Ahmed. Not anymore. Instead, she'd keep it for her own master plan, the grand strategy which would improve her standing.

Alahu Akbar! Allah is Greater!

She called up 'The world's most popular Islamic fashion website'. These clothes were at the other end of the price scale and far more affordable than the luxury items she used to buy. Zinah could get ten bat sleeved abayas for the same amount as one labelled bag. The site was also where she could find cotton shawls and headwear which could be delivered directly to the door. They came in lovely colours.

But while it was Zinah's dream to wander the London streets in a pale pink designer scarf, she couldn't do so. It drew too much attention. Ahmed was right about some things and this was one of them. *Keep a low profile.*

Just because there'd been no knock on the door or mention of Zinah's undercover activities in the papers didn't mean the authorities were not on to her.

She took out her one-layer niqab and tied it around the back of her head. This Saudi chiffon head cover was the best item of her disguise. The forehead part was peaked. It hid her eyes away from others, but it still gave the advantage of good vision. Zinah actually loathed the burka, but it varied her look.

There was an encrypted message on her phone from Fatima about making plans. She told Zinah she'd been working on how to skip school and was hoping to talk someone else she'd met recently into going with her to the Caliphate. Zinah messaged back to warn Fatima to *keep it down* and be cautious.

Zinah bristled as she sent it. Fatima was acting erratically and in a competitive manner. Who did she think she was all of a sudden? Did Fatima see herself as more important than Zinah all of a sudden?

Zinah never mentioned Westfield to Fatima because, if she'd done so, it would have been an acknowledgement she had not only stolen her idea but it was Zinah who had carried out what was being seen as a second-rate bombing. A fiasco. And that wouldn't do.

But Fatima had put two and two together anyway because she pre-empted Zinah's avoidance of the subject. She sent her the message next. 'So it worked. Cool.' Smiley face.

Later, when they skyped a few minutes on, Fatima was full of her upcoming trip and how excited she was becoming just thinking about the escapade. 'Oh my God they will be so shocked when I, like, go missing!'

It was clear to Zinah then that Fatima had had another row with her parents.

Zinah knew these girls needed treating with kid gloves. 'You will miss your mother.'

'She is evil, I tell you. I will not.'

But having heard this so often, Zinah smiled to herself. *You wait.* Once they travelled to Syria from the West the girls usually pined for what they had left behind.

'Have you been studying the words of Allah?' Zinah asked.

'Yeah. I am like so ready. This place is, like, so bad. If you are Muslim and you cover your hair, you are like so *second class.*'

'But there are so many Western comforts you won't

find out in the desert.' Zinah did her best to warn them about how a downside to being brought up in liberal London was it made them vain and effete.

You will see.

Zinah al-Rashid did her best to prepare girls like Fatima because there was no point sending brides who whined about rubbish mobile phone reception and bad coffee

'You girls will not find things cushy. Listen.'

But she also knew nothing would deter them. By now they were desperate to travel out to Isis mostly because they craved the fame that came with it. And Fatima was no exception. She fantasised like they all did, there'd be a before-and-after picture like the Page 3 model in the *Metro*.

Zinah knew Fatima was thinking this way because she kept telling Zinah how important it was to get the right shots on Facebook early on in case the press wanted to run a story. 'From glitzy night clubber to a girl in purdah.'

Zinah knew better however. The bride thing was no longer newsworthy. And few Westerners cared much anymore anyway. European girls travelling to Syria was already becoming old hat. The public attitude was, bugger off.

'You're Muslim and you want to travel to Islamic State? Then, go and see if we care,' she'd even overheard in the street.

These non-believers couldn't even spell Koran, the sacred text of Islam, so what did they know about it?

Zinah thought to herself, that's the difference between the kaffir and the mumina, the disbeliever and the believer. Lack of knowledge, ignorance.

Ignore us at your peril.

Luckily, nothing would deter these sisters like Fatima and Amirah from going if Zinah continued with the slick role she played. She knew how to work them.

Sell the glory but warn of the difficulty. It was the Zinah strategy. Whether any of them listened to the downside or not, at least they couldn't say they hadn't been fully warned.

And how could you tell what'd concern them, anyway? It wasn't what was expected. The hard journey, blazing heat or being pestered by terrorist fighters for sex every five minutes that seemed to get to them. It was far more trivial matters.

One post. 'I can do your hair and makeup coz I know how you like it to look and they don't here.'

What did they damn well expect? Beauty salons and nail bars?

Enough multi-tasking for the day Zinah thought, as she became more and more wound up over Fatima and her arrogance.

If we do not seek to increase our faith, it will decrease. It's forever fluctuating, never steady. She performed salat.

Maybe she would cut back a bit on mentoring brides because it was beginning to do her head in.

Anyway, soon she'd move on to Plan Big.

CHAPTER 31

Even talking to someone in a morgue was disarming. Karen had rung Quacker straightaway she'd heard about what they'd assumed was Miller's death, but pressed FaceTime by mistake.

The words 'connecting you now' came up before she could stop it. There was the familiar linking up noise and the ruddy-faced DI was all at once smiling into the screen. 'Karen? You realise you're on FaceTime?'

'Is it Robin Miller?' she asked, holding her head for support. Haruto had made the point Karen may well have suffered a mild concussion from the crowd evacuation at Westfield because she'd been having these dizzy, forgetful spells. Maybe he was right.

'No it's not, as it happens. You'll be relieved about that. The Millers certainly were when I called them, as you can imagine they would be. The guy they found is probably a young drug addict.'

'And the political leaflets?'

'They were dumped in the corner and the fact they were there at all may be completely unrelated to the case. I can't imagine the crowd that lives around there would be too interested in conservative party stuff.'

At the time, Quacker was standing in a special viewing area of the morgue where the public can observe autopsies via a screen. It was all silent, not like the TV shows one little bit. 'Have you ever seen inside one of these places? Let me give you a tour.' He rotated the phone to show her the layout.

However, the relief it wasn't Robin Miller was short lived.

'No, we can rest easy on that one at least.' Quacker checked his notes. 'It's a young guy by the name of William Wan.'

Karen couldn't take the words in. Perhaps her ears were playing tricks.

It's a young guy by the name of William Wan.

He repeated it for her, several times. But the shock was so extreme, her voice was weak. She couldn't cut through his talking, anyway.

'On first glance, the victim exhibited all the signs of a cocaine user. There was a strong likelihood, a very strong one, he was an addict. The place he was found is notorious for gang stabbings and fights. Do you know a drug death lets the place down? In fact, London does pretty well on that score.' He gave a grin. 'This city has a lower rate than other parts of the country for deaths by drug misuse. Would you believe that?'

'I know William Wan.' This time Karen emphasised her words so they got Quacker's attention. She went on, 'William was a friend of Robin Miller's. He was the Chinese guy I met at the Churchill bunker. And there has to be a connection. It can't just be a coincidence.'

'I see,' said Quacker. 'Keep this information about you meeting up with him and also his friendship with Robin Miller to yourself, won't you? At least until all the Wan family has been informed.'

To the side Haruto had been straining to listen and take in all Karen had been saying. When she finished the

171

FaceTime call, they looked hard at one another.

Karen's heart was still in her throat. She didn't know what to say. 'I only talked to Wills yesterday afternoon from the top of the bus.'

'You should have told Quacker that.'

'I forgot.'

Also, as Haruto kindly reminded her, it'd been particularly difficult to get a word in edgeways. Whatever, the nice guy who called himself Wills who'd been so friendly and concerned about Robin, was himself now dead, lying on a metal gurney and being prodded by strangers in latex gloves.

Haruto picked up the remote and flicked on the TV. Nothing reported on the death. There was an overseas property programme on one channel and an auction game show on another. No news.

They hit the internet. Twitter is always ahead of the papers. But no further mention there either. It seemed William Wan was unimportant, one more statistic and that's all.

As Quacker was too busy to meet straightaway, Karen and Haruto busied themselves about the flat. They agreed then and there that Haruto should move in with Karen. It'd been his suggestion and on the basis he could help her with the mortgage. She told him she thought it a great idea.

The spare room he'd stayed in the night before was small but adequate. It required someone clearing and after that effort disposing of packing boxes. But who better to do it? Haruto seemed pretty happy with the arrangement.

Karen lay down on her own bed to absorb the ramifications of what'd just happened. It was still hard to believe. But two minutes later her new flatmate emerged from the bathroom with a live Hunter spider cradled lovingly in his palm.

'Look what I found near the plug hole.' He then opened the window and tipped it out onto the sill.

Oh great. Haruto was a Buddhist.

'The Gods consider if you kill for no purpose it's sinful,' he said and smiled.

They ducked up to Marks and Spencer to stock the fridge, avoided two more calls from Hailey and then got back down to business.

They needed a plan and a good one at that, Haruto told her. He fished out a cream coloured folder from amongst the office clutter, scrawled in large print on the front 'Find RM'.

The death of Wan and his connection with Robin Miller gave the case a new sense of urgency. Haruto was spot on with his view they had to organise themselves and fast. Plus more questions were now being posed which they couldn't answer easily.

'We must itemise and prioritise.' Haruto scribbled a list on the white board which included 'drugs?' and 'Was Robin a user too?' What if his disappearance had nothing to do with politics or being bullied? Were they possibly on the complete wrong track?

There was a further perspective to consider. Maybe Robin Miller was himself involved in William's death. Maybe even responsible. Inconceivable, unlikely, but nothing at that stage could be ruled out because now there was far more to reflect on than they'd originally expected.

After all, Miller and Wan had planned to meet up,

hadn't they? Was Robin Miller the lost soul they'd imagined, or, in contrast, a cold and calculating killer?

Haruto and Karen kept watching on the net. They checked the usual places. Robin's Facebook page remained the same state of non-activity as it had done the week before. Nothing added. His last Twitter post had been the bunker event details, which they now knew hadn't been written by Robin, but by Wan.

Wan was now dead and therefore would be posting no more messages.

Any further tweets would show Robin was still alive and hiding up somewhere. Of course they hoped he was.

Next Karen made a full list of Miller's followers on social media, aware only a portion of those would be personally known to him. That's how Twitter works.

They then sorted from those people, who amongst them were connected with the Tories. This was following up the bullying scenario.

An hour later Haruto and Karen were looking at a list of over fifty people from different ages and backgrounds. A jigsaw puzzle to complete.

By the end of the day, they'd transformed the flat on Devonshire Street into one of those TV drama sets. Out went Karen's poster of Trafalgar Square in the nineteen fifties and in came a Ryman's stick board. On it was Miller's picture, a photo of where he was last spotted crossing the road to St James Park Tube and an oversized map of London.

Now what?

CHAPTER 32

Haruto finished stocking the food cupboard with essential Japanese ingredients such as dried shiitake mushrooms and sesame oil. Bonito flakes. Konbu seaweed, Mirin and sake. As a live-in side-kick to a private investigator like Karen Andersen it meant being also chief cook and bottle washer. Karen wasn't equipped that way. If he was to be the chef, he figured he might as well enjoy his favourite home cuisine as part of the package.

Haruto Fraser had a strong emotional interest in helping find the missing activist when he heard how the guy had been bullied. Thirty years back, before Haruto was born, his half-brother Masi had committed suicide after being through the same ordeal at school.

Also, Robin Miller's disappearance was an intriguing mystery and Haruto liked working things out. He considered himself a pretty shit hot puzzle solver. Then the death of William Wan, close on the heels of Miller vanishing into the ether was even more than bizarre. It added urgency to everything. So he was pleased to be involved.

'Who's the boy? 'Karen asked when he'd laid a photo of Masi on the kitchen bar in front of her.

'My mother's son by her first marriage. In Japan bullying is known as ijime. It's a big problem. The start day of term, which is September 1st is when so many kids have taken their lives rather than go back to school.' Haruto explained Masi had been one of them.

'And my party was September 1st.'

'Yes, your party was September 1st.'

It occurred to Haruto that Karen was the only girl he'd ever confided in over this issue. 'It started with two guys and then others joined in and ganged up. They'd decided Masi was their target because he wasn't as bright as them.'

Haruto rolled up the empty plastic bags as he spoke. 'Where do you keep these?'

'Anywhere.' Karen hadn't any system, clearly.

'He was so sloohhhhhhhw,' he said, taking off how they slurred their speech and mocked him. 'Like he had Down's syndrome. Not that he did.' He was searching for fridge space. 'Then once when he'd tried to walk away, they pushed him into a wall and wouldn't let him move. The rest of the class stood by laughing and cracking up.'

'And the teachers did nothing?' By her pained expression Karen was not really enjoying the green tea Haruto had made her.

'The teachers said if they sided with the clique it would not help Masi. It would show the class he was different and then they could label him a teacher's pet.' He opened the fridge again and replaced old jars from the back of a shelf with fresh ginger and spring onions. 'That's what they told my mother, anyway.' He washed and dried his hands. 'Who's saying they were wrong?'

Karen was quiet in thought. She was listening without interrupting.

'One day he got to class to find his desk had been turned into a memorial, complete with a large funeral wreath and a picture of Masi in the centre. They'd even lit a stick of incense and left a condolence card written by students and teachers.'

'And teachers?'

'Yup.'

'And September the first was when he killed himself?'

'After he killed himself, all the children and staff involved said it'd been a joke. Masi had taken it all the wrong way. It was his *fault*.' A sarcastic edge. 'If you research the net, you can read about him.'

Haruto then sat beside her. She touched him on the arm. 'I am very sorry and the coincidence is odd, isn't it? Me holding the party, Robin Miller disappearing. The Hailey issue. I'm surprised you came along that night.'

He smiled. 'Maybe I wanted to see you again.'

Karen flushed at this. It looked like she'd been fishing.

They continued talking about bullying. 'It's a big problem in Japan,' he repeated. 'And a pet hate of mine. To make matters worse, this behaviour didn't even stop them. Despite the agony it caused my mother,' he went on, 'After Masi, they picked on another guy. He suffered exactly the same way with all the taunting and beating. They forced him to shoplift for them. Then made him eat dead bees. He killed himself too exactly twelve months later.'

After Masi's death, Haruto's mother and her husband had split. She'd married a Scot and Haruto had come along. When he got to school age he was sent away to board in the UK to avoid the same thing happening to him.

'And? How did here compare with back in Japan?'

'Not too bad,' he grinned. 'Better than eating dead bees, anyway.'

Probably because of Masi, by his own admission, Haruto had been thoroughly spoilt. After university he'd trekked Asia, Burma, Nepal and Borneo, all at his mother's

177

personal expense. He wasn't proud of living off her. And then her second marriage had also failed.

'She can't blame Masi for that one,' he said with a flash of mild rebellion.

There were tears in Karen's eyes as she listened, which Haruto read as genuine empathy. He kept his locked on hers. Usually, he was pretty cynical about any other person's concern for him, but she was proving different. Karen Andersen was a bit of an enigma. He genuinely wanted to help her. Was it her sense of independence and sheer guts to do the job she did which appealed? Or, the very opposite? The fact she complimented him, and her face lit up when she saw him walk in the room. The vulnerability, smudged makeup if she bothered with any at all, the way she played with the back of her hair even though her highlights were growing out. When she attempted a joke, she gave up before the punch line. Plus she looked a nervous wreck half the time which didn't exactly fit with her being a private investigator.

All said, once they'd located this Miller guy, Haruto would pack up and move on like he'd done so often before.

He didn't want to be tied down by anyone, not even Karen Andersen.

CHAPTER 33

Karen Andersen was a millennial. This marketing label describes someone born between the early nineteen-eighties and the late nineteen-nineties. In addition, they're called Generation Y, Generation Me, Echo Boomers, and Peter Pans, narcissistic and self-centred. They need employment with meaning, not any old dead-end job and even this has to have an element of creativity about it. Globalisation handed these semi-precious souls everything on a plate. On the plus side, millennials are also confident and tolerant. And, having grown up during the Twin Towers attack and weaned on computers, this crowd are pretty inured to cyber threats.

Quacker was the complete opposite. As a Baby Boomer he was raised in the era of steady jobs and modest behaviour. He viewed the internet as the frontier for all modern crime. Karen was trying to explain him in this way to Haruto in preparation for their eventual meeting.

'He claims he knows nothing about the net. But that's not quite true. He certainly knows about its impact on stalking. Quacker was behind the first harassment conviction in 1999 which changed everything for victims. It involved a woman knocking back a security guard at work who'd access to all her personal data. The guard posted her name and details on a chat room saying she harboured rape fantasies. Several men showed up at her flat and she was getting phone calls nonstop. A message pinned to the door explaining it was a hoax stopped it for a while. Then the guard went further. He wrote on a sex forum she'd only put the note up to sort out the men from the boys and she still welcomed being raped. Why this case was so significant was the guard had invented an online profile in the woman's name, which was something which couldn't be done before the cyber age.'

They were discussing the internet together and how, since then, even school children were adapting to the normalising of stalking over the ether. Karen showed Haruto what she knew about how it worked. How hashtag hounding led deeper into a labyrinth not dissimilar to Alice through the Looking Glass.

This was all necessary if she was to pull him in to help with some of the cases she was working on.

'Google the hashtags and you'll still see it. #FakeRape #MenMatter and so on.'

In the middle of this exploration of the dark web, Haruto Fraser was called back to the kitchen. She heard, 'Just in time.' A short while after there came a whooshing noise and smells of a Japanese curry immediately wafted through the flat.

Karen was at the point of closing off the trails and following Haruto out of the room to be able to continue their conversation when a post caught her eye.

'Some guy called Robin Miller enjoying himself Tory Activist. #MenHavingFun and #Masturbation. Sick.'

What was this?

She clicked on the link attached. It came up with a video. While the Twitter promotion was only recent, the bit of film it led to was obviously not. It'd been well viewed, hundreds of times, by the looks of things.

As onions sizzled in the other room, Karen watched her screen in front with mounting unease. The clip showed someone who looked very like Robin Miller performing a sex act on a young girl. How had they missed this vital piece of information? Haruto, hearing her wail of surprise, rushed out to see what the fuss was all about.

'Robin Miller was being bullied, all right. A video like this is bloody bad if it's him, isn't it? Do you think it is? We won't know until we find him. Could be one reason he's disappeared,' she said.

They acknowledged between them there could be multiple explanations for the film on the net. Had Robin posted it himself as revenge porn against a girl? No. Surely not. He didn't strike them as the type to do that. But perhaps someone else had. 'She's young, isn't she?'

'The girl is underage for sure.' Haruto was not disagreeing.

While they fixated on the laptop, Karen's WhatsApp imported a stream of new messages. It was Fatima going frantic with excitement because Zinah al-Rashid had finally agreed to meet up in person to interview the latest recruit. 'Don't let me down, Sister.'

Quacker called next thing. Having told them only hours before he was too busy to meet up with them, he now needed to see Karen right away if she could find five minutes to spare. Could she make it over to his office? Oh, and had Robin Miller showed himself at all?

At this Haruto rushed back to the kitchen and turned off the cooking, it was time they upped and left.

Everything about the past few days had been happening faster than either of them could have imagined. They raced out the flat, down the stairs, now very aware of why Quacker needed Karen there and then. He needed a statement about William Wan because Karen had become a witness in a murder inquiry.

All the time she'd wanted to acquaint Haruto with the facts of her other case, Tessa Clark, Zinah al-Rashid. Bring him up to date on death of the feminist Alesha Parkhurst. But the opportunity hadn't yet presented. Now it had. Having seen her WhatsApps, Haruto asked Karen straight out, 'Who is Basilah?'

CHAPTER 34

The verdict was still out on William Wan's cause of death. Self-inflicted or murder? The coke in his pocket suggested an accidental overdose, though there'd also been signs of a struggle. But Karen couldn't learn much. It seemed to her something had happened even since she'd last spoken to Quacker on the phone. He was definitely distancing. There were even slight indications he wanted to actually move her off the Robin Miller case.

Why had he lost interest in him all of a sudden?

The two events, the apparent vanishing into thin air of Miller and the then death of William Wan surely had to be linked?

First, she'd met up with Wan by accident chasing news of Robin. She'd established via Wills a close friendship existed between the two of them. For example, if William Wan used drugs, what about Miller? Did he use them too? Karen was trying to help. These were sensible suggestions. But even so there was almost nil response from Quacker. Even the bombshell of the sex tape online didn't seem to move a muscle. What was relevant about Robin Miller performing for the camera? Not interesting enough. It came back with a big fat nothing from him.

Instead, Quacker was keen to emphasise, and repeatedly at that, they were meeting over William Wan and that was it. What Karen could tell him about Wan like when and where she last saw him would be useful. But he didn't want to talk about Miller right now, thank you.

He only took the most cursory of looks at the video on her phone. And even then it produced a rather atypical reaction. 'Good Lord. Didn't know Robin Miller was that sort of lad.'

'We can't be sure it's him,' said Haruto.

Quacker wasn't as forgiving. 'Bears a very close resemblance to the pictures I've been shown of him.'

'He could have been set up,' Haruto offered, stroking his tiny beard, rising to Miller's defence.

'Or maybe he was just unaware it was being filmed. You can't be too careful these days, can you?' He got off the subject as he usually did by telling a story.

'I remember the first case which I had to deal with. I'm going back a few years now.' He reclined in his chair and stretched his neck.

'Jilted boyfriend stuck his ex's name and number in a phone box where prostitutes leave their visiting cards. The girl found the advert, took it down, thinking that was it. But next, it's up in another kiosk. Same again, discovers that one. Turns out the bloke had pinned it up in over forty boxes round the City. He must have walked for bloody miles!' Quacker was enjoying telling this tale as an excuse to lighten the conversation.

Haruto later told Karen she looked as if she would explode at that moment.

Karen, put back in her box, mumbled about holding a meeting with Miller's father.

'Ah.' As if to call things to a halt, Quacker gave hand on table gestures. 'Well, I'm backtracking a bit, Karen. You probably won't have to go down that route anymore.'

'Not go down which route?'

'We've already filed a missing report on Robin Miller.'

'But there's a lot we still don't know about him.' Karen felt the colour rise as she petered out of reasons to keep herself involved.

Quacker tapped on the desk with his pen. 'I had a call today from a Simon King from CCHQ, Conservative Party Headquarters. He also deals with all internal complaints about the Tories.' Haruto and Karen waited for what was to come next. 'William Wan was out delivering their leaflets at the time of his death. I don't consider the two matters are in any way related though.'

'But they could be,' Karen interrupted. Then she saw Haruto send a 'calm it' warning.

Quacker showed a small smile of thanks in Haruto's direction. 'I raised the subject of Robin Miller with him as they were both activists for the same party as we know. King was surprised, Karen, we were still searching for Robin Miller. His understanding is that he's away somewhere. I also brought up how you were looking into the bullying issue.' Karen felt instantly on guard. 'He told me all that stuff had been sorted out weeks ago. And if there is party discord, which apparently there isn't, it's been dealt with. They always take reports of bullying seriously.'

'That's it?'

He crossed his arms. 'He was even a bit indignant, I have to add. None of our business. That sort of attitude.' The irony obviously amused him and he chuckled quietly to himself. Karen was still expecting Quacker to go on a bit and fill in some of the gaps. So, where is he? What was sorted out? But that was it. There was nothing else. He'd finished.

'Did he say what type of bullying they had investigated?' she asked, more concerned about what she'd tell Robin Miller's father who would want to know stuff in a bit more detail.

'A storm in a teacup was his view and what's more all dusted and done. And anything of that nature, harassment or abuse, is an internal affair which they don't discuss.'

'But Robin Miller is still missing, isn't he?' There was silence. Clearly, her opinion was not wanted. Quacker was even making signs of leaving. 'Karen, as far as Robin Miller is concerned, many thanks! You may as well lob in an invoice now, I guess.'

'I've prepared a report.' She propped her head on her fist to display her discontent.

'Put that in with it. We've got a possible murder case on our hands, Karen, with William Wan,' he said.

Karen wasn't the police, was his tone. She was untrained, untested, probably unhinged with it, was his offish manner.

What he meant evidently was Karen Andersen was now surplus to needs. Also, don't undermine a criminal investigation by bringing up lesser issues. She'd heard all this before on other cases, mostly involving bullying matters.

Bullying is not illegal, more a moral issue. It's been around forever and goes on daily. Nowadays everyone claims being bullied when they assume they are being slighted or laughed at.

Then Quacker excused himself and left to go about day-to-day police business. Haruto and Karen sat and waited. Half an hour later one of the uniformed officers handed her a typed statement to sign, and they too made their way back home.

It seemed everyone other than Haruto wanted Karen to give up on Miller. But she couldn't just drop it. At the very least she felt obliged to meet up with his family as she'd already promised to do so. Her only concession to Quacker's request was she might avoid the sex tape issue. She doubted Robin Miller would want his folks to see it anyway.

Also Karen Andersen, who would happily have sidestepped the whole affair some while ago, was being told in so many words, don't go there. And that got her back up. Having determined to see the job through after her self-talk in Chiswick Park, she intended to do so. By the time she left the meeting with Quacker, Karen had decided, by any means, she'd find out for herself what had happened to Robin Miller.

Then, posing as Basilah, Karen would sit down with Zinah al-Rashid and discover why, by the sounds of things, this home-grown terrorist wanted to blow everyone in the UK sky high.

CHAPTER 35

Quacker entered the dimly lit café next to the Polish Cultural Centre in Hammersmith. It was a favourite haunt. If he was in the area, the bustling coffee shop and restaurant was somewhere to drop into for a quick bite. He was meeting his wife there for lunch, not that Chris would eat much. It was lunch in name only. Her new-fangled starvation diet to prepare for a bikini forbade it. So Quacker thought he'd better get in early with his order. Otherwise, it'd be two lettuce leaves and a carrot for the both of them.

The other reason he'd arrived earlier than her was to give himself time to think. It was an ideal opportunity to make difficult bloody decisions, like choose between whether to help the Miller family or placate the Tories. Simon King had spelt out clearly enough just how Quacker's investigation into the missing activist was angering higher authorities. He'd hinted at national security. No questions asked. Quacker knew only too well how treading on toes at the top could lead to more trouble than it was worth.

In front of him in the queue were two painter decorators decked out in white overalls, both built like brick shit houses. They recognised a bloody good meal deal when they fell across it. Know something he didn't? Probably. So Quacker copied their order of beetroot soup and a stewy-looking dish with sauerkraut. 'Same as these lads are having,' he told the staff.

'Bigots.'

'That'll do.'

188

He took out his wallet, slid out a ten-pound note. A newspaper clipping floated out and down to the wood floor. It was a two inches square piece of print on the Parkhurst incident, which someone had clipped out of the Welsh press and sent on. Quacker's quote was starred and underlined. 'It is my opinion that further investigation should be carried out regarding this unexplained death.'

So Quacker had his fans. Nice gesture that.

The Alesha Parkhurst affair still niggled as it had done from the start. But he had too much work on as it was. Overload. Perhaps it was time to let go of a few matters. Beginning straight off with the Robin Miller one. But it was not that simple.

As he tucked into the bright red soup, his mind was on the reason why. Karen Andersen. He'd commissioned her to find him. Maybe that wasn't such a great idea.

Sometimes you can get yourself in deeper than you want.

He'd come across Andersen by chance, engaged her for all the right reasons, mostly the setting up of 'Partridge Security' in view. Twenty years younger than him at least, she was bang up to speed with modern bullying issues and the tech world which Quacker knew bugger all about. Yes, he could Google and text, but not much more than that. Cyber research was her forte which was very handy as most offences these days involved the web. Today criminals were as creative as they were crooked.

In addition, this Karen Andersen was keen as mustard. Didn't take no, did she? Looking at his phone, he could see she was requesting another meeting with him, there and then.

Chris arrived, pink-faced and puffing from her brisk walk to get there, a bottle of designer water in hand. 'Bit noisy in here,' were her first words. The grinding coffee beans sounded like turbines of a Boeing 747 starting up.

'That'll stop in a minute.' He pushed his empty plate to the side. The jet engines died, but a loud clattering of dishes then filled the room.

His wife slid a Portuguese phrase book from her bag. She still harboured dreams of a six months in the UK, six months in Goa deal after Quacker retired. Her next holiday there with her sister loomed, which would only encourage her more.

'Funny how things happen, isn't it?' he said, searching for some tactful means of moving the subject off Goa. But as they'd met Robin Miller's father and mother there, and since he'd gone missing, it was all she spoke of. It'd been Chris who'd slipped the Miller wife Quacker's business card and suggested they all stay in touch back home. Something to do with them all house hunting. Maybe, after a night of cut-price rum and cokes with them, it hadn't been too well-timed. 'This Miller disappearance is impacting on security issues, Chris.' At this, he crumpled up his paper napkin.

It seemed to do the trick. She paused what she was reading. 'Oh dear, in what way?' She knew he was referring to MI5, and that wasn't good. 'I thought you'd passed Robin's case on to this investigator? So as not to get too involved.' All of which was true.

'Might order that apple pie if you're going up,' he got in before Chris left him to get her black coffee. 'I'm having a few concerns,' he raised once more after she sat down again. 'About Karen Andersen. This Miller enquiry is touching on a sensitive matter. All these claims he's made. Then Andersen's investigating is treading on toes. I suppose when describing her operation the phrase 'bull in a china shop comes to mind.' He wanted to add a few other things had Chris's response to this not cut in.

'That's rich coming from you.' She laughed out loud.

He gave her a knowing grin. What Quacker was now drinking tasted far too sweet and milky after the heavy lunch. He left it to one side.

There's a lot grown men cover in public, but share with their wives. Chris Partridge was a smart, intelligent and sincere soul-mate. She recognised Quacker, or Donald as she referred to him, was not an unsympathetic person. But yes, he sometimes came out with things he shouldn't. As he would have put it, his job was to protect people, not placate them.

Quacker thumbed obligingly through the travel manual. The waitress removed his plate when she brought him the pie. He was eating slowly, ruminating moodily over his apple. He knew he was in a spot. He needed now to distance from the Miller's, but his wife was plonked right in the damn middle. There was even a photo of the four of them, the Partridges and the Millers, as a featured image on her personal Facebook account.

'You're a father yourself,' Chris said, knowing exactly what he was thinking. She raised an eyebrow. 'Remember that. You can't just turn your back on David Miller, can you? Not until the boy is found. No matter who' is breathing down your neck. You can't.'

He chewed on, partially agreed it was wrong to drop an enquiry you were bang in the middle of. 'He's no longer a boy, Chris, and perhaps not as innocent as first thought.'

'Even so. Having someone you love go missing is horrible. And that's why you hired Karen Andersen, remember?'

'I'm only concerned, Chris, she's getting a bit ahead of herself.' Quacker crossed his arms for definition. His wife wasn't letting him off the hook. This was not turning out as he'd hoped. 'The girl needs a tight rein.'

'What did you expect her to do, for God's sake?'

"Search the hospitals. Compile a list of Miller's friends. Perhaps drop by his daytime workplace.'

'All of which she's done.'

'And more.' Typical of a novice, Karen was champing at the bit, over eager to perform. 'Maybe she sees herself as that Danish detective in the ugly jumper.'

'Sounds to me as if the political party is trying to sweep the bullying issue under the carpet and she's not letting them do so,' said Chris. Quick as a flash.

Quacker conceded that. However, Karen caused ripples where she needn't. Then there were these other incidents. Westfield had happened, and Karen just happened to be there in the shopping centre as the explosive detonated. William Wan died and there's Karen claiming to have met up with him just before, which made her one of his very last contacts. Quacker had only Karen's word for the fact she'd done all this. Another coincidence, or a fantastic stretch of the imagination?

However, the more Quacker tried to suggest Karen was over-meddling, the more his wife rose in her support. Why? What was all this about? Girl power? Or did Chris have a sixth sense about her?

So rather than have his wife help him find a way of getting rid of Karen, she'd worked on getting Quacker to bloody promote her. What next?

What's more, the retirement flat in Goa hadn't gone away. More discouragement required.

CHAPTER 36

The plan was for David Miller to meet Karen at Robin's bedsit. Quacker's backsliding on the case didn't stop that. *I stick to my commitments, Karen had told him.* But Quacker had also set exact terms. If Karen continued, she was to stay well away from the Tories. Despite Simon King's denial that they'd received any formal bullying complaint from Robin Miller, which was being challenged by Andersen, she was to steer well clear of CCHQ.

'It's one thing having an activist go missing. Now another's died while out delivering their leaflets. Simon King doesn't want to give the media a field day,' said Quacker when he called her with his conditions.

And there'd been no extra money, which wasn't an issue with Karen. She felt paying David Miller the courtesy of a proper conversation was the very least she could do for the family.

It was the second visit to the property involving Miller's disappearance. The earlier time it had been someone from the agents, Sampson and Sampson, who'd gone round with the Police to check for a body. But on this occasion the property company was short staffed, so Karen and Robin's father were granted permission to visit alone, but only for one hour.

The morning was not as forecast, but overcast and spitting with rain. It was pretty foul. Karen, having rehired the motorbike, had left it in a supermarket loading zone close by. It was a ten-minute wait on the step before a car whizzed up with David Miller at the wheel with the keys to the whole building. He'd driven in from out of London and told her the traffic was abysmal. Having made initial contact, he'd then sped off to find a park. Karen was aware by then they were running way over time, but at least there wasn't an estate agent hovering in the background, cramping their style. It was some consolation at least.

David Miller trotted up three minutes later wearing beige trousers and a short-sleeved collared shirt, no tie, clean-shaven, in his mid-forties. He apologised for being late. 'Have you been waiting long?' He then fished through the tangle of keys which he'd collected from Sampson's on his way through to find the right one.

'Where does your son get his red hair from?' she asked.

'My wife's Irish colouring.' The Millers also had a daughter, fourteen, but she was blonde and took after David.

They entered the building, and Karen checked the pile of discarded mail to see if there were any bills or letters for Robin. Could he have been in debt and maybe that had been the reason for his sudden departure? His father didn't think so.

Then they climbed the stairs to the top floor. The property was rough, but in such a great central location Karen knew it would still cost a bomb to rent.

David Miller said several times how thankful he was they'd shown such a keen interest in his son before he found the correct key and opened the door. They peered into a small, almost spooky space. It was the stink of damp towels and clothes which did it. Made it seem too private. How would Robin feel about them poking around amongst his personal belongings?

He flicked on the light, which helped. The teeny room was part of a house typical of so many like it. Carved up into miniscule living spaces where zero thought's gone into the design and far more into the short-term profit potential. Everything plywood banged together. Plus the bedsit was a complete and utter tip. They were straightaway knee deep in boxes of political leaflets and bunches of time expired survey forms.

'This is the first visit for me here,' Robin's father shoved his hands in his pockets, raised his eyebrows and gave a sad sigh. 'He's quite tidy at home.'

'It's not a big room,' Karen said. She peered into one of two black rubbish sacks filled with clothes. 'Nowhere to store things is the main problem I see.'

On the light-framed single bed was a pile of political tee shirts and, if it was even possible, more paperwork. The only small table in evidence was sticky with spilled coffee, littered with empty plastic bottles and unwashed mugs. Student living.

'I am surprised he'd live like this,' said David Miller after opening the cheap microwave and finding it filthy inside

'Should we take a look around?' Karen suggested, for instance the shared bathroom on the second floor.

'Passable,' said Robin's father, which it was. It had all the hallmarks of a regular cleaner who tended to other parts like the public area. The bath was half-decent, and the shower. But it was short on airing shelves or places to hang wet laundry.

'It's always hard to find somewhere to live in London.'

They returned to the bedroom. 'He's been hoping to

move in with some of his colleagues, maybe into a house.'

'This is typical of any young guy on his own. Nothing that out-of-the- ordinary,' Karen said kindly, having noticed the high stack of takeaway boxes. 'Does he come home often?'

'Once a month. Depends on whether there's anything better happening here, of course.'

'Perhaps I'll take pictures on my phone.' Karen pulled back a pair of flimsy curtains. The extra light made a slight difference, but not too much.

'Good idea.' Mr Miller, still absorbed with the state of the place, was quiet. But Karen assured him he shouldn't have been because the room could have been far, far worse. For example, there were no drugs, pills or even alcohol, just two empty beer cans.

'Can you pick anything missing?' She was referring to Robin's phone or any other personal items he'd mostly likely have at home. Not an easy call. But underneath a discarded hoodie, Karen found his laptop. By his expression, this worried David Miller too. It's not something you leave behind these days for too long on purpose.

'Not a great sign,' he said.

'You're sure he's not gone off on a trip?' It was obvious he hadn't, and she regretted asking him this the minute the words came out of her mouth. *It didn't look that way so why say it?*

They had to face facts. Robin Miller last left his flat expecting to return a few hours later. For example, there were signs such as his phone charger cord was plugged into the wall socket and a new tea bag in a mug as if he had

197

just boiled the kettle.

Also, there was something else. This was the home of a fairly clean living, normal young man. Not someone who'd knowingly participate in the filming of a sex tape.

Now came all the unpleasant stuff she needed to tell his father.

CHAPTER 37

They decamped from the stale-smelling bedsit to the local Costa and took Robin's laptop and the paraphernalia lying beside it with them.

'Have you done many missing people cases?' David Miller asked Karen, as she was trying to fire the thing up.

'Brides to the Islamic State,' came out. And as they'd hit the obvious stumbling block to getting into the computer, she was reminded of her conversation with Linda Clark about accessing her daughter's phone.

'I don't suppose you know Robin's password?'

'No idea,' he said.

'It's not letting me in,' she finished with, shutting the lid.

'What upsets me and his mother is the political party's attitude to all this. Robin idolises them and there's no doubt they've taken full advantage of that for their own purposes. Now he's vanished into thin air and they don't want to know anything about him all of a sudden. Shut off all communication.'

David Miller said he felt like he was between a rock and a hard place. 'I've got a good mind to take those bloody leaflets and make a bonfire with them outside their HQ.'

Karen agreed getting rid of the boxes of campaign flyers would help with Robin's space problem, but perhaps there were other ways to go about it. 'Are you a member of the party too?' she asked him.

'No. But we've never discouraged Robin becoming involved with them or any other political group for that matter. The Tories were his choice, not ours. We've even gone out delivering with Robin on occasions to help him. Under sufferance, I might add.' Miller paused for breath and then went on talking again. 'And before you ask, there's been no falling out at home.'

Karen lifted her coffee cup. 'And you've phoned around family and friends? Yes, I'm sure you have.'

'We don't know his London crowd though. That's where you come in.'

'Does Robin have a girlfriend?' She was inching closer to raising the subject of the sex tape if she had to, but dreading the moment.

He shook his head. 'Not that we've been aware of. But it's possible he has someone we haven't yet met.' He produced a warm smile. 'That would be a lovely outcome, wouldn't it?'

She was mirroring his actions. They were both cross armed, fixated on the beige laminated surface in front of them, trying to fathom what to do next.

He tutted. 'If a girl goes missing, then everyone's up in arms and it's all panic, isn't it? But not if a boy disappears. The rules for them are different and no one sees them as vulnerable too.' He coloured and fell silent. 'Forgive me, I didn't mean to rant.'

'Not at all. Many people would agree with you,' Karen said. 'Obvious to ask this,' she took out her pad. 'How often is he in touch with you?'

'Look, he rings every few days. Or, if he doesn't do that, he messages his sister or his mother. There's always some contact on WhatsApp or by text.'

'Mr. Miller, you're aware Robin made a bullying

complaint against some of the members of the party shortly before he went missing?'

'He mentioned it once, and we were conscious he was having problems but it was then only said in passing. Perhaps he didn't want to worry us. He is borderline autistic, which some people find hard to deal with. Then again, knowing Robin, he'd not dwell on something like that because he knows how I feel about political parties and the way they spin things to suit themselves.'

'So you don't know if Robin made an official report?'

'Some of his colleagues were unpleasant to him, that's all I knew.'

'But he'd not lodged anything in writing?'

'Oh, he wouldn't do that. Robin is also dyslexic. He doesn't put pen to paper unless he has to. And he's not the type to fuss about tittle-tattle. He's always had to stand up to ribbing over his red hair. Also, when he was at school he was small for his age.'

'But the videotape may have upset him.'

David Miller winced. What was that?

'There's a video on the internet that's gone viral involving Robin and a young girl. Did you know about that?'

They fell silent, and Karen left him to absorb what had obviously just come as a bit of a shock.

'A sex tape?'

'I'm afraid so.'

'It wouldn't be Robin.' David Miller was adamant. His son was far too prudish to act in sex films.

Karen pushed thoughts of the video out of her mind as she listened to David Miller defend Robin, who could be bloody annoying and obsessive but certainly never ever lewd. It wasn't him. No way.

She then decided to leave well alone. At least she'd raised the subject. It was an investigation after all and she needed all the help she could get. Yes, Quacker wanted her to wind up the case. But all she could think of was a scared young man with a ruined reputation afraid for his future. She mentioned the possibility of amnesia or abduction or even, God forbid, suicide.

He and his wife had given this last option plenty of thought, he told her. But he thanked Karen for raising other options. They'd not considered memory loss, for example.

'When children go missing the first thirty-six hours is crucial,' she said. 'Adults are the exact opposite because the majority of them turn up.'

He gave an appreciative sigh, and it was obvious to Karen she'd raised the man's spirits a bit. Good thing. She was happy to have given him hope. 'You're not alone with Robin's situation. People go missing a lot. The only cases that hit the media are high profile and involve big money and you don't hear about any of any others.'

He smiled. 'Thank you for that.'

'There are support groups too because ultimately it's usually always the family and friends who do the spade work.'

Or maybe even something worse might happen. Her next thought, for example, was of the Chinese guy who'd grown close to Robin Miller and was now lying dead in the morgue.

But Robin Miller was no druggie or sexual abuser. He sounded to Karen more like a home-loving boy who'd moved to the City and lost his way. He deserved *someone* to look out for him, even if it was only her.

CHAPTER 38

Zinah was feeling sorry for herself. Westfield had disappointed her. It'd been frustrating and demeaning to be considered such a non-event. A shame the human stampede she'd created hadn't been bigger and better.

In addition to this, from his domineering manner on the phone, it was clear Ahmed massively undervalued her. And now, with her father dead, it was possible the Brotherhood no longer respected her as much as they did. They'd fully factored in her generous donations. Also the brides were no better. No respect. It was evident these girls prized themselves far and beyond their true worth with all their absurd requests and silly expectations. So typical of them to take good people like Zinah for granted!

When she was this upset, she usually retreated into one of her many powerful fantasies to raise her mood. Today this meant attending a rally.

At school, Zinah had studied social psychology and human behaviour and got great marks for it at the end of the term. Initially, it was to learn why the other girls often shunned her. But she liked the subject and carried on with it. The science behind mob mind-set fascinated her. So why had she tossed it in at Uni? She would've been brilliant at it. Who knows where it might have led? A masters, a doctorate? Certainly nothing less.

While she didn't get the tee shirt in a qualification, she gained valuable insight into what made men and women tick. Crowds. Gangs. Groups. She could even still recite by heart the article she stole off the internet for an essay.

'The principle is that, in man and in the gregarious animals, each instinct, with its characteristic primary emotion and specific impulse, can be excited in one individual by the expressions of the same emotion in another, in virtue of a special congenital adaptation of the instinct on its cognitive or perceptual side.'

Zinah loved Poppy Day and the Queen's Birthday. Not for the sentiments they expressed, which were linked to western privilege, but for another reason altogether. These occasions gave reasons for people to gather in one place. That's why events such as Changing of the Guard were a magnet to the pickpocket, the possible rebel, the Zinahs of this world. So, what to do? She googled the net. There was a Refugee Welcome protest happening that morning she could join.

'In the crowd, the expressions of fear of each individual are perceived by his neighbours. This perception intensifies the fear excited in them by the threatening danger.'

Zinah caught up with the five thousand strong march after it had just begun. 'Nothing can beat the surge of adrenaline from a full-blown riot,' she'd heard.

How she itched for this experience! Maybe today would be the day. She was no longer an isolated voice of injustice but a part of a stirring chorus.

Sadly, they didn't flare up. No hurled Molotov cocktails or bricks, nor too dense a crowd. But shuffling along amidst the others she was part of the throng, a living organism, something potent and unpredictable. Zinah found it thrilling all the same. As she walked forward, pacing the protestors, she turned over the analysis on riots in her mind.

'In the prescience of danger, a mass of frightened individuals can transform themselves into a mob, united by the evocation of one emotion: fear.'

Demonstrators get off on these probabilities. They thrive on being teargassed, beaten with a truncheon, and screamed at by cops. Zinah was one of them. She loved the drama. Take the police shooting of Mark Duggan! How quickly it had boiled up and over. It had started calm all right, but then a bus had been set on fire and a shopping arcade looted. Copycat insurrections the following morning. By day three, these riots had spread to the whole of the UK. She almost wished she'd not been in Syria at the time.

'Each man perceives the symptoms of fear, the blanched distorted faces, the dilated pupils, the high-pitched trembling voices, and the scream of terror of his fellows; and with each perception his own impulse and his own emotion rise to a higher pitch of intensity and their expressions become accentuated and more difficult to control.'

Crowds had such potential. No one had fully assessed the latent opportunities in groupthink, football fans all jumping up and down in triumph. Pop Idol audiences. Soldiers parading in step with one another. Marching in step produced such strong bonds between the people involved that rarely did anyone ever ask your reasons for being there.

They take for granted you're the same as them.

This fact could be capitalised on.

'Individual psychology is very different to group psychology. Emotions heat up in a crowd to reach fever pitch. This was not achieved in any other way. Crowds.

Incapable of respect for individuals. Self-consciousness, restraint, morality and refinement evaporated in a whiff. Panic was a natural consequence. It was the crudest and simplest example of collective mental life. In a crowd, emotions such as terror and hatred were highly contagious. It was known as primitive sympathy.'

It'd been during the protest that day, coming fast out of her mood of despondency, she'd resolved to fast forward. She would ditch the failures of the past and move on swiftly to the next phase. Three weeks only until the Birmingham Conservative Party Conference. Not long. So could Zinah really go through with the project in time? *It was huge.*

So despite the bomb which didn't feature, and the nonviolent protest which didn't erupt, Zinah al-Rashid left the march that day on a new high. She took the Jubilee to Bond Street and then the Central Line on to West Acton.

Once above ground, she stopped at a convenience store and bought a wrapped sandwich. She was starving, drained in a way only pure emotion can deplete the body of calcium. It had left her ravenous and shaking.

The jihadist-in-waiting upped her stride so she could get back to the basement as soon as possible. Much had changed since Zinah had joined the march. She'd even forgiven Ahmed. In fact it was time to check in again with him, if only to discover what was being planned for the Midlands.

At home she put on the kettle, prepared a cup of tea, and devoured her egg mayonnaise. Zinah al-Rashid was ready for work. She was buzzing again. There was another potential jihadi wife to meet. Her name was Basilah. In Arabic, that meant fearless. Cool.

CHAPTER 39

Karen's bike was waiting for her when she got back to Sainsbury's after meeting David Miller, but so was a tow truck. The loading bay was being cleared for renovation work and she'd not spotted the sign. To argue her corner and prevent her bike being impounded, she had to buy a ticket then get it stamped inside the supermarket. Before that, purchase two items she didn't want. All this added up to a half hour delay Karen could well have done without.

The trip from Paddington to her meeting place with Zinah al-Rashid in Edgware Road should not have taken more than twenty minutes. If anything, less. However, finding somewhere to leave the Honda and not risk being towed away twice in one day meant locating a parking station. Having had plenty of pad before, Karen was now tight on time.

She parked the bike and hot-footed along the busy thoroughfare arriving with only minutes to spare. She'd been going over the narrative in her mind endlessly. Having scraped together a fantastic tale only seconds before meeting Fatima in the alleyway a week ago, meant it hadn't been exactly a perfect plan. From that point, she'd continued to embellish it. Big time.

But, at the time of making all this up, Karen had never expected to have her identity tested out by the one and only Zinah al-Rashid. Now it was too late to alter her backstory too much. If it didn't hold water, and Zinah realised she was snooping on her secret enterprise, Karen's life could be in peril.

As far as the bridal network knew, Basilah was a twenty-eight-year-old white convert who'd become disillusioned with the West. She'd married an abusive man. He was also an alcoholic and drug user, an out-and-out racist and a BNP supporter. However, he was a creep with a trust fund and this had given her access to stacks of money through their many joint accounts. The diamonds and jewellery he'd bought Basilah held no value to her since she'd learned of his womanising. He was also a sex addict and a con artist. This cash would serve the Caliphate better than pay for hotel rooms for her husband's trips away with his slutty assistant.

Her deep love of the religion had been inspired by her grandfather who'd converted to Islam when he was working in Kuwait in the 1950s. Though Basilah's Arabic was sketchy, she could read and write three or four sentences after taking a course at Ealing College. She'd met Amirah online, and Amirah had in turn put Basilah in touch with the gracious Fatima, who'd arranged the hook up with Zinah al-Rashid in the coffee shop that very day.

The prospect of developing a relationship with the woman who may indeed have murdered Alesha Parkhurst was not a fun one. Nor, sitting opposite the failed Westfield bomber. But despite that, Karen saw becoming Basilah and learning all this as a part of her national duty. Zinah was radicalising young British women and sending them out of the country to the Islamic State and it seemed then and there Karen was the only agent who'd learned of her methods. So meeting Zinah in person was the first step to obtaining vital evidence.

There was also another reason. Karen now needed to impress Quacker with something new after her trail on Robin Miller had grown cold. Zinah al-Rashid was maybe a big fish. Certainly she could be a threat to the public. Because of the importance of the meeting, her anxiety level was high. Because of the personal risk she was taking, Karen was also terrified out of her wits.

Edgware Road had been suggested because it was an Arab area where Zinah al-Rashid would integrate smoothly with her surroundings without drawing attention to herself. Basilah would be just one of many Muslim women who hung around there. How would Zinah recognise her, she'd been asked? Simple, she'd messaged back. Basilah would be the one in the pink hijab and black leather jacket. Since her husband had denied her the use of his Mercedes sports, she'd been forced to get around the city on a motorbike.

Zinah had been right. Inside the coffee shop there were several who met the same brief, though only two were in full Islamic garb. However, they were not responsive to Karen in the least.

'Which one was Zinah?' after a while became, 'Where the hell was this Zinah?'

Karen bought a cappuccino and perched at a small table near the door looking this way and that, watching for any Zinah type person to approach.

Half an hour later she had a message through from Fatima on the WhatsApp group. Her date with Zinah was postponed. No reason was given.

CHAPTER 40

Quacker was more anxious than he let on to Karen about the disappearance of Robin Miller. His feigned disinterest had been merely a subterfuge to get her to step back a bit until he'd reassessed the position for himself. Several scenarios were likely, the cheeriest of which was he'd pop up with a suntan in a few days' time. Miller most likely got sick of knocking on bloody doors for nothing. Probably gone off to get his leg across in Ibiza.

Another was he'd met with an accident after consuming vast quantities of alcohol and his body would wash up somewhere downstream. Or he'd topped himself and all the same would apply.

Then a darker explanation, that William Wan had not died of an overdose, but been strangled and it'd been made to look like a drug incident. The two of them were supposed to be leafleting together, as Karen said. Could Robin Miller have been responsible for killing him?

'Going postal' is a common phrase for workplace stalking. This is because there have been occasions in the US where ex-postal employees fired up by revenge have gone on killing sprees. Both Wan and Miller were out delivering, weren't they?

Making a crack like this was typical of Quacker's rather unfunny remarks, his wife had told him.

Until Karen had filled him in on the relationship between the two boys Quacker hadn't picked up on it. There'd been a large turnout for the local election that night with over thirty activists involved, including Wan. No one had batted an eyelid when Wan had speared off alone. Activists often did streets individually. Wan wasn't even that closely associated with the local Tories. Described as a nice guy but a bit of a loner, William Wan had only turned up to support the Westminster West crowd twice before.

Quacker decided a phone call to Robin's father would be in order, if merely to bring him up to date on events. Let him know what was happening. David Miller was on speakerphone when he took the call. The man was fuming. But being at the wheel in particularly heavy traffic was not the only reason for his atypically poor humour. His phone calls to Simon King, who'd be the last one to meet up with his son, were not going through. He reckoned he was being fobbed off. Didn't they care?

'I suppose they don't consider there's very much more they can do at present,' said Quacker.

'Answer the phone might be a start.'

'How's your wife coping?'

'Not well, not well at all. She has this feeling something bad's happened to him. And then there's this video which Karen told me about.'

Karen. 'Karen Andersen told you of a video?'

'Yes. Apparently, there's some sex tape on the internet with Robin in it. She's doing her best she told me to get it taken down, but it's not that easy to do.'

'Haven't seen it yet,' said Quacker thinking maybe it was time he did. He fired up the tablet he kept in his car and followed the links he'd been given by Karen until he got to the video. She was right. It'd clocked up thousands of views.

Not having met the young lad and only seen photos of

him he couldn't be too sure it was Robin Miller. But if it was, the twelve seconds clip showed him and a young blonde girl engaged in a sex act. How on earth did the boy get duped into doing something like that?

But Quacker had kids himself and, as Chris had said, what if it had been one of his own? Yes, sickening to have this circulating on the internet. People felt safe telling strangers their innermost feelings, opening up over the internet. It was as if they thought they were insulated by a phone line. But so often what begun as something remote, ended up as actual physical abuse. Sometimes even death.

CHAPTER 41

Haruto was not home when Karen arrived back after her encounter with David Miller followed by the botched attempt to pin down Zinah-al-Rashid.

But in her hurry to return to her bike, she'd left Mr Miller to take Robin's laptop back to the bedsit. Then he'd handed the key back to the agents. It'd been the deal they'd struck with them. Nothing touched or removed, father or no father. However, Karen was sure the Apple computer contained vital information on Robin's whereabouts. In David Miller's position, she would have hung on to it, regardless.

Karen was chipper all the same. She'd avoided a clamping fee and being rumbled by a possible terrorist before she'd shored up her fabricated identity. Also, Karen had satisfied Robin's father there was plenty of sympathy for his son and the Millers too, if not from the party then from the rest of them. As promised, Karen compiled a summary.

MISSING REPORT DETAILS

Robin Miller

February 24, 1995

White, British

Red hair, 5'7", slim build.

Jeans, blue sweatshirt, Brown lace-up Eccos.

Last seen: Tube station, Westminster, August 31st, 2016

Borderline autistic. Dyslexia.

History of Asthma, HSBC debit card

Address: Flat 3, 93 Bradiston Road W9 3HN

Consent was given to search residence

Consent to publicity

Place of work: Phones Unlimited, Harrow

Assumed heterosexual, no named girlfriends

Friends, contacted

Social media, Facebook, Twitter, Skype, LinkedIn

Mobile phone number 07768 007999

NB Recently anxious as a victim of cyberbullying, the subject of a viral sex video, having been side-lined by political association, shunned by peer group, frustrated by menial employment, solitary living situation. No official bullying complaint though raised concerns with parents

Lines of inquiry taken already:

Preliminary search of RM's flat

All local hospitals checked

Other tenants in block notified by flyer

Trace on a mobile phone owned by him at Westfield Shopping Centre. Now showing no results

Laptop available for further analysis, but no password known.

There was a knock on the door and it was Karen's neighbour, Elspeth Cochrane, who despite claiming otherwise, looked in robust health.

'You know how you helped me out yesterday? I have another small request.'

However, in the time Karen needed to shoot to Boots and back, matters took an unexpected turn for the worse. And all because she'd suggested David Miller get more up to date with modern media so he could help with the hunt for his son, Robin.

It takes about five minutes max to open a Twitter account. David Miller had set one up the year before. But like so many new users, he'd created one and then done nothing with it. But after Karen's little pep talk and since she'd left Bradiston Road and got back home he'd already posted: 'Anyone know whereabouts my son Robin? @karenandersen Last seen central London Thursday afternoon #MenMatter #MissingPeople'.

Being a newcomer to Twitter David Miller was only being followed by a handful of people. Karen had several thousand. So the only decent course of action to take when the message popped up was to retweet it, which is what she did. She never reflected on the hashtags or the ramifications of her actions. It was that quick.

'When a girl goes missing people are more likely to take action,' David Miller had said to her. *No one cares about boys.*

Within seconds of Karen's retweeting the post, while she was collecting Ibuprofen up the High Road, she'd attracted a swarm of trolls. Men's rights activists like Justice for Rape Lies were on to her. So too were the campaigners. It seemed now anyone who followed the #MenMatter tag such as anti-feminists in support of men's rights or pro-feminist in opposition to men's rights had a strong opinion to express. They'd let rip.

Karen's inbox was full of hate mail including one from Zinah al-Rashid condemning feminists for their misinterpretation of sharia law.

No wonder Alesha Parkhurst went round the twist.

What was coming through from the net was the 'we know where you live' style of message. Karen then googled

'William Wan' as much to avoid the cyber abuse as to find out the latest details on his funeral.

William Wan's sister had posted a RIP tweet which was touching and had kick-started interaction within the Chinese community. In addition, Karen counted three retweets and fifty-six 'likes'.

At least not everybody on the net is abusive, she thought.

It was while sliding the cursor over the profile pictures of the people who'd engaged with Wan's sister, she came across a familiar one. A redhead.

Robin Miller!

The page had been 'liked' by Robin Miller!

Her mind flashed back to the conversation she'd had with Wan and how he'd known the login for Robin's account. He'd even used it on occasions to post messages. But with William dead, the only person who could have 'liked' the tweet was Miller himself. That could only mean one thing. Robin Miller was out there somewhere and deliberately avoiding all contact with everyone he knew.

Karen jumped for joy and relief. It was her first reaction. She couldn't wait to get on to the Miller family and pass the good news. Her second thought was how to backtrack on surly messages she'd sent Quacker about being taken off the search. So next she concocted a quick sweet as pie text in draft ready to attach an invoice before he went cold on paying her account.

From then on, however, she grew angrier by the moment. With Robin Miller out there all this time, it had cost Karen credibility. She'd driven important people wild for no reason trying to trace him. Now it was clear he'd treated them all like a bunch of clowns.

No wonder police don't act on missing individuals, willy-nilly.

The following hour Karen spent dawdling about the place and not getting on with anything special but puzzling over her relationship with Haruto. What was going on between them?

Doubtless, the trolling wasn't calming either. All things combined, she grew more and more irate when Robin's number still didn't connect.

He owed them all some explanation.

Then, sitting fuming, Karen was suddenly inspired to take matters into her own hands. She reckoned if Robin Miller wouldn't tell them where he'd been, she'd damn well discover it for herself.

In the investigative business, it's essential not to break the law. But there's a fine line crossed all the time and by now Karen was more than ready to step out of her comfort zone. Robin Miller had a Gmail address, didn't he?

She logged into Google and then the box which prompted 'add another account'. When she typed in his name, it called for the password.

There are illegal login busting systems, but if you don't have one of those, it's down to the old trial-and-error technique. The majority of people use the same passwords for all their transactions. Or perhaps three or four combinations based on the same word. Otherwise, how do you remember them all? As the internet has taken over and we've all set up more online accounts, it's become a nightmare to memorise too many different ones.

Karen tried to recall what William Wan had told her

about Robin's Twitter account. Wills Wan had known the password, and that's why he'd tweeted information on the War Rooms event on Robin's behalf. Karen remembered the 345 bit. But what about the word? She recalled when he mentioned it there was some link between the combination and what was happening at the time. There'd been an association of some sorts. What was it again?

They'd been at the Churchill bunker. That was it. It wasn't the word Churchill itself, but something or someone related. Another prime minister? Such as Thatcher. *Thatcher 345? Could by any chance Robin Miller have used the Thatcher password on his Gmail account?* It was worth a try.

She tapped in 'Thatcher345' and hit 'enter' but nothing. Wrong password. *What about Churchill345?* Again she drew a blank. She returned to the word Thatcher and tried combinations around the numbers working on the likelihood Robin set up a Gmail account before he did his Twitter account.

Thatcher123? No. Thatcher234? *Bingo.* Seconds later the account connected, and Karen Andersen was into Robin Miller's Gmail account.

CHAPTER 42

Gaining access to Robin Miller's Gmail account was for Karen like winning the lottery. Now she could learn what he'd been up to. As expected, it was a rich cache of information.

Robin had not picked up emails since the afternoon of his last sighting. But he'd interacted only two hours back on William Wan's RIP tweet and that showed out of character behaviour.

The inbox was stuffed full of unopened promotions and newsletters. Amongst them were the notification of retweets and emails in from Karen, his parents, even William Wan asking where he was. But what about before that time?

She scrolled down the main page. It was clear straightaway there was a close relationship between William Wan and Robin Miller. The two guys had been in regular email contact over several party matters. One string, which was about a mile long, had 'bullying report' in the subject line.

So there was a formal notice, after all.

From the tone and content of the emails, it was soon obvious William Wan had authored the report. But why?

Being dyslexic, Robin needed the editorial input.

The document which made up the bullying complaint had been the end result of substantial editing and restructuring. It appeared William Wan first drafted it, sent it to Robin Miller, who had added his comments and sent it back. So on and so forth. There'd been a fair bit of modification before the final finished paper had been agreed on and printed out. Printed out? From the email string it was clear the report had been sent through the post and not emailed. So who would they have sent it to? Plenty of back-and-forth discussion on this too. The recipient they settled on was Simon King MBE. He was the director involved in the candidates department.

From the dates, all this had happened at least six weeks earlier.

More recent exchanges showed there'd been no response to the letter. There was an email from Robin to William asking 'Should I chase it up?' To which William had replied, 'Not yet.' Then three days before his meeting with Simon King at The Buckingham, Robin had received a message from William with 'What the fuck????'

What William Wan was referring to was a hyperlink to the sex tape.

Straight back from Robin Miller to William Wan, seven minutes later, was 'How do I get this crap removed, mate?'

The following emails were short and to the point. Phrases included 'party revenge', 'a shit to get down' and 'devastating'.

A double-click on the original message and link brought up a YouTube site where the film had been first uploaded under a pseudonym Pegga Pig. Now nothing. Just a notice the video had been removed because it contained offensive material. Obviously not in time.

A later email from William Wan to Robin Miller enclosed links to other platforms. The sites were multiplying. People had watched the film and posted it on other forums. No doubt it was still doing the rounds of social media.

It wasn't the first time Karen had seen the tape but now she paid closer attention. After all she had a formal report to complete. She wrote up her notes.

The clip begins with a beaming Robin Miller, head askew, who wears a cap and tee shirt, party logo. He does thumbs up into camera. There's a girl by his side, youngish, dressed the same, about fourteen, maybe even younger, pretty, enjoying the attention. She throws her arms around his neck in playful wrestling. He pulls a face. Pan back to see a bus, political banners prominent. A lot of Coca Cola toasts, but no alcohol. The backing track being played to the film is 'Girls Just Want to Have Fun'.

Next, the production moves indoors, the backdrop a cheap hotel room and probably early evening, Summer. The same girl, eyes bleary, looking wasted, maybe drunk too much and acting nauseous. Drugged perhaps?

Close up of a party tee shirt crumpled on a pillow. Hers? A shot of a female upper torso and lace bra. The kid rolls her head over, moaning, followed by wonky ceiling action to suggest head now spinning. Artistic, ha-ha. Camera focuses on a quarter full bottle of wine suggesting good time had by all but then returns to feature girl. She raises her right hand half up in lame protest and then drops it again.

A man moves into field. We see only a back view and the blue shirt from behind, and that he's wearing the campaign cap. He pulls back. Maybe he is standing a distance away? The camcorder pans to show the area around the waist as the guy lifts his tee, unbuttons his belt and unzips his fly. Next he runs thumb and four fingers up and down his erection, time and time again, faster and more furious, his shoulders heaving. He spasms. Close up of a female torso now covered in semen.

While unwilling to clock up more views it took six plays and several stops to get all this down. It also needed that number of run throughs for Karen to realise the film was a clever spoof. The second actor appeared to be a much bigger guy than Robin with dark arm hair. But the deliberate dubbing wasn't the shocking aspect. Nor even the content, if you'd been forced on occasions to view internet child porn as part of your job. There was something else.

It wasn't Robin's girlfriend in the shot. It was his sister.

Maybe she'd overindulged or was spaced-out before the film was taken. Either way, she probably wasn't aware she was being videoed. Did she even know this sex clip with her in it was now circulating freely on the net?

Karen's breathing slowed and her stomach caved in. What had she done? Only passed the video link to David Miller unaware that the person Robin Miller was protecting was not himself but his fourteen-year-old sister Sally.

Instead of cooling matters down, Karen had fanned the bloody flames.

She wanted the world to swallow her up. Things were going downhill rapidly, and it was her fault entirely. She'd ignored Quacker's advice to leave well alone and blundered on, regardless.

Karen called Robin's father at once. He recognised her mobile number because when he picked up he used her name.

'Mr Miller, David, please don't look at the film I told

223

you about,' she said, welling up. 'Because -'

'I just have,' he replied to cut her off. 'It's our Sally.' He sounded too upset to go on with the conversation.

'I'm so sorry, I had no idea it was your daughter.'

Karen had wanted to convey the good news that earlier on Robin had 'liked' William Wan's RIP message which meant he was at least alive somewhere. Also that she'd got hold of a copy of the bullying report and this would serve as evidence Robin was being pressurised by people in his own party. But she couldn't even do that without confessing to hacking into Robin's Gmail account. So David Miller finished up none the wiser on those matters when he closed the call.

When Karen re-opened the latest email exchange between Simon King and Robin, it read:

'Dear Robin, I have received a report which you sent into the Conservative Party in July and apologise for the delay in response. We have now had time to review it and I suggest we meet first as a matter of urgency for a chat about events. I am free this afternoon to see you at the Buckingham Hotel at 5 pm. Apologies for such short notice. Simon King MBE.'

Robin's reply had been sent on his Gmail account literally minutes later from his iPhone. He'd probably been out and away from his laptop. It was a brief response. *'I would be pleased to meet you at the time and place specified.'* This was Robin's last email to anyone.

Karen had had no luck herself in contacting Simon King despite her many attempts to get through on the switchboard. What was he hiding? Was it that underage girls like Sally Miller got wasted on the party canvassing coach?

Was it not wanting the unwelcome media intrusion?

It wouldn't have been common knowledge that William Wan had helped Robin Miller compile his complaint. But Wills Wan was now dead and murder had not been ruled out. Miller was still missing or in hiding and no one from the Tory party wanted to talk about the connection between the two guys, let alone the bullying. Why not?

Despite having emphatically promised Quacker she'd have no more dealings with them, it was time to break the rules. Obviously, Simon King knew more than he was letting on because of the constant fob offs. Her emails to him had met with the standard 'out of office' autoresponder. There was only one communication King was likely to answer. Reopening the email chain between him and Robin, Karen posted another 'reply'.

'Further to our last meeting, I have reflected on what was discussed. Would you be free to meet at the same time and place tomorrow afternoon?'

Robin's outfit for the Buckingham Hotel get-together with Simon King on August 31st was documented in the police report. He'd worn a similar anorak to the one Haruto used for photographic shoots. So when Haruto came through the door later, Karen was ready to involve him in her audacious plan whether he liked it or not.

'Can I borrow your coat?' she asked.

As her new flatmate he was hardly in a position to refuse.

CHAPTER 43

The bullying statement put together by William Wan on behalf of Robin Miller, was the fullest Karen had ever read in her investigative career. The standard document is usually around two pages, so it was also long.

It began with a clear introduction.

My name is Robin Miller and I am making this statement as I have been bullied and harassed by a person I know as Oli Harrington. My testimony can be corroborated by six other people who themselves have been intimidated by Oli Harrington. I have had a long time to think about what has happened and I am prepared to attend a party meeting to discuss this matter. I have been advised to make a formal complaint of harassment to the police but would like to allow the party to act on the matter first-hand. I have no wish to bring about embarrassment or unwanted publicity to the Conservative Party.

Background.

I am twenty-one years old and I have just obtained my degree in Business Studies with a class 2:2. I am severely dyslexic so I have difficulty with spelling and numbers. I enjoy presenting and public speaking and my ambition is to follow in the footsteps of Winston Churchill. I am working for Phones Unlimited in St Anne's Road in Harrow. I worked there since July of this year after I left university. During the weekends and after work I volunteer for my local political association Westminster West where I am an officer. My life is dedicated one hundred percent to the

Conservative Party I represent. All my friends and colleagues who help out with me are of the same political persuasion and mostly in the same age group. We all have a laugh together and enjoy a pint and a debate on the current political situation. We are all Brexit supporters. The bullying activity I will describe began twelve months ago just before the last election. At first, the bullying directed against me was subtle. I didn't think too much about it because I thought Oli Harrington was just extrovertist. I have known him for one year. I met him when he set up an initiative to bus young campaigners around the countryside to help with the general election. Oli Harrington is thirty-two years of age and works for a sports marketing company. He is a senior party activist and once stood as a candidate for the party in a general election ten years ago. I believe he is hoping for a return to active politics.

After meeting him for the first time, one of the other female activists, Tammy Smythe-Kell, warned me about him. She told me he gossiped about people and advised me not to tell him anything about myself that he could use against me. When Oli saw Tammy and I had become friends on the campaign bus was when the problem first surfaced. Tammy told me Oli had made several sexual advances towards her, which didn't come as a surprise because Oliver Harrington's father, who is a serving MP, was involved in a sexual abuse case twenty-five years ago.

Incident One Introduction

On Saturday, April 24th, 2015 I was out delivering leaflets on behalf of a party candidate in Nottingham South. His name was Eric Smith. It was a forty forty seat, and we were told he had a good chance of overturning the Labour

MP's 3,028 majority. We had to distribute addressed envelopes containing a letter written by Mr. Smith asking the constituents for their vote. There must have been two thousand in total. There was a group of thirty activists to do this. Oli Harrington had organised the bundles and we were divided up into teams of four. That meant there were ten teams. I had arranged to go with John Rogers, Mathew McClurren, and Tammy Smythe-Kell.

When Oli Harrington saw me standing with that group he said, 'Not you, Robin. You're in my group.'

I replied that I didn't want to go with his group but stay with the one I was in. He responded, 'I said you are with me.' He looked annoyed because I had answered him back in front of all the others. He flushed red and angry. I eventually said, 'Oli, why don't you come out with our group too?' but he ignored me and then snapped back 'Do what you want.'

When we left to distribute our leaflets, he was already heading off in the opposite direction and had five other people with him. I thought nothing more of it. We returned to the coach an hour and a half later having made our deliveries. We were all standing around in the sun and I decided to get my Facebook power charger out of the pocket of my coat which I had left on my seat on the bus. I wanted to take pictures of the campaigners for my Twitter account and my phone battery was flat.

I climbed the steps of the coach and was leaning into the place where I had been sitting. I could hear footsteps coming up behind me and suddenly I felt a sharp pain in my back and my head was forced forwards. I fell between the seat and the floor of the coach and my forehead struck the metal. I felt dazed. I could taste blood in my mouth. I got up and made my way to the front of the bus and stood at the top of the steps. Tammy Smythe-Kell looked up and saw me. She said, 'Robin, you're bleeding. Are you all right?' I responded 'Yes, yes.' I looked across and Oli Harrington was standing slightly side on to me and his face was pale. I asked the group, 'Which one of you struck me in the back?' Everyone looked confused and embarrassed. They were all looking in Oli's direction. He just said, 'Sorry, I was putting the forms back on the coach and I didn't see you. It was an accident.' Everyone went quiet. Then Oli said, 'Come on. I'll buy you a pint'. I heard someone say to Oli, 'Clumsy bastard'. I felt uncomfortable telling people I thought it was intentional and therefore I didn't make a fuss.

We went on to the pub where we had fish and chips and Oli was nice as pie as if nothing had happened.

Background to the incident.

At the pub the following morning after Incident One, Oli walked in on a conversation I was having with some of the other activists. We had been discussing whether the campaign bus touring the country came under the candidate spending quota or not. It wasn't me who had raised the subject because I was getting cornflakes at the time. But having come in on the end of the discussion I asked one activist, who is a lawyer, the legal position on the matter. Oli glared at me as if I was a troublemaker and by then it had all gone quiet around me.

Incident Number 2.

On Saturday, April 30th we had arrived at a pub in the west of England. We had been delivering calling cards all day and everyone was in a very good humour. I had my sister with me on the trip and Oli was filming us all on his phone for campaign footage. We were looking forward to the evening. I went up to speak to Oli Harrington, but he looked away from me. I could tell he was annoyed with me and I asked him had I offended him? He fully turned his back on me. I left the room to use the toilet. As I was coming back into the bar, I heard wolf whistles and laughter. Oli was being very loud and there was a lot of hilarity. I was pleased that he was enjoying himself. I lined up at the bar to get my pint and saw Oli with two of the girls relishing a joke with them. He was showing them a photo on his phone and then the phone was passed around. I caught a glimpse of the film. It was of a naked man engaging in an indecent sex act. The girls looked over at me once and turned away. I asked to see the picture myself, but he refused. Someone told me later that it was a picture of an activist who had been duped into performing a sex act and it had then been posted on the net. I went up to Oli and again asked to see it. He wouldn't let me. He held the phone up to stop me. As he is much taller than me I felt humiliated. I told him it was not appropriate to be showing those films. I had my fourteen-year-old sister with me on this trip and I didn't want her to see that sort of thing.

The report continued for several pages. Incident four was about phone calls during the night to Robin from several unrecognisable mobile numbers.

Five was a text in capital letters from Oli Harrington's number to say. 'YOU ARE GETTING ON MY NERVES. I WILL FINISH YOU WITH THE PARTY'

Six was where Robin had incensed Oli Harrington with

his support for Tammy Smythe-Kell's opposition to the Iraq war when he had been pushed in the shoulder. Seven was a feminist incident. Even though it was Wills Wan who'd said he thought the campaigner Alesha Parkhurst had been murdered, Oli had turned on Robin Miller about it. He'd mocked Robin about his dyslexia. The newspapers had clearly stated Parkhurst had committed suicide. Couldn't he even read?

Eight concerned a rumour that Robin had been colluding with the opposition over exposing the fact the party was not declaring the campaign bus expenses.

The next bit caught Karen's eye.

Incident Nine background

Oli Harrington is a very ambitious man. He is hoping that his campaign bus strategy will be rewarded by the party with another place on the Parliamentary List and then a safe seat. He competes with everyone who is also in the running to stand somewhere winnable and makes up malicious stories about them so he can bully them into standing down.

Incident Number Nine.

June 1st, 2016.

I received a text at 3.45 pm from Oli Harrington which said 'THANKS TO YOU I'M OFF THE CANDIDATES LIST.' I responded with a text to say I was sorry to hear that and asked why he thought it was my fault. He answered with another text saying, 'SOMEONE HAS REPORTED ME FOR BULLYING BEHAVIOUR'

I texted back to say I had nothing to do with any report on bullying. I had made no such complaint in writing. He never replied.

Incident Ten

This took place on 10 June 2016. I had just moved to a new bedsit in Bradiston Road. It is small and cramped and the address is not known to many people as I do not intend to stay there too much longer. I am waiting to move in with some activist friends but it is important I live within Westminster West because of my immediate political ambitions.

On that day I got up and dressed. I went to the bathroom on the second floor and brushed my teeth. I then walked across the landing and down the stairs. These are situated directly opposite the front door. I could see a small parcel lying there. I bent down and picked the packet up and saw it was addressed to me. The parcel measured approximately 20cm by 20cm. I opened it. A book was contained within the wrapping. I pulled out the contents. The title of it was 'One Hundred Ways to Kill Yourself'. I threw the book on the floor. I felt physically sick. Later I put it in the rubbish bin. I wished I had kept the book as evidence but I did not think of that at the time. You must take my word I received it.

Incident Eleven Background

By this stage, I was becoming very afraid. I was not sleeping well. I was concerned, as I still am, that my career in the Conservative Party is at an end. The bad feeling between Oli Harrington and myself was threatening my sole ambition which is to become an MP. I tried to call Oli Harrington to discuss the issue, but he was not taking my calls. After several attempts, I finally got to speak to Oli's father, James Harrington MP. I told him the full sequence of events and how I thought Oli was blaming me for things

I hadn't done. I hoped he would speak to his son on my behalf. James Harrington was very understanding. He even suggested to me there could be a position coming up in his parliamentary office which might suit me. He says it would look like nepotism to give it to Oli.

On 10 July I received a text message from Mrs. Harrington saying PLEASE DON'T KEEP CALLING HERE. I don't know what this is all about. I did not call them again after that.

Incident Twelve.

July 23rd. At 4.45 pm I received another text message from Oli Harrington. STOP STALKING MY PARENTS. This is the same accusation.

Stalking is a serious offence. While there is no proof of my having harassed Oli Harrington's parents I am concerned that evidence could be fabricated to suggest I did and my reputation impugned. I would like to state in this report that I am the victim in this matter and certainly not the perpetrator.

Because of all the above, I am now making a formal complaint of bullying. I am concerned the intimidating behaviour coming from Oli Harrington will not stop unless I report it. I am on the local council list and looking forward to building my career with the party. I should therefore like this matter resolved and put behind me.

The bullying report concluded by naming several people within the conservative party and not just Oliver Harrington. But it most certainly had been written and most certainly had been sent.

Could the detailed complaint have anything at all to do with Robin's sudden disappearance?

CHAPTER 44

Simon King got a big surprise when he received an email out of the blue from Robin Miller. It was the last thing he'd been expecting. There'd been all this talk of him vanishing. So that countered that damn theory, didn't it?

He'd never made it home after visiting Westminster West Association. Instead, King had booked himself into a hotel in Marble Arch and then gone on a cocaine bender. Since then other work had come up at headquarters constructing narratives for future campaigns. He simply hadn't been able to get away. Plus, he was dealing with the added fallout from the death of the Chinese volunteer William Wan. The press were trying to link it with the party in some way. Of course they couldn't, because King had used his well-practiced blocking tactics. *There is no connection.*

Yes, Simon King needed to get home. So after this session with Robin Miller, he resolved once again, he'd hightail it back to Bishop's Stortford.

Robin Miller's most endearing trait, if he had one, was his damned persistence. He was hard to dump. So when King set off for The Buckingham that day, albeit on that occasion the restaurant and not the lobby, he was retracing his steps almost exactly from the time before. He reckoned he could've walked the path in his sleep.

Then out of his peripheral vision, he caught a flash of ginger. It directed him to the very far corner. The dark anorak, short reddish hair. It had to be Miller. King manoeuvred his way into the tight wooden booth and took the seat opposite. But when he looked up, it wasn't Robin Miller there but instead a youngish woman who wore a carroty coloured wig. It made her appear slightly deranged. But by now Simon King was stuck rigid, wedged firmly between the bench and the table. He couldn't move.

The girl offered her hand to shake as if she'd been awaiting him, *expecting him.* 'Mr. King? I'm Karen Andersen. I've been hoping to catch you. My calls keep going straight to voicemail.'

When King didn't take her hand, she withdrew it.

He adjusted his glasses which had slipped on an angle. 'Yes. You've been calling me a lot, haven't you?'

'I have.'

'We've been flat out recently. And now you're out of luck again. I'm afraid I've got an appointment.'

'With Robin Miller by any chance?' she asked.

How did she know that? Was this Miller's rep?

King consoled himself with the fact that sitting squished as he was he at least had an excellent view of all people coming and leaving the restaurant. But this was highly irritating all the same. As if to make a point he picked up his phone and flicked through. Maybe good to double-check the details he'd received earlier on. But nothing. There'd been no update from Miller and certainly no mention this girl would be joining their meeting.

'Ah. So what can I help you with then, seeing as you're here?' King was being heavily sarcastic. But with Andersen sat there bang in front, he may as well discover why she'd been bombarding him with phone calls. What did she know? What did she want?

235

At this, she whipped out a wafer-thin visiting card. 'My details.'

He checked her out with a quick once over. She was better looking than he'd expected.

What's with the silly wig?

She drank nothing, nor wanted anything when he finally offered her a drink.

King tapped his watch face to emphasise he was limited by time. 'I've got just up until Miller arrives. Or if he doesn't show five minutes top whack. It's essential I make it to Bishops Stortford tonight. But seeing as you're here now, fire away.'

But he'd not discuss confidential matters nor personnel procedures. He'd made that plain as punch to Partridge who'd raised the issue of Robin Miller's bullying when they'd spoken earlier about William Wan.

'I thought as much,' she said.

So why was she here?

King recognised her voice, staccato. 'You sound familiar.' He finally put the facts together. *Robin Miller, DI Partridge, the TV broadcast.* 'Were you on the news recently?'

She flushed. 'I was on the BBC last week. But that was before Robin Miller went missing.'

So King couldn't get her off the subject. What would it take? 'He's officially missing, is he?' More sarcasm.

Had Miller requested a meeting with King or hadn't he?

She stopped short. 'Well, he was reported missing. Now I'm not so sure.'

Simon massaged his palm. *Four minutes left.* 'You were talking on TV about internet bullying.'

'It was about Alesha Parkhurst that time. But the situation is the same as Robin Miller's.'

'Well, as you probably know, otherwise you probably wouldn't be here, I'm expecting him shortly.' He looked over to the door constantly, trying to fathom what was going on. 'So what was your link with Alesha Parkhurst? The feminist who died?'

'I was asked on to the programme to discuss the seriousness of bullying on the net.'

'There's been speculation recently Alesha Parkhurst was murdered. You heard that? She was a woman who made enemies with her strong views.' Karen thought he was fishing for her opinion on the matter, so she gave it.

'Helping victims of sex abuse and harassment doesn't make you friends of criminals. And Alesha Parkhurst was organising a trafficking forum in the UK. The conference is still going ahead. One of the speakers coming over may even know who killed her because she was on the phone to Alesha fixing details of her travel the very night she died.'

Simon King leaned back in his seat and pushed hard against the table. He fixed the girl in the red wig with a stony stare.

'If she was killed, I know who it was anyway,' she added.

'You do?'

'I can't prove it yet.'

If so, this was something King definitely wanted to hear!

'What's the death of Alesha Parkhurst to do with this meeting about Robin Miller?'

'There are many similarities, actually,' Karen said. 'Do not deny you're unaware of a sex tape circulating and the impact that would have had on Robin? It's classic cyber bullying. I don't think you and your party take these matters anything like seriously enough.'

At this she was off like a rocket pressing her unwanted liberal viewpoint on the fragile state of Miller's mind and how the party alone was responsible for it. So that's what she was doing there. Wanting to dig up that damn bullying report again. 'So you're here to fight Miller's corner for him, are you?'

That's when Simon King's stomach rumbled. He needed food and fast, and they served the rarest steaks ever in the restaurant, right there on the spot. 'You hungry?' Without waiting for an answer King cast around for a menu. As his mind wandered, he let it drift and settle on pleasant recollections, tasty steak dishes and even elaborate on the last time he dined alone with a feisty woman. What they'd ordered and why. Where it was. Her look. How she'd smelt of fresh, sweet perfume and had smiled. So much so he was smiling now. He'd just invited Karen Andersen for a date!

His romantic plot was interrupted by her diving for her phone. 'No thanks. He's here now.'

Karen Andersen seemed well aware her statement was ambiguous and it would leave King wondering who exactly she was referring to. Robin Miller?

Simon had barely noticed him approach but a lanky, half oriental chap with a goatee beard was all at once standing by the table, camera in hand. There was a supercilious grin etched the full width of his face. Karen introduced him to King as her boyfriend. Then she slid out from opposite him with no trouble at all, being wafer-thin.

Damn. He'd been looking forward to having a steak with her!

CHAPTER 45

The illegal hacking of Robin Miller's Gmail gave Karen a significant edge. It confirmed there'd been a friendship between Miller and Wan. Also, how the Conservative Party, and Simon King in particular, knew only too well of the bullying allegation and had attempted a cover-up.

It'd allowed Karen to set herself up with the elusive Simon King. Emailing from Miller's personal account had done the trick in fooling King into showing up at The Buckingham.

Karen and Haruto had planned it all. Haruto's suggestion to arrive as support was smart. He'd called it insurance just in case Robin Miller had logged into his Gmail account, picked up on Karen's fake email and arrived himself at The Buckingham. She would have had to pretend she was there accidentally, meeting up with Haruto. As it was, him showing up when he did had been perfect to get her out of a developing tight spot with King.

'You called me your boyfriend' Haruto said when they left. He was grinning like the cat that'd got the cream.

'Sorry. I thought he was hitting on me.' Karen removed the red wig at this point and poked it into her messenger bag. 'What a complete creep.' When she'd knocked back King's dinner invitation Karen had noticed a personality shift. His face had turned a beetroot colour from the neck up and she got the sense she was looking into the eyes of someone with a serious rejection complex.

When Haruto and Karen arrived back at Turnham

Green Tube station the place was hopping. Across the road, a funfair had set up camp. Despite Haruto having accrued enough accoutrements and ingredients to open a professional kitchen, they settled for takeaway again. The route from the tube station at Turnham Green to Devonshire Street is just too convenient for fast food. Despite the big talk about Haruto being shit hot in the kitchen, this was becoming a regular pattern.

Back at the flat, Haruto imitated King as he twisted the cork on a spicy white wine. He'd seen King's mood shift for himself so Karen hadn't imagined it.

'So how about it, Karen?' He popped the cork. 'You up for a bit?'

'Did he expect me to say yes, do you think?'

'Depends on how much you wanted the info.'

'Oh, stop it.'

'Did you discuss the sex tape?'

'Only that I'd promised David Miller we'd get it taken down. Maybe I shouldn't have done so.'

'Maybe not. The dark web is five hundred times bigger than what's searched on the surface on Yahoo and Google.' Haruto folded his arms across his chest in silent reprimand. 'The internet is a digital rabbit hole! You know that.'

'Yes, I shouldn't have made such a claim.'

'You mean well,' he said. But what he implied by his tone was the opposite, that Karen was becoming a pain in the arse and causing far too many unnecessary problems. *It stung.* It also sounded as if Haruto would lose patience with her if she continued.

Karen opened her Twitter account to come clean and show Haruto the abuse still pouring through. 'Can't even look at my own profile, can I?'

'I know where you *live*?' He cocked his head in disbelief. Did this girl get herself into some trouble!

'Probably because I called this utter arsehole something I shouldn't have.'

'You know never to feed the trolls.' They both went silent for a couple of beats. 'Let's take another look at the film again,' said Haruto crunching on a dry poppadum. He knew she was feeling wretched and was trying to cheer her up.

Karen thought the opposite. That he was rubbing it in, emphasising her gaffs. 'Had I known it was Robin's sister I'd have kept my mouth shut.'

'But Robin's father had to know.'

'But not from me.'

'But if that's why his son disappeared you *had* to tell him. You are not responsible for his sister being targeted because of Robin's unpopularity.'

'The family knew nothing about it before me. To them Sally was an innocent fourteen-year-old. They didn't know she was doing all those things. Maybe they needn't ever have known it.'

Karen's mood was worsening by the second. So much so she almost wished Haruto would up and leave her to her self-imposed misery.

'The upside, Karen. At least it wasn't how it was made to look at first. A sex act with her brother.'

They were bickering a bit. It was horrible. She'd not had cross words with Haruto before about anything. Now this.

At least they had the same view about the internet, they agreed. It was a will-o'-the-wisp. A misleading ecosphere where nothing was real.

'And nor is this tape,' said Haruto pointing to the desktop computer. He slapped his thigh in extreme delight. 'Karen, it's fake through and through.'

'It's not Robin. I know that.'

'More than that,' he said. Then he squealed like he'd discovered something hilarious which made her jump.

'What?'

'Karen Andersen, you have redeemed yourself.'

She slid back into the chair and stared at the screen through watery eyes. She didn't know what on earth he was shouting about or why he was clapping his hands. So he said, 'Run it again. I'll show you.'

Frame by frame, they worked through the film. The opening sequence was as described in the bullying report. By now Haruto had printed it out and it'd become a permanent fixture on their work surface. He found the place in the document and read out, '*I had my sister with me on the trip and Oli was filming everyone on his phone for campaign footage. We were looking forward to the evening.*'

It was all there. The film showed Robin Miller on the bus, sister by his side, arm around her shoulders, thumbs up into the camera. This was the footage taken by Oli Harrington described in incident number 2 in the bullying report.

Then the film moved on in jerks to the grosser part, the unbuttoning of the fly, the full frontal action. 'Study it,' Haruto ordered. 'We know this isn't Robin.'

He laid a hand on her shoulder and she felt her skin burn, shiver at the touch.

'But the girl–'

'Take another look.'

She flinched. 'It's Sally. It's his sister.' *What's your point?*

'Karen, it's Sally. Yes. But she's not on a bed. She's asleep on the coach.'

The film was a clever splice. It had been dubbed to make it look as if Sally Miller was lying back on a divan. Her head reclined, slightly to the side, eyes half closed, mouth drooling. *The Miller girl had dozed off on the campaign coach while someone filmed her.*

'The campaign bus.' Haruto waited for the relevance to sink in.

How could they have overlooked that?

'Nasty.' She blinked. 'That's really nasty.' Then the full tears flowed. They streamed down her face. It was a relief for Karen to know she hadn't caused the family more suffering than necessary through her blundering. The whole thing, the sex act, the sister, was a nasty hoax. They checked the bullying report again.

'I lined up at the bar to get my pint and saw Oli with two of the girls relishing a joke with them. He was showing them a photo on his phone and then the phone was passed around. I saw it was a naked man engaging in an indecent sex act.'

'So that's where it started.'

'The report tells it all.'

'I told him I didn't think it was appropriate to be showing that sort of film. I had my fourteen-year-old sister with me on this trip and I didn't want her to see that sort of thing.'

Haruto's hand was still there, all this time, growing heavy and warm on her shoulder. With his other arm, he leaned across and urged her up and into his arms. He tightened his grip, squeezed her into his chest. She could hear his heart beating.

'You shouldn't cry. You're a private investigator.' And with that, he lifted her head and kissed her on the mouth. She held on to him and kissed him back. After a few seconds, after the tenderness, awkwardness gathered between them and they both grinned. After what seemed like an eternity they were still holding one another in the silent room with a never-ending sequence of spicy You Tube films running on and on in the background.

Karen turned and led the way as Haruto followed her into her bedroom. He lay on the bed with her. An hour later they were in the same position, but naked and snuggled in each other's arms.

So there was Karen with someone she'd referred to as her boyfriend that afternoon without thinking too much about it who'd since become her lover.

Now what had she done?

As she was trying to fathom the physical relationship which she'd never meant to happen, Karen's phone went. It was Quacker.

'Didn't disturb you, did I?' She was instantly guilt-ridden and befuddled. What did he want? Where was she? What was happening? For a moment Karen couldn't think straight.

What if Quacker learned she'd hacked into Miller's account?

Since the time Karen had stuffed up and put him on

FaceTime and not speaker phone she'd become paranoid about cameras and calls.

Could Quacker see Haruto and Karen lying in bed together? Or had CCTV picked out Karen in a hijab meeting up with the girl who'd stolen the keys to his hockey club locker hut?'

'I thought I should bring you up to date on affairs, Karen. From the coroner's report it looks like William Wan was strangled. Also that the drugs found on him seemed to have been planted. Someone wanted to make his death look like an accidental overdose. Also apparent he was more than just a colleague. He was well-known to Robin Miller. Apparently, they were often seen out together.'

What have I been trying to tell you?

'As you suggested in the beginning, of course. So we must now find him as a matter of urgency. Bring him in for questioning. He's become a prime suspect in this murder. I've heard you've been working more on the case on your own as you said you would. Any more leads from your end?'

Robin Miller had been bullied, dubbed into a sex tape and now the security services were trying to frame the poor guy for his friend's murder. No wonder he'd gone to ground.

CHAPTER 46

Quacker had sworn blind to his wife Chris that from now on he'd refuse crack of dawn interviews, particularly those from the other side of the country. But here he was doing another one! There was a method behind his madness, however.

On this occasion the radio station he was doing the piece for was BBC Cymru. He'd seized on their offer to put him up wherever he liked and requested The Cardiff Hotel. They never questioned why.

The idea to stay there had come to him on the spot. It was the place where Alesha Parkhurst had taken her life six months earlier. Quacker thought it would be useful to eyeball the hotel.

The radio interview was not linked to any killing for once. Overall crime levels were doing well and had even fallen to their lowest level in thirty years. However, there'd been a rise in violent rapes in Wales. That was Quacker's specialist subject.

If the interviewer asked why sexual crimes were up Quacker would answer as he believed. The surge was more likely due to increased reporting than added crime. Victims were coming forward at long last and testifying. Good thing too.

Had it not been for the wet weather the television interview would have been quite pleasant as a break from the office. It wasn't even too bad for an overnight. The Cardiff was not too far from the studio. The hotel was a tad battered with worn carpets and scratched furniture but those little touches actually gave it more of a friendly feel. Still it did have a proper cafetière as opposed to the usual kettle and a packet of granules, and even a bowl of fresh fruit in the room.

Not that grim. Or somewhere so dismal you'd want to commit suicide either. Surprising.

There was another reason Alesha Parkhurst was on his mind. A conference she'd been working on up until her death was about to kick off in Central London. It was still going ahead. Aimed at raising awareness of sex trafficking and the modern trend in acid attacks, it would be well supported. No doubt the media would use it as an excuse to dredge up her story again and Quacker thought it would pay to be prepared. So in travelling down to Cardiff he was taking a proactive stance. As a hotel guest he had the perfect opportunity to probe a bit. At the same time, he could avoid the local police thinking he was intruding on their affairs. It didn't pay to tread on toes.

Quacker sought out the manager as soon as he was back from the interview. The Cardiff's thirty something boss had only worked there for nine weeks, returning home for family reasons after a seven year stint in the States. But, all the same, he couldn't have been more agreeable.

'Do you by chance still have a staff rota for the morning of twenty second of March?' Quacker flashed his ID.

'If you give me a minute.' The manager, Gareth Jones was a short muscle-bound man with black hair and pale skin. Despite the time in Florida his brogue was still distinctly Welsh. 'See what I can find for you,' he said and then ducked out through a side door to check records.

The rain pounded on the pavement outside with no signs of stopping but Quacker had no plans to wander out in it again. Instead he quietly took in the ambience of the place, picked up the vibes. Within ten minutes the paperwork was set out in front of him.

The manager leant on the counter to look through the description of the day's events back in March. He was trying at the same time to avoid drips from Quacker's raincoat. 'Sad matter, this. She was well-known, I believe?'

Quacker took out his note book. 'Indeed. She was a leading feminist campaigner.'

Clipped to the Parkhurst account was an unpaid restaurant bill, which they both noticed simultaneously.

'So she ate with you that night?' Quacker had already checked out the bistro menu though he hadn't actually sampled it. He'd arrived too late the night before, missed out by just a few minutes. Annoying. It was reasonably priced and varied. Not the out-of-the-freezer blandness which you got at most of the chain hotels. 'You close quite early here, don't you?'

Jones said, 'Yes, boyo. It can catch you out if you're not aware of it. Apologies for that.'

'Mind if I take a look at the bill, please?'

The manager was happy to help. He was also feeling awkward about the account. 'I'd have thought under the circumstances it would have been written off by our hotel.'

'I could do with a copy of that for my records if you could spare it.' Quacker was on the point of taking out his Visa card to pay the outstanding amount when Gareth Jones made an executive decision. He put a sharp line through the total, detached the restaurant bill and handed it over to the inspector.

One of the room girls who'd clearly been summoned arrived in the lift and was in a strop for having been taken off bed making to answer questions. She told Quacker she'd not been on duty that day but had heard plenty about the awful incident during smoke breaks out the back from other staff. They'd discussed the suicide for days. Therefore she didn't have much extra to add. Just that the convention held on the fifth floor had made them busier and left them even shorter staffed than normal. The stretching of resources was obviously a constant gripe amongst the staff.

'We were crazy busy.' So much so, two of the cleaners had been asked to cover the restaurant as well that night.

The manager was combing through another book of records. 'Who was on duty that morning, Anna? Who found the guest? Do you recall?'

Anna glanced from her boss to Quacker then back again. 'It was the Filipino.'

'The Filipino?'

'Mary. The girl with the wrist tattoo.'

'Right. Is she still here?' asked Quacker.

'No. She left the hotel straight after that and never returned.'

Two elderly guests waiting to query their room charges started fidgeting. It was time for the manager to break off and attend to them. He made a polite escape, leaving Quacker and Anna together.

Quacker wanted to know more about Mary. They knew she'd taken the train to London after finding and reporting the body. The staff had tried to contact her after that, but her phone didn't pick up. However they all understood why. It was something to do with her thinking the local press would want to take her picture. In reality that wouldn't have happened. But she was paranoid about it. Everyone knew she'd escaped from an abusive Arab family the summer before. The chef had said Mary was terrified she'd be traced if her photo appeared in the paper and sent back to them.

'Can I take a look at the room Ms Parkhurst was staying in?' asked Quacker.

Reluctantly, because she wanted to get on with her work, Anna agreed. She then told him it was the second time she'd showed the room to an investigator which caused Quacker to wonder who'd been there first.

She took Quacker back up in the lift to 325 and waited impatiently in the corridor while he studied the layout, the overhead fan, heavy drapes. By then Quacker had seen enough. He reckoned he'd better let the girl get on with her job. The room wasn't too dissimilar to the one he'd had himself. Only in that this one had been freshly decorated, probably following the Parkhurst incident.

Quacker returned to pack up his things and leave. He handed in his key at reception. It was time to return to the Big Smoke.

On the way out the strong aroma of fried bacon left over from breakfast lured him back into the now empty restaurant where the tables were already set up with red cloths for lunch.

So this was where Alesha dined the night before she died.

An energetic member of staff was restocking the shelves. But he cut off to study the picture of Alesha Parkhurst on Quacker's phone. He peered down at her bill, by now laid flat on the polished bar top.

'I wasn't on that night. Sorry.' He went back to bottling up. 'Who was she dining with by the way?'

Quacker cleared the iPhone screen. 'She was alone from the looks of it.'

The bottle stocker gave the counter a quick polish. 'No, Sir, she wasn't. She'd have been with someone else, that's for sure.'

Quacker raised his eyebrows. 'And what makes you think that?'

The bar tender snatched up a menu and opened it with a flourish. 'Chateaubriand, that's what.' He laid the menu out on the by now glistening surface. 'We only serve Chateaubriand as a meal for two.'

'My favourite,' said Quacker.

'Thick, juicy tenderloin fillet, white wine, shallots demi-glace, butter, tarragon, lemon juice.' It was obviously his too. He smacked his lips. 'Gorgeous.'

Quacker was salivating just thinking about it all. Together they stared at the menu like a loved-up couple choosing a ring. 'So someone went halves with her.'

'You're sure about that?'

'Absolutely sure.'

'Thank you. In that case, I'll trouble you no more.'

'My pleasure.'

Quacker wrapped on the bar counter with his knuckles. This was new information, new information indeed.

He folded the restaurant bill and put it away. But Quacker was still puzzled. What Alesha Parkhurst had ordered was a trifle unusual. It was heavy meat. Maybe he was just being old-fashioned in his thinking but surely this was not the dish two women eating together would have chosen.

Did Parkhurst then, have dinner with a man just before her alleged suicide? If so, wouldn't he have picked up the tab? Paid the bill?

The thought struck. As an ardent feminist, surely she'd insisted on going halves!

Quacker was now off and running. His hunch that Alesha had not simply taken her own life but had in fact been murdered was at last beginning to shape up nicely. But why, after he'd questioned the room girl further and worked out it was Karen who'd been there before him, had Andersen been enquiring about a woman in a burka?

CHAPTER 47

She hated this place. Why had she allowed Ahmed to talk her round again when it just meant more hours cooped up in this damn dungeon? Applause and flattery, that's why. 'You're doing a great job, a fantastic job,' he'd lied, when she'd told him she felt undervalued. Like the slime ball he was, he could heap praise when it suited.

Ahmed, the silver tongue. What was this? Why had Zinah ever doubted their gratitude? She was a shining star and Isis treasured her contribution. The girls looked up to her as a symbol of perfection, the white convert who'd surpassed herself, turned her back on a life of privilege, chosen the rightful path. Keep on, keep on doing it. *Like that old hit record.*

On the other end of FaceTime that morning was Fatima. Why hadn't Zinah kept her meeting with the new sister Basilah? Was something wrong? Fatima crowed on and on about the convert she'd recruited and how great she was. So much more engaged and positive than some of the ones Zinah had sourced. Amirah, for example. Basilah was different. She took a real interest in Fatima and 'totally got' her. Basilah was really, like, really cool.

At this, Zinah felt another spasm of jealousy, because Zinah al-Rashid was the leading figure around here. Hadn't Ahmed said as much?

She didn't like one little bit the way Fatima talked of recruiting people because that was *Zinah's* role.

'Basilah will have another opportunity to meet me,' said

Zinah. And yes, she completely understood Fatima was aching to join Isis but she would just have to sit on her hands, wouldn't she? Yes, she knew Amirah had dropped out. So what? But now Fatima was asking to join forces with other sisters going from the West. She'd promised Basilah there were enough of them travelling out there to help one another.

'There are plenty of others,' said Zinah al-Rashid.

But that's not what Fatima had learnt, which was why she was calling Zinah. Fatima had been WhatsApping with a bride called Jamilah from Istanbul. It seemed getting company on the trip from Turkey was not always in the offing. Jamilah, for example, had asked what to do next and had been told to board the bus to Urfa and make the eighteen hour journey all by herself.

Fatima was right. Jamillah was indeed in a bad state when Zinah finally contacted her. Why weren't there any other brides, she was asking? If not brides, what about the fighters? How did they expect her to travel all alone and cross into Isis territory without an escort?

Jamillah's WhatsApp's were fast and full of misspellings, but that wasn't all. There was another problem which was making her cry. It concerned her future husband.

'Has he been in touch?' typed Zinah.

'Sister, he is *sexting* me. He wants to see me naked.' That was not Islamic, was it? The groom was telling Jamilah to show herself to him. As they were only twenty-four hours from getting married, he couldn't get how there was anything wrong in asking for that. After all, Jamillah was to be his wife, and he was a soldier with needs, wasn't he?

Jamilah had cried on and on. She'd wanted to be a good

254

wife to a good husband. Zinah had assured her, promised her that much. How she'd marry a perfect Muslim. 'Sexting was not part of the picture, was it?' Jamilah was typing as fast as she could. 'Brothers lie to get a wife.'

But Zinah's networking skills knew no bounds. She always got the most satisfaction out of the biggest challenges. So she swore to Jamilah she'd hook her up with someone on WhatsApp. And within seconds she did. A sister called Karimah.

'It was the sickest thing crossing that Turkish border,' Karimah messaged Jamilah when she came online. 'I'll never forget that night.'

'I want it to be ok. I want to serve Allah.' Jamilah typed back.

'It's time for action, sis. You must cross. Your faith will get so high during the crossing. Big adrenaline rush. It is sinful for u to be staying in the UK whilst there is a khilafah.' A successor to a prophet of God.

'I'm not in UK. I'm in Istanbul.'

'You have to cross then.'

Jamillah came back with, 'I will cross.'

Victory achieved.

Going to the Islamic State was a starry-eyed adventure into the unknown. It was a Mills and Boon style picture of romance.

Zinah told the recruits what they wanted to hear. Becoming a jihadi bride was less about submission and more about the promise of a life of no inequality. Wasn't that the very opposite of what the West said about them? The Caliphate vowed no poverty which was appealing to all these girls who thought the Times Rich List was, like, so unfair.

No government with humans in charge could ever completely avoid corruption. The brides-to-be liked the clear-cut laws of the Koran. Modern life and society was so, so confusing. No mere humans could fully conform to Sharia which was why they must serve Allah. Allahu Akbar.

Zinah told them, 'You can have this perfect world, and it's there for you right now. But you have to try harder.'

'I want to serve Allah.'

'The West has done too much damage already with its consumerism. It has tried to corrupt you too. There is plenty to overcome. By joining Isis it shows real character and true commitment. You will become a perfect person.'

The girls all believed her word for word. Zinah al-Rashid's delivery was that smooth and unbroken. Perhaps it was because what Zinah needed more than anything else herself was to be that 'perfect person'. She told them all, 'I am committed and I want to serve Allah above all. You must too.'

When Zinah had finished on WhatsApp she went on Twitter and retweeted a post 'the most amazing experience of my life was crossing with a family of ten and new-born.'

Afterwards she dealt with her sales from eBay by packaging them up in Jiffy envelopes ready for delivery. She'd sent out in total twelve pre-owned designer bags over the last two months alone. Not only were these from her own collection, they included ones she'd borrowed or stolen. For example, her grandmother's vintage Gucci taken from the upstairs bedroom closet. It was as well the elderly woman had creeping dementia. She'd probably never discover her diamond choker and earrings missing either.

All these Zinah had already sold online to aid the cause. *Allahu Akbar.*

Yes, Zinah had done well, but not well enough obviously. Now too many others were starting to copy her. She needed the buzz back and to know she was the best of them all.

When Zinah cleared the sideboard of dust and circular mail, she found a political leaflet which had been lying there for far too long. On it was the face of a fat man with teeth grey as tombstones. He had his vast arm around the shoulder of a small kafir, a non-believer. The picture irritated her so she ripped it in two cross-ways.

Zinah didn't want to think back. But it was hard to forget when the pamphlet had come through the door, her *private* door followed by the wrap on the window. It'd caught her unawares. And then the old, 'Can I count on your backing? It means so much.'

No, it didn't. It didn't mean a thing. Because it was *Zinah's* support he was asking.

If only the people who had penetrated her bastion had known Zinah al-Rashid was a future soldier of the Caliphate!

When she felt bad about things, she spoke out loud a mantra. Focus on the end game. Raise cash, serve Allah, and complete the task.

Zinah al-Rashid was as bold as brass and gifted at what she did for the cause. But that was not all. Alongside her relationship with them, she also maintained a high-profile Western identity. All this was key to her proving to them her ability as a master tactician and leader.

Since she'd embarked on *Plan Politico* Zinah had

discovered her *real* power. This was what now coursed strongly through her veins and drove her onwards daily towards her destiny. When it flowed, like right now, she felt more alive than ever before. Her idea for fame and religious fulfilment was epic, massive and greater than anyone else's. Euphoria and self-belief drove al doubts aside.

CHAPTER 48

On Thursday Bea Harrington was one of the chief panellists at the London conference *Combatting Acid Violence Face On: Stigma, Survivors, and Solutions for Domestic Abuse.* Because of this, she dressed in her blue suit, white blouse, and heels. The cream lace handkerchief which didn't match was more for practical reasons than appearance. She reckoned she might need it.

While marital rape was not on the agenda that day, they'd discussed it before. Assault in the home was a hot topic at the last domestic violence symposium and as such Bea had been even more vociferous than she usually was.

However, after her recent ordeal Bea didn't want the subject to raise its ugly head. Otherwise she'd feel a fraud.

Bea Harrington was always hammering hard the message you've got to report abuse or it won't end. Now she'd herself become a victim, it was a different story. So much so, as the taxi stop-started in the sluggish traffic she kept breaking down.

Talk about double standards!

But Bea couldn't afford to grizzle, she told herself. It was vital to keep body and soul together.

Problem was, it was hard for her to avoid thinking about the rape and every time she did the damn clouds descended.

The memory of the night it'd happened would strike without warning. If Bea was eating, which was less likely since then, the food stuck in her throat. She didn't sleep much anymore. In social settings, even in full flood, she'd suddenly forget what the hell she was saying and her sentences would fade away to nothing.

Read the script out today or you'll never remember it. A moment of sheer terror at drying on stage hit her.

Oh, please no, not now.

She couldn't breathe. She was trying to fend off the panic attack before it started, knowing once it kicked in she'd be totally bloody useless all round.

After Bea's personal ordeal, she had a deeper insight on just what domestic assault felt like when it happened to you. The shame and self-loathing it brought to the victim. But how could she tell anyone? With her public work chairing committees on women's rights and James's impending ministerial promotion, it was all too difficult.

They'd just become the laughing stock. Or get the sympathy vote. Whichever was the worse. Mega embarrassment either way.

And if she did confide in someone, which she knew she wouldn't, what to say anyway? A shit of a thing to explain. Right after it'd happened James had tried the line 'I thought that's what you wanted', meaning rough sex. Then the following morning he'd used another totally different approach and sat by the bed, head in hands, sobbing. Could she ever forgive him?

Bea Harrington sank way back in the cab seat, wiped her nose and studied the conference programme. At least she'd successfully dodged sharing a cab with him which would have meant having to put up with his cutting sarcasm about feminism. Even worse, his self-sympathetic regrets and excuses. *How sorry he'd been.*

Would life together ever be the same again? Everything

since that night had turned bad. No wonder the following evening she'd hit the bottle and staggered to the spare room drunk as a skunk. Then the washing machine had flooded, and the boiler broken. The weather had turned foul, and it had bloody chucked it down.

The misery wouldn't lift. She could neither look her husband in the face anymore nor bear to listen to his lies. It was of no interest to her to know what he'd discussed with Simon King when he had dinner with him that night, or hear about Robin damn Miller or the late-night phone calls. Sob stories, all of them. She didn't want to be taken in by him again.

Maybe people already suspected something was wrong. Bea had dodged three major internal meetings in as many days in case she'd been lost for words, or worse than that, started blubbing in public. Then again, she wasn't alone. Everyone she knew in the Tories were short-tempered and jumpy ever since the William Wan death because of the party connection. He'd been out delivering for them after all.

They didn't all take it out on their wives though.

Despite her earlier doubts at whether to attend, Bea was pleased to be there once she actually arrived at the conference. Half an hour later, seated and spooning sugar into weak coffee, she relaxed a bit. *Well done me for not pulling out.* Bea Harrington had a constitution of iron. She was even smiling for the first time in a week.

Having been organised by Alesha Parkhurst before her tragic end, the event had an ever more solemn edge. There was a great cross-party crowd but the diverse delegation gelled perfectly. They paid lots of hard-earned tributes to the feminist.

Strong females put themselves out there despite the hostility.

Women in the public eye make natural targets, she thought to herself.

Everyone attending the Acid event was fronting some form of anti-abuse campaign or another. There were plenty of male attendees too. Surgeons, psychiatrists, social workers, police, politicians, activists, and local community leaders were all there to learn what the Government could do to tackle one particular item on the agenda, modern slavery. Oher topics included child sexual grooming, unaccompanied children being trafficked out of Calais, domestic rape. *Oh no.*

It was noisy as hell and Bea counted on two hands the times she shouted 'get involved' or 'call me' at someone over the din. With one hundred and sixty-eight bods crushed together in the reception area, it was nigh impossible to catch what anyone was saying. A welcome hush descended when the programme began. Local councillor Merry Lear, who'd set up a rape helpline the year before, was first on the platform and of course began by banging the drum about funding.

Next, a celebrity activist was heralded in. She used the 'women should run the world' approach. Whether they agreed or not, the audience lifted the roof in support of such a great PC principle.

Then a woman, late twenties, launched herself up onto the podium and introduced herself as Karen Andersen, an investigator. But she might have been Dolly Parton because Bea's paranoia kicked in straightaway. Every word seemed aimed at her. So when this manic character spoke about how she checked on a boyfriend or potential husband to see if they had a criminal record or not, it got her mind racing again. Did James have an abusive past she didn't know about? Was there something she'd overlooked before which she shouldn't have?

No matter the topic, from sex trafficking to stalking in the UK, Bea Harrington found a personal link that day. She grew more wretched by the second.

Her hypersensitivity was stifling. *I will never do this again.* Throughout the coffee break and lunch of small sandwiches and fizzy water, she tried to switch modes. But nothing would shift her mind. *Stop Abuse Now* was everywhere—posters showing rape victims and sex slaves were on the cover of every leaflet and the back of every toilet door.

In the afternoon Bea pulled herself out of her mope. What did it was the film of a Pakistani girl with third-degree facial burns. 'Most victims are women and children,' said the film's commentator. 'Acid dissolves bones. Targets are blinded for life and scarred.' *Bea's rape ordeal paled in perspective besides these girls.*

The cosmetic dermatologist who treated scalds pro bono struck Bea as a genuine and decent human being. Not *all* men are bad. 'Half the injuries are from accidents. The rest are deliberate wounds from knives, fists, petrol and even fire.' But, anyway, in her post-traumatic condition, all this was far too close to home.

The organiser introduced the main event. 'My next guest knows only too well what it's like to be stalked and intimidated. She still lives in fear of her life. She was scarred by an abusive partner and is here to talk about it to us. For safety reasons, we'll only give her first name. I'm delighted to announce as our speaker today, everyone, please welcome Nala.'

At this, a Somalian stepped up to the platform. Horrific acid scars had left her skin looking like parchment. She began before the applause had faded, drowning out her words. She giggled and her white smile flashed and enthralled the audience. Nala put hands on the sides of her head in a thank you gesture.

'I'd first like to say how grateful I am to Alesha Parkhurst for bringing me across here to speak to you today.' The applause began again. Several got to their feet. 'She was a wonderful woman.' Nala stammered, raised a finger to the damaged cheek and stopped a tear. The audience murmured and fell silent.

The facilitator who'd introduced her, now jumped up and brandished the conference booklet. 'There's a piece on Alesha Parkhurst in the program for those who haven't heard about her.'

When she sat down Nala continued her compelling story. How her attacker had scarred her as a teenager because she'd backed out of an arranged marriage. 'I always look over my shoulder. My life is in constant danger.'

As she listened, Bea thought about her own situation and how anyone, simply anyone, could have something horrid like that happen to her unexpectedly.

'Even as the innocent victim I was shunned. Not one person spoke to me or took my side. Not my friends, not my relatives. Not one.'

What if I told someone about James and no one believed

me?

Nala went on. 'Because nobody wanted to know me anymore, I didn't want to live.' Her voice broke and the front row shuffled, awkward with compassion. 'I stayed indoors for eight years. My attacker could leave *his* house. But not me. No, no. I was the prisoner.' She made big eyes to stress her point. 'Can you believe, he returned to normal day-to-day life after just six weeks?' The audience shook their heads in disgust. 'Today he is married, and he has had a family.'

'When the attack happened, I was too poor for surgery. Then my father died and that forced me to become the breadwinner so I had to have it done.' But it hadn't been the skin grafts, or the bereavement, or overcoming poverty which had changed Nala's world for the better. It was Alesha Parkhurst!

This stirred up fresh clapping. They applauded the inspirational figure, the selfless icon, a fearless fighter for feminism who had helped Nala rediscover her true worth and the ambition she had which had been buried. She went coy when she then spoke of the new relationship she was now in and the good man in her life who'd encouraged her as well to campaign on domestic violence.

Nala closed with 'People feel sorry for me because of my face. They can see my scars for themselves. But what about rape victims? Often there is nothing to show for their pain at least on the surface. That doesn't mean it is not there. These women too have internal wounds we don't know about. They need our help.'

Bea fidgeted in her chair knowing she was up next to speak. At that moment she'd rather have locked herself in a lavatory and wept. But bravely she mounted the stairs and grabbed the microphone, wondering what would come out of her mouth. Then, as much as she had dreaded it, Bea was off and running in automatic mode. Her off-pat speech went better than ever. What are we doing, folks? Her party would implement great programmes, certainly if she had any say in it.

Bea Harrington shook at the knees, but no one either noticed or cared. She rolled out the usual pitch. Spiel about how the Tories were passionate, with a capital P, about helping women, and how they abhorred domestic violence. Too many wives suffered in silence, didn't they? Too much happened behind closed doors.

La de da de da.

When she dropped back exhausted into her hard seat in the second row, Bea had a new neighbour. Someone she'd love to have avoided if she damn well could have done. But despite the earlier press of numbers, several people had already left and as a result there were now quite a few empty chairs in her row. Tammy Kell, who she'd taken an instant disliking to from her *Political Woman* course, was now sitting in the one right alongside her.

Just Bea's luck!

However, Tammy Kell was full of compliments on her speech which right then was exactly what Bea needed. 'It was truly superb, Bea. Domestic abuse is one cause that really needs addressing, doesn't it?' As Bea had noticed before, Tammy dressed almost the same as her. This copycat behaviour and obsequiousness should have sounded alarm bells but, under the circumstances of the day, it did the very opposite. It sealed their future relationship. From then on

Bea Harrington was all over her. She'd not hear a word said against the female candidate, her new rising Tory star.

CHAPTER 49

It had been a risk. Karen Andersen had expected Zinah al-Rashid to show up at the Acid conference because her venom-packed tweets were full of mentions of the event. She would just have to hope, if she was there, al-Rashid would not recognise Karen as the jihadi impersonator called Basilah. But as they'd not yet met up, it was a chance worth taking. Much to her disappointment, Zinah never appeared anywhere near the area.

Again, the person Karen was least expecting to run into on her return to Andersen HQ afterwards was Hailey Wren. Fortunately, still in possession of the hired motorbike, Karen was driving up Devonshire Road when she spotted her standing outside the front door astride a large box and with her parents' dog on the end of a lead.

Trouble lay ahead.

Not in the mood for a showdown, Karen opened the throttle and took off towards the southern Embankment. She reckoned after a sixty-minute spin, Hailey would have got bored with waiting and moved off the spot. Damn right! By the time she got back she'd gone.

Karen leapt lightly up the stairs to the flat, relieved to have avoided conflict. But when she turned the key in the lock, it was clear straightaway she'd been sprung. The dog was inside and now barking like crazy. Karen assumed it must have been Haruto who'd opened up to her. But Haruto was nowhere to be seen.

'Your neighbour let me in. I've brought your box.'

Hailey pointed to the carton she'd been storing in her apartment which Karen had been hassling her about for weeks. It was a terrific relief to see it back. Hailey Wren sprawled herself across the sofa with the dog going mad. 'Karen, I'm not here about Haruto, if that's what you think.'

Hailey embarked on a sorry tale about how she'd lost a whole bundle of rings, necklaces and designer bags. She'd held a party at her home asking a crowd of top social types. But it was after this *well-attended event* she'd discovered half her exclusive wardrobe had gone missing.

Hailey worked four days a week in the jewellery department of Harrods. She spent everything she earned. In addition, she was working through a small trust fund outlaying on show off items which seemed to Karen a complete waste. But Hailey Wren was a dedicated social climber, so she had completely different priorities. It was ironic therefore she'd been targeted by a thief. One reason Karen, private investigator, had been glad to move on from Hailey's flat was the niggling idea that her flatmate was shoplifting on the side to fund her expensive life style. No wonder Karen reeled when she was asked, 'Can you help me recover my stolen goods?'

'Have you reported this to the police?'

She hadn't. Hailey's explanation for this, was that she didn't want her set of smart friends put under suspicion. It'd mean social death. And there was another factor too. Amongst the lost pieces were a few of Karen's which she'd tucked inside the pocket of a forties bomber jacket. There were two old Parker pens, an engagement ring and a gold Hunter watch of her grandfather's. It seems they were all gone as well.

'Isn't that what you do? Private investigations and "stuff"?'

They both agreed the culprit had to be a guest at the party and most probably a woman. Then, because Hailey reckoned she'd actually seen one stolen item put up on eBay, the other things would most likely end up there too. All at once Hailey put her hands over her eyes and sobbed noisily.

Finally, they struck a deal. Hailey would keep a look out on the web for all the items taken, including Karen's bits and bobs. They could then bid together to win them all back and Hailey would cover all the costs. Both would come out ahead. Hailey would save face with her friends and Karen get practice for her little job, whatever it was.

Haruto walked in about ten minutes after Hailey left which saved the embarrassing scene Karen had so far managed to avoid. He could tell straightaway Freddie the dog had also paid a visit. 'Shit, what the hell, Karen?' The jigsaw puzzle they'd been doing together was scattered all over the carpet and there was the unmistakeable residual odour of canine fur.

Karen would have told Haruto Hailey's other news but Quacker, for some reason, was now banging at the door downstairs.

When Karen showed him into what now passed as her office Quacker was straight away into it, completely ignoring Haruto. It was as if Karen was the one under questioning.

'How's it progressing with the research, anyway? Have we found Robin Miller yet?'

He didn't need to be so direct. Karen felt bad enough as it was without being reminded she was going nowhere fast with the investigation.

'You've put yourself around London a good bit searching for him, haven't you?' What Quacker meant was she'd been *annoying* people around London, having been clearly warned to back off.

'He has to be somewhere. If he is, I will find him.'

'So I hear you were at the Acid conference?' Was Quacker checking up on her? 'Buildings have ears and eyes. What did you make of the event, anyway?'

Karen had in fact been there to get a fix on Zinah al-Rashid, for *certain* the killer of Alesha Parkhurst. But there had been a Robin reason too, which is what Karen used on Quacker. She'd noticed the line up on the conference programme featured Bea Harrington, the stepmother of the guy who'd apparently bullied him. She'd wanted to get a word with her. However, the woman had proved less than co-operative. She'd cut her dead! But also, there'd been another link. Karen had learned William Wan had been connected with Nala, the Somalian acid victim, who reckoned she knew who could have killed Alesha. But telling Quacker all this would mean fessing up about hacking into Miller's official bullying report. She didn't want to do that. Anyway, hadn't she been unceremoniously hauled off the case?

So, on the spot, she made up a story about her passion for supporting the feminist causes the conference was about, like stopping the trade for sex of women into the UK. Quacker seemed to swallow it.

'Human trafficking is up by forty percent. Criminal

gangs have been exploiting the EU free movement. It's a growing problem.' He put his pad back.

Karen sensed Quacker had yet another reason for his visit and the questions about the conference.

'You know that event was organised by Alesha Parkhurst?'

She did.

'I never told you about my trip to Wales, did I?' With this he filled in the blanks on an outing he'd made to the Cardiff Hotel. Quacker told Karen and Haruto he was by now trebly certain the feminist had been murdered and the crime covered up to make it look like a suicide. One big clue had come from her having eaten dinner with a partner in the restaurant the night before.

'Someone very much fitting your description, Karen, had been there earlier asking questions about a woman in a burka. Mean anything?'

He was by this time also taking in bits of the bullying report which they'd foolishly taken off the clipboard to study. It had formed part of the post Freddie file demolition process and Haruto at that very moment was busy salvaging the remains. It was then Karen told Quacker about her illegal hacking and how she'd got the document in the first place.

'I wondered where you were getting your leads from. You say William Wan knew Alesha Parkhurst?'

'His sister lived next door to her and was an ardent supporter.'

If there was one particularly useful thing she'd learned from Robin's statement, it was the fact Nala had spoken to Alesha Parkhurst that night on FaceTime. Karen had even managed a brief word about it with her at the Acid conference. What did she remember?

Only how Alesha had appeared to be in a particularly upbeat frame of mind. Not suicidal in the slightest.

'So we should arrange to meet with the Somalian lady,' said Quacker. 'Well done.'

They called the Stratton Hotel in Pimlico. It was where the seminar organisers had booked Nala a room. There was no answer, but Karen suggested maybe this was because Nala probably had evening arrangements. They next tracked down her mobile via someone working for the conference crew but their call went straight to voicemail. So where was she?

It seemed, finally, that rather than dismiss Karen as a waste of space, her work had begun to be appreciated. So much so, he actually wanted to use her again. This time to track down the Filipino hotel maid who'd been the one to discover Alesha Parkhurst's body. The wannabe singer was somewhere in London and that's all he knew. She'd doubtless changed her name from Mary Mendoza too. In fact all they had to distinguish her from others of her description was a tattooed wrist and the singing voice of an angel.

Karen finished the day content on several fronts. At long last it was official. She was working on the Parkhurst death. Ok, there was also the little matter of the theft of her grandfather's gold Hunter, but she was dead certain she'd get it back. *Somehow.* What concerned Karen more was that Quacker had told her MI5 was interested in speaking to a young Muslim woman by the name of Basilah if she came across her in her travels.

CHAPTER 50

Nala ran the tap, and the bath filled with hot water. She'd dreamed for so long about getting to London and now here she was right in the heart of it. She'd done better than expected. Her talk had been so well received. The audience clapped as if they'd never stop. 'You are a natural at public speaking,' they said. Yes, Nala loved every minute.

'In good old London town, the sun was shining' Nala sang out loud what played inside her head. Her skin soaked up the rising steam. She emptied the soapy gel into the bath and the sweet smell of orchids filled the room.

At that moment the thirty-two-year-old from Mogadishu believed she would melt with happiness remembering how everyone had been so kind. Hello, world, I'm back! She slid down into the tub and wallowed in the water's warmth.

She counted seven more events to come in the following three days and wondered if the organisers of these would all send flowers to her room like had just happened?

Next on the agenda was a fashion show!

No one knew the dreadfulness of living with such a big scar on your face, so what a turnaround.

'What did you look like once, Nala?' she'd heard asked so often. Her answer was, smart enough to land a job but not good-looking enough to take it up! But everything had changed. Now Nala was the belle of the ball and she'd not be shunned anymore. *Thank you, Alesha.*

Ten years ago she'd lived a prison like existence because

of her disfigurement. Today the opposite. Free as a bird flying around the globe to voice the message that violence against women was wrong. Maybe she'd become an icon like Malala. *Thank you, Alesha.*

In her speeches Nala often spoke about her mentor, Alesha Parkhurst, who'd made all this happen. How sad Alesha wasn't around to share in the day's success. She'd read about her suicide online after it'd happened, but why had she done it? Alesha seemed so happy the night they went on FaceTime together.

Anti-feminists had posted hate messages on the internet about Alesha Parkhurst and had threatened to kill her. But Alesha had been bullied because she stood up for women like Nala and exposed men who scarred and maimed their victims. Their cruelty knew no bounds. *Thank you, Alesha.*

When the bath cooled, Nala got out and dried herself. She sank into the green and white coverlet on the bed, clearing aside several visiting cards she'd collected. Women's organisations, an agent interested in a book, new friends. *People cared what happened to women here.* Then there was the presenter and speaker who'd followed her round and round the conference hall and wanted to talk to her when she was free. What exactly did she want?

What did she remember about her last conversation with Alesha Parkhurst?

Nala needed to collect her thoughts. By focusing on them, the facts came rushing in. It was in a restaurant that she and Alesha had gone online about her coming to the UK. Alesha had showed her round the room on her phone. 'You'll love the UK. We'll have dinner together somewhere like this when you're over here.'

At the time there was a man seated across the table from Alesha and Nala had seen him and even exchanged a few words. But who was he? Could she describe him? *What were the details again?*

The more she tried to remember, the harder it was because too many other positive thoughts flooded her mind. For example, how Nala had been described as 'inspiring' by the head of a burns charity.

What was the guy like? Nala tried to refocus again.

Who knows what the result of this trip could be? She might make a fortune or end up on TV. So long as the attacker who'd ruined her face hadn't heard of what she was up to in London and where she was staying then her prospects were rosy. She got up from the bed and danced in front of the mirror. *Thank you, Alesha.*

Despite her best efforts, Nala could not recall the facial details of any man but the one who had destroyed her life. And he was still a threat, even here in London. If he found her somehow, he'd surely want to kill her. By Nala speaking out like this would bring shame on his wife and kids. But not to worry. He was in Somalia and she was safe in the UK.

As she was fastening a white bra, dressing for the party thrown by the conference organisers, there was a light tap on the hotel door. 'Housekeeping.'

It must be even more fresh flowers!

Nala, wrapped in a towelling robe, opened up with a ready smile. Immediately she was struck hard. The shock of the blow combined with the weight of a male body threw her back into the room. As she fell, she heard the door slam shut and was just aware of her head hitting something, the sharp edge of the set of drawers, perhaps. Her vision was clouded. Her ears rang, and she screamed but nothing sounded.

She was now alone with the attacker who dragged her up on to the bed like she was nothing. Nala felt the blood spurt from her wound and her vision greyed. Panting for breath she was again at Taleh Road and reliving the terror of the multiple rapes, the pitch black nightmare. *She hadn't chained the door.*

She braced herself for more violence. 'Please don't kill me' she pleaded over and over in a soft, choked voice. She stared up at him but it was not the face she expected. Who was this?

The details she'd been trying to remember flooded back. It was the same man who'd been with Alesha Parkhurst.

CHAPTER 51

The Headlines. 'Somalian Acid Victim Model Found Strangled in London Hotel.'

News of Nala's killing came through on the morning broadcast when Karen was still in bed with Haruto. Quacker called as she was using the bathroom. The roar of the shower meant he had to repeat himself several times until she turned off the water.

Hotel management had first been alerted when Nala hadn't shown up at her charity reception. When staff opened her room at eleven thirty that night and found the body, they'd also seen the green answer light flashing on the hotel phone. Karen and Quacker's call was not the only one which had gone unanswered, but that's how the hotel had got back in touch with Quacker to alert him.

'Tell me again what you discussed with her at the women's conference.' Quacker demanded a damn good debriefing. As he reminded Karen, two of her contacts had been killed just after she'd spoken to them and therefore there had to be an explanation. 'And, does the hashtag #MenMatter mean anything to you?' The killer had scrawled this social media label in permanent marker on the bedhead.

Karen told him the tag had been used by Robin Miller's father and on countless occasions by many Twitter users like Zinah al-Rashid to shaft feminists.

Karen thought back to the death of Alesha Parkhurst after the feminist conference in Wales. She remembered what The Cardiff had told her about a woman in purdah being sighted in the reception area. She recalled the tweet from Zinah al-Rashid threatening to silence the lies of feminists who criticised Sharia law if they dared to do so at the Acid conference.

Zinah al-Rashid had been in Cardiff when Alesha died. Zinah al-Rashid was in London when Nala was killed. Did she have a motive to kill them both?

Quacker said he would think about what Karen had to say.

After she'd shivered through a phone debrief with Quacker, there came a similar grilling from Haruto. He was also pretty irate. It was absurd. He'd devised a concise plan of action to find Robin Miller, which was the only job she'd been hired to do. Not tearing around London on a motorbike trying to track down a radical Muslim, wearing a hijab. 'Gut feelings are all very well but what we need are solid facts, Karen. Otherwise, people like Quacker will continue to see you as a lightweight.'

'Oh.'

Chastened, unfairly so from her viewpoint, Karen dressed in a plain skirt and top in case they had to visit the police. Like an old married couple, Karen and Haruto sat together in the kitchen, drank tea and bickered. What next?

Karen went through as much as she could remember about Nala's speech at the Acid event to help throw light on who was behind the killings *other* than Zinah al-Rashid. 'She was worried about her abuser in Somalia.'

'She underestimated the dangers of this city. Besides Mogadishu, London seemed harmless, safe.'

The UK is a haven for abused women in relation to

other parts of the world like South America or the Middle East.

'Men who abuse women are wimps.' Haruto was slouching against the wall looking depressed. All his work assignments had been disrupted since he'd started the affair with Karen and got entangled in her messes.

They agreed to keep the news of the latest killing from their ageing neighbour, not wanting to worry her. But when Elspeth Cochrane swept in five minutes later, announcing she'd opened the door to Hailey Wren, she appeared to be as up to date as they were.

'A Somali girl found strangled. Have you heard?' She even knew all the details. How the girl's jaw, already burnt to the bone with sulphuric acid had been broken in two places. 'Her ex-partner had threatened to kill her if she travelled to the UK to appear in the media.'

Elspeth refused tea, instead demanded coffee. Karen and Haruto would have been happier had she not stayed. But Elspeth Cochrane was one of those people who can pick up vibes they're not wanted but tough it out anyway. Trying to head her off the topic and defuse the growing tension, Karen apologised for Hailey's dog barking its head off.

'Felt sorry for the girl struggling with such a large load. It was good you'd left your key with me.' She fixed Karen with a silent stare and poked into the box still open in the centre of the room. Then, 'You staying on?' She gave Haruto a probing look.

No doubt Hailey had given Elspeth her own version of events.

Haruto directed a half smile at her which let on nothing whatsoever and continued polishing the lens of his camera.

At this Elspeth adjusted her glasses, raised eyebrows, got up and left the flat to return to a TV show she'd been watching. As she did, she slapped a six-item list of shopping errands centre table. This was grating.

Haruto said, 'She's hardly bedridden!' But until that point, he'd been deep in thought, not about the neighbour imposing on Karen as she was, but the crime. 'It doesn't sound like the ex-partner with the scrawl on the bedhead. What's the hashtag about, anyway?'

'Men's Rights Movement.' Karen explained how the tag crops up often now boys get the raw deal compared to girls as regards suicide prevention and anorexia. The stream also gets its fair share of hate mail from those who are bitter about pro-feminist legislation.

Haruto said, 'Perhaps the killer was trying to frame Men's Rights just to throw investigators off the trail.' As he said this, he cleared the table and ran the tap.

Karen agreed, finding it hard to imagine who'd do such a thing and also how long it would take for social media to get involved. Not long. When they checked Twitter, Nala's nasty death had already been dubbed the hashtag killing. The #MenMatter murder.

Anyone posting under the stream tag was a potential suspect. Because of David Miller's tweet and Karen's trolling, she was one herself as Quacker had been quick to remind her.

CHAPTER 52

It was like something out of Kafka. Karen Andersen could sit there and wait for the shit to hit the fan or she could act on it beforehand. Robin Miller was still missing and while she had no clue where he was, she'd hacked into his email account. That was illegal. His friend William Wan and fellow contributant in a bullying complaint and investigation was in the morgue. Karen had met up with *him* only hours before his death. Nala, according to the press, had been raped and strangled.

Karen's test case, cyberbullying victim Alesha Parkhurst, who she'd sworn blind on TV had committed suicide hadn't. She'd most likely been the subject of a murder cover-up. The main suspect *in Karen's mind*, but no one else's, was the illusive Zinah al-Rashid.

Zinah had been avoiding all contact and requests to meet up. But everyone including MI5 now had wind of Karen's meeting with jihadi brides. Unless she could prove her hunch, Karen Andersen was in serious trouble.

On the positive side, Quacker, convinced someone had murdered Alesha, needed her on the investigation at long last. Karen's work load was building. The one person who could shine added light on the Alesha Parkhurst saga was the Filipino hotel worker who'd found the body and she was tasked with the job of locating her.

While the room girl had been known in Wales as Mary, she'd before that been called Joy. She favoured changing names all the time to conceal her identity. So no doubt

Mary, or Joy, would be called something completely different again. But what? As Quacker had told Karen, explaining all this, she'd once upon a time escaped from a Saudi family who'd brought her into the country and considered herself to be still on the run.

Haruto was on board to help. They needed the address of the hideout in Willesden where Mary had been headed that day. But this alone took days to track down. As expected, Mary had by then met a guy and moved on. Apparently he had a flat of his own above a pub where she could sing on Saturdays. She'd also purportedly found work as a manicurist. One of the other house inhabitants who threaded eyebrows for a job gave them a list of some likely beauty salons to try.

Haruto and Karen finally traced her by the tattoo on her inner wrist. She now called herself Regine after a pop star and had it not been for that distinguishing mark it was unlikely they'd have had much luck at all. Her appearance had changed drastically since the photo taken at The Cardiff Hotel. She'd dyed her straight hair Barbie blonde, was made-up to the hilt and had also gained about ten kilos.

Even though there was nothing left of her nails, Karen allowed herself to be buffed with an emery board to open up a conversation. 'We know you used to work in a hotel in Cardiff?'

At first, she refused to talk. Instead she entered into a loud vocal exchange with another manicurist in her mother tongue, and then went all coy. But there were promising signs by the little girl looks she gave Karen and Haruto that they would eventually get information out of her. 'Why I tell you?' She teased, 'Your hands very dry.'

She had no reason to believe they were not working for the Saudis. That was genuine. She'd worked in their household. The wealthy bosses would use private investigators at the drop of a hat. They'd pay them to hunt out a lost sack of laundry if it was important to them. Why not over a girl like her?

She snipped away at Karen's sore cuticles and listened warily for a false note.

'We're not with the family and promise not to tell even the Refuge where you are. Why'd they bother to search for you after all this time?'

'The son wants to have sex with me. I refuse him. He become crazy like obsessed. That's why.'

When Karen and Haruto convinced Regine their only interest in her was finding out what happened the morning she found the woman dead in the hotel room, she finally opened up.

'I've run before. I am always running.' Regine used her ready smile. For someone who'd had a shit of a life, she'd somehow maintained her sense of humour.

'The Saudis would punish me for leaving them.' Her face darkened as she took Karen into her confidence. 'Police mean trouble. I don't want to go back to that house.'

As part of the nail deal, Regine had taken it upon herself to give Karen a technicolour job and was busy lining up little bottles of varnish in a range of clashing colours.

'Did you see a woman in a burka either the day before the death or that morning you found the body?'

At this she went all coquettish on them again. 'Many women wear the burka. I am not talking to you.' She dunked Karen's right hand in a shallow bowl of water.

'What was the Saudi house like? Were there many other girls?'

'It was a big one in Knightsbridge. One other. There was a chef.'

'Were they unkind to you?'

'No, not at first. They were nice, like my family. Joy, we love you.' She tutted and rolled her eyes. 'They took me to Bahrain. Abu Dhabi. Then one day the boy slapped me and then slap, slap, slap all the time. There were three wives. So all the time I'm rushing around for one and then another. I don't want to go back to them.' She shook a bottle of colourless cuticle oil and fixed Karen with a warning glare.

'Joy - Regine, I mean. You won't have to go back to them again. I promise.'

'So why you ask about the woman in the burka?'

'Because I think she may have -' Karen began until Haruto tossed her a look.

She massaged Karen's right hand and her eyes watered, but at least *she was talking*. She was pleased Karen had used her new name. 'So when I came to London I had to run. Only place you can get away.' She'd caught the eye of another Filipino in Harrods Food Hall and they'd spoken in their own language. The other maid had shouted back her mobile number.

'So that's when you learned about the refuge?' Karen asked.

Regine told them she'd opened the front door of the Saudi house one night with all her possessions in a black bin liner. She'd pretended to be taking out the rubbish. The African chauffeur had been parking the car at the time. The coast clear, she'd sprinted out of the gate, down the mews, round the statues, through the garden squares, on to one bus, then another bus and another. She'd made the shelter. After that she'd taken a train to Wales to work at the Cardiff.

'Why did you think it was safe to return to London?' By this point in their questioning, Regine was working flat out on Karen's left hand, the final one. They knew they would soon be running out of time. 'Six months before I come back. Six months! Maybe more. But I worry they still look for me.' She slapped Karen playfully. 'You not tell them!'

'Was that the last date you worked there?'

'Yes, when I found the lady.'

'And the morning you left you cleaned two rooms?'

'Two?' She corrected her. 'No, three. Three early checkouts.'

'Because you had to catch the train to London?'

She opened the nail polish, and Karen wrinkled up her nose as the pungent smell hit. She was sick to the teeth of going through the same manicure routine. 'Yeah, the smell is strong.' She laughed and tapped the side of her right nostril with an index finger. 'Bad as the room I cleaned at the Cardiff Hotel.'

At this point Regine was hunched over Karen's hands, so it was hard to hear her. She was flowing like a tap so Haruto had moved forward on his wheelie chair to sit alongside. He wanted to know what was the smell she was on about and which room was it?

'Like bleach. They do my job for me.'

'Are you telling us the person who had been in there had washed it?' He leant in closer as she told the full story. According to her, whoever booked the hotel

286

accommodation had checked out early. Not even used the bed.

Could that have been Zinah al-Rashid?

'Your woman in the burka,' she said letting on nothing. Then, 'Why you want to know all this?'

Karen thought perhaps Regine needed to be filled in on things a bit more. She'd got the feeling that Regine or Mary or Joy was likely to shoot through after this and that would be it as far as they'd go tracking her down again. So she asked, had she followed the Alesha Parkhurst case at all?

Haruto was smiling at her in a suggestive manner. He'd found that worked well as a method of keeping the chat from drying and her breaking into song. He repeated, had Regine read the story in the paper about Alesha Parkhurst?

She couldn't remember. Maybe if she saw a photo of her, she'd help more.

Haruto flicked through the photos on his phone. He was on the verge of tapping the internet icon to call up some Wikipedia coverage on Alesha when she jabbed a finger at a picture of Karen. 'You look silly with the red hair.'

Oh great, thought Karen. *She's taking the piss. Laughing her head off at me and flirting outrageously with Haruto!* It seemed to be the shot of Karen with Simon King which had got Regine so cracked up.

Karen didn't like it too much.

'The big man, your friend, he was in Wales at the hotel. He your boyfriend?'

Haruto and Karen exchanged deep looks. 'Him?'

'Your boyfriend? You take the big man and I take this boy for me, ok?' She pushed her chest forward and tickled Haruto on his goatee beard.

287

'Mary - Regine, I mean, this man in the picture. He was in Wales, you say?'

'Yes. Your boyfriend.'

They were nearly at a breakthrough even though it was not what Haruto and Karen were expecting. If only they could keep her on track, serious. Was she absolutely certain she saw this man? Because it was all very, very important.

Yes, sure, she repeated. She'd been working in the restaurant the night before she found the body. The man in Haruto's photograph was dining with a woman and it'd been at one of her tables she was on and so yes, she was very sure.

They next showed her the news clipping of Alesha Parkhurst. 'He smiles at her like he loves her.' She looked over to Haruto, more than a little suggestively Karen thought.

At this, Haruto pulled up yet another story on Alesha Parkhurst. 'Was this the woman you saw the man with?'

She took a long look. 'Yeah.'

It was. They couldn't believe what they just heard.

If it was Simon King, what was he doing at the Cardiff Hotel? And also, what was he doing with Alesha Parkhurst? Why was he with her the night before she died?

It took another agonising twenty minutes for the nails to dry. But when they got up to leave, Karen asked what she meant by 'like he loves her'. She described the sloppy expression Karen had seen on Simon King's face when she'd tricking him into meeting up by sending a message from Robin Miller's Gmail account. The look wasn't one of love, but lust. Karen was surprised Regine hadn't picked it as that. If anyone could recognise a leery, lascivious grin, she reckoned it should have been Regine or Mary or Joy with her backstory.

Was Simon King, party director, upstanding citizen, MBE, also a killer? They hurried back to Devonshire Road to recheck a part of the Miller report.

'William Wan, who was sitting beside me, then also got up and left the table. I told him that his remark was offensive to William whose sister had known Alesha Parkhurst personally and who had been one of the last people to speak to her on the night of her death. He said he hadn't known that but still refused to apologise.'

Had Simon King learned William Wan knew Alesha Parkhurst from the bullying report? Had he killed Alesha? If so, could he have then met up with Wan and murdered him to cover his tracks?

Karen had told King about the Somali speaker visiting London.

Alesha Parkhurst, William Wan, Nala were all dead. The party director who'd been handling the bullying report had also been the last one to meet up with Robin Miller before the activist himself had disappeared.

There could only be one conclusion.

Simon King MBE was a serial killer.

Zinah al-Rashid had nothing to do with the murders.

CHAPTER 53

The right to silence has a long history in England and Wales, first having been codified in the Judges' Rules in Nineteen Twelve. But Simon King had no wish to keep quiet. One rare specimen, a murderer who fesses up, he was keen to talk. It was a need to pour it all out and empty a guilt-ridden conscience. The interview lasted only four hours and based on his confession, the CPS was sure of an easy conviction. He pleaded guilty to murder the next day at the magistrates' court. Then he was off to Wandsworth Prison where he'd be remanded to await trial.

Simon King was not sorry. However, Quacker believed King was relieved to be caught. Perhaps Andersen's findings had stopped a killing spree spiralling out of control.

King's major concern and his ready admission of guilt were purely to limit the damage to the Tories. He insisted his crime had nothing to do with the political party in any shape or form. He was that brainwashed.

Like many stalkers, King was keen to share the minutiae of his preoccupation with Alesha Parkhurst as a way of continuing with the obsession. But King was only interested in his own feelings, not hers. The irony for him was he'd fallen in love with a feminist. For someone who'd had his life torn apart by the lobby she represented, it was bizarre.

'Tell us about that.' While Quacker had by now read plenty on King's acrimonious divorce, he wanted to hear it from King himself, straight from the horse's mouth.

'I'd rather talk about Alesha.' Tears welled in King's eyes

and one rolled down as far as his double chin. 'I know it sounds doubtful, but it was an accident.'

He'd started out antagonistically, loathing her brand of gender politics and even blaming her for what happened in his earlier life. She was a spokeswoman for feminists after all. He admitted sending abusive texts and hate mail under the tag #MenMatter. 'She personified everything bad that had occurred to me I suppose. In the beginning, anyway.'

King was the sort who blamed all his personal failures on others rather than his own piss-poor behaviour. He'd done nothing that wrong in his own eyes. At least before the killing started. The suburban accountant and Falklands veteran who married at thirty-two years or age, mowed lawns on Saturday and read bedtime stories to his kids was a great guy. Then came a divorce which he'd never wanted nor expected. The smart Surrey wife who manipulated the court but fibbed and made up total garbage had led the whole thing.

King claimed he'd covered up time and time again his wife's indiscretions, not his own. It was her temper, not his, to blame. Her phone slamming and tantrums at parties lost them friends and finally ended the marriage. In addition, there'd been the physical attacks launched after she'd downed a few drinks, which he'd kept quiet about. The domestic abuse King's ex-wife accused him of simply did not take place. That was his story. It was all fabricated. 'I did none of that back then,' was his line. 'I'd never have hurt a woman.'

'Did you not think to tell someone about your wife's physical assaults?' Quacker tried to empathise on this point. King had considered it his duty to cover for his abusive wife before the divorce and would have continued to do so had she not made up child sex claims. 'She didn't need to lie.'

What this amounted to was his destroyed life, isolation, a twenty-kilo weight gain and estrangement from his children. He blamed everything on lefty policies based on political correctness which were anti-men and pro-feminist. The F-word.

Once King was talking, it was a matter of letting him get it all out. Quacker was concerned he'd clam up before they'd got the full details. 'So did you kill Alesha because she was a feminist?' he'd asked straight out.

At this, Simon King buried his large head in his hands and there was total silence in the interview room.

'I often listened to her on the radio. Then when I heard she was on at this event in Wales, I followed her. It fitted with some party business down there. We were thinking of holding a Spring conference at a cheaper venue. I booked into the hotel where she was staying in the hope I'd bump into her.'

'Tell us more about that day.'

Anti-Sharia protestors had been targeting Alesha Parkhurst because of her views on women's rights and there'd been a woman in Islamic dress loitering by the lift. There was a risk this person meant her harm, so King warned her. It was an opportunity to speak to her, to engage.

'You had dinner with her. Can you tell us how that happened?'

'She thanked me. Next thing I knew she'd grabbed her bag and was off and talking into her iPhone.'

'What then? Did you follow her?' Quacker asked.

'Yes,' he answered in a whisper. 'That's when I saw her in the corner of the restaurant sitting on her own. The tables were chock-a-block.'

King continued with how she'd caught his eye while she was on a FaceTime call. He'd been searching for an empty place at the time and she'd gestured to him to join her table as a thank you for warning her about the Muslim woman. She was even affectionate towards him.

'One of the waiting staff came to take the order. She'd asked about chateaubriand. When I heard it was a dish for two, I said I'd share it with her.'

But by now Simon King was off into his reverie and twisting the story to suit. How her signals throughout the dinner were misleading and more than friendly. How much she'd sparkled and was so animated and vivacious he'd just assumed she found him attractive. He'd offered to pay for the meal, but she'd refused. 'Feminists insist on paying their share'.

'You took the friendly behaviour as a green light, did you?'

King said nothing, continued wiping the tears from behind his glasses with his fingers while Quacker fixated on him knowing he was close to solving the mystery. 'What happened then?'

'I walked with her afterwards up to her floor. I told her my room was further down the corridor.'

'Was it?'

'No. I lied. We'd already passed where I was staying. We got to her door. She slotted her card in and it flashed green. I think she thought I'd gone by then and I sense she was just turning to say goodbye.'

'But you didn't leave?'

'There were the signals. I took hold of her and went to kiss her and she dropped back against the door which was open. As she fell, she shouted out at me something I couldn't make out. Thought I was going to rape her.'

'Can you tell us what took place then?'

'I never meant to harm her in any way.' He put his hand to his own neck to show what had happened. 'I grabbed her to stop the noise, and that was all. But sometimes you don't know your own strength, do you?'

She'd crumpled up under his weight. Then he'd panicked when he realised she was dead. 'She'd told me about the abuse on the net. That's mostly all we spoke about at dinner. How the woman in the hotel who was wearing the burka was probably the one who'd sent her hate mail, and she feared her because of the threats against her life. Everyone knew she was prone to depression because she'd written about it in a magazine. So I made it look like she'd killed herself. Took a suitcase strap and used it to suspend her from the overhead fan. Then I placed a chair on its side to make I look like she'd kicked it away herself. I reckoned if they suspected anyone of killing her anyway it'd be the woman in the lobby. She was in Islamic dress. The hotel management saw her too because they made a point of staring at her as if they knew she was there to cause trouble. I was surprised they didn't investigate the cause of death more deeply.'

He'd got away with killing Alesha Parkhurst, he thought. Because nothing happened after that until six months later. Then Robin Miller's complaint had arrived on his desk. It was on reading through the bullying report that he'd learned William Wan knew about the FaceTime call with the Somali because his sister volunteered at Alesha's charity.

'The FaceTime call which identified you?' asked Quacker.

'Yes.' King explained how Alesha had rotated the phone to give the girl a landscape view of the restaurant. He'd even been prompted by Alesha to say hello to her. 'She had a horrible scar on her face.'

'Is that why you wanted the bullying report to disappear?'

'Yes. That and the fact I don't like that type of tittle-tattle because it makes for bad feeling all around. But Miller wouldn't let it drop and he kept on and on. If he hadn't, then none of these other deaths would have happened.'

'Only Alesha.'

Even though it was unintentional, he'd met up with William Wan when he'd gone over to Westminster West to serve notice on Miller. Wan was in a lather about Robin Miller having disappeared and even accused Simon King of having swept the bullying issue under the carpet. That turned into Wan challenging him on why he'd done so. One thing led to another, and he'd suspected King was with Parkhurst on the night she died.

'He was threatening to expose you so that's why you murdered him? And then you put the cocaine in his pocket?'

'No. He was high on the stuff when I met up with him. The coke was already in his jacket. Afterwards, I took some out for myself.'

'Karen Andersen let slip about the speaker attending the

Acid conference. Which is why you murdered Nala?'

'I would have found that out anyway because William Wan had mentioned her.'

'What about telling us what you have done with Robin Miller's body? I assume you killed him too after you'd met up in the Buckingham? Before he exposed your cover?'

At this King seemed genuinely confused and affronted. He shook his head from side to side. 'Why would I do that? If nothing else, Robin Miller is at least faithful to the Party. Unlike William Wan who was using Tory connections for his own ends.'

If Robin Miller wasn't one of Simon King's serial killings, then where the hell was he?

CHAPTER 54

After the arrest of Simon King and although Karen had inadvertently tipped him off about Nala coming to London, she was back on top of her game. Quacker was even kind about this. He reckoned King would have wised up to where Nala was staying whether Karen had leaked it or not so the result would most likely have been the same.

During this period Zinah al-Rashid made several attempts to arrange a meeting with Basilah, but they were usually last-minute arrangements. Having been wrong about her involvement in the Alesha Parkhurst murder Karen had become less interested in Zinah. As Haruto said, her major assignment had been to track down the Filipino maid which they'd done. Through that, they'd nailed Simon King for three murders. Karen Andersen was getting everything right for once. She had only to concentrate on solving the Miller mystery to keep winning further accolades.

He was right. By now, Robin Miller's family were kicking up bobsie-die. Their son was still missing and Simon King had been the last person to have spoken with him. But King continued to deny all knowledge of what had happened to Robin Miller after he left The Buckingham that late August afternoon.

The Millers had ample reason to create a fuss. While it was now clear Simon King buried their son's bullying report to cover potentially incriminating clues on the murder of Alesha Parkhurst, the party were not apologetic in the least.

297

The Tories didn't care tuppence about using and abusing activists, particularly the younger ones, did they?

David Miller needed to keep Robin's disappearance in the press, but apart from resulting in someone's death, bullying was pretty small fry. And not newsy enough. Also when an establishment is attacked, it closes ranks, and that's what the party had done. No one was talking about *anything* at CCHQ and certainly not something as insignificant as the bullying of an activist. They even all agreed Simon King had been wise to bury the matter. Was it only Karen who saw the irony in all this, she asked Haruto. The Miller bullying scandal had been the catalyst for three murders.

Eventually, local media ran something again on Robin Miller which hit the net and stayed online. This led to several party members contacting Karen directly with offers of help in locating him. Alert to any name mentioned which stood out in Robin Miller's original bullying complaint, when Tammy Kell contacted her and offered to meet up Karen was straightaway up for it. This person reckoned Robin Miller was still alive for sure. On hearing this, Karen told her she could be anywhere she wanted within the M25 in five minutes flat. *As if.*

Tammy Kell was tall, elegant and oozed charisma. When they eventually got together it was at the esteemed Carlton Club in St. James where Kell was a member. Karen knew she'd seen her before but couldn't think where their paths had crossed.

Karen Andersen ordered a large glass of wine at Tammy Kell's invitation expecting her to do the same. But she refused to join her. Karen assumed this was no more than a sensible precaution for a politico watching her words.

Compliments can be an effective device and Tammy used the technique liberally. But Karen wasn't too fooled by that. Charming, but false. She'd made it on to the approved candidates list for the party, she'd just heard. 'How can I help?' she asked.

Karen brought up the event in the bullying report which involved her. *He tried to squeeze past Tammy Kell and as he did so he grabbed her breast. She got up and left and was visibly upset.* Had she been offended by Oli Harrington? What could she remember about this incident and how well did she know Robin Miller? So far Tammy Kell had offered her nothing at all.

She shrugged and sipped her water. She couldn't even recall the groping bit. 'How do you know all this information in the first place? 'she asked, fixing Karen with her steely blue eyes.

'He submitted a formal complaint about bullying and I've read it,' Karen replied. 'He was obviously in a fragile state when he went missing.'

'He was a restless type,' she said, referring to him as if he was dead.

So why did she think Robin was still alive like she'd said on the phone? 'Everyone wants to be a star, don't they? Including him. Terrified he'll do the wrong thing and not be noticed. Over anxious about everything,' she replied, picking up on her own error by speaking about him in the present.

Karen fired a whole heap of questions, too many at once. Did she know Robin Miller well and was he a hypochondriac? Did she have problems with Oli

Harrington and how often did she join the battle bus? Why would the party not make more fuss about William Wan's murder? What got her involved in politics?

Tammy Kell stared back at her. 'My stepfather Archie was my way into the Tories. They're open to relatives of past MPs even back to the 1980s just as most political parties are.'

Then she told Karen a long tale about how she'd been sent to an austere boarding at six after her mother's death. The man her mother had married possessed a dual personality and on one side a predilection for privacy. His secret war against convention which included dressing in women's clothes, how he'd wear Mummy's dried out mascara into the House of Commons and even her underwear. His ghastly set of child-molesting friends.

Karen's mind veered back to the report where Tammy was mentioned. 'People who claim sexual abuse often make it up.'

She told of Archie's vision to see himself as a great statesman right at the top. And finally about his untimely suffocation with a Sainsbury's carrier bag when an extreme sex game had gone wrong. There was little left to the imagination.

Her eyes were dancing with raw emotion as she entered a tirade of abuse against her stepfather for everything bad in her life. He'd been a hideous stepfather to her. Karen Andersen would have liked to learn more about his wardrobe choices but Tammy was off on a different rant altogether.

Then suddenly it was back to the Robin Miller subject. But it was Tammy Kell questioning Karen and not the other way round. What was *her* relationship with him? What did Karen think had happened to him? Then, had she told her anything helpful?

Before Karen could answer, she shifted in her chair in readiness to leave. It was completely back to front. Tammy Kell was fishing for info from *Karen Andersen.*

'Anyway, you strike me as very on the ball over all this.' *On the ball.*

Robin Miller was still missing, and Karen had squandered a whole sixty minutes listening to the grievances of Tammy Kell. She gathered up her smart, designer handbag, 'I have to leave I'm afraid.'

Damn. Karen Andersen was about to blow a chance if she didn't think fast. The party weren't responding to her any longer, and she needed inside contacts, anybody. At that second of panic she recalled where she'd seen Tammy before. It had been at the Acid conference. *Why was she there?*

This question stopped her just as she was rising in her seat. Yes, she'd been there. Why? Because it was important to keep up on developments in women's rights, didn't she think? Wasn't it dreadful that Simon King had killed Alesha Parkhurst, and no one knew he'd done so but Detective Inspector Partridge? She'd read that in the papers.

How no one, no one, had spotted Simon King at the Cardiff feminist conference. Not even her.

She'd been to that one as well?

Of course she did. Went to them all. Tammy's views on feminism seemed to take her over. The burka was a matter of choice, didn't Karen agree?

Anyway, Tammy Kell insisted Karen let her know the

minute, the very *instant* anyone heard from Robin Miller. She gave Karen her card and rushed away.

Leaving the dark interior of the club Karen stumbled into the blinding bright sunshine of Jermyn Street. She lost her bearings for a second. Which way to turn? Left or right? And that had been Karen Andersen's overall impression of Tammy Kell. In need of direction. But also of someone who could maybe lead her to Robin Miller.

CHAPTER 55

When the Tory Party said they took bullying seriously, technically they were correct. All the standard policies were in place but Simon King, a self-confessed serial killer, had been the author of the legislation. He was now the butt of sick jokes.

Police who deal with violent crime consider bullying activity trivial and a waste of their time. 'Come down tough on the criminals and sex abusers. Leave society alone on anything else,' was their general philosophy. Maybe there's sense in this because the subject has become a political hot potato and has almost developed into an industry in itself. When you reflect on how the first test case was only back in 1988, the year Karen Andersen was born, that represents a huge change in public thinking.

'Do you think Miller was after money?' Quacker cut a blueberry muffin with his knife and offered her half. 'Twenty-odd years back a crime squad detective got a hundred and seventy-five thousand quid for bullying. She suffered permanent inner ear damage after her supervisor forced her to wire up all the time. A child abuse worker won a similar amount. She reckoned stress overload gave her two nervous breakdowns'

Karen rose to Robin Miller's defence. 'He doesn't strike me as after money.'

'No, I don't think Miller's like that either,' said Haruto backing her up. 'Revenge maybe but nothing more than that.'

Quacker was keener to show Karen his caring side these days, and so she told him about what happened to Haruto's half-brother Masi.

'Sad that, he said, 'Well, I have some sympathy with the Miller chap. But you can't do much about it, can you? While bullying is a nasty little crime, and it is a crime really, it's hard to tie it up with laws. And anyway, only five percent of cases need to go down the court route.'

But while giving his opinion, he noted how the flat décor had been changed and the fact that curtains had been closed against the light. Only on leaving did he bring it up. 'You been doing a bit of meditation, have you?'

Haruto was into Zen big time. So not only were there pictures of William, Nala, Alesha and Robin on the wall, it also had a Buddha statue on the shelf. Haruto believed some form of psychic art would help Karen deal with the difficult people she encountered, like the Simon Kings and the Hailey Wrens of this world. The lotus flowers and candles were her girly additions. However, as a novice, and with her hyper personality, the more she tried to let go of her thoughts the more they rushed in.

The bully torments you because his actions reflect how he or she is feeling about himself, not you. For example, if he or she is angry, he or she will act with anger and resentment. The bully transfers this negativity on to you. You will then feel negative and upset.

Haruto had said. 'We can't stop our thoughts, Karen. Zen meditation helps us notice them without judging.'

'If our mind is peaceful, we will be free from worries and mental discomfort and so we will experience true happiness and relaxation. But if our mind is not peaceful, we will find it difficult to relax and find happiness. Bullying destroys our peace and happiness.'

The flickering wicks that day did little to wipe out the memory of dealing with a serial killer who'd murdered three of her contacts.

Bullies will often communicate indirectly when looking to criticise you. They will do this by asking questions. The questions make you consider yourself.

The sweet woody scent from nag champa wafted upwards in a smoke trail but still, the meditation did not work on her.

It is not nice when someone continually asks questions.

Something Quacker had said replayed in Karen's mind.

'The victim wants to get back at someone who has turned their life into a total fucking misery. They want them punished for bullying them and will often threaten suicide to make the bully feel like shit.'

You can feel as if you are on trial. To turn a situation around you must go on the attack. You must ask the bully a question. Get him or her to state something. Once he has stated his case and you know his or her view, you can then force them on to the defence.

Did Robin Miller ever go back to demand answers from his bully, Oli Harrington?

CHAPTER 56

In the West it is all about money! Everything centred on it. The more you spent the further up the totem pole you went and the more acceptable you became to your peers.

Rich women in burkas treated like celebrities! Poor ones treated as scum.

You shop for a pashmina in Harrods? Cool. But buy your hijab on Whitechapel Market and you're a lowlife, an oppressed woman, a suicide bomber, an uneducated, NHS grabbing, multiple-kid-producing immigrant.

Serves you right if I can scam rich people.

Serves you right that my comrades can withdraw from my PayPal account your money and use it to fund missions for Allah.

Where Zinah made deliveries that day was a bit of a pain. There were a hundred and one other things to do back at Acton. The drop involved a hike up the Lea Bridge Road. This part of the city was a million miles in style from the glossy West End.

Next time she'd wear trainers, she thought, looking down at her tired feet in the flimsy pumps. But Allah urged her forward. Allahu Akbar! Doing this painful walk would please the Prophet.

As the obedient soldier of Islam marched across the River Lea, a dog sniffed the marshy ground below and seagulls cawed overhead. This particular circuit was a long one, but by now Zinah knew the route well. The old Cinema with its bare hoarding. Then, a few houses later, the red-brick building with its unlit fairy lights and shabby fittings. The mosque.

Inside, she made her way straight to the announcement area. The felt board had pinned to it a laminated notice which was an appeal for Syria. On a table below it, there was a plastic box half filled with flyers printed in Arabic in support of various causes. Zinah al-Rashid topped up the leaflets from her bundle, calculating quickly how many she could leave at the mosque and still not run out before the rest of the circuit. Whatever, it was time to get rid of the lot of them one way or another. Someone else had left similar advertising material. 'Thinking of returning to your country?'

Zinah refastened her messenger bag and stepped back out of the Islamic tiled corridor. No, Zinah wasn't the only servant of Allah. Her sisters were everywhere.

Included in her remaining delivery schedule were the letterboxes off Ilford Lane. Flyers shoved through letter boxes were a part of her everyday life, weren't they? Zinah weaved her way quickly through the back streets. On to Henley, right into Windsor, and then Hampton.

The windows said plenty about their inhabitants. Some were decorated with grubby net curtains others orderly with ultra-neat frontage to match. They varied enormously. Yes, you could pretty much tell who lived inside by the state and condition of the front of the houses. Like the home with the discarded mattress and washing machine in the road facing garden. Then it was back into Ilford Lane again, the sari store, cash and carry, the house with a Palestinian flag roughly nailed above the front door. Zinah al-Rashid could have done all this with eyes closed. She knew the route backwards, the place that sold Halal chicken, the travel shop where you organised your Hajj, and the jewellers with its window full of gold bling.

She looked at her watch. Six o'clock. She'd not do this patch too late. After midnight this was the locale where the heroin dealers and Romanian hookers hung out and the Sharia Patrol marched up and down shouting, 'This is a Muslim area,' trying to clean the place up.

The work of the faithful believers who volunteered for the patrol to keep the streets safe made the newspapers, but for all the wrong reasons.

No one who read the Daily Mail was interested in the other side of the story, were they? Which was that seventy-five percent of all British converts to Islam were women like Zinah al-Rashid. And why was that? They weren't forced. They converted because of the higher status it gave them, not the opposite. It returned to them the dignity modern living had stripped away with its ever-increasing vulgarity and low morals.

If Islam was a cult, then it was a good one.

CHAPTER 57

The mystery surrounding the death of Alesha Parkhurst was at last solved. But Robin Miller was still missing. Oli Harrington, who'd bullied him, had come up trumps with the sex tape. He vehemently denied he'd played any part in making it, but knew enough about technology to remove it from the web. But during the conversations they'd had on the phone, he'd also warned Karen, 'Stay away from Tammy Kell. She is poison. None of her stories stack up. She'll say anything about anyone to get her where she wants to be.'

But Kell's political website was impressive. In addition to the usual sections on campaigns, 'about me', and contact details, she wrote a well-researched blog on children's mental health. The background blurb didn't mention her stepfather. She played hard on the selling point that she'd grown up almost as an orphan.

What the site emphasised instead was her A category status on the Approved Parliamentary List. The rest was self-adulation. Tammy Kell promoted herself as a star candidate and stressed she was someone who'd not had a leg up but worked her way right up through the ranks into the inner sanctum.

The photo gallery contained pictures of her smiling while posing with government ministers at cocktail parties. There was one of Tammy standing in an arc with other female politicos commemorating Emily Pankhurst and another holding a placard high above her head flanked by

Hindu worshippers. Another with Muslim women in full-length black dress. Delivering surveys. Door-knocking. Folding flyers. Even a picture of her with Oli Harrington, William Wan and Robin Miller on the Tory battle bus.

Thursday afternoon Karen Andersen called her on the pretence it was a wrong number because of this strong gut instinct Tammy could lead her to Robin Miller. As Karen hoped, Tammy was ready to open up. Robin was mentioned. The last thing Karen was expecting to hear was Tammy had spoken to him recently.

'How about we meet where we did before?' she said. 'Say six o'clock upstairs in The Thatcher Room at the Carlton Club?'

Friday afternoon was sultry with a promise of rain and the long days were closing in. Tammy Kell was soaking up the people vibes when Karen Andersen entered the ornate drawing room. She sat in a beige velour armchair straight across from the entrance wearing a pinstriped grey suit which Karen had seen her in on her Facebook page.

Karen got the distinct impression Tammy was watching the door and not just for her arrival. While Karen was curious about past politicians whose portraits were all along the wall, Tammy Kell was more interested in the present ones who came and left all the time.

For the first ten minutes they went through the usual platitudes and Karen complimented her on the fullness of her website.

'In politics, if you don't get a photo of the event with you in it, you haven't done it,' Tammy said, adding, 'The pic tells the story.'

When Karen was once again wondering why Tammy

Kell had been so keen to meet again, she came out with 'He's gone to ground, you realise? Robin Miller is who I'm talking about.'

By now Karen Andersen had learned Robin owed on his bedsit rent and also that he'd not been back to Bradbury Road since the disappearance. David Miller was thinking of clearing the flat of his things.

Then, bold of brass Tammy claimed to have an opinion on him. The twenty-one-year-old activist and former choirboy was running scared because he'd uncovered a historic paedophile ring. Didn't Karen believe her? It included several senior members of the Conservative Party. It was why he'd been bullied, obviously.

'How do you know all this?' Karen cut across her.

Tammy Kell fixed a gaze and Karen could see one of her blue eyes was out of alignment.

'Is he mentally stable?' In this Karen was a hundred percent serious. One of the major reasons people go missing is a healthy dose of paranoia.

'Very definitely. He is absolutely in his right mind. Why wouldn't he be?'

'You said you'd spoken to Robin Miller so where is he?' Things were growing curt between them.

Tammy Kell gave a half grin. Karen had a hunch she'd not get a straight answer even if there'd been one to give.

The political candidate sidestepped the direct question with, 'You sound sceptical about the sex ring. Why don't you believe it?'

When you hear something like this, where you hear it is as much a key to its plausibility as who said it in the first place. And they were sitting in one of the oldest established

311

bastions of conservatism.

Tammy looked around rather pleased with herself. 'Simon King used to come in here all the time.'

She raised her glass with a ring festooned hand. Out of the corner of an eye, Karen could see even more Carlton members shuffling in for a stint of pre-dinner drinking. They wore musty old suits or floral dresses with vintage crystal around the neckline. She wondered if any of them featured on this imaginary list of sex offenders.

Tammy Kell now unleashed on Karen her theory as if it was Gospel. And the story almost stacked up. King had murdered Alesha Parkhurst because she'd been working on sex abuse and could nail him and some of his cronies in a huge scandal.

It was unsurprising King's name came up. Tammy Kell wasn't alone in wanting to discuss him. Everybody did. It took little to get the subject going. Behind them someone else was murmuring King this and King that.

'Vile man,' Tammy said, fixing on Karen again.

The tabloids were at the time running with allegations of sex abuse of children by public figures dating back to the early nineties. Tammy Kell mentioned this and said, 'Well, it happened to me.'

Through her work Karen had known adults who'd been molested. Victims often describe the effects as a locked away pain that won't come through. They don't talk about it much. But instead, Tammy was flowing. 'I was abused at seven by an MP who still dines here every week.' At this she glanced again to the door and at the same time held up her glass of water. Because of this, rather than listening, Karen had fixated on her ring. It reminded her of the one she had lost.

Tammy Kell was trying to engage her in some personal sob story. But Karen Andersen was determined she would not be side-tracked this time. Tammy had lured her there with the promise of information on Robin Miller and she wasn't delivering. Nor likely to. So now Karen wanted to swing the subject and leave. She said 'I'm looking at your ring. You have lovely rings.'

'You get superb stuff on the net.'

'To buy online you'd have to know something about it,' Karen said.

'I used to run a jewellery section in Harrods. A long time ago.'

There'd been no mention of shop work on her website so Karen was curious. And as of now there was another connection. She asked quick as a flash, 'Ever know someone called Hailey Wren?'

'Course,' she said. 'I trained her.'

At that second Karen noticed Tammy's mood shift as if she'd let something slip she'd wanted to keep to herself. She flushed red, opened her collar and complained of being hot. It was getting late, and she had to be going. She made a move.

But it was definitely a blunder, maybe a silly, insignificant one. The roles reversed, Karen was all at once fired up to know more. What was it? She was determined to discover the answer, what it was she was hiding. But it meant engaging with her more. And here she was trying to slip away. But right then Tammy's phone flashed, and she took in the message. 'Oh shit. One of my panellists has dropped out for the Tory Party Conference.'

The topic was cyber abuse of female politicians. Despite Karen's gut-wrenching at public speaking, she now needed any link to keep in contact with Tammy Kell. 'Could I help out?' she heard herself say a bit too quickly.

Tammy Kell clapped her hands. 'Oh perfect. Yes. You were on the BBC, weren't you?'

Karen had all the credentials to fill the slot.

CHAPTER 58

Bullying facts: Predators of the air are unconsciously programmed to decide what they should hunt. Hawks, eagles and buzzards will seldom seek a healthy adult as their prey. They don't want to risk injury by fighting an opponent of equal size. So they target the young.

Take a lion. It kills a competitor to take control of the pride and mate with the females. In the process the male kills all the cubs of the deposed lion. So the motive is not food (antelope is the dinner). Their action does away with the genes of the former lion king.

Female polar bears must defend their young against males who will devour them. An opportunistic seabird may eat the chicks of its neighbour. The barn owl will swallow whole the smaller brother or sister. And the female praying mantis bites off the head of a mate during copulation so he is more fertile for her. Nature is full of examples of bullying as an essential part of the survival of the fittest process.

In humans it is about abuse of power. Not a one-off impulsive event but a pre-planned and persistent harassment, putting a weaker subject down and making them feel humiliated or tormented. The bully mimics the girl or boy with a handicap. They will call their victim names. They will persecute someone who's different, who's not in the cool crowd. School bullying is hard to identify. Kids play pranks on one another all the time. Boys wrestle and girls compete with hairstyles. Pushing games are fun, aren't they?

'Have you no sense of humour?' Oli Harrington had said to Robin Miller.

Calling names can be used for bonding, can't it? Not if it's establishing a pecking order or when fun turns to fear. The moment a group turns against an individual, it's no fun. Bullying pushes boundaries further and further and there is a tipping point. It can drive a young person or child to kill themselves.

Was what happened to Miller so bad that he just wanted to hide, disappear completely?

Nothing made sense anymore.

CHAPTER 59

Quacker was forty-eight hours on from his hip surgery. He watched *Skyfall* on the hospital screen and grumbled to himself as James Bond picked up his personalised pistol and a miniature radio transmitter. Is that all he gets? Where were the exploding pens and other clever stuff?

Today 007 would be a computer hacker with a Facebook page. Secret agents hang out on Tinder, not at casinos. He flicked off the TV in protest at the way things had gone. It was a changed world, indeed. Modern spies are now all online. Not just them. Also novice investigators such as Karen Andersen. At this he reopened the get well card she'd sent him. The bright fluorescent lighting had its uses after all, if only for reading the unfathomable scrawl which passed as her handwriting.

He put it back on the nightstand and resolved to call her later to thank her.

Quacker was as puzzled by Robin Miller's disappearing act as Karen, but not enough to spend more brain time on it right now. That was her job. She'd not found the lad, but in looking for him she'd led them on to nab a serial killer and a most unlikely one at that.

He checked his phone messages and news feeds. M16 needed a thousand more spooks and were scouring for suitable women to fill the roles. Not out of political correctness for once, but because they were often able to penetrate the jihadist cells more easily than men. *Let's hope they're correct, shall we?*

He reflected on the July terrorist attack on the city in 2005 when he'd seen for himself the iconic London bus with its torn off roof. Trouble was, Islamic State supporters plotted attacks on UK soil from just about everywhere else on the planet. Intelligence via modern media was a must. But, Quacker thought, you can't beat the traditional methods of getting information talking face-to-face. *Life changes but nothing changes*

He was as restless as a kitten. The controls of the adjustable bed were worth playing with at least twice, but no more than that. He picked up a Grisham novel then laid it down again. Thrillers and old movies didn't calm his fidgets and by now he'd read the newspaper cover to cover. It was back to his news update and time for further deliberation. If the secret services needed original thinkers, Anderson might fit the bill. Original? *Half barmy, more like.* But he'd put a word in for her. He wondered how she was going with her highly unorthodox jihadi bride investigation.

At that point his wife Chris stuck her head in.

'Now, this is a pleasant surprise.' Quacker's spirits soared at the random visit and the mattress creaked as he adjusted his position to welcome her.

'I've only got five minutes, love. I'm parked on a double.' She rushed to open the small closet and deposit a set of fresh pyjamas. 'I'll take your others home when I go.'

'I think your judgement on Andersen was correct, dear,' he said, hopeful of opening a conversation. So when she told him to lie back and keep quiet he ignored it. 'Karen did a thorough job after all that, didn't she?'

'Let's talk about it later, shall we?' She fluffed up the

pillows. 'You feeling better?'

Before Quacker could intake breath to answer, Chris was off and out through the door to avoid parking charges and he'd missed out once more on a chat. Instead he was left to mull over on his own the series of back to front events and Karen Andersen's practise of following hunches which had brought in the Cardiff hotel worker and eventually nailed Simon King.

The private hospital room was too still for Quaker's liking. Only the intercom in the corridor broke the long silence. So he fired off a text to his nephew, Mark. 'Languishing in the lap of luxury for a week.' *Anything* to fill in the day. His son and daughter were visiting separately to avoid the scrapping which happened when they were together more than three seconds. Maybe his sister's lad could combine with one or them. That'd be good. Quacker was sure he'd want to pop by and say hello.

Ten minutes later, having finally secured a proper car space, Chris was back. 'Given up on you. Taken that much time has it?'

She poured him a beaker of water. 'Tidy this up, shall I?' She rearranged the reading material on the rolling table. 'You don't know who will drop in, do you? Don't want the place to look too bad, do we?'

Quacker wanted to talk over the Alesha Parkhurst case and he started up on it. But he knew his words were falling on deaf ears. 'You're not listening, are you?'

'No. You're supposed to be resting.' Chris kissed him goodbye. 'I'll be up again at six for those pyjamas.'

When the door closed behind her, he flipped on the TV again. Perhaps he could scan for a half-decent news channel.

But scenes from Simon King's story still played havoc with him. How'd they ignored the parallels between Nala Nassér and Alesha Parkhurst? Why had they missed the connection between King and William Wan's killing just because cocaine was involved? If there was something out of this to teach the kids it was 'Don't carry drugs. You may be strangled by a psychopath and they will get off scot-free by making it look like an overdose.'

A week's rest might do him good.

Quacker preferred to be out on the hoof doing something useful rather than lying in bed for a week. And there was plenty to do. They'd settled the King murders, but were still puzzled about Robin Miller. For example, why had his phone signal died at Westfield the afternoon of the locker blast? Had Robin Miller been in the shopping centre at the time? If he'd damaged his mobile, then surely he'd have replaced it with another by now. And why had he not come forward after William Wan's death? Never mind Miller's bloody state of mental anguish, there were serious questions to be asked. Was the boy even still alive? What had Karen said? She wouldn't believe Robin Miller was alive until she'd eyeballed him.

Quacker shuffled under the white sheets. Lying in isolation there was little else to do but keep fixating on these missing facts. According to Simon King, Miller had left the meeting at The Buckingham in high spirits. This was because King had led him to believe the party would review his case favourably when in fact it was quite the opposite. Simon King had never had any intention of taking action on the bullying complaint. But in the conversation, if King was to be believed, he'd actually told Miller that if they were to caution Oli Harrington, it'd have to go to a full board meeting first. In that case Miller would need to corroborate the facts with witness statements.

Robin Miller had assured Simon King he'd be able to get backup support from at least two other party members. William Wan was one, but who was the other? What member of the party would risk putting their future career in jeopardy by adding their name to an official complaint against Harrington? Who did Robin Miller have in mind? And importantly, where did Miller go after leaving the Buckingham?

As Quacker wondered if he was himself suffering post-traumatic stress syndrome there was an audible rap-rap and a physiotherapist bounced in a second later. 'Are you ready for me?'

Whether he was or not, she started to work on Quacker at once. There was no messing about. 'Lie on your side with legs bent.' She barked out orders in rapid succession.

'Got a train to catch, have you?'

'Put the pillow between your knees. Feet together. Don't use your back muscles. Up with the top knee. Hold for a count of three.'

The Detective Inspector groaned loudly and made reference to the upcoming week of torture facing him under the physio's pummelling.

'What's all this about seven days? We'll have you up and out in forty-eight hours.'

Quacker could tell she was a sadist who enjoyed his suffering, and he told her as much. But laughing apart, there were now several hospital visits to call and cancel. He didn't know whether to laugh or bloody cry.

CHAPTER 60

Mrs Ladipo wore plain black trousers and a yellow blouse. Zinah al-Rashid could have picked her out a mile off. The teacher was mingling with the children in the enclosed area of the Modani Academy fanning her broad smiley face when Zinah pitched up at the school gate.

It was muggy and almost too hot to breathe so going indoors was a welcome relief. Zinah and Mrs Lapido shut themselves away in an empty room near reception. The closed shutters kept it cool, but they then needed the overhead light. Small gains.

Mrs Ladipo was her usual cheery self when they discussed what was happening in class and she mimicked the students as if she enjoyed it. 'You know what one twelve-year-old said to me yesterday? Mrs Ladipo, I'm gonna fight for my country.' At this she lifted a pretend machine gun. 'I'm gonna fight for my religion because that's what Allah says we got to do. I will kill all the Christians.'

Zinah's introduction to Modani Academy had been via Ahmed. He'd built ready ties with the chief governor, and the head was also particularly keen on Zinah's visits. It was part of the school's anti-extremist programme and bolstered the reputation.

If only they knew!

Children from every country under the sun, Albania, Nigeria, Romania. All were here. It was one of the many learning institutions in London where eighty percent of students only spoke English as a second language.

The classes were on a drop-in basis and were all part of a plan to look out for pupils at risk of being radicalised. On her first visit, Zinah al-Rashid had addressed teachers on tell-tale signs to look for and had made such a hit with the staff they'd given her unsupervised access to the girls. The head teacher directed the talks with the boys. The system worked well as far as they knew.

Zinah was a perfect fit for the role, as far as the school was concerned. She wore full Islamic dress. She also communicated easily with children which meant she spoke their everyday lingo and so could reach out on a one-to-one basis.

The community was one hundred percent Muslim. Some of the girls arrived at the school in headscarves and shot straight to the toilets to remove them. These were the ones who changed into minis, used cosmetics and wore high heels. 'They rub off their eyeliner before they go back home. I know they do because it's my cleanser they borrow!' Mrs Ladipo adored all her kids.

However Zinah al-Rashid interpreted this behaviour as brazen and disobedient. She looked down on girls who came round her door in mascara-coated lashes and kissed boys in the playground. But she couldn't let on. So she found these chats with Mrs Lapido particularly testing. She didn't want the teacher to sus her out for real. Today she longed for loopy Lapido to quit talking and leave her to get on with things. Eventually the Nigerian picked up on the hint. 'Can I get you a drink before I go, dear?'

Giving the interviews was one way Zinah sourced future brides. Ahmed's inspired idea was already bearing fruit.

They'd found two potentials.

When she was out of earshot Zinah called Ahmed. It was her first opportunity since she'd heard about it to complain to him about the fighter making sexual demands on one of the bridal recruits.

'It's the internet, innit?' Ahmed said. 'But Zinah, bad behaviour spreads quick. You don't want sisters passing on these stories. He's totally of line, this guy. Out of line. It's sexting, innit?' After that he told her they'd received a money transfer from an MP in the Conservative Party. 'That's one of yours, innit?'

Great news. Zinah al-Rashid wanted to sing out loud, whirl around the room. What a win.

James Harrington MP was now financing Isis warriors.

Since the country had held a Referendum on the EU, everyone in the school was focussed on British values. Along with Morris Dancers and red white and blue bunting, drawing pictures of the Queen and PG Tips, all were great ways to promote Britishness and to counter extremism. So, no surprises when Mrs Ladipo returned with a mug of weak English tea made with skimmed milk. There was no escape from this nosy woman with her fawning manner!

The sessions were fifteen minutes or thereabouts. The timing was long enough for Zinah to learn what she needed to know about the girls' home habits. Who'd been their best friend since birth? What did their parents feel about the UK? How often did their family say prayers? Did they sympathise with the so-called Islamic State?

That day Zinah al-Rashid had twelve students on her list to interview which was longer than usual, so she shot through the first batch as fast as she could. It took six girls to arrive at the first promising pupil. She wore a knotted scarf and was demure. Sixteen years old, a clever student and devout. The school had told the parents her grades were slipping and causing concern and she'd been sent to Zinah.

'I dream of marrying a fighter. Is that bad?' she asked when they were alone.

'No. They are very brave.' The girl's rust colour eyes widened at this. It had been unexpected. Then Zinah spoke of the fearlessness of the warriors, the beautiful orange sunsets in the desert. Everything the young girl wanted to hear.

It had been a promising start. But after her, it was an hour and a half before Zinah found another.

This is how it worked. The girls who revealed their support for radical Islam heard more to excite them, not less. They learned in even greater detail the prowess of the handsome young soldiers who served Allah. Their strength of character. How these perfect men selected only the best wives for themselves. And crucially, the importance of secrecy. Everything they spoke about was confidential.

Zinah played her deception well and followed the plan which had worked so well up until then. That day for example, she underlined the names of two girls who despised the Caliphate. She told the school exactly the opposite. That they needed watching closely as they were showing signs of radicalisation. The diversionary strategy worked to perfection.

She practised the perfect answers if they ever grew suspicious. How her methods were tried and tested to work on the type who'd been brainwashed and groomed online. It was her special technique, and she bonded instantly with

325

young people this way who were hard to read. Zinah al-Rashid was there to counter evil, not condone it!

But on that particular day Zinah had a very narrow escape when the Nigerian teacher stared at her and asked in a questioning tone, 'What are you telling them exactly?'

Zinah was packing up at the time and it came out of the blue. She'd thrown her pens down on the table in protest and went back strong. 'What are you suggesting? Mrs Lapido, don't you know there are recruiters combing London constantly just looking for Isis brides? Why do you think I talk to them as I do? I talk to them as those people would talk to them.'

Mrs Lapido obviously hadn't been expecting such a robust reply. So she apologised straightaway. 'I wasn't accusing you, my dear. I get concerned about the girls too much I think.' She even tapped her chest and gave a sigh of deep relief as she said, 'You are doing fine work, I am sure of that. Don't let me stop you.'

Zinah, however was unconvinced this wasn't an act and Mrs Lapido might report her to the head all the same. So just to be sure she followed it up again with, 'It's important the girls know the lies they will hear, don't you think?'

But Zinah had butterflies fluttering in her stomach which was a sign she was swimming in dangerous waters. Anyway, it'd been a productive session and the two teenagers she'd identified would make worthy recruits. They were also super keen. Zinah planned to put them in touch with Fatima and even this new sister Basilah once she'd checked her out. Encourage them more.

However, it wasn't just the near miss at her school operation which freaked her out, there was more. Someone was hard on her trail. A woman called Karen Andersen, who she knew to be a private investigator, had bid for several designer items she'd put up on eBay. She'd been forced to buy them back rather than risk being tracked down by the Counter Terrorism Internet Referral Unit. Andersen had become a risk to Zinah's plans. But at least she was now on to her.

It was time for a showdown. *Alhumdulillah.*

CHAPTER 61

On Tuesday afternoon Karen Andersen got a call for Basilah from Fatima requesting a get-together between them somewhere in North Acton. Fatima was worried Basilah had grown cold on plans to travel to the Caliphate because Zinah al-Rashid had not been able to meet Basilah and vice versa. Basilah assured her she hadn't at all.

Quacker had confirmed by now the hockey club locker key thief fitted Fatima's description. Someone in the club had seen at the time a girl loitering around the shop area where the keys were kept on a hook. If Karen could get her hands on them, could they have them back, please?

Karen got the bike out on rental again. Quacker had handed her a report on bride recruitment when she'd visited him at the hospital. She'd stuffed it in the pannier to read later. So the meeting with Fatima had to go ahead and there were no excuses. It was a chance to do her small bit for MI5. She was by now shit scared of the danger she was putting herself in, but equally of losing the reputation she'd been quietly building. So she agreed to attend.

Fatima had changed her image completely from the time before. Gone were the stiletto image and in its place the full black Islamic attire. Today her only nod to fashion was a pair of bright suede trainers not dissimilar to the ones Haruto wore. She told 'Basilah' she'd got them from Zinah's online business. Did Basilah want Fatima to get her some too? The two of them could wear the trainers together and they would both match. Also they'd be perfect for the trip to the desert. Cool.

Reflecting on the operation ahead, Karen knew Fatima was just not important. A cog in the wheel, a pawn on the board.

But Zinah al-Rashid was Queen Bee. Although she had not broken the law technically speaking, all the same, grooming young girls to leave the country had evil intent. Hadn't Amirah's mother commissioned her to save not just her family closeness and daughter's future happiness, but even possibly her life? Selective scenes flashed through her memory, none pleasant. The lipsticked face of one girl whose head had been blown off in a suicide attack. The images of children in Ariana Grande T-shirts caught up in the Manchester bombing. The YouTube clip of a pilot burnt alive.

Zinah al-Rashid needing stopping. Karen swallowed hard and pushed through her own wall of fear. She *could* do this.

Fatima had a best friend Mia, and she was the far more radical of the two. So when Basilah and Fatima met up at the coffee shop in Victoria Road they straight away left for Mia's house around the corner to exchange ideas while her parents were out.

The three women sat at the kitchen table, with Islamic paraphernalia all over the walls and smoke clogging the air. Mia, seventeen and wearing skinny jeans, was a chain smoker. Her school books lay open on the table and inside one Karen glimpsed a doodle of Islamic State, the iconic single finger pointing upwards.

Mia spoke without stopping of how she loved some supporters of the Caliphate, but not all. She turned her back on the girl called Basilah and addressed Fatima directly. White western converts couldn't be trusted because they were far too extreme. She also disliked Amirah, loathed Malika, Aida and Yasmin, and hated *Zinah al-Rashid.*

This got Karen's full attention. Not only was Zinah al-Rashid a white woman but, by the sounds of it she was planning far more than just grooming girls for Isis and carrying out witch hunts on Twitter. She was dangerous.

'So when do I meet her?' Karen asked Fatima who at least was facing in her direction.

'Look, I don't think this,' Fatima said, helping herself to one of Mia's cigarettes while the other girl was doodling away. 'But like, you could be anyone, couldn't you? Like, you could be the secret service. I must convince her first you are ok.'

Underneath her veneer of calm control Karen had a sense of growing panic. Was Zinah al-Rashid aware of who Basilah really was? Had Karen's cover been blown? And if so what threat was she under right then and there sitting in the kitchen of a potentially psychotic teenager with no one knowing where she was.

As the two teenagers chain-smoked they talked to each other about 'green birds' and 'dusty feet' which Karen learned later were hadiths about martyrs. The other language was easy to decipher. 'Taking a holiday' was the vernacular for the trip to Syria. It was as if Basilah, sitting there, didn't exist.

Whether they were indeed harmful or not, neither girl was any more talking bridal talk. That seemed to have dropped right off the radar.

They got back on to Zinah al-Rashid and her ears

pricked up. Fatima complained to Mia how Zinah had laid the blame for the balls-up at Westfield on both of them, which was totally unfair. It'd been Fatima's device, and she'd made the base part of it. But Zinah had stolen it off her. Then when the bombing had failed, she'd shifted the guilt back to Fatima and it'd been so wrong to do so. It wasn't her fault. Mia enjoyed the Zinah-slamming.

Basilah agreed it was a shit not to take responsibility when she would have certainly grabbed the credit if it hadn't gone wrong. 'Who's doing the blaming?'

'Ahmed.' Mia explained this was a guy Zinah reported to in Birmingham.

With that Basilah was welcomed back into the fold. Seconds later Mia was venting to them both about Zinah stealing their glory, upstaging them. It was humiliating for them to be blamed for a small job just so Zinah could plan her big one.

Karen Andersen left Mia's house on the motorbike, looking over her shoulder all the time. Her mind was racing through everything she'd learned and how she'd ever managed to become involved in such an undercover operation. From wanting to avenge Alesha Parkhurst for the hate mail from Zinah al-Rashid which'd actually given Simon King his excuse to cover up her murder, all the way to Tessa Clark's radicalisation. But however it had come about, she'd been let in on a potential terrorist plot linked to a Birmingham cell.

Basilah was the only person who could penetrate the North Acton jihadi brides circle. Quacker dubbed it the NAJBC. To date, miraculously enough, Fatima and Zinah and co hadn't rumbled Basile's true identity. But Zinah al-

Rashid was no fool, and she was also dangerous. If she worked out who Basilah really was, Karen had no illusions about what might happen to her and it would be sticky. But if she managed to remain under cover, she would save many lives.

If Zinah al-Rashid's next mission was to commit mass murder, Karen Andersen had to stop her somehow.

CHAPTER 62

The last thing Karen wanted was to be drawn into some other Miller related scandal involving hearsay from Tammy Kell so she promised herself to move on from the whole mystery. Even take a clean break. But that was before she received an email from the man himself.

It was a stark reminder. The case was open. Karen still hadn't found him. She needed to gain closure on it all.

Did she need her head read? Why was she at the Gerry Carter Fun Fair that night? To meet up with a guy who'd been missing for several weeks and not bothered to be in touch with anyone. What should she be interested in? An explanation. Questions to be answered, that's why.

So that muggy, sultry, rainy evening Karen trudged out with Haruto when they'd far rather have stayed indoors tucked up in front of the TV.

By now Karen had accepted Robin Miller was exceptional at vanishing acts. Also that he'd likely be planning to stay in hiding for a while longer. Too many bad things had taken place since the afternoon he'd gone missing. Was Tammy Kell right about a high-profile paedophile ring? Was that what he had uncovered? If so, Robin's life could be at risk. And to want to meet amidst the flurry of showground activity he was sure acting like he thought his life was in danger. The rendezvous was perfect for a guy who might need a fast getaway.

So everything seemed plausible enough.

Karen went along with the bizarre message. She

reckoned she'd been on every sort of roller coaster of emotion over Robin Miller. Now he wanted her to ride one for real. Was that odd or just how he operated?

The mood of the fair was light-hearted and relaxed and families trooped in to use the dodgems and take last advantage of the late summer evening. No matter how annoyed Karen was with Robin Miller's strange request, she couldn't be too unhappy. She was hand in hand with Haruto. Is this what it felt like to be in love?

Once inside the fairground, they'd agreed to split. Haruto would spear off to take action photos which suited him fine. Robin Miller had demanded that Karen Andersen be on her own. There was something else too. Robin wouldn't give a mobile number. Instead he was using a new Gmail address to send the messages. Only control freaks force you to do that. It means you have to keep updating your inbox.

The instruction came. Karen was to make her way to the entrance to the Ferris Wheel ride, then stand by the place where you alight. Miller would be in touch again once he saw her there.

She did exactly that. And when an empty car arrived Karen got in as further directed. But there was no Robin Miller. What had gone wrong? Before she could alter course, a woman wearing full Islamic dress had slipped in alongside and blocked her in. She held her shoulder bag close in front on her lap with one hand and carried a small bottle of coke in the other.

'Excuse me. I have to leave the car,' Karen said. She'd had enough of women in burkas by then.

Where was Robin Miller?

Ferris wheels wait for nobody and so despite trying to slow things down to get out, the eager thrill seekers behind were doing the very opposite.

Karen's travelling partner either couldn't or wouldn't budge, surrounded by all her paraphernalia. Instead she stared out and away from her as if looking for someone in the crowd, and deaf to Karen's demands. Before they knew it, the Ferris Wheel pulled ahead with a forceful jerk.

More customers packed in from behind. Children's happy howls filled the air from right across the field. It seemed everyone was having fun but her. So Karen hauled herself up from the seat now frantic to get out. 'Excuse me,' she repeated.

The woman now turned her head towards her and Karen spoke straight into the black veil. Thoughts of Zinah al-Rashid briefly entered her consciousness. But she dismissed them to remain sane.

The woman unscrewed the lid. *Fizz.* She passed over the coke bottle.

This wasn't happening. *I don't want a drink.*

'I have to get *out*.' Karen shrieked. Then, 'I will be sick.' But nothing shifted her or was getting through. Perspiration streamed and her flee or fight response kicked in. Karen did her best to keep her balance and climb out of the rocky seat at the same time.

Instead of moving, the woman urged her to sit down. She held the bottle up to her mouth. *Bloody Robin Miller. Where was he?*

The ride lurched forward as Karen tried to keep her footing and just as suddenly stopped, the car swinging to and fro ten feet in the air. The woman in Arab dress grabbed her again.

'I need to get OFF this thing,' she screamed.

Ok, so the Arab woman was trying to prevent her falling. Her grip was like a vice. What was with this Good Samaritan? Karen needed to leave the car and if not by the normal steps then by any other means possible.

'Sit down,' someone yelled from behind, eager for the ride to get underway.

It was about to take off again. She had to act. Do something. It was now or never.

Karen pulled with all her weight and strength away from the Mother Theresa figure. In two seconds she was free of the bar and had clambered over the side. *Don't stop. Close your eyes. No way back.* The ten-foot drop was over in a second. *Quick check. Both legs still intact.*

Karen's final scream crossed the ground so even Haruto heard it loud and clear just as he was setting up his tripod. Landing in the mud, she cursed. A few strides and the real danger of being crushed was behind her. With a huge sweeping motion, the fairground ride continued on its jerky way.

Leaving the cart had been the correct decision for Karen to take. Robin Miller or no Robin Miller, she hadn't wanted to sit out a stomach-churning experience just for pride. She hated heights.

Above her the woman in black robes kept climbing higher, ascending in superiority, looking down as she did so. *Ok, thought Karen, so she has a cooler head for altitude.* So what?

From far above a half empty coke bottle missed Karen by inches and exploded on the ground. Coke went everywhere, on her clothes, face and in her hair.

'He didn't bloody show again' she said to Haruto when he caught up with the bedraggled figure.

They continued to search the crowd for redheads, for Robin Miller. But what if he was wearing a hood? By then they were both exasperated.

Haruto rubbed his long fingers together, stroked his beard and shivered in the cooling breeze. 'Let's let it go, shall we? Enough for today.'

CHAPTER 63

The fair was a damp squib. Robin Miller must have run for it when the Ferris Wheel arrangement hadn't worked out. Karen was hopping mad. It had not only been a waste of time, it'd come close to costing her dearly dangling from the structure. She should never have gone along with the plan from the start she told herself.

Any thought of Miller maddened her. All sympathy had been lost. He now only replied to emails when he could quite easily have given a call. Ok, so he would have cottoned on to the hacking of his Gmail account. Karen couldn't log into it anymore because the password had been changed. Same with the Twitter one. He'd continued sending out party dogma as he'd done before. But that was it.

Robin had also failed to contact his father, or his mother. Despite all the fuss about his sister and protecting her from the dummied-up sex tape, he'd not bothered with her either. Nor had they heard a word from him at his work. And the agents had even relet his bedsit which hadn't taken long.

'Yes, we've seen the Twitter activity too' said David Miller when Karen called him. It was a relief to them he was ok enough to message on social media but still felt something was very wrong. What had they done to him to be so rejected? 'It's out of character. He's traded us in for this blessed Tory party.'

But even that wasn't the case. Despite Simon King's arrest and confession which cleared Robin Miller on a range of issues, he'd not once turned up at CCHQ to help out like he used to. He'd missed canvassing sessions and the local constituency office and other colleagues hadn't heard a beep. For someone who ate, thought and slept the party that was abnormal behaviour.

Karen had spoken to Oli Harrington once before but called again after the funfair fiasco, to thank him for his work getting the sex tape removed. Had he perchance received anything from Miller? No. There'd been a big fat nothing.

'Bloody party's now pissed me off. I've pulled out.' He'd made what he referred to as a life-changing decision and was quitting politics. The reason? Oli Harrington had just heard he'd been culled from the List and the party might even go further and expel him. He'd turned very anti. 'The Approved List is not only a secure source of easy revenue but an instant captive army of by-election foot-soldiers.'

'Did they tell you why you were dropped?' Karen asked.

He'd failed the interview set for anyone who reapplied to stand for a national seat next time round. The party refused to admit it was Robin Miller's report which had cost him. 'They do this all the time. The candidates' department perpetuates a type of fraud that the harder you work the more credits you clock up and that's one hundred percent untrue.'

'Can't you appeal the decision?'

He gave a cheeky laugh. 'There *is* no appeal process. They know you're screwed when you put in the reapplication which is why they ask you to do it. Loyal recruits aren't even deemed worthy of common courtesy let alone basic levels of natural justice. The likes of Simon King and his cronies act like arrogant discourteous apparatchiks. If it hadn't been the Robin Miller thing, it'd have been something else they'd get me for.'

He wasn't the only candidate to be kicked off. Others, who didn't deserve it as much as maybe he did, had been dropped too, dedicated hardworking, loyal members. 'They pass their PAB which costs real money and pay an ongoing annual subscription for the privilege and then continue putting in for nothing. Despite all this, they're still able to be arbitrarily vetoed by the likes of Simon King who we now know to be a serial killer. All because someone like him or one of his cronies hasn't taken a shine to them.'

'It seems wrong after all your initiatives.'

'I wasn't on the A List, which isn't supposed to exist, but does. Those on it are aware who they are. The others who aren't are left to pick up the clues via phone calls which are ignored and emails which are also ignored and no advancement.'

'I'm sorry to hear that,' Karen started to say, but he cut her in mid-speech.

'This happens all the time. The party changes to whatever is the latest zeitgeist philosophy. Sometimes it's promoting women or ethnics. Those who suddenly don't fit the revised model are still expected to pay the annual subs, still travel hundreds of miles and still dedicate hundreds of hours to 'the cause'. It's ok for the A-listers, but for everybody else, it's a scam. A deeply shameful and profoundly un-conservative, anti-meritocratic modus operandi with a propensity toward injustice promoted by the likes of my bloody stepmother.'

He was talking faster and faster. 'Never mind that I

organised the best campaigning initiative they'd ever bloody had. Never mind it was a Labourite who made the Miller sex tape, but it was me who got it down. I'm made the scapegoat. Bloody pisses me off. And, from what I hear Robin Miller is even back on the scene somewhere.'

He told me he was thinking of going abroad before the whole Brexit issue took hold. He'd had a final falling out with his father's second wife over the Robin Miller affair who he thought could have done more to support and stick up for him. Instead she'd dumped him in the shit.

The mention of Bea Harrington got Karen's interest because of how the MP's wife had pointedly shunned her at the Acid conference when Karen had introduced herself. In the bullying report it was Bea Harrington who had complained of Robin Miller harassing them at home with late night phone calls. So Karen had expected her to be more cooperative.

'Turns out she wasn't sure it was him all along,' said Oli Harrington. 'So that could have spared me half of this crap to begin with.'

Oli Harrington did not understand who else it could have been calling night after night. 'My father wants to move on and get out of politics and do something else. I was lining up to take his seat but now all that's gone.'

'I didn't know your father wanted to step down,' Karen said.

'My stepmother won't let him. She can't let it go. She's typical of the older party crowd. They've delivered in the rain, spent thousands on the conferences, and do the phone canvassing seven days a week unpaid. Stood for some shitty seat years ago. They've been abused outside the Pound Store and had human shit put through their letterbox. All that and then the party dumps them off the List like they've just done to me. But they still continue as before. You've got scores of men and women in their fifties and sixties hanging around doing anything they're asked to do. Like being scammed out of money by an internet lover, they feel too embarrassed they've been conned by the whole party process to admit it to anyone.'

'Why did your stepmother think it was Robin Miller who kept phoning your father?'

'Robin Miller wanted a job in Dad's office and she assumed he was hassling him and told me about it. Otherwise I wouldn't have sent him that message to back off.' Oli Harrington was adamant he never bullied Robin Miller any more than anyone else. 'Look, you have to understand how this system works. Robin got hooked on the party and becoming an MP like all the others. They're like groupies and the party is their life. They rush around fundraising and they drive their neighbours mad. They haven't any friends outside politics, anyway. He was shit scared I would shaft him and he'd be out of the process. Guys like that become hypersensitive to everything.'

'No one's forced to volunteer their time and put in unpaid hours or run up phone bills. It's like any other cult. They don't force you to offer to work at a drug rehab centre like Robin did just to make the rest of them look less like the nasty party. So why do they do it? Because they want something back for themselves. Or to belong. There's always a personal motive.'

He asked me to pass on his best wishes to Robin when Karen finally spoke to him which he was sure she would.

Relay his apologies again if his actions had offended or been misunderstood. He was genuinely sorry. Robin Miller was a decent chap underneath, but hellishly naïve.

CHAPTER 64

By now Karen had gathered a range of impressions of the twenty-one-year-old who'd vanished. Some good, some bad. She still wondered what type of guy he really was. When Haruto got back from a photographic job, she told him how Oli Harrington had spoken well of Robin Miller and with no resentment about what had happened between them.

Karen told Haruto also how Oli hadn't recognised his behaviour as anything out-of-the-ordinary. But then he'd not seen the complaint. And bullies don't always accept or understand the impact they have on others.

Haruto had still not formed his own opinion. He wanted to check out the drugs centre where Robin had volunteered. It was as much more curiosity as fact finding and to hear from the workers there what they thought of Miller and reserve judgement until then. Also, before they gave up the search for him and got back to normality.

Working in a shelter is not for the faint-hearted, even if you're only manning the phone. What duties did he have to do? It sounded gross and meant Karen playing Ralph McTell's Streets of London to get her in the mood.

If you ever go to a careers evening at a school, it is unlikely you'll hear much about the perks of a job in London's social care. It's a tough calling and those who do it generally come from the margins of society. They might eat MacDonald's and rarely drink anything stronger than ginger beer. They've come via churches and immigrant

344

centres. They may be reformed junkies or ex-prisoners who've seen the light. They might have done a stint selling The Big Issue. To them, the drug rehab drop-in is a positive career move. Not quite the thing for an aspiring right-wing politician.

The centre was run by a Croatian and his assistant, a rather shortish man sporting a beard much too long for him. The four of them sat around the kitchen table, like the one at Mia's house. Only, this time Karen wasn't wearing a cloak and hijab.

Karen had expected the fob off and to learn Robin Miller was a shirker who didn't show up for shifts. That would have fitted with his recent behaviour. But it was a hundred percent the opposite. The Croatian hadn't set eyes on him for weeks. But when Karen suggested could he maybe have lost his bottle, they defended him strongly, having none of it. He was a great bro'.

Robin Miller was not the sort to slip through because he couldn't hack the job. In their opinion, if he had disappeared, it was most likely he'd taken a well-earned holiday.

Someone had to be tough to work there amongst the addicts and the homeless and also for no money. They were adamant Miller was the best worker they'd had in years. Drug centres are like care homes. Full of people doing graft nobody else wants to do.

They crunched into Danish biscuits as they heard about Robin's strong work ethic and were emphatic Robin never took drugs himself or would ever, ever break any law. But his friend William Wan?

'The Chinese guy who was murdered? Now there was a

user. Robin brought him down here once to see how bad things could get.'

The boss of the centre then ran through the daily chores and activities, told them what Robin did there. They described him fondly. He was fastidious about his yellow gloves but happily went about cleaning up a druggie delivered by the Street Pastors with a warm smile on his face all the time. 'He never complained once about *nothin-k*.'

Haruto pulled his chair up close beside her. 'Do you remember anything else about who he worked with when he was here?'

'Robin was great with the addicts because he listened to them,' the manager explained. 'He got one man to see a psychologist. Talk through life goals and all that well-meaning stuff.'

So who was this Robin Miller? Nor as vulnerable as they'd first thought. You couldn't be to work amongst the excrement, the stench of cleaning fluids and the putrid smell of homeless men's clothes. He was quite the contrary. Like his father said, Robin Miller was compassionate, reliable, self-effacing.

So wherever he was, he could most likely look after himself.

CHAPTER 65

As soon as Simon King was arrested, everything turned upside down because anyone who'd been close to him was under scrutiny. *Did so-and-so know anything? Were they involved in any way?*

In addition to dodging awkward questions, Bea Harrington was inventing ways to hide the fact she'd split from her husband James. She didn't want that aired about. It was a horrible time. Harder still was keeping the news from her toe rag of a stepson Oli, who'd had the gall to blame her for his deselection and potential expulsion from the party. He'd brought that all on himself. There was no love lost between the two of them anyway but if he found out, he'd air it about.

She told colleagues she'd moved out of Dolphin Square because it was being redecorated. Of course it was nothing of the sort. Bea had changed everything from carpets to curtains only the year before. Not that it was any of their effing business what they thought. But she had to invent some excuse.

Dolphin Square, a once glamorous housing complex, known as home for celebrities as well as both real and fictitious spies, had now assumed a 'den of iniquity' image as far as Bea was concerned. Bad vibes and all that. She no longer saw it as a cosy London nest. The two Union Jacks which guarded the entrance, once a symbol of pride, now filled her with shame and self-loathing. Politicians liked Dolphin Square for its proximity to the House of

Commons. Not any more did this suit Bea Harrington. That James could slip home for lunch or dinner in just twenty minutes, once something she relished and adored, drove her up the wall with anxiety. She never knew when he'd show. And then when he did, that awful conversation would start up again.

Too much bad personal history associated with the ruddy place.

James Harrington and his first wife once owned a flat in the imposing block back in the 1980s. Then there'd been the rumour of a paedophile ring and somehow James's name had got connected with it. It was only a news scandal. But it'd cost him his first marriage and very nearly a career.

They'd been bloody fools to move back to some place with such bad Shui. Idiots.

It was a bastard having to hide away from everyone, but Bea Harrington's life with her husband was fast unravelling. She wanted no one to know, not yet. But living on at Dolphin Square was a constant reminder of the ghastly night it'd turned so ugly between them. And the purple bruise which appeared down the inside of her left upper thigh and refused to fade was another.

There was something else too. Money was missing. Bea had checked their bank account the day after the assault. There'd been two large sums withdrawn. But now was not the time to question James. It'd only open that bloody subject again when she'd prefer to wipe it totally from her mind.

For the last few days, Bea had commuted up from the Coast. But with the party conference looming, this eventually became impractical. Rather than incur extra expense, the Harringtons agreed between themselves they'd share the Dolphin Square flat on a strict 'his and hers' basis. So Bea moved back in and threw herself into her work. She promised herself at least a successful convention. She'd not let James Harrington or his bloody son dampen her spirits. *Like Gloria Gaynor, she would survive.*

One overcast, rainy afternoon, James came over to the flat. He wasn't supposed to be there, and apologised for the intrusion. His excuse for dropping by, not knowing she was in, a bald-faced lie, plopped out of his mouth. Bea Harrington was neither happy to see him nor hear another string of lies, but as they were adults there was little she could do about it.

He sat on a chair in the tiny kitchen. 'Who'd have thought Simon King capable of murder?'

Bea shot him a look. James had lost weight and looked drawn. 'Well, you for one.' She stopped after that, turned her head away. 'Sorry.'

All conversation between them now led back to one of two things. Either, how James had forced himself on her, or the latest on his old army buddy, Simon King. 'But *did* you know he was capable of murder?' she followed on. If he insisted on talking about it, she might as well let him learn how revolted she felt about his friendship with that monster.

'No, of course not. But I knew he's never been able to take rejection. There are things I think you should know.'

After the tone he'd adopted. Bea wasn't going to allow James to patronise her with his defence of men behaving badly. Even raising the fact Alesha Parkhurst had knocked Simon King back which is why he'd killed her was provocative in itself.

'It's very difficult for me,' she said, wishing he'd now just drop the damn subject and go. Alesha Parkhurst was strangled. Horrible. But hadn't James tried to choke Bea? What was the difference?

'I'm not usually like that.'

'I know.'

'We've been together fifteen years.'

She knew that too. He didn't need to remind her of it. 'You look bloody awful.' He'd become a shadow of himself.

'Thanks for that.' He hadn't lost his sense of humour.

But this was no laughing matter. She could see, by his pleading looks and watering eyes he was suffering big time. However, at least they were talking a little easier now. But then she remembered the money. 'What's with the cash, James? Where's it gone?' She was quick to add, 'Not that it'll make any difference.'

He told her he'd received an email from Robin Miller a short while before, asking for money.

'The guy who phoned you up over Oli and who's gone missing?'

'Yes. He wanted me to give five thousand pounds to a sex abuse charity.'

'And you paid it? Are you mad?'

'He'd found out about the paedophile ring.'

'But, James, you were cleared of that?'

'Yes.'

'So?'

'You know how things are today. Witch hunts. These historic cases. And there was a girl who–'

Bea stopped him. 'I don't think I'm ready for all this

350

now.'

'I should have told you beforehand. But we agreed never to mention the past, didn't we?'

'It was twenty-five years ago. Move on.'

She'd never believed the stories, but she wasn't going to say so again today. He'd lost the right to her loyalty.

'I shouldn't have paid it,' he said. 'You're right.'

'It's blackmail. Which charity?'

'I assumed it was the one he volunteered for. He told me once on the phone he worked for some charity. '

'Which charity?' she repeated.

'I don't remember the name. Only what it did. Looks after Syrian orphans. I was just given the account details.'

Bea paced the room, rubbing her head. 'Was Simon King aware of this?'

James rocked in the kitchen chair. 'I told him about it the night we met in case Robin Miller stirred up trouble through the media. Don't need that sort of thing. Simon was sympathetic because his wife had accused him of something similar.' There was a brief awkward silence. 'And allegations of sex abuse can bring a party down. Can't it? But it was wrong to tell Simon before you. Sorry.'

'And you weren't to know then he'd committed a murder. Three in fact. And also we'd agreed never to mention that period,' she said repeating what he'd said earlier. Letting him just a tiny bit off the hook.

'She was a seven-year-old, and she was playing around.' he went on.

'What were you doing with a seven-year-old, anyway?'

Ever the politician, James had suckered her in once more. Once he'd sensed the softening, he'd gone on as if he

351

was fully exonerated.

Why was she listening to this?

He came out with how James had interned for an MP who'd asked him to take his kid on some scary ride but then what this girl had later told people was a pack of damn lies.

It didn't explain his paying silence money.

'You know how bad it can be for men these days. What with these charges going back years so they can't defend themselves.'

James Harrington ran his eyes over the conference agenda Bea had spread across the table and took in the various women's issues, FGM, child brides, sex trafficking, pregnant prisoners. 'What are you speaking on this time? Sexual abuse, no doubt.'

She tried to grin but instead, her eyes watered and the tears flowed. What a prick. But by the sorry look on his face, he most likely thought she was crying for him, for them, for their bust up. Which she certainly wasn't.

She had no feelings for him anymore. It was relationship grief she was feeling.

He went on with the historic sex abuse topic as if nothing had happened between them. 'You can't judge the standards of twenty or thirty years ago by those of today because it's a different world, isn't it?'

'I think you'd better go. Or if not, I should.'

'That came out all wrong. I didn't mean to say it like that.'

'James, I don't want to be with you anymore.'

He was searching for clues in her face and still not reading them right. He went on with, 'Men are confused today. You've said so yourself. Other than that occasion, the night–'

'I'm not ready to talk about it.' Bea Harrington knew her husband was such an adept master of spin he'd turn her words whatever came out while she was in rabbit mode, upset.

He said again he understood. How he wasn't surprised at her reaction. Whether it was marital rape or not, he didn't know.

It was, and she did.

He cursed and took out a handkerchief to blow his nose.

Oli, her obnoxious stepson was right after all. Bea shouldn't have interfered with his father's plans to leave politics. She wouldn't have done so if she'd known some damn scandal was about to erupt. Why should she care a toss if his son got put up for his seat or not? James had probably only stayed on in politics because Bea had battled for him to do so. Knowing all this, yes, maybe he should have stepped down.

James started up again. He'd never wanted to be with anyone else but her because he loved her, adored her. Even their recent problems he blamed on Robin Miller for stressing him out, making such a big deal of Oli's behaviour.

Typical James. Always someone else's fault.

Before he left, she agreed that when they were up at the Birmingham conference if she had twenty minutes free, no pun intended, they could grab a coffee. But it was just to get James to the door, any ploy to get him out of there.

She didn't tell him she was travelling up on the train with Tammy Kell. Why should she? None of his bloody business, or so she thought at the time.

CHAPTER 66

Zinah completed her upstairs chores with lightning speed by following the rigid routine she'd established whenever she filled in for a carer who'd gone sick. It sped things up having a tried and tested system. This morning it took less than thirty minutes, despite the fact the front room was overcrowded with junk and china ornaments and she longed to dump the lot in the dustbin.

Her grandmother stood watching on, dressed in blue slacks and a pink cardigan, looking absent and vague. The seventy-six-year-old woman's thin white hair was the same shade as the plastic tulips in the Wedgewood vase.

'I can't bend down like I used to.' She raised a bare foot showing she'd lost a slipper and performed a curious pirouette.

Zinah located the shoe under the sofa and they sat side by side in matching armchairs. Then came the inevitable photo routine which happened every time Zinah kept her grandmother company. 'What did you say your name was?' She lifted the silver frame in her direction. 'You look so like my daughter. Have you ever met Miriam?'

Once upon a time, Zinah bothered to answer with, 'Yes, of course, Grandma. She was my mother.' But she'd long since tired of the pointless repetitions and at the elderly lady crumpling up her brow in concentration, trying to recognise who the cleaner was, desperately trying to pull a name from her destroyed brain cells. So Zinah kept quiet and said nothing. She knew too what was coming next. The phrase, 'You should meet her.'

'I should.'

That's what Alzheimer's did, didn't it?

Had she been able to, Zinah al-Rashid would have liked to discuss her father with her grandmother, her *real* father. But that'd never happened even before the disease struck and she lost her memory. He was non-existent to her since her daughter's first husband had changed his name to Mohammed.

The front bell rang. Standing on the step was the good-natured Jamaican care assistant to take over from Zinah and tend to Ann Bishop's needs. So Zinah handed her a repeat prescription, the card of a home hairdresser who'd be calling in and a bit of paper notifying of the change of rubbish collection that week.

'Did you find your package yesterday?' the care worker asked with a still-strong Caribbean accent. 'The man who delivered the parcel said it was for your dressmaking. Ann, over there, was itching to open it, weren't you, my dear?'

Zinah felt the blood drain from her face as the horror struck. *What if they'd opened the parcel which contained the bomb-making materials?*

'But I told her to leave it alone. It wasn't her delivery but yours. Not to touch. I took it off her and put it outside the door downstairs myself.'

'Thank you for that.'

'What do you get up to making down there, m' dear?' The Jamaican crossed her large arms and looked at her with a twinkling eye and sympathetic smile. 'I could do with some couture myself. I've got a wedding coming up. You could make me something special. I'll look in some time.'

355

'Best I know if you're planning to visit,' Zinah said. She avoided eye contact. Just in case her extreme alarm was on open display.

Zinah declined the Jamaica's insistence she kiss Ann Bishop goodbye. She wanted to get out of there.

Her grandmother answered anyway with, 'You will come again and see me, my dear, won't you?' Then Zinah heard her turn to the carer and said the predictable. 'What's she called again? She is *frightfully* nice.'

'She's your *granddaughter*. You don't recognise her today?'

Zinah scampered off thinking the carers were beginning to probe too deeply into what was going on downstairs. Fortunately there was only so much they could discover in their half hour work slot. *Alhumdililah.*

CHAPTER 67

Karen Andersen got to break the news to Hailey in person which was that she'd failed to win back any of what they thought were her designer bags on eBay. Their bids had just served to push the price up higher and then they'd still lost out on them.

Hailey had watched as the value of her Chanel bag sky-rocketed and was going crazy. 'Terrific. You told me you were good at this detective work, didn't you?'

Karen reminded her then she was a private investigator and not a mystery shopper.

'I know they fetch a fucking bomb,' Hailey said.

There had been words exchanged. How Hailey had saved thousands by losing out on a load of overpriced bags worth fifty quid tops, which she had once owned, anyway. It hadn't gone down well. Hailey looked as if she'd dropped into a large hole.

Karen informed her she'd come by the office at an inopportune time as she was midway through packing for the Conservative Party Conference in Birmingham. It was not a good moment to discuss the theft which, as if Hailey had forgotten, included Karen's bequeathed diamond ring and her grandfather's old Hunter pocket watch. It didn't stop her. It went over her head.

'How did you agree to do this? You HATE public speaking.'

Because of a rash and hasty offer to Tammy Kell, Karen Andersen was now a speaker on a panel debating online bullying. Thanks to her uncle, the five-minute speech he'd written she was sure would be shit hot. Quacker, who was still in recovery after his hip surgery, was all for her attending. Cyber abuse was more relevant than ever to female politicians and indeed the practice of speaking at the conference might help improve Karen's poor delivery.

In addition, Quacker thought Karen's attendance could be useful for career advancement. He'd become her mentor. What was not to gain, Karen? She'd get to meet the Justice Minister and learn how they planned to stop kids carrying six-inch kitchen knives into geography lessons. Plus everyone in Government would be attending. Candidates and activists as well. Therefore, the perfect opportunity to hold an open clinic on Robin Miller.

So Quacker was a hundred percent for Karen going north. Hailey Wren was not. 'I still think you'd be better off spending the time getting our property back,' she said. 'I did house your bloody stuff after all,' she continued, heaping on the guilt.

While they pursued this farce, talking rings and bags and watches on eBay versus delivering political speeches, Hailey was taking in Karen's flat, the array of meditation props, looking no doubt for signs of Haruto. Of which there were plenty.

It was because of this talk about the Tories Karen recalled her conversation at the Carlton Club. 'A girl called Tammy Kell told me she once worked with you at Harrods.'

'Never heard of her.'

It took a few seconds before the response penetrated, but this was because Karen had noticed one wheel missing from her case and monetarily her mind was on that. 'She

358

said she trained you.'

At this Hailey came alive. The sudden realisation caused her to leap up from the sofa and circle the room, taking in the old prints propped against the wall with a dismissive eye. 'Oh, Tamsin Smythe-Kell! That's who you mean. She's only been Tammy since she became a Tory hopeful.'

Hailey lit a cigarette and dangled it from the open window to let the smoke out, insisting Karen understand how upset she was about everything that had happened to her. *Everything*. But now Karen agreed to accept what Hailey had to heap on her in return for what she knew about Tamsin Smythe-Kell. There was plenty.

Hailey Wren had known her first seven years back at Harrods when she'd been very different indeed, dowdy as hell. But she also recalled how Tamsin had born a grudge against an MP who she reckoned had touched her up when she was a child. 'But she's uber-glam now,' she said. The Carlton Club, Harrods bags and black cabs lifestyle impressed Hailey no end. She'd been *delighted* when she turned up at Hailey's party.

'Tammy Kell was at your party?'

They reached the same conclusion simultaneously. Tammy was one hundred percent Hailey's thief! How could she have not picked it straightaway when Tamsin had been the one who'd been shoplifting in Harrods all those years ago?

When Hailey dropped Karen off at Turnham Green Terrace it was as if they'd never had a falling out. Karen agreed to track Tammy down at the Conference and confront her. Then Hailey dropped the bombshell at the Tube when Karen was least expecting it.

'Harry still planning to go to Japan, is he?'

It was a punch in the guts. Haruto had never mentioned to Karen he'd been offered a Tokyo job which would take him away.

Karen put on sunglasses so Hailey didn't get the satisfaction of seeing the tears start to form.

Yup, she's found my weak spot again.

The trip should have been relaxing. Karen had a speech to rehearse and even a book to read. But she spent it churning over what she'd discussed with Hailey. How Haruto was planning to take off as she'd always suspected he would after a while. He'd never even mentioned it, which was what hurt Karen the most. Why not?

When she took a surprise call from Quacker, Karen wasn't ready for it in the slightest. Nor what he had to convey. 'Decided to travel to the conference after all seeing as I've got my security pass through. With some luck, Robin Miller will show up there.'

'Erm.' Karen muttered.

'Well you never can tell, you know.'

Karen's mood plummeted to rock bottom. In her present state she didn't want the extra pressure, the need to socialise with him up there. Quacker was bright about it.

'Are you ok to walk, though?' Karen asked, hoping to deter Quacker, needing space for her private thoughts.

'Definitely not up to a train ride under the circumstances.'

Karen smiled with relief. 'Certainly not good for you to make a long journey on public transport.' But she hadn't picked up on the trap he'd set for her.

'No. Exactly. So I've hired a car and I'll get Haruto to

drive me up.'

This too was not what Karen needed. Haruto was the last person she wanted to see. Their affair meant nothing to him, obviously. Everything Karen had tried to avoid hit her with full force. The emotional pain was extreme. As the train hurtled through countryside the blurred green images made her giddier still, added to the heaviness of disappointment. Nausea. It confirmed her sense of dejection.

The harder you fell, the more misery it caused.

Karen's iPhone chimed as a message came in on her WhatsApp, which she expected to be from Haruto, but wasn't. She could barely take in the words. It was from Fatima. Somehow Basilah had convinced Fatima she was deadly serious about travelling to the Caliphate. While it'd still be ok to arrange a meeting with Zinah, even though she'd stood her up so *many* times, she wouldn't be available until after a trip to the Midlands. Word had come back Zinah was in Birmingham herself and could meet Basilah in the Bullring while she was up there.

Karen got straight onto Quacker.

'I think there's going to be an attack at the Tory Party conference.'

CHAPTER 68

Quacker gripped the passenger seat of the hired Vauxhall. It'd seemed a good idea at the time to get Haruto to chauffeur him up to the conference. Now he wasn't so sure. As the fields flashed past, he wondered about the numbers of others who would be en route at the same time. However many, no one would be doing it in such a reckless manner. Although he didn't ever exactly exceed the speed limit, Haruto Fraser was a terrifying driver.

Quacker had tipped off security after Karen Andersen called to warn about the possibility of jihadist activity by Zinah al-Rashid. It stacked up. Several senior ranking Isis soldiers had recently been eliminated in Syria. There could feasibly be a revenge attack from a cell operating out of the Hadley Road area of the city aimed at targeting the high-profile national gathering.

Quacker clasped his hands across his stomach to stop it churning. The journey hadn't been all bad. Haruto had picked him up at the door exactly on time, jazz blasting from the car radio, and ahead lay the prospect of good grub once settled on the motorway north. 'Are we going for the full works?' he'd asked Haruto after a while. 'The bumper English sounds good.'

How long they stopped was at Haruto Fraser's discretion because he was the damn driver. But the motorway pit stop was also a perfect opportunity to extend a bit, to get the lie of the land before they arrived at their destination. Breakfast was a chance to catch up on all fronts.

For example, Haruto didn't know anything about James Harrington MP, who'd surely be attending. He would be worth questioning. Simon King had suggested in the interview his old army friend Harrington may have been the target of a blackmail plot by Robin Miller relating to sex allegations way back. Recent gossip supported it. 'Rumour has it the Harrington marriage is at a breaking point. And Robin Miller was in touch with them quite a bit before he went missing.'

'I don't fathom the connection myself,' said Haruto forking down the beans.

'Miller wanted help over his bullying issue so he turned to Oliver Harrington's father to get him to tell his son to back off. Can't see why he'd do that myself. My son won't do a thing I tell him.' He chortled. 'But now there's been a fresh development which may shed new light.'

Once Simon King had suggested the idea to Quacker, he'd been straight away on the phone to Bea Harrington who'd confirmed the details. She'd also had something else to add. 'She believed there'd been an extortion issue as well. It was to do with 'reputation control' was how she put it.'

'It explains the large sums missing. You said five thousand pounds were withdrawn on two occasions from their joint account?'

'Or of course the removal of money could be different altogether. Maybe nothing to do with Robin Miller,' said Quacker. 'James Harrington had quite a serious gambling habit once upon a time. Addiction to betting is something the gaming industry tries hard to hide. The Government too. Harrington sits on a select committee looking at the issue. He's a prominent figure. Also, he campaigned for

Brexit, didn't he? Now the UK's up and leaving the EU the gaming crowd in Gibraltar are unhappy. They're not beyond outing any Brexiteer who hasn't declared a conflict of interest. Harrington is one of those. Turns out he was once a director of Jackpot. Kept nice and quiet about that. Maybe his blackmailer, be it Miller or someone else entirely, found that out and used the information to squeeze him for a few quid.'

'Possibly. But I don't think Miller is after money,' said Haruto. 'He's being scapegoated, I'm sure of that.'

'Perhaps Harrington gambled again and the ten thousand was to repay his debts. He doesn't want his wife to know about it so he makes up a story as cover.'

'So then why blame that on Robin Miller?'

'To pay him back for having complained about his son? Revenge is sweet.'

Quacker thought Haruto far too easy on Miller. But after Haruto told Quacker about the visit to the drug centre, his opinion softened. It wasn't what he'd been expecting to hear.

'The guy they described doesn't sound like someone who would get involved in any criminal activity,' said Haruto.

Quacker decided the matter could be resolved with one quick call to James Harrington which he then made. It was a brief conversation because the MP was driving too and set to arrive ahead of them at Birmingham.

Harrington confirmed what his wife Bea had said. That James had received an email from the missing activist asking for money. Like it or not, the pieces fitted.

'Sorry to disappoint you but it seems Robin Miller's

motive is money. Even if it not for his own purposes, an extorted donation to charity is still blackmail.'

'Well then perhaps James Harrington has something on his conscience,' added Haruto, not letting go of his defence of the twenty-one-year-old activist.

Quacker was off again. 'Then it could be that Robin Miller found out about Harrington's connection with the paedophile ring back in the 1980s. Seeing as his son Oliver had been such a prick to him he thought he'd take advantage of this knowledge. Also the sex tape with his sister in it was the last straw. If he's the great social worker you say he is, this adds up. James Harrington pays a handsome sum to a kid's organisation. The motive? A compassionate act plus revenge. Kill two birds with one stone.'

By the time they'd finished their eggs and bacon, Quacker had talked through the complex case. 'The account belongs to a Muslim charity run by a certain Zinah al-Rashid. This is the woman Karen has been investigating over her involvement in the jihadi brides' operation. On the surface, the charity collects funds to help kids used for sex in the refugee camps, and no doubt Miller would have believed that. But in reality it is not destined for children at all. We now know these donations get sent on to fund terrorist activities.'

When they'd finished breakfast Haruto picked up the keys meticulously wiping off the tomato sauce his passenger had dripped on them. As they drove out of the service station and back onto the road to the Midlands, he and Quacker recapped on the two scenarios.

One pro Miller.

The other, the opposite viewpoint.

The first anti was Robin Miller wanted everyone to believe he was a nice guy trapped in some bullying nightmare. And while people now knew Simon King, who'd been dealing with his case, was a cold-blooded killer that didn't necessarily make the political activist a saint, did it? The two matters were unrelated.

Quacker's second *anti* scenario was how Robin Miller had discovered James Harrington's past record and the scandal when he first applied for a job in the MPs office and wasn't successful. Miller had then taken out his disappointment on Harrington's son Oli at not being hired by needling him whenever he could. Then Oliver Harrington retaliated, and bullied back. After that Robin had hounded the MP and his wife with phone calls over Oli's bullying. It was a 'give me a job' or 'pay me some money'. Miller knew historic sexual abuse was a hot potato.

Quacker by then was alive with speculation. 'Or, how about this one? The calls are so frequent that the wife thinks it can't be Robin Miller, as her husband told her and perhaps it's a woman calling and he's having a bit on the side. She finds money missing. That confirmed it in her mind. The tension results in her leaving him and eventually a broken marriage.

'How do you know there's a broken marriage?' challenged Haruto, narrowly missing the back end of an HGV.

Quacker pointed a shaking finger at the next threat as Haruto refocussed on his driving. 'Because Mr and Mrs Harrington have booked separate hotel rooms at the conference.'

'Or, maybe James *was* having an affair with someone.

366

And it wasn't Miller calling, but a dumped lover harassing him because he'd flicked her off.' Haruto's suggestion contained shades of Hailey Wren.

'Ah, yes, there is that possibility isn't there? You had trouble yourself like that, didn't you? How's that going?' Quacker added, 'Harrington's wife mentioned she *suspected* at one time he was having an affair but that was a long while ago. And she couldn't, wouldn't comment on it, anyway.'

'Still doesn't explain the money sent to charity,' said Haruto.

'No, but it does explain the late phone calls to the house designed to alarm and upset the missus. The MP tells his wife it's Miller to cover his tracks. I suggested this to Mrs Harrington when I spoke to her. Maybe there'd been a woman with a crush on her husband. Could she think of anyone?

All she could come up with was how Harrington had once mentioned he'd written a reference for an aspiring woman politician and then wished he hadn't. Maybe that's how it began? A reference? Then it'd gone sexual? Perhaps James Harrington was trying to break off this stale relationship and didn't want Bea to find out.'

Haruto's posture stiffened. 'Or possibly he's overlooked something in the girl's past?' His eyes were bulging and his foot hit hard down on the accelerator reflecting his excitement. Weaving in and out of the middle lane Haruto, his memory jogged, told Quacker about the dialogue between Karen Andersen and Tammy Kell. How the alluring blonde female candidate had told Karen how she was abused as a child.

'What if the person she'd been waiting to walk through the door of the Carlton Club and confront was James Harrington?'

Quacker hung on to his seat as they whizzed past another ten cars.

Who gave this guy his licence?

'But if that was the case,' Quacker came back. 'Why would someone like James Harrington, who was caught up in a salacious sex scandal years back, help his accuser?'

'To keep her quiet.' It was a strange, quiet moment between them. Haruto went on with, 'An MP gives a woman a character reference knowing her to be the step-daughter of a colleague who's now dead. She climbs the parliamentary ladder. He later discovers she's harbouring a personal grudge against him for child abuse, one he wasn't aware of before or had forgotten about. He confides in his son Oliver about this because he doesn't need his wife Bea to find out and build a drama when there was no substance to it in the first place.'

Haruto stretched his arm over to the back seat and fished into his messenger bag. Quacker saw the driver ahead check his rear mirror. 'Want me to hold the wheel for you while you do that?' He had visions of a multicar pile up.

After a few more one-handed swerves, Haruto found the page he was looking for in Robin Miller's report. He passed it across to Quacker. 'Read that.'

'When Oli saw Tammy and I had become friends on the campaign bus that is when the problem first surfaced. Tammy told me that he had made several sexual advances towards her, which didn't surprise her because his father who is an MP was involved in a sexual abuse case twenty-

five years ago.'

Therefore, the individual behind the blackmail plot was most likely Tammy Kell. Miller was her accomplice.

Haruto broke into his signature dazzling smile. 'Where was Robin headed after he left Simon King at the Buckingham?' He didn't need to complete the sentence because Quacker was ahead of him.

'To see Tammy Kell and get her to dash off a witness report,' he said. 'If so, she was the last person to have any contact with him.'

When they arrived at the conference, the usual band of protestors was gathered ready to spit and hurl abuse at anyone going through the security gates. While Haruto hared off to park, the car-sick detective joined the snaking queue. He had several new lines of enquiry. James Harrington, Tammy Kell and Robin Miller himself, if the lad ever surfaced again. He reckoned he had things just about sussed now. But first he needed to find some milk of magnesia to settle his stomach. He was amazed they'd made it in one piece.

CHAPTER 69

Bea Harrington met up with several of the older female candidates at the conference. It was a prime opportunity to dish out unwelcome news when the four of them were together and also in a place of mutual support.

'There will be a seat reduction, ladies, as you all are aware. I've been helping the candidates' department. It's no good having everybody in the running so we've reassessed the numbers and in particular talked about our senior activists,' she told them. 'Sometimes older candidates feel they want to pass on their experience and help the party get the younger women ahead. I'm sure you agree with that. Us older crew know what works and what doesn't. That it's time to give something back.'

So they were to be promoted to mentors.

Bombshell. None of the women bought it. They knew it meant being put out to pasture, not getting their applications for safe seats looked at. They weren't too happy about it at all. Two were resisting, hands on hips. The others hadn't quite got what was being said. But the decision was made, and they had to accept it.

It was bloody unpleasant having to deliver this news.

Tammy Kell, who'd not caught the train with Bea because she'd travelled up instead on an earlier one, was damn useful indeed. Right now Tammy was by her side and an excuse for Bea to talk to someone else and avoid the unpleasantness.

'Anything you need?' Tammy asked.

'A coffee would do go down well if you can manage it.'

Tammy rushed to oblige. But she also made a fuss, unwrapped the plastic covered biscuits, fetched chairs and set out leaflets. She was a godsend.

As soon as one room of people vacated, the next lot trooped in. There was no time for recrimination or deep discussions with disappointed candidates, thank goodness. Everyone was on the move.

Bea Harrington felt bad for the older ladies after all they had put in over the years. But it was only realistic. The likes of Tammy Kell represented the future of the party which had to be considered above all else. It was far better to back winners. Tammy's chances of seat selection were about as good as they get and she prepped well. Bea noted with admiration how she could change her look on a sixpence. Plus she was staying at the top hotel and not short of a bob or two. That helped.

Bea thanked her for the help. 'Tammy, you have been terrific.'

'That's what I'm here for.'

It was genuine. Bea was impressed by Tammy and not just how she put up her hand at the conference whenever somebody was needed. Not like the others, who did the minimum unless it was a hundred percent in their interests, Tammy attended *everything* Bea spoke at. It was flattering. And right now Bea needed a shadow like that. Ever since the rape, she'd shied from her usual crowd, people she'd known for years. She didn't want them sticking their beak in, thank you very much. It was time for new allies. New beginnings. So she plain forgot Tammy Kell had not too long ago given her the shivers.

'I'm proud of you, Tammy. One thing I like about you is how trustworthy you are.' Yes, Tammy Kell should be up for a secure seat next election and Bea Harrington would offer her personal recommendation. Tammy was well up on affairs in the Middle East, was young and had the right skills for the cabinet eventually. What was her name again, the full one? Tammy Smythe-Kell.

The Smythe part rang a bell.

The scheduled event *How to get started in Politics* began exactly at ten. It brought in a hundred and twenty-three women and even a few guys. They were all fishing for clues on how to make it to the next rung of the ladder. Because of that, they hung on Bea's every word of introduction.

Why does Smythe sound familiar?

The speakers included 'superwoman' who'd held sixteen public committee positions and a newly appointed Police and Crime Commissioner whose only experience of the law had been winning an appeal for a parking ticket. On their panel they were joined by two newly elected female MPs. It promised to be a good discussion.

The gist of the message behind the discussion was personal planning. Everyone wanted to be an MP, didn't they? You have to be inventive, creative. That's why you're here at this event, to get ideas on how to go forward in politics.

Wasn't a chap called Smythe once an MP?

'There are plenty of roles and loads of ways to get involved with the party without standing for public office yourself,' Bea said in a low voice. *La de da de dah.* She blurted out the same old thing she always did. The speech was on autopilot which was just as well. Her brain was tussling with a problem.

Didn't James once work for Julian Smythe MP?

Ten minutes from wrapping up the event, Bea decided to ask Tammy directly about her connection with the deceased MP her husband had assisted on starting out in politics. She would do it the moment she finished the speech. But just then she noticed two police at the back of the room. What did they want?

Standing right in the rear of the marquee structure, one in uniform, the other a big plain clothes officer, both stood with arms crossed and grim professional expressions.

They made hand signals in her direction that they needed to speak to her.

'Me?' she gesticulated holding up five fingers to signal she'd be there in so many minutes.

Bea Harrington should have been listening to the panel so she could wrap up in a half intelligent manner but her heart thumped so loud she couldn't make out a word. A surge of bile rose in her throat. *What do the detectives want with me?* There could be several reasons. Conference security for one. To back up the Police and Crime Commissioner for another. Or, God forbid, sex abuse. Maybe the threatened scandal had broken as her husband James had warned her it might. After all the shenanigans of Robin Miller, nothing would surprise!

Then again, Simon King may have implicated her and James in some fashion because they all went back a long, long way. *Horrors.*

Bea Harrington was desperate for a heads up and her stomach was like melting jelly. What did the Law want and what should she tell them? What about the rape? Should

373

she pretend it never happened? Was it relevant anyway? *Depends on what James has done.*

So just when she could do with sending someone over to find out ahead what the Police wanted, it appeared Tammy Kell had slipped away.

Bea finally excused herself from the top table and made her way over to the police. The plain clothes detective introduced himself as Donald Partridge. They'd spoken on the phone twice before, he reminded her.

James Harrington? Yes, he was her husband, but she doubted she could speak on his behalf because they'd not talked since London two days back.

That's when she heard how an hour ago he'd thrown himself off the Bromsgrove Highway footbridge. James Harrington had left a note for her to read to explain his actions. But first, if she didn't mind, they needed her to identify his body.

CHAPTER 70

At just past two in the afternoon Karen Andersen was in Birmingham. Once she'd got into the conference area from Centenary Square and distanced herself from the demonstrators it took another twenty minutes to clear security. There were four search channels operating. Armed police were everywhere. The processing was more thorough even than at Heathrow on periods of high alert.

While Karen was waiting in line she received the follow-up WhatsApp message from Fatima to say that Zinah al-Rashid would meet Basilah the following day. As her mobile disappeared into the X-ray machine, with the potential for it being confiscated and analysed, the full implications of her position came home. She was caught up in a potential terror cell. Other than Quacker and Haruto, no one knew about her undercover operation.

Ahead of her, security refused entry to a woman who wanted to take her Samsonite through. Karen smiled to herself. She'd at least read the rules. No luggage whatsoever allowed.

Inside the secure zone a seething mass of delegates, going twenty directions at once, made it hard for Karen fighting her way to the cloakroom to check in a bag filled with her laptop and a change of clothes. Despite the thousands of attendees only two interested her in the slightest: Blonde Tammy Kell and the red-headed Robin Miller. She began immediately to comb through the crowds looking for them.

Maybe the programme would be helpful in finding

where they might go. If Robin Miller was there, he wouldn't just stand in the foyer waiting for Karen to spot him. Where would he be? What about the event *How can we make a positive difference to the state of student politics?*

Another which might have attracted him was 'Your first steps to becoming a Parliamentary Candidate' but that was by invitation only. Karen was certain Conservative Campaign Headquarters would suffer from their super recruiter Simon King being behind bars, but she was wrong. Future hopefuls still clustered around the stand. The negative publicity on Simon King had had the opposite effect. There'd been a fresh recruitment drive. The usual smiling and nodding from those hoping to pick up an encouraging tone, but Robin was not one of them.

With Miller not turning out to be easy to find, Karen turned her efforts to Tammy Kell. If she was the sneak thief Hailey had identified Karen was certainly in the right frame of mind to catch her out. So where would she go? Karen ran her eyes over the agenda. The teaching union was pushing for more gender equality in the classroom. 'Women and girls must no longer be subject to sexual harassment, abuse and bullying, in person and online.' They were all there. The Huffington Post, the Legatum Institute, Girl Guiding, Christian Fellowship, and the Wildlife Trust. All the charities. Action Aid, Christian Aid, every other sort of aid.

She'd heard the conference was a big hooley and drink fest. There were receptions for the Green Belt enthusiasts, brownfield campaigns and blue flag beaches. Many organisations rights were being debated, including animals and even trees. Woman's Aid conversed with politicians on the toxic trio of substance misuse, domestic abuse and mental health. There was even an enlightening talk on partnerships, preventive strategies and support services. But all Karen cared about right then was confronting either Tammy Kell or Robin Miller and preferably both.

After that, because of her mood of doom, she had been planning to deliver her presentation and then head on out of there back to London. But now Karen had a date with Zinah al-Rashid which meant she had to stick around longer. *Damn.*

She walked miles pausing at Starbucks and Smiths, both set up to capitalise on the captive customers. Loitering a while in the spacious seating area in the Entertainment Zone, she absentmindedly studied the faces around her, hoping for a break without any great confidence.

It was while standing by a stall selling local craft, that she got a voicemail prompt on her phone. Quacker and Haruto had arrived on the scene and were looking for her. They needed to speak as a matter of urgency and it concerned Tammy Kell.

After years of denial, Karen had finally recognised Hailey Wren's technique. She was a mistress of lightly veiled personal attacks and fake news. A highly effective combination. And Karen still hadn't got over the last example, about the rumour of Haruto going back to Japan. Was Hailey up to another one of her mind games designed to destroy their relationship or was it true? Had Haruto been making plans and if so why had he not told her? Whatever the case, it had worked. She couldn't face Haruto at the moment. Maybe later. So she ignored the call.

Karen knew she could not avoid them for too long. But

she didn't want to explain anything until she'd figured out her own priorities. Which were the theft of *her* property, the agonising speech which had gone clean from her memory, and meeting up with Zinah al-Rashid to sus out any terror plot if it existed. In that time order.

She saw the flash of bright blonde hair first and all of a sudden there she was. Tammy Kell stood looking up at a television screen, along with a group of delegates, taking in some announcement. She looked as blow-dried and stunning as ever.

'Hello, Tammy.'

'Hi, Karen. Isn't this place full? When did you get here? Have you heard this report?' She was wearing a very expensive looking suit and had a Michael Kors handbag which, from what Karen had learnt would not have been hers to carry. It hardly fitted with her new toned-down look which she said the party had asked her to adopt, in order to present herself as one of the people. But by now, Karen was puzzled by everything she did and said. 'Apparently, some MP has committed suicide on their way to the conference and we are all waiting to hear who it is,' she delivered in a matter-of-fact tone. 'Have to go,' and without waiting for a response Tammy disappeared off into the crowd.

Karen's WhatsApp went. It was Fatima again messaging 'Basilah', who'd agreed at their first meeting she'd be prepared to sell her valuable jewellery to support the cause. Obviously Fatima hadn't forgotten. She messaged, 'Zinah sells stuff online. Designer bags and rings. The cash goes to Caliphate. Give her your things tomorrow when you meet.'

Karen knew she was on the verge of an intuitive breakthrough. The adrenaline charge fuelled by danger kicked in. She always got her best ideas when her back was against the wall. WhatsApps were popping in, chiming nonstop. Meanwhile Tammy Kell edged away through the press of people.

Zinah al-Rashid sold handbags on eBay to support Islamic State. Tammy Kell stole handbags and bought jewellery on eBay.

It was a wild hunch. Could Tammy and Zinah be connected? If so, could Robin Miller, who Tammy claimed to be in touch with, be the link between them?

CHAPTER 71

It was hard to hear yourself speak above the high pitch mumbling of the crowd, so very few words had been exchanged between Karen Andersen and Tammy. But as Tammy pulled away from the monitor to distance and make a convenient exit, Karen tagged along determined not to be flicked off.

Tammy Kell didn't want to be chummy. So she used a turned shoulder to block Karen from walking with her. Which acted like a red rag. Now Karen was fired. She wanted answers. She knew Tammy Kell was guilty of something other than just the theft at Hailey's flat but she couldn't finger exactly what.

They entered a coffee area where there were a handful of tables and stools but all were taken. Delegates were even staking out parts of the wall to lean against. The wait for cappuccino was at least twenty. Perfect. But *how* to confront Tammy Kell? Karen still wasn't a hundred percent, but she knew she was on to something.

Tammy Kell stole things for Zinah al-Rashid. But why?

'Can you line up for me and get a coffee? I'll hold your stuff so you've got hands free.' Delivered confidently and quickly such an approach can work like a charm. So in a sweep, Karen thrust the startled woman forward and at the same time whipped the Kors from her arm. Tammy Kell looked back aghast. For the first time since Karen had met her at the Carlton Club, her carefully managed mask of composure slipped, caught unawares by Karen's audacity.

In a matter of moments, Tammy had been buried in the queue by other customers pressing up behind her.

Seizing the opportunity, Karen turned away, opened the bag, took Tammy's room card which lay on top. The Hyatt Hotel was the only one within the compound and the top spot where the Prime Minister stayed. That was typical of Tammy. Keep in nice and tight with the VIPs.

Tammy turned back towards Karen, her face flushed with growing anger at Karen's move and being put in a patronised position. 'Are you quite all right standing there, waiting comfortably?' Tammy's face distorted with a tight-lipped smile. 'Give me that. I can manage it myself, thank you very much.'

A cold chill ran over Karen. The stiff and rigid stance had run a bell. *Where have I seen that before?*

Karen had to go. She invented a quick but weak excuse. 'Look, I'll be back in five. I just have to go to the loo.' Tammy Kell's face registered scepticism that again Karen had taken the initiative.

Shaking with adrenalin, she darted off through the dense crowd without a backwards glance. Dodging and weaving, she sprinted the length of the exhibition hall, through the lobby, out the entrance door. Karen took the outside steps three at a time and charged across the forecourt towards the Hyatt as if her life depended on it. She flew like the wind.

It was vital to focus just on the task ahead and not stop for an extra breathe. If she could get in and search Tammy's room, she'd find answers. *If.*

The sight of someone running flat out is a common one at conferences because organisers time events to the second and speakers are often late. So nobody batted an eyelid.

She ducked behind a post because she *had* to fill a lung before they both burst. Was Tammy following her yet?

Karen needed to work on her hunch before speaking to Quacker or Haruto. It would have taken far too long to explain. Also, she knew they wouldn't approve. Stealing someone else's room key at a top political event crawling with armed police was not very wise. If Karen was right, Tammy Kell was a mole for Zinah al-Rashid and the Islamic state.

She entered the lobby of the Hyatt at high speed and pressed forward to the busy reception. 'I've forgotten my room number. Can you please remind me of it again?' She held out the card.

'Woo, I see you've been running. You're who, Ma'am?'

'Tammy Kell.' She panted. 'I've got an event starting any second. My speech is still on the desk. I'm a total blank today with nerves.'

The receptionist swiped it. 'Number 453. Hope it goes well.'

'Of course, it is, 453. Thank you.'

Time was against her and she didn't have long to get in and go through Tammy's things. Was she missing Karen yet? If Tammy opened her bag and discovered the key gone, she'd most likely come straight back to the room to see what the hell was going on.

She took the lift to the fourth and raced down the hallway, heart pounding. How could Tammy Kell afford this place? These rooms were the most expensive during the conference season. Being connected to the complex, guests could avoid the inconvenience of going through security every time they went to and from their hotel to the

Exhibition Hall. That saved at least forty-five minutes a day.

The other attraction was the razzamatazz. It had a champagne bar where candidates like Tammy Kell could hang around networking to improve their chances of selection.

Karen slid the card into the portal and the light flashed green. She was in. The queen size bed was still unmade which was a further incentive to hurry. The maid was in the throes of servicing the floor and would be there at any minute. Apart from the bed, the room was tidy, disappointingly so, certainly no odd diamond rings lying about.

She threw open the drawer nearest to where Tammy slept, but there was nothing. The sofa was swathed in clothes which she lifted one by one to see if there was a gold Hunter beneath, which there wasn't. The chest of drawers was covered with neat stacks of seminar materials. In the top one, there were visiting cards, hotel paraphernalia, two bibles, and a map of the city. Karen quickened her movements. There was the closet to check. Blue mid length suit, blouses, a long dark gown. A range of shoes. She'd unpacked and assembled everything in typical Tammy orderly fashion.

At the back she found a hand luggage-sized Samsonite at the back. She pulled it clear and tossed it onto the bed, but found it securely locked. The combination would take forever to break. The bag had the usual front panels which weren't covered by the combination lock. Karen dived her hand into the compartment and straightway found a chamois leather pouch. Inside, amidst a cluster of glittering sets of Hailey's jewellery and goodness knows who else's,

Karen found her grandfather's Hunter and the diamond ring. Her heart was thumping and banging with excitement. *Mission accomplished.*

The busy hum of a vacuum cleaner out in the passage panicked Karen. Extracting half of the contents and stuffing them in her pocket, she returned the pouch to the case and pushed it down deep. Feeling some silky material at the bottom, out of natural curiosity, she couldn't help pulling it out to have a look. Karen stared in disbelief at the black headdress.

Why would Tammy Kell have a niqab?

Memories of the fun fair rushed in. The look, the vice-like grip, the woman travelling in the car who wouldn't let her out. Was she going insane?

What had she seen hanging with the stuff in the closet?

A long dark gown.

Karen raced back to the closet and flung the door open. She pulled the hangers apart and tore through the sets of clothes and finally found what she was looking for. A full-length black dress which hung down to the carpet. She'd assumed it was an evening gown, but it wasn't. It was an abaya. *Why would Tammy wear an abaya?*

And two bibles in the drawer?

She ripped open the drawer. One copy was a bible, the other a Koran. *Was this property of the hotel?* Next to the Koran lay an envelope addressed to the BBC World Service, stamped and sealed, ready to send. She ripped it open. Inside was a USB stick, which she put in her pocket. Were Tammy and Zinah working together? Or were they the same person? She was about to find out.

384

CHAPTER 72

Karen's heart was booming away at a tremendous rate. She needed to view the tape somewhere private. Still no wiser on just what the terrorist cell was planning. She'd escaped from the hotel room before Tammy Kell steamed up with the cleaner to bust the door and catch her red-handed looting her stuff. When Karen Andersen didn't return for the cappuccino Tammy had put two and two together and realised she'd been outwitted. Karen had made off with her key card.

'I need my bag in a hurry.' Karen kept looking over her shoulder as the cloakroom attendant slowly took her ticket away for the sack in which she had her laptop. A full conference is not the perfect place to find an empty room but eventually she found one. The USB was certain to have clues about just what Zinah al-Rashid's organisation was planning.

An MP3 file on the stick confirmed her greatest fears. Tammy Kell speaking into a camera, covered head to toe, but in an unmistakeable voice.

The words were few and chilling. 'My name is Zinah al-Rashid. You'll know me better as Tammy Kell.' Karen's heart galloped as she continued to watch. 'I will shortly carry out my mission.'

Karen Andersen sat there viewing a jihadi suicide tape, her pockets stuffed with stolen goods, some even her own, when the door burst open. 'This is a security check.' A heavy-weight fire arms officer with a semi-automatic announced there'd been an explosion outside the conference building. 'Everything is in lockdown. Everyone must go to the central area for their safety so rooms can be searched.'

Karen's initial thought was of Tammy Kell. How could she have been out in the streets if only minutes ago she'd seen her at the Hyatt Hotel as Karen tried to hide behind the room service cart? *Impossible.*

'I have to get out.' She ducked under the arm of the police officer and out through the open door. TV monitors in the main lobby area were already screening the street scene. Outside the security zone there was complete pandemonium. What had happened? Terrorist attack? It was a rerun of the vehicle-ramming incident at Westminster.

'At least two men have been shot dead and many pedestrians killed,' splashed across the monitor. The red message ran continuously on the TV. The police had killed the attackers but not before their truck had ploughed into scores of conservative party supporters and demonstrators.

The screen showed scenes of total destruction, bodies scattered everywhere, with small groups of people around them trying to give assistance where they could.

Karen's fight-or-flight instinct was on red alert. Wailing police vans and ambulances raced to the scene drowning out the news commentary. Where to run? People in the lobby waited for further instructions as events unfolded. The display, which previously had been covering news of an MP's suicide, now showed graphic images of the panic and chaos outside the conference area. The public ran in long files from the area, hands on heads to let the police know they were not involved. A stampede to safety.

Karen asked the nearest man to her, 'What's happened. What's going on exactly?'

'The area's under attack. Terrorist attack. Best remain inside.'

But it wasn't best to remain inside. Everything was crystal clear. Karen was sure what was coming next. The outdoor incident, however atrocious, was a prelude to the main event.

The guards herded people into the auditorium unaware of the future threat.

'We have to get out of here.' she screamed.

'No one's allowed out.'

'But Tammy Kell?' She trailed off because it was hopeless explaining. Who'd listen? Tammy Kell aka Zinah al-Rashid was the big deal. If she wasn't involved in this part, she was about to do something on her own. Commit mass slaughter within the conference complex itself. The delegates in the chamber were sitting ducks.

Karen was on speed dial to Quacker as the guard caught sight of the video she was watching. What was playing through her computer linked her directly to the terrorist network not as Karen, private investigator, but as Basilah the new recruit. The following day she had been due to meet up with Zinah al-Rashid. But things had changed in the last hour. Zinah would be pushed into acting earlier than she'd planned. *Like shortly.* But Karen couldn't hang around to explain how she'd got drawn into all this. They'd not believe her in time. She needed to find Tammy Kell who was no doubt heading for her main target the Prime Minister and those in high government office near her. Nobody would suspect a parliamentary candidate of being a traitor and set on mass murder in the highest degree.

Karen could hear the guard calling after her as she raced out of the room. 'There's an attack coming from inside,' she shouted to him. 'You've got to clear the hall.'

Flinging herself forward, she shoved and pushed her way through the crowds. Her focus was on one thing alone, to find the tall girl with the blonde hair, who Karen knew would be within the inner section, the *safe* side. While security were busy checking other vehicles for explosives, Karen had her mind set on just the inside of the building.

She jostled forward through the press of dazed delegates. Then she saw her. Kell. Al-Rashid. Her body shape thicker and rounder. She was stood amidst colleagues. Ready to kill. Karen knew straight away the reason for the instant weight gain. The smart blue suit concealed an explosive vest.

Their eyes met. Karen in a split second saw her twitch and put a hand inside the jacket. Decision time. Karen could charge her. This ran the risk of Tammy exploding the device immediately. The alternative was no better. She could turn and run, save herself. But that would allow Tammy the time to tuck into the densest part of the throng and detonate her bomb killing even more people.

'What's the connection?' Hesitating, Karen's brain had new ideas. They slammed together in her mind. The girl so keen to meet at the Carlton Club to talk about Robin Miller had another identity completely, as a jihadist intent on terrorism. Had he found this out too? If so, was Robin her accomplice or her victim?

Pushing towards her through the crowd, Karen yelled out at the top of her voice, 'Tammy, stop!' Even though resigned to the fact these would be her last moments on earth Karen tried to reach her. Adrenalin powered her on. If she didn't try, she'd never live with the consequences. But Tammy had dissolved away into the crowd.

Karen listened for the sound of a blast but none came.

She paused for a moment before she was shuffled on through the door into the chamber. Karen was sure Tammy had not gone in that direction. So she turned and weaved her way through the crowd, getting an angle on people's faces, looking for the one who'd got mass murder on her mind. Where was she? Where would Tammy Kell go to next?

She checked out the toilets. No, she wasn't there.

And then all at once the lobby was deserted and silent. Karen's mind veered back to the suicide tape and how if Tammy saw it she'd know for sure the game was up. So Karen returned to where the USB was plugged into her laptop.

She entered the room, to be immediately struck from behind with terrifying force.

Karen realised it was Tammy. Before she went down, she got a look at the laptop and saw the USB had gone. Still conscious she seized Tammy. Locked together they dropped to the floor with a crash, scrambling, rolling, fighting.

Her vision clouded. There were stars bouncing around.

Tammy broke free and got up again. Karen lay on the floor, rebuilding her strength. Finally, she clambered to her feet too.

But now there was nothing left in her but fury and the desire to save herself and everyone else.

These delegates were supposed to be Tammy's allies, fellow activists who did not know she was amongst them for only one reason which was she wanted to kill them all.

'Karen Andersen. So you got me figured out?'

Karen could see Tammy's eyes bulging as she shrieked at her. 'It's not too late. You've still done nothing wrong. It's time to stop, Tammy. Zinah has killed no one. Not yet.'

'Don't take that away from me. I'm a servant of the Caliphate and I have committed jihad on Robin Miller. You cannot ruin my plans. The Brotherhood will acknowledge me. You'll see.'

Was that what had happened? Had Robin Miller been her first victim? Karen was sickened and giddy but at last, she had her talking.

'Tammy,' she yelled. Tammy Kell was intent on martyrdom with or without Karen Andersen and she had to break her down while she had her engaged. *Everyone wants to be a star.* Was committing an act of terrorism all about getting acknowledgement by her own party system? Maybe. 'The Brotherhood doesn't need stars like you! Can't you see that?'

'What are you talking about? The Brotherhood worships me.'

'They didn't coordinate with you. They didn't want you to take their limelight, can't you understand that? Have you seen the attack outside? You weren't in on it, were you? If you had've been, you would have been ready. And you weren't, were you? And why not? Because you didn't know about it. Because they didn't want you in on it, that's why.'

Tammy was struck dumb by this. The Brotherhood had stolen her thunder, not Karen. In the split second it took for Tammy to absorb this, Karen renewed the attack and threw herself at her. She was stronger than Karen imagined and also the padded vest protected her. Twisted and turning Tammy grabbed a pair of scissors off the worktop and jabbed at Karen viciously who screamed as the blade caught her open palm.

'Shit.' Her gut was telling her to put her fencing training into place. Tammy's sinewy body writhed as she stabbed at Karen dodging about the room. The wannabe terrorist had wound herself up tight as a top, ready for her moment on the world platform, but the Birmingham cell had beaten her to it. Now she would take out all this frustration on Karen.

She threw herself to the side as Tammy Kell rushed her again. A glint of light caught her eye. The scissors would have sliced her upper torso, had she not parried and grabbed hold of her opponent. They fell. The impact of them hitting the hard ground sent the only weapon they had shooting across the floor. Karen grabbed them as they whizzed past. They both clambered to their feet, but this time Karen was up first. She performed her riposte with the stumpy blade. The blow caught Tammy centre chest, but it was useless. It made no impression whatsoever on the impenetrable layer of padding. Instead she screeched back in Arabic 'Allahu Akbar' and reached for her belt. The exposed wrist received a direct hit from Karen.

'Drop the weapon!' Crash! An invasion of bodies and noise broke up the fight. In seconds there was Tammy Kell on the ground with uniformed security on top of her and there was Haruto right with them. How had he found her? The racket they caused was deafening. She clutched at her throat and felt a sharp pain grow stronger. Her hands were covered in blood.

Karen couldn't see her as she shouted out, 'She's Zinah

391

al-Rashid. She's got a bomb.'

Zinah gave a final primordial scream again. *Allahu Akbar.* Then ear-splitting cries and cursing filled the air. Karen just had enough strength to get the words out to Haruto, 'Why are you leaving me and going back to Japan?'

She raised her head to hear his response and the room came down to meet it. Blood pooled on the floor, Karen's blood and she gasped for breath. She had a sinking sensation, and felt trickling down from the wound. She wanted to stay conscious, but faintness took over.

There were three positive outcomes from it, which Karen reflected on later. Firstly, she didn't have to give the dreaded speech. Secondly, rather than admonished she'd been commended for her room invasion episode. Having been in a hurry after Tammy Kell returned to the hotel and realised Karen would blow her cover, she'd rushed to connect the suicide vest and got the wires back to front. So the explosives had failed to detonate. And thirdly, when Karen told her she was Basilah, Tammy Kell acted stunned. How could she not have known that?

Tammy Kell was a master liar who prided herself on her ability to conceal her secret identity as a jihadi from everyone. But Karen Andersen's double act as a convert to extremism was even better. *She'd outwitted her.*

CHAPTER 73

One of the guiding principles in police work is that ninety percent of crimes are solved because someone made a mistake. In Zinah al-Rashid's case or Tammy Kell, as she was known in the Tory party circles, she'd underestimated how observant Karen Andersen was. She'd noticed the diamond ring she was wearing in the Carlton Club. But Zinah had never mentioned a boyfriend, denied it even. So where had it come from? Then one thing had led to another.

Security found extra bomb-making equipment in the Samsonite because Zinah had been in too much of a hurry to plant it when she'd rushed off with her suicide vest.

So Zinah al-Rashid didn't go to Paradise to meet up with her *abu* as planned. Instead, she went to Holloway to reflect on where she went wrong.

As a pathological liar nothing Tammy Kell said stacked up when carefully checked. But, as often happens with a con woman who invents such cool and fashionable aliases, no one questions them too much. And she was excellent at the art of disguise in every way.

Karen Andersen spent the rest of the conference in Birmingham City Hospital recovering. Meanwhile, the Met were busy at Tammy Kell's house.

Here she was operating as Tamsin Smythe-Kell upstairs and Zinah al-Rashid from the basement. Archie Smythe MP had been the second husband of Ann Bishop's only daughter Miriam. He'd become Tamsin's stepfather.

While a female officer cooed over a silver-framed photo with the elderly lady upstairs an anti-terrorism police patrol unit searched the floor below. They quietly unravelled the chic operation Tammy ran from there, sending British born brides to the Caliphate and UK funds to jihadist fighters.

The evidence was all there on her PC, the maps, rehearsal tapes of her video message. There was the template for the leaflets she delivered. Her contact Ahmed al-Mustafa had been one of the terrorists killed in Birmingham.

Investigators also found a badly spelt letter from Robin Miller amongst the debris.

It was a brief note scribbled in blue biro. 'I ned you as a witness. We can stop Oli bulling. Culd you sign you saw him come down the steps after I was kicked and they will speak to him. It's for the god of the party.' David Miller verified his son's dyslexic writing.

They discovered Robin's body packed into a chest freezer. His throat had been slashed and his ginger hair was matted in black blood.

They learned how Robin Miller traced the address where he knew Tammy lived and had seen a light on in the murky basement. That's how he'd come across Tammy/Zinah in full Islamic dress. When he'd rapped on the door, she'd opened it without thinking. Tammy lived upstairs, Zinah down. That was Robin's fatal mistake. Getting them back to front.

While the outcome of Robin Miller's disappearance meant a family torn apart with grief, his death at least served well. In an indirect manner, it'd stopped one of the most ambitious atrocities in UK history.

Tamsin Smythe-Kell, aka Zinah al-Rashid created two

battle plans for her final ascent to the top of the terrorist hierarchy. The first was to saunter up to the PM as she made her way through the packed bar of the Hyatt and detonate her vest.

And if that opportunity didn't present itself she intended to kick the second into play. She'd gained prime seating at the front of the hall for the PM's speech at the close of the conference on the Wednesday. This was arranged by her new best friend Bea Harrington. It could have worked. No one checked who exactly were staying at the Hyatt Hotel and thus they could effectively bypass security completely as they were already within the security cordon. Had Tammy got into the hall, this home-grown Islamic extremist in her explosive vest would have been seated right in the centre of the full British cabinet.

Zinah as she insisted on being called from then on, agreed to talk in person. She was keen to pick up on where she and Karen Andersen had left off at the Carlton Club though this time it was against the less salubrious backdrop of a woman's prison. Tammy picked up the large sticking plaster on Karen's neck, but chose to ignore it.

Seated opposite Karen's hands trembled in a wave of nervousness. 'Tell me how this all happened.'

While the Tammy Kell side of the woman's personality felt remorse for Robin Miller, Zinah al-Rashid not a bit. That's how strange it all was.

It was her as Zinah when she said. 'You and I have much in common. You had a father you loved. So did I. My dad was killed in a drone strike. It took years for me to track him down. Then he was gone in a second. I was heartbroken. You understand that.'

They faced each other squarely, Karen a free woman, not her. But all the same Karen felt Zinah still had her pinned like an insect on a display board. Her powerful persona and manipulative instincts still there, but the dazzling smile had faded.

'I committed myself to jihad at that point. Then Robin Miller came by. He'd have blown my cover for sure. I'm superb at disguise. He barely recognised me at first.'

Poor Robin.

'So why did you set up the Ferris Wheel meeting at the funfair?'

'You were getting too close. You knew someone was doubling for Robin Miller. I saw it in your eyes at the Carlton Club.'

That was the last thing Karen thought she had in her eyes that evening. She hadn't even come close to rumbling the deception by then. 'So, for that, you would kill me?'

'If it was the will of Allah. It wasn't. Or it would have taken place.'

Karen was beyond speechless, her jaw trembling.

'In the beginning what I wanted to do was to become an MP. I've been a Tory activist since sixteen. After Archie died, I gave it a go. James Harrington did not understand who I was when he sponsored me. Can you believe that?'

'You approached him for a reference?'

'Years ago. You must get referees on your application. He'd worked for my stepfather, Archie Smythe. When I reminded him of that he was only too happy to write me a glowing recommendation.'

'So what did he do to you as a child?'

In a rare moment of weakness, Zinah's eyes filled with

tears. 'I don't want to talk about that.' Recovering quickly, her face hardened and changed almost beyond recognition. She aged visibly.

'Didn't he remember you? Or what he was supposed to have done to you?'

'How would I know? He acted as if he had never ever seen me before. Maybe that was the worst bit. I think finally he cottoned on. You don't believe me, do you? That he abused me?'

Karen felt sick with disgust. It's hard to listen to someone who's plotted to send you to their version of Paradise and feel compassion for them. It's even more challenging to work out the difference between lies and fact from a habitual liar. Was James Harrington ever guilty as charged? Or was the extent of her sex abuse just another of her fabrications?

As Oli Harrington had said, 'Tammy is poison.'

Was she telling the truth? That's what men's rights and Justice for Rape Lies were protesting about. Not all accusations are truthful. It was one reason Simon King had grown embittered over the years. Then he'd taken it out on innocent Alesha Parkhurst. *Too many deaths.*

'The fact is by then I was doing pretty well without James Harrington's help. Thank you very much. Standing by his wife at a fundraiser when I was first on the List I introduced myself to her and she, in turn, presented me to her husband. She seemed put out he hadn't mentioned he'd written my original reference. I told her we went back a long while. Maybe that's when he twigged it. After that, I did everything to speak to him about it. Instead, he did everything he could to avoid me. Do you know how that feels? You do, don't you?'

The way she spoke as if they were two old girlfriends together discussing a one-night stand, was uncanny. Had Karen ever had the flick off? Well, had she? She answered her yes. She'd had plenty. But Karen added, 'I've never felt the desire to take it out on the rest of the world though.'

'Archie used to fob me off on anyone so he could go on one of his sex splurges. Couldn't care less what they did. Seven, I was. I believed Harrington would have wanted to make it up to me. Give me his blessed parliamentary seat at least if he could. But then he tried to distance. You know what it's like.'

I did know what it was like. 'He didn't want the trouble.'

'Probably not. But think about it. If it hadn't been for Archie, none of this would have happened. My stepfather's original name was John Smith. He changed it to Smythe because it sounded more highfalutin. It was then I tried to find out more about who my real father was.'

'And that's when you went to Syria?'

'It was the turning point in my life.'

'And by that time you were well into the political system?'

'Yes. I could bring about change. My dad impressed that on me. In fact, my stepfather too.'

Karen felt numb, but she listened to her story carefully. It was important to connect the dots. She heard the background. How Tammy's mother had tossed her left-leaning first husband Jeb/Mohammed aside for the stylish young member of parliament. 'I don't blame her. It's done a lot. Even I liked the nice things Archie offered. Eventually

Miriam ruined herself with too much high life.'

'By that you mean Harrods and the Carlton Club?'

'By drugs and alcohol.' She went quiet for a bit. 'I regret nothing I've done.'

'In the Islamic State Archie would have been pushed from the top of a tower block,' Karen said.

'In the UK it wasn't much better until a few years ago. Archie lived a secret life. Why do you think was? You all consider yourself so liberal. He was beaten up more than once. Gay bashing they called it back then.'

There was still a tiny part of the riddle missing. It was how she'd led Karen such an effective, merry dance for the last few weeks. 'How could you pass yourself off as Robin Miller for all that time?'

'It was the bit you missed, wasn't it? That day on the campaign bus the three of us agreed to help Robin stand up to Oli Harrington. Everyone hated James Harrington. They recognised he was a lecher and his son a damn bully. He picked on Robin's spelling problems. We knew Robin had dyslexia. William and I both wrote down his password and login details so we could correct posts for him. Doesn't look good on Twitter to keep misspelling things. After William was killed, I knew someone new had got into the Twitter account. And the Gmail. I worked out it must be you. Who else would it be?'

She folded her arms across her chest. She was reliving it all, revelling in her own cleverness.

'And the phone?'

'Westfield. I needed to get rid of the mobile. So I attached it to the explosive device and put it in the charging unit. I assumed someone would ring the number sooner or later.'

Me. I'd detonated the shopping centre bomb when I'd called Robin Miller.

'How could you not feel bad for Robin's family?'

He was lying just three feet away from you in a freezer and you could ignore it. How could you do that?

Zinah swung her leg to and fro in a manic fashion. 'Robin's death couldn't be helped.'

'And what about all the other families you destroy when you lure their teenagers out of the country? Amirah, Fatima, for example.'

Her face contorted with bitterness. 'I don't need to lure them away. It's what they want. What they dream about. Hundreds. Their fantasy is to cross the desert. One day they will be citizens of dawla. You don't get that do you?'

Karen's own personal memory of teenage ambition was making a new top from a remnant off the market. Not joining a killing regime. She told her that. How could these kids even afford it for a start?

'What are student loans for? The Kafir wealth is halal for us.' She explained it meant getting funds from non-believers and not ever having to repay them. All for the glory of a holy war. 'A form of Jihad Seekers Allowance.' She grinned at her own joke.

'So did James Harrington know he was financing your operations?'

It was the first time there was the slightest acknowledgement of failure. 'Probably not. I'd done too good a job convincing him I was Robin Miller, and I was still alive and ready to expose his past. My only regret was not making him suffer more. He never knew it was me.

400

Taking his own life was an act of cowardice.'

She could read the irritation in Karen's eyes which she'd been trying to mask if only to learn the full story. Tammy's brainwashing had been complete. Climbing the slippery pole of the UK political system wasn't big enough or fast enough for her. She craved fame above all else and the Islamic cause offered that.

And if her idea to bomb the conference hadn't panned out? What then?

'I would have cancelled the operation rather than muck it up like what happened at Westfield,' Zinah continued. 'My long-term plan after that was to travel to the Caliphate and become the wife of a shaheed.

'What's that?' Karen asked.

'That's a martyr to you.'

It was as if high status was another of the great driving forces in her life. She'd be looked up to out there, for sure. There was a three-month mourning period expected of bombers' wives. After that the proud widows receive a healthy pension provided they study the Koran and its messages, the 'fiqh' and 'hadeeth'.

'At least you would have practiced what you preached. Do what you've been telling these young girls? You'd give up politics and ambitions associated with western life just as they give up their education to become terrorist wives?'

'I'm a feminist, you know, like Alesha Parkhurst was. But you wouldn't see that would you? Not unless you looked at it through our eyes and not yours.'

'You are the opposite. The subjugation of women is the counter of everything Alesha Parkhurst stood for.'

'In the Caliphate, we see women's role differently.' She

explained how there were plenty of choices if girls wanted to work. She talked about the al-Khansaa. This group enforced the severest interpretation of Sharia law on other women. 'And you can even take part in these hisbah patrols if your husband is away fighting. It's enjoyable.' Zinah was toying with her, enjoying herself.

In a voice rigid with determination, Karen said, 'I will stop you, you know.' Their eyes locked together in an eye war. 'I will.' *I will stop you.*

CHAPTER 74

After her arrest, Zinah's bride recruiting scheme was completely dismantled, in part because of Karen Andersen's work as Basilah. But there were other reasons which had a more enduring effect on its operation. The jihadi wives, married off straight away once they were widowed, often to multiple husbands, were returning from the Caliphate with stories of being caged up, abused, treated like living slaves. It was not what they'd bargained for. And the war had turned against the fundamentalists who now found themselves on the wrong side of a big power play.

Amirah reverted to calling herself Tessa Clark again, took up art and started planning a career as a graphic designer. Fatima and Mia got a call from the security services. They admitted straightaway knowing Zinah al-Rashid was a recruiter but denied active involvement in any extremist plot themselves. The girls were in the clear. For now.

Zinah al-Rashid continued to believe in what her real father did, that a global war between true Islam and the Kafirs, the disbelievers, was underway. Muslims had to choose a side, and she'd chosen hers. It had cost Robin Miller's life and destroyed many more. Guided by the wise words from her mullah at the local mosque, her inspiration had been the following:

'You can't live your life waiting for the next weekend to come; your aspiration should be far, far greater than that. It should be paradise and that should be sought every day.'

Karen Andersen acknowledged that Zinah was a super saleswoman. She could sell ice to an Eskimo. Also that black robed heroic women, armed and charging into battle, had a sexy winning resonance for feminists. But much to Zinah al-Rashid's disappointment it wasn't her name being feted by the Islamic propaganda machine. They had side-lined her completely. She'd undermined the Birmingham operation by trying to upstage it with her own. Karen Andersen had done the rest by spoiling her plan.

The montages of Muslim suffering had helped Zinah al-Rashid's cause. They showed poignant pictures of the bodies of Syrian children lying amongst the rubble of rebel cities and young men suffering from nerve gas attack. All were used liberally as justification for their own brutality. *Muslims who failed to support violent jihad were colluding with the West, were like coconuts. Brown on the outside and white on the inside. Do not take the kafirs as your friends, they are your enemies.* This was the message of hate Zinah al-Rashid had been broadcasting to potential recruits.

As Karen Andersen dashed stop-starting through the London traffic to return the hired motorbike, she wondered who would replace Zinah al-Rashid as the next firebrand. Also, if Robin Miller hadn't crossed her path that night whether she'd still have felt compelled to plan her major attack. Circumstance and chance had combined to produce a tragic outcome.

CHAPTER 75

Quacker, Haruto and Karen lunched together a fortnight later following her recovery. The men settled on rancheros and Karen picked away at a few of soggy tacos while they ran over the events of the past few weeks. Haruto was still puzzled as to why Quacker had insisted on catching the train back to London from Birmingham. Despite the DI insisting it had nothing to do with Haruto's driving technique, he was slightly offended. But it was a lunch when the three of them philosophised more than they ate.

Karen said, 'How did all this begin anyway?' And they went from there. How the circle of bullying and the game of multiple aliases had finally ended, but where did it begin? Was it Oli Harrington with his heavy-handed approach to the younger activists? Or Daesh, which had brainwashed Tammy Kell into believing its mind-numbing ideology. Perhaps Simon King with his confused ideas of loyalty. However it started, it had highlighted flaws in national security as well as those in human nature.

Bea Harrington was left with questions and not knowing where to go next. Following the death of her husband, several women came forward to report James Harrington for sexual harassment. Some months later, she withdrew from politics and began voluntary work as a counsellor in a Rape Crisis organisation.

However much they spoke about it there was no way of avoiding the figure of the tragic activist Robin Miller always right in the centre of the whole spinning sphere. The family were understandably grief stricken and angry at the indifference to the matter of the party he served so loyally. And his death affected everyone who heard Robin's sad story.

After the long lunch Haruto stretched over and squeezed Karen's hand. Once they'd finished with the debriefing, Haruto and Karen left and went off on a romantic London bus ride.

The trip took them in sight of Tower Bridge, the Tower of London, Monument, and St. Paul's. Blackfriars Bridge, Fleet Street, the Royal Courts of Justice, Waterloo Bridge, the Strand and Trafalgar Square.

Relaxed on the open topped bus, Karen and Haruto soaked up the late summer sunshine and took in the sights. It was when they were smack bang in the centre of the city Haruto mentioned he was going to Japan.

'I know. I hope you have a nice time. It's cool with me.'

It came out smooth as silk because by then Karen had had enough time to absorb the ideas Hailey had planted. That their affair was to be a short term one. And Karen could live without him. It'd been factored in.

Haruto seemed hurt and even confused by her reaction. 'Would you not consider coming along for the ride?

Karen hadn't been expecting that. 'I can't leave all this.' she said, looking out the window to cover her surprise and as if she didn't give a damn. Despite her heart doing drum beats.

'But it's two months at the most. You may well need the space, which I understand. But I want you to know from my point of view I'd like us to stay together because I think I've fallen in love with you.'

'But I assumed you were going for good.'

He smiled. 'I wonder who gave you such an idea? Don't tell me. I can guess.'

So Karen Andersen bought a brand new suit case with the latest three hundred and sixty degree working wheels and packed straightaway.

Back in Chiswick they both stopped at the George IV and went over the top with a glass of champagne. Then it was off to do Elspeth's Cochrane's shopping. It was only neighbourly.

She had to be well stocked up if they were to be gone for eight weeks.

ACKNOWLEDGEMENTS

None of this would have been possible without the help of others. Firstly, my campaign manager and extraordinary husband Donald Burfitt-Dons who loyally supported my 2015 candidacy in the UK General Election. The experience gave me a practical knowledge of party politics and provided adventures to write about in future books.

Thanks to the wonderful work of Nottingham Rape Crisis Centre which gave me a feeling for Bea and Alesha Parkhurst.

Heartfelt thanks also to Reem I Abdelhadi for her patience with my Arabic and my fellow students at Ealing, Hammersmith and Weston London College who provided invaluable insight into the realities of life for Muslim women in the UK. Their private lives, secrets and taboos helped me enormously with Zinah and to bring Fatima, Amirah, Jamilah and Ahmed to life. Grateful thanks to RUSI, the world's oldest independent think tank on international defence and security for their helpful research into jihadi brides.

Appreciation goes to Hamish Browne MBE, Detective Mike "Duck" Proctor, the forensic psychologist Gill Merrill, sociologist Ian Flett, who advised on coping with stalking and bullying. They've supported my work with Act Against Bullying for nearly twenty years which shaped the background to the central character in this book, Robin Miller. And Google which is active in helping us promote cyber safety. Also Ania Roberts, Monica Monni, Celeste

Ekerick, Kathy Scholfield, Lenka and Marcus O'Neill, Vivian Zink, Alexandra Eversole, Wendy Georgetti-Remkes, Mark Garrity, Dennis and Mary Williams.

The excellent team at Victim Support who are unsung heroes deserve a shout out, particularly Jane Mather. Likewise Acid Survivors Trust International who aided with the character of Nala. For the advice on medical matters, I'm indebted to Dr Ivor Burfitt. Thanks must go to Simon McQuiggan and Muse Strategy for their design skill and assistance online.

Finally, my beloved daughters Arabella Burfitt-Dons and Brooke Williams. And my terrific son-in-law Rhys. Thank you.

Made in the USA
Columbia, SC
21 June 2022